WHEN HALLOWEEN WAS GREEN

A NOVEL BY
BERNARD K. FINNIGAN

UMBRA

Livonia, Michigan

Puka horse cover illustration by Alli Kappen

Cover design, interior book design,
and eBook design by Blue Harvest Creative
www.blueharvestcreative.com

WHEN HALLOWEEN WAS GREEN

Published by Umbra
an imprint of BHC Press

Library of Congress Control Number:
2016953384

ISBN-13: 978-1-946006-16-5
ISBN-10: 1-946006-16-5

Visit the author at:
www.bhcpress.com

Also available in eBook

TABLE OF CONTENTS

To Elly and Ian
Because October just got a lot more exciting for all of us

A NOTE ON PRONUNCIATION

Samhain - Has a silent m:
"SOW when"

Puka - Has many variations in spelling:
Pooka, Puca,
but all spoken "POO-Ka"

Dulluhan - Is spoken as "dull," as in a dull blade:
"DULL Li Hun"

Ankou -
"AN Koo"

MacCumhaill - Has three syllables:
"Mac KOO Wul"

Sluagh - Has two syllables:
"SLOO-ah"

The First to Die

A SCREAM IS A WINDOW to the soul.

It is the most honest sound one can utter, revealing in an instant every fear someone spends a lifetime trying to conceal. The entire self reduced to a single naked exclamation. Everyone is afraid of something.

Scotty O'Brien was terrified.

He screamed within a nightmare, and he couldn't wake up.

Howling echoed over the forested hills.

A young mother clutched her child to her chest at the sound. Cool wind irritated the crows, who cawed to each other in annoyance. But there was no one to hear them.

She was alone.

Her small cottage held no light. As the orange of the sun died by inches over the horizon, only a candle held back the dusk. Open windows let in the wind, a low moan in a dead silence, in the single room with only mother and child.

And a corpse. Her father.

The corpse lay staring up at the thatched ceiling. His last breath had locked open his eyes in one moment of perfect clarity. The mother had seen his last moment, when he saw one glimpse of what lay beyond. And he died.

The howls returned. Closer. From beyond the forest. Shrieks that came from no mortal throat. The howls heralded the passing of the sun as the wind grew stronger, easily penetrating the cottage. It prickled the woman with whispers in her ears and a frozen bite on any exposed skin.

The child whimpered. But the mother couldn't leave the cottage. She huddled on the floor next to her father and collapsed in her own sobs. The child wailed louder.

Pounding. Outside, across the field, something was running towards the cottage. She couldn't see the source, but each footfall pounded her ears as hammers on stone. Her grip on her child turned into a painful vice but the pounding continued. Through the field. Up the path.

To the door.

Scotty didn't have nightmares. Some arrogant corner of Scotty's mind scolded himself. He didn't get scared! But this nightmare tore so deep into his mind's eye that it broke into his waking world, dragging him out of his bed, even out of his house! Cold night air bit his skin as he awoke with a start running down a deserted street in the deep of night. How did he get outside? He had no idea even as the visions ensnared his mind again and this time didn't let go.

The door smashed open, bringing a rain of dust out of the ceiling timbers. The woman screamed, her eyes locked on the shape standing at her door.

It was a man. An ordinary man. Well-calloused hands smeared with farmer's grime. A man with a pockmarked face betraying a lifetime in the fields. A face that now looked down upon her with anger.

Why are you still here? It's The Night! Save your child! You can't tarry here! Your father is almost—

The man's gaze reached the father. He saw the sunken eyes and lifeless body. The man spun to see the sunset give up its last. The orange was all but spent, leaving a cold blue that got darker yet. It was The Night.

Samhain.

He heaved the woman to her feet.

RUN, WOMAN! RUN!

With gruff hands the man forced both mother and child out the smashed door into the cool dusk. The mother turned back to the cottage to wail for her lost father.

He's GONE, woman! He was the last to die! RUN!

Grabbing the child with one arm and dragging the woman with the other, the man shoved them across the field, Her feet tripped in the deep grass. She couldn't leave her father's body. The man dragged her all the harder over the fields. No time to mourn. The sun had abandoned them. But there was light, across the hills, on the tallest peak.

A human fire. High up the peak, people hovered around a fire and waved down to the trio at the bottom of the hill The man pushed the woman towards them.

GO WOMAN.

Tripping across the fields, mother and child wept...until the howls reached them. Rolling through the hills, riding the wind that blew all the fiercer. The howls bit their ears with the chill of the grave.

The man ran through the field. Scarecrows were the only witness to their flight amidst bales of the harvest, motionless sentinels to be avoided as the man pushed the woman toward the fire on the hill. The Puka's Share lay unmolested as the people on the hilltop called to them.

Tonight, the only value was the community.

The man shoved the woman and child up the hill. But he stayed a moment, surrendering to the pain in his chest. He risked a glance behind to see how far they had come. Tiny fields were below him. The mountains turned black with the final dusk. And he saw the woman's decrepit cottage, still holding a single candle within. The tiny light held back a darkness that now swept across the valley floor, freezing branch-

es and grass in mid-rustle. In the man's ear, the darkness whispered, an infinite scream passed through the world.

They were here.

Coming out of the forest. White forms against the black, howling as they blew like wisps of balefire, catching the wind and rising into the Night. THEIR Night.

They found the cottage. Swirling forms engulfed the tiny shell and the corpse within. Cackling with hollow laughs they extinguished the candle, drowning it in the darkness of the fields.

But the cottage burned bright. Not with light, but with a white that cast no shadows and gave no warmth. The white burned through the cottage walls, and a form emerged. From up on the hill, the man strained to see, he could almost see a form step out of the cottage, a form no mortal was meant to see, the fate of the Last to Die—

NO. HE DARE NOT LOOK.

He ran. For his life.

Get to the Fire! Woman!

The man reached the woman. Her child tripped and collapsed, wailing. Her cries were echoed by howls in the fields, and by the lifeless white that now flowed up the hill.

The man grabbed the child with both arms and pushed the woman. Behind he heard the swirls fly to the chase. He felt their gaze in his back, boring through his flesh to gaze in delicious temptation on his soul.

But above the man, the circles of fire were close. Bones of slaughtered livestock blistered with sizzling cracks, funneling ash and ember into pillars of orange, reaching into the sky. Yellow flame blazed through the eyes of a hundred grinning skulls, laughing at their own cremation.

Men stood in the circles, holding torches high. Animal skins adorned their thick bodies, ash smeared into their faces. Reaching for the man and woman, they pulled them across the circles into safety. The man felt a tickle of a single finger up his spine just as he crossed the boundary of skulls ringing the central fire. But he made it.

The woman fell across the boundary with her child. She was grasped in sobbing arms and cried together on her knees with her child. The fires shot spirals of flame into the night, surrounding them. The people surrounded them all in protection.

The shadows could not touch them.

Men stepped up to the boundary with skulls. Carved skulls. Carved with their own hands from their harvest. Carved faces filled with sizzling animal fat blazed with orange shining eyes, scorching away the night. The men presented these skulls boldly against the shadows. The howling forms shrieked and screamed. They taunted the unseen boundary, slicing the smoke and ash.

But they couldn't enter the circle of fire. The man rose, safe.

Below, the hills were bathed in a wispy smoke seeping from the ground. For an instant, the smoke betrayed a glimpse of a mortal face before being whisked away. The dead were rising from their graves, obeying the call, HIS Call.

Looking, the man saw Him, a skeletal frame, bathed in white, feet hovering above the grasses, repelled by the Earth which rejected his unliving essence. Long spindly white hair floated above his head. With his arms outstretched, he called to the dead. The wisps from the graves whirled and fell in behind him.

It was the Night of the Harvest. The mortals harvested the land by day. And HE harvested the souls by Night. The Harvest of the Dead held his reason for being. He called and the dead obeyed Him. He was the Last to Die.

He approached, and the people recoiled from the flames. Their boldness quaking at the sight of His white grinning face...

ANKOU! ANKOU!

His white hair caught the wind of the fires and flared into the air. His white arms and impossibly long skeletal fingers caressed the flames. But he could not enter.

This was the Night of the Dead, but within the ring of fire the living were safe. The bone fires and carved skulls protected them. Their songs and chants protected them. The carved skulls guarded the circle,

11

staring out into the white shadows with unblinking eyes. The shadows could not pass the fire.

ANKOU!

The people chanted in the center of the flame. Their chants echoed across the hills, catching the flaming wind to be born of the fire and ember's racing through the wind. The people protected themselves as they had done since before memory.

But the woman...

The man looked for the woman, still cowering on the ground. Sobbing. But now she looked up. She saw Him. She saw His Face.

He smiled at her.

Dadai?

Yes, her father's face. Her father clad in the white rags of smoke. Who now stretched out a skeletal arm, reaching for her... The woman arose.

Dadai?

Yes. Yet beneath His face was the outline of a grinning skull. Her Father. The Last to Die. The man also saw Him. The man would not be taken, nor beguiled. The man knew the danger.

But the woman forgot.

She walked towards the border of skulls. The man shouted and jumped to seize her before she touched the hand of smoke.

WOMAN! DON'T! THE ANKOU!

He grabbed the arm of her child and pulled. But the woman stepped too close. Reaching for the hand of her father, she crossed the boundary...and a victorious screech pierced the ears of the people as the woman was pulled into the swirls of fog. Her shriek spun high into the air and was lost in the fire and ember, her final cry arresting the chant of the people. Nothing but a whistling scream on the air.

She was gone.

The man looked to the woman's child, crying for her mother. She was young. Too young to know the dangers of the night. The man gripped her in both arms, surrounded by the fire and the people. Outside, the triumphant spirits returned, mocking with delight, looping into the night sky. The man held the girl and rocked her, soothing her fright. Pulling her close, he whispered.

You don't have to be frightened of The Night.

As long as you remember.

Outside the circle, the shrieks of the dead returned. The great fire threw glowing ash high into the clouds. The carved skulls kept vigil with eyes of flaming orange. As the embers spun, centuries of the world passed beneath them.

And passed.

And passed.

And man forgot.

Pain shocked Scotty awake. His bloodshot eyes stared at his lacerated hands, raw flesh throbbing. His bare feet slipped on gritty concrete, leaving red streaks on the pavement. His legs burned and chest wheezed as he collapsed on his knees on a wet road in the dead of night.

Maybe not so dead as a large shadow reached across the street. Scotty fought to his feet as the wind roared with crackling tree branches and buildings towered over him as monolithic tombstones.

Last to die.

Scotty's mind screamed with those words as his bloody hands groped brick walls, reaching for somewhere, anywhere to escape as vision after vision pummeled him. He finally found himself in a dead-end alley, cornered by a huge shadow towering above him. The shadow focused into a black mane whipping in the night air with eyes of red flame glaring through him, eyes of a monster Scotty O'Brien had no name for.

Last to die!

No, Scotty was not going to be the last, but the first. As the horror reached for him with black arms, Scotty had one last vision telling him exactly why.

Because forgotten monsters can come back.

OCTOBER
28TH

ONE

ONLY IN THE DARK corners of a Haunted House is the honesty of human emotion ever truly revealed.

People scream. Then laugh. Then scream all over again, and pay for it. Haunted Houses happily take anyone's money. Scaring is their business. Some people scream at buzzing power-tools or wriggling spiders in claustrophobic hallways, others just scream at the dark itself, at the grotesque shadow just waiting for someone to reach out only a little too far.

In the heart of this haunted house, the *Scare Asylum,* terror gripped Benny MacCool Bensel. Not from anything in the house however. Far from it, for despite his 18 years of age he was now face to face with the greatest terror of all.

A girl.

Two in fact. One on each arm. Cute. Pony-tailed and giggly, squeezing his arms with every squeal they uttered, and they squealed at everything, from the noxious clouds of fog that tickled the lungs to the screams of the ax murderer behind the wall that might, just might, actually be real. Their bare hands on Benny's arms send shivers into his brain.

Haunted Houses were fun. Girls? Those were terrifying.

Dear Lord let me get through this. He'd had a rough day already. He had a nightmare last night that had hit him pretty bad. Benny hated nightmares.

Especially ones of blurry shadows whirling like ADHD overload: *Someone running...being chased on a windy night in a panic, leaving bloody footprints on a deserted street, then being trapped.*

Over and over. All night. Benny hadn't slept at all, and now just wanted to lie down. But Fate didn't let Benny off so easily. Shuffling down a hallway with green-glowing skulls and choking fog, the girls stumbled and tripped him, propelling him forward arms flailing toward the hard cement floor. At the last instant a hand shot out to catch his wrist, then placed him back on his feet. A dark shadow leaned in to whisper above the din.

"Strong and steady. Never let them see you scared." With feline grace, the form moved back to the front. Keith was good at that.

Keith Finn MacCool. Benny's uncle.

Keith wasn't afraid of anything. Not in this haunted house anyway. Keith had a haunted house of his own, the *HallO'Scream*, and toured the competition as much as possible. He often left disappointed. He prided himself on having the scariest house in town, and had been awarded "Scariest in Town" for multiple years. But not last year. This house had beat him. Keith was going to find out why. He took Halloween seriously. So seriously, in fact, as to have Edvard Munch's *THE SCREAM* tattooed on his right shoulder, rising up his neck to peek out from a black leather jacket that Keith wore everywhere. He had other tattoos up and down his arms, each of another terrifying monster from world history. Benny hadn't even heard of most of them.

So Keith led the way, fearlessly blazing a path through a dark foggy hallway with howling monsters around every corner.

Whereas Keith was Benny's uncle the two of them were only a decade apart in age. Benny was a jeans and hoodie kind of young man with brown uncombed hair and fashion sense limited to whatever shirt he found on the floor. Keith was at least a head taller than Benny. Benny didn't need to duck under the faux cobwebs. Keith did.

So did Connor, who took up the rear. With his shaved head and goatee, Keith's best friend Connor was even taller and more intimidating than Keith. Connor could never be accused of being related to either one of them, as other than his lack of hair Connor's single most distinguishing feature was having five times the mouth. Whereas Keith went through every room with a stare of grim analysis, Connor broadcast a huge contagious smile. Drooling monsters who assaulted from behind were greeted with a handshake and a chuckling, "Well done."

Connor also owned a haunted house. *The Fright Zone,* not far down the road from Keith's *HallO'Scream.* He'd known the MacCools for years. They went to the same trade shows, bought from the same wholesalers. Friendships in the business were inevitable. And what else would haunted house friends possibly do with their off hours? Tour haunted houses of course. Connor also helped Benny move the girls along, even as another fingernail pierced Benny's arm.

Entering the latest room, Benny admitted that it was indeed worth a sizable scream: a masked psychopathic charging around a corner with a screeching buzz saw.

Naturally, the girls shrieked. But before Benny even blinked, Keith planted himself directly in front of the monster, blocking his attack. This let Benny and the girls slip by without being accosted. The rubber mask didn't like being blocked and roared with ape yells and arm pumping grunts as Benny bit back pain in his arm and pulled the girls through to the next area. They'd be safe now. Haunted House Rules were unassailable: Monsters could not follow past their assigned position. Once the party went around the corner the girls stopped screaming. Keith caught up without a sound and resumed his place in front. He was good at that. With his black-leather jacket he could vanish into the dark and reappear at will.

Directly ahead of the group, the hallway glowed with a dull orange. Tensing his arms, Benny escorted the girls around another corner into the next room of the house. Right into what looked for the world like a linoleum-laid kitchen.

No. An operating room. A very bloody one, with a single orange bulb in the ceiling. Everything dripped blood. The walls. The counters. The operating gurney. Words such as "red rum" were smeared on the walls. Disembodied heads and hands swung on meat-hooks from the ceiling. The girls caught just one glimpse of the entire gory mess and hugged themselves in terror, refusing to open their eyes until they were out. Benny sighed and walked them toward an exit in the far wall, then looked back.

Keith wasn't following. In fact both Keith and Connor were standing in the center of the orange room, faces locked in disappointment. Infallible Haunted House Rules had been violated. The rubber mask monster of the hallway was supposed to have been *in here*. He had left his post, leaving this room without a punchline.

Keith would never let that stand.

"Newbie. No business jumping out until we entered."

Benny could hear voices of other patrons through the walls both in front and behind him. They had to keep moving and there was nothing left to see here. For anyone except Keith, that is. He just stood there scanning the whole thing, every blood droplet, every swinging chain.

"Well it was a well-oiled buzzsaw," Connor piped in, earning a scowl from Keith. Connor always tried to find the best in everything, but Keith didn't have that kind of patience.

"It's a rerun from last year. They didn't even change the lightbulb!" Keith scowled. "These heads are right off the rack from the Shriek Bootique! I've told them 50 times, you *can't* use the same props that any idiot can buy at Walmart."

Connor motioned as the group behind them got too close, so Keith finally moved on. Around another corner, the scenery changed to a hallway in complete darkness. It went straight several meters before hooking back onto itself. A maze. Mazes were simple time-killers that didn't require any actors. A few boards and a bucket of paint, and the room scared by itself.

Keith never paused, turning dark corners without the slightest hesitation, forcing Benny and the girls to keep up. Connor helped Benny move the wide-eyed girls along. Even the girls knew this rule: The longer the maze went on without scaring them, the more likely that eventually something would. And the longer the wait, the more dreadfully monstrous the unspeakable horror would be. Certain their inevitable death awaited around every single corner, the girls only moved in six-inch shuffles.

Worse, they insisted on speaking to Benny the entire time.

"Why aren't you scared?"

"Because... I do this a lot," *Please don't talk to me...*

"You like haunted houses?"

"I work in one." *But you'll never see me there.*

"Really? Which one?"

"The HallO'Scream." *The best in town.*

"We heard that's too scary. What monster are you?"

"I work backstage." Short single-sentence answers. Benny's preferred communication.

"You're not a monster?" They sounded disappointed.

"No. I just build props."

"What?"

"I build monsters. For my uncle. The guy up front in the leather jacket."

"He works there too?"

"He owns it."

"Really? That's why he's not scared either, right?"

"Right... and... we're not in danger here anyway. Haunted houses don't put two scary rooms back to back. Better to space them out so they don't give each other away."

"Oh," the girls straightened up, and covered their mouths, looking embarrassed.

Oh. That about described girls in a haunted house. And that conversation was the longest one he'd had with one since... since he last saw Bridget. His sister. She wouldn't have been scared of this place. Not one tiny bit.

21

Girls like *these*, however, always were. Benny never wondered why hyper-frantic girls would voluntarily enter a spook alley. No matter the time or the day of the week, some girls were always there at the ticket booth, *pleading* for an escort to take them through, an available dateless male. Like Benny. Benny dreaded it. As an alleged adult, Benny appreciated the possibilities of being hugged by females in darkened rooms, and of maybe even a goodnight kiss for a job well done. But harsh pride would step in and chastise him.

A haunted house was certainly no place to have one's first kiss.

Besides he wasn't in the mood for any of this, that bad dream last night...

But Keith's loud voice broke into his thoughts. More observations.

"The ceiling's too high. Should've made us get on our knees and crawl."

"That's what they did last year," Connor piped up.

"It was scarier last year," Keith replied.

Benny actually smiled. Haunted houses did actually make him feel better. The *Scare Asylum* was doing its best, but as the party passed from one room to the next, Keith and Connor continued to give each room their biting critiques:

Torture chamber. Red glow-stick juice and a strobe light, hiding yet another psycho: "Bad planning with the electric chainsaw. Couldn't chase us because the cord was too short."

Guillotine. Illuminated under flickering candles, casting ghastly shadows over the executioners and pleading victim, who screamed like a hammy actress: "Tennis shoes under the black robes."

Haunted graveyard. A large room peppered with cardboard tombstones in a sea of golden maple leaves, filling the floor a foot high. "They'll jump out there, there, and there," whispered Connor, his pointed finger whipping across the room. With perfect timing, rotting zombies hurled themselves out of the same oversized leaf piles Connor had just predicted.

But if Connor was observant, Keith was jaded. Case in point, the Dracula room. Velvet coffin, Bach's Toccata and Fugue in D Minor blaring from a hidden speaker. Bela Lugosi opened the lid and waved delectable claws at the girls as the party passed through without a sound.

"Oh my GOD. That was corny," Keith exclaimed.

Benny knew one thing about Keith. "Corny" infuriated him. The word was his most blasphemous profanity, and he had no tolerance for it in his house or any other. Leaving the Dracula room for another hallway where yet more spiderwebs caught his head, Connor brought it up.

"Seen anything better than the RedCap yet?"

"Nothing'll be better than the RedCap."

The "RedCap" was Keith's new scare at the *HallO'Scream*, debuting tonight. Few others knew about it. Keith wanted it that way.

"Darryl hasn't shot it down yet?" Connor asked, and Benny shivered. Darryl was the co-manager of the HallO'Scream, Keith's partner. It was Keith's land (via his brother-in-law), but Darryl provided the cash and paid the actors. It was a marriage of convenience, and once the house was established they had agreed to disagree on virtually everything. Keith's many gripes with Darryl included imagination. Mainly that Darryl didn't have one. He creeped Benny out to no end.

"He doesn't get to. The 1st floor is mine."

"Until he says it isn't," Connor continued. "His promises only last as long as he says they do."

Keith grunted.

"Think Darryl would ever have said yes if he knew your first idea was the Puka?" Connor laughed at his own question.

Puka? Benny had only been paying half attention. He usually kept quiet most of the time anyway. But this hit his curiosity dead center. His question was out before he even knew his mouth was open:

"What's a Puka?"

Connor laughed. "That's *exactly* what Darryl would have said."

Which didn't answer Benny's question. He thought he knew every Halloween monster. Zombies. Mad Scientists. Slash killers. Those

23

he had heard of. The MacCools had the biggest horror DVD collection in town. But Benny had never heard of anything called a 'Puka.' *Funny name.* So he asked again.

"What's a Puka?"

Keith stopped and turned around. Looking at Benny, he spoke in flawless authority.

"In the country where Halloween was born, it was the scariest monster of all time."

That was Keith's absolutely dead serious voice, and it was the only answer Benny got as Keith turned back around. *He's talking about Ireland.* Benny thought. *An Irish monster? Never heard of it. I'll look it up later.*

Keith stopped to admire a lavishly painted diorama of skeletons having a family dinner, glowing under a blacklight. Connor moved up to join him and to Benny's relief, so did the two girls. They released Benny's arms as they moved up to Connor, Benny happily let the girls go and enjoyed circulation flowing back into his limbs.

Alone. He wanted to be alone. Last night's nightmare still swam in his head. He'd hoped a good rip-roaring haunted house would flush it out, but the girls had interfered. He needed to enjoy his favorite activity *his* way, so he left the crowd behind to peek around at what was next. Rounding one last corner of bare plywood that should have been painted like a haunted castle mosaic or bare black at the very least, he ran right into a thick black velvet curtain covering a door bathed in a red bulb. Dark. Foreboding. The highlight of the *Scare Asylum.*

The Grand Finale.

But before Benny could enjoy the sight, a black form peeled itself out of a corner and pushed Benny back with an aggressive shove. Benny caught himself from tripping, but didn't object. It was only a guard, here to give the Finale time to reset between guests. However, the guard took the part way too seriously, wearing the predictable costume of another vampire. The corny kind, the tres chic vampire of the Blade movies. Slicked hair, leather trenchcoat, biker boots, ear rings, and cheap plastic clip-on fangs. He towered over Benny by a good 8 inches.

Looking down, the vampire gave a snorty laugh.

"Well, hello, Benny."

Crud.

Through the red haze Benny's eyes focused on a male he knew as Marcus, someone he knew from school. Someone he had no wish to ever see again.

"You're awfully brave to come in here alone."

For the first time that night, Benny wanted to scream. Benny had had to endure Marcus for years, as his ridiculed plaything. Marcus had always been taller and meatier than Benny no matter what school they were in. From junior high onward, he'd been a bully.

Benny's graduation last spring was supposed to be the end of it. Apparently not.

Out of all the haunted houses, in all the towns, why did Marcus have to work here?

Benny wanted to talk back. Wanted to shout "I am NOT alone!" But he kept quiet. He always did.

"Going in? Don't get hurt in there. Never know when something might happen to you," and Marcus raised his palm, reaching out to give Benny another minor shove that Benny knew far too well. With Marcus's flair of clawed fingers (painted) and sharpened canine teeth (plastic), Benny's mind flashed through several comebacks, but he said nothing. He just did what he always did, closed his eyes and waited for it to be over with.

It never landed. Benny opened one eye...

Keith held Marcus's wrist in a twisted grappling hold. Marcus's painted nails flailed. Yes, Keith was REAL good at appearing out of nowhere. Benny heard Connor and the girls coming up behind him, but Benny fixed on Keith, who spoke to Marcus with dripping sarcasm.

"Your mascara's running," Keith said with cold eyes.

Marcus's other hand was halfway to his face before he caught himself. His eyes narrowed in anger. Marcus was taller, but Keith held him firm, daring Marcus to move even one muscle.

"Sorry. I didn't know if you were supposed to be a vampire or a male model," Keith's voice dripped. "I didn't recognize you without your sparkle."

Benny inhaled, bracing for Marcus to throw a punch. But Keith didn't budge, and gripped Marcus's other hand all the tighter until Marcus averted his eyes. Keith dropped Marcus's hand in silence, then motioned behind as Connor came out of the red gloom with the girls. Marcus moved back to his corner as the group moved past. Benny felt Marcus's eyes burn him all way down, but then he faded into the dark.

Keith watched him leave and huffed. He was not going to be interrupted. Not here. THIS was allegedly the scariest scare in town. THIS was getting all the attention. Keith wanted to see it. Connor wanted to see it. Benny wanted to see it.

The two girls absolutely did not.

They grasped each other behind Connor, bulging eyes unanimously agreeing that they were *not* going in there. Connor laughed and for once Keith joined in too.

"Ladies, ladies," Keith adopted a fatherly voice as he and Connor leaned in to talk softly. "Right now you're perfectly safe. Think about it. Nothing ever scares you going *into* a room." The girls blinked as Keith gestured towards the dark door that hid god-knew-what. "They have to wait until you're in the middle. They can't scare you before then, because the whole idea is to chase you out the other side. Not trap you back here."

Only Keith could use Haunted House logic as a counseling tool. He engaged both girls eye to eye and spoke in as reassuring of a voice as the surrounding cacophony of spectral laughs would allow.

"So here's the plan. You stay here. We'll run in," he pantomimed his upcoming dash through the door. "You listen for the scare, then run in right after. The monster will be in plain sight, and you'll see how to run right around him. If you're fast enough, he'll even see you at all. But you have to run. Don't wait."

Too hasty nods from the two girls telegraphed *I just want this to be over.* Connor laughed again, gesturing Benny to join him at the

26

door behind Keith. Connor had his own advice for the girls before readying himself.

"And whatever you do, don't scream. Or it'll know you're here. Trust us, ladies." Connor stood proudly. "We're Haunted House connoisseurs."

Keith groaned, then huddled everyone up.

"On the count of two, we charge." He pointed to Connor. "You run straight through and stall him. I want to see everything."

Benny had been looking forward to this room all night. Keith obviously felt the same. Zipping up his leather jacket, checking his pockets for loose items, Benny saw Keith give the nod of *Get ready*. Keith had been the black sheep of his mom's side of the family. Mom's little brother didn't scare easily, if at all. Benny watched as Keith pulled the door open to stare into the darkness beyond.

"OK, Scare Asylum," Keith tensed, "I dare you. Scare me."

Keith and Connor dove through the door together. Benny took a breath, then jumped in one step behind, leaving the two girls in clutched panic behind them.

A strobe went off.

A shape jumped out of the corner.

The girls screamed.

WALKING TO CONNOR'S CAR in the parking lot, Keith's face was one of downright dejection.

"That was not scary."

It was hard to impress Keith. The Scare Asylum had tried its best and failed. Keith's adventure was over. Benny's was not. The two girls wanted to talk to him.

"Thanks for taking us through."

Benny cringed. The encounter with Marcus had shot his desire for socialization through the kneecaps. He just wanted to go home.

"Sure... no problem."

"Maybe we'll see you in school on Monday."

Benny's eyes flicked up as...anger flared inside him.

"Sure." Then he turned aside, and the girls walked away. Benny didn't want to look at them again.

School? Great idea. If he hadn't already graduated last spring.

Benny was 18, but still baby-faced and waiting for his final growth spurt. He could still pass for a high school freshman with a year to spare. Maybe when he was 30, he'd finally pass for an adult.

Your own fault you know. If you were in college like you were supposed to be...

But he wasn't in college. He couldn't go alone, not without Bridget. His sister was supposed to have gone with him.

Now that will never happen,

Benny just wanted to go to bed. He had slept horribly last night and still had a Too-Little-Sleep headache that burned behind his eyes. Tomorrow they'd see another Haunted House and he could forget tonight ever happened. Benny's internal stewing almost made him miss Keith's next pronouncement.

"Well thank God that's over. Now it's the home stretch."

Benny's head clicked back to the here and now. They weren't done yet, "Wait, weren't we going to the Field of Screams tomorrow?" He looked from Keith to Connor.

Connor's eternal smile vanished. "No. It closed."

CLOSED? Few things could get Benny talking, but the unexpected removal of an entire haunted house in late October?

"That's the best one! What happened?"

"An accident. Scotty's gone."

"Gone? Where'd he go?"

Connor looked away. Keith turned to his nephew.

"Scotty was killed last night."

"Killed?" A hundred thoughts flew through Benny's head.

Scotty was killed? LAST NIGHT?

He'd known Scotty for years, a professional costume maker. Scotty had taught Benny the art of Halloween prop construction. He couldn't be gone, he couldn't be—

Dead.

But Scotty was. And it freaked Benny out. Not the fact that Scotty was dead...

But because the night before, Benny had dreamed the whole thing.

TWO

YOU COULD TELL A lot about someone from their favorite Halloween monster.

Dry-cleaned suits and knotted ties? That's the fakery, the fantasy of someone pretending to be a responsible adult when they're not. But a monster someone lovingly creates with their own hands? That's their real face.

On the way home from the *Scare Asylum*, Keith put on his real face in the passenger seat of Connor's car. Visiting another haunted house the same night that your own house is open necessitates multitasking. Keith could multitask his multitasks.

Such as now, attacking his face with globs of gooey latex even as Connor blasted his car through congested traffic out of the *Scare Asylum* parking lot and out of the Big City. Keith's haunted house, The *HallO'Scream*, opened in fourteen minutes. With Connor driving, Keith would be there, ready for the show, in six. And damned if any sissy drivers fumbling at the speed limit were going to stop him. As Connor wove through blaring break lights like a maniac playing Tetris, Keith kept half an eye on Benny in the backseat. Benny's eyes were open in either terror or exhilaration. *I should have told him about Scotty earlier. Looks like he's taking it bad. I'll talk with him later.* Meanwhile Keith's fingers pockmarked his face with layers of zombie goo. Long-learned muscle memory did the work for him, letting him digest the night events.

Leaving a haunted house depressed him, as bad as 2 pm on Christmas Day when all the presents are opened, the house is quiet, and you realize you have to wait another 365 days to enjoy it again. This hurt even worse.

"Taylor's not scary any more."

The *Scare Asylum* was the brainchild of Taylor O'Neil. Keith and Taylor had been friendly rivals for a long time. But Keith was stupendously jealous of Taylor's word of mouth. And what was Taylor's stupendous new monster that was leeching all Keith's buzz? A psycho clown. A Joker. A la Heath Ledger in *The Dark Knight. That's* what had been awarded "The scariest fright in town." Ten foot tall monster clown with eyes of blood and wicked chainsaw to be sure, but still a clown.

"A freaking clown," he muttered, even as he applied swatches of gray and fake blood to transform his own face into the walking dead.

"And you're mad that you didn't think of it first," Connor surmised while steering around an overloaded semi-trailer. "Judging by the screams, it's the best chainsaw monster Taylor's had in years."

"It was a leaf-blower."

Using a leaf-blower in place of a chainsaw was a time-honored switcheroo. In the darkness they sounded darn near identical, even if Keith ranted about it being a cop out. His house used a real chainsaw and always would. With chain removed of course.

"If Heath Ledger knew what haunted houses were doing with leaf-blowers in the Joker's name, he'd claw out of his grave."

"A Joker is exactly what I expected from Taylor," Connor said.

"The Joker *was* Taylor. Don't tell me you didn't notice him under the paint," Keith all but snarled. "Taylor doesn't want to be scary, he wants to be a star. He used to know better."

"Could have been worse," Connor gave a pregnant pause. "Could have been a vampire Joker."

Keith groaned. He had no patience for the current sexual metaphor overload of Halloween. "Please don't give the world any more bad ideas."

"Everyone wants to be a vampire."

"I don't."

When it came to scary Keith always put his money where his mouth was. His face stared back at him from the passenger-side vanity mirror as a terror of worm-rotten flesh. Sneaking a peek out the window, Keith could see the lights of cars flying by at suicidal speeds in this race out of town. Connor had earned his driver's license from the school of "Brakes are for sissies." Potholes were bumped, curbs skidded, but Keith's eyes stayed on his face in the visor mirror.

"Just be glad Darryl didn't go with us," Connor said. "He would have hired the Joker on the spot."

"Darryl's problem is that he never goes with us. Too busy with his empire." Keith's complexion was now a sickly gray with red splotches of decaying pores. Slices of loose latex flapped and swung like so much decayed flesh. Connor slowed to negotiate a curb and a girl walking on the sidewalk saw Keith face-to-face. She double-taked with a hand over her mouth. Keith grinned. That's what Halloween should be.

"Well, tonight's the night," Connor remarked while gunning his engine again. "Is your Redcap ready?"

"Would I have wasted a night with the chainsaw Joker if it wasn't?" Keith retorted. He had been working on his new Grand Finale a long time, and it would be the best in the city. Certainly better than a dumb Joker.

"If Darryl doesn't blow it back in your face."

"He doesn't get to. The Grand Finale is mine."

Whipping around a last few residential streets, Connor's car spun gravel on a dirt road leading out of town. The HallO'Scream lay beyond.

"Would you have liked Taylor's house better if he would have had a cute ticket taker at the front gate?" Connor snickered.

Keith turned to face Connor as a flesh-eating ghoul with rotten teeth.

"Do I look like I like cute?"

Bzzzzz Keith's pocket rang. The ringtone of *Grim Grinning Ghosts* from Disneyland's Haunted Mansion filled the passenger seat as Keith fished into a cavernous pocket in his leather jacket and yanked out his black android, seeing—

"Why in the hell do I have ten texts from Jack? And three missed calls?"

"No coverage inside a haunted house, remember? Fine print in the terms of service." Connor chuckled as Keith fiddled with his screen and his eyes went wide with righteous anger. Darryl had done it again.

"Get me home." Keith all but shouted. "NOW."

From the backseat, Benny moaned. Keith turned around long enough to make sure he had survived Connor's escapade. The road was a straight shot now, deep into the boondocks of the countryside. Benny lay huddled in a ball, but would be OK.

Darryl wouldn't.

YOU KNOW THOSE DREAMS that just... nauseate? That smudge your mind all day and then make you feel dirty just for remembering it? Benny's dream the night before had been that kind.

Someone panicking... being chased like an animal and being run to exhaustion in the dead of night...until being trapped in a claustrophobic alley with nowhere to go, as the walls closed in and black form rose above to smother him...and ...and ...

And he had Scotty's face. *Why didn't I see that before?* In the backseat of Connor's car, Benny's queasy brain insisted he wanted to heave, but not because of Connor's driving. The nightmare kept flickering over his eyes.

Scotty is dead. And I dreamed about it. You're not supposed to have dreams like that. Scotty's worst fear was to be smothered.

33

Wait, how did I know that?

Benny could only wonder, and looked to Keith. He wanted to tell Keith everything, but he didn't have the courage. Benny envied how Keith could transform himself into a blood-drinking ghoul in the passenger seat of a car going 70 mph. Nothing scared Keith. Benny however, could only groan. Between the girls, Marcus, and the nightmare, it had turned into yet another perfect Benny day. Right now he wanted nothing but to hide in Keith's basement and not come out for a week.

Except, what would his sister have said about that?

He knew exactly what Bridget would say.

"Benny! Stand still and talk to me. Someone told me she was going to say hi to you today."

She did.

"And?"

And what?

"WHAT did you say to her?"

Hi.

"And then what?"

That's it.

"A girl says Hi to you, and that's all you said?"

Well, what else is there? I just can't start jabbering away whenever someone mouths off to me in a crowded hallway! I have places to be!

"Like hiding in the basement until midnight? Don't you want some friends?"

They just get in the way.

"Brave to come here alone," Marcus had said. Except with Bridget dead, Benny preferred alone.

We're almost home anyway. Just outside the city, the road gave way to cracks and grit, the glow from Keith's magnum opus finally came into view.

The *HallO'Scream.*

Keith's haunted house began life as an elementary school, decades past when all buildings were square with sealed windows, reminding one less of education and more of incarceration. With shifting demographics the school had sat abandoned for two decades before Keith found it.

And in the finest Frankenstein tradition, resurrected it. A golden sea of carved pumpkins filled the entire front lawn of a red brick edifice two stories high. Happy faces, scary faces, malefic faces glowing with sinister intent. The flickering of orange lay so thick one might step from the street to the front steps and never touch unlit ground. Crucified scarecrows with pumpkin heads lined the walkway to the front door, flaunting piranha teeth that dared guests to enter. The entrance itself flickered orange firelight, a gate to Hell inside a cavernous double door. The *HallO'Scream* opened later than other houses in the area, allowing Keith to cater to older clientele. Keith had a responsible crew working for him, enough so that he could drive into his parking lot mere minutes before opening and find his house already up and running. His people knew their jobs, and he let them know when they didn't.

Speaking of his good people...

"Why's Jack standing there like he wants to get run over?" Benny heard Connor ask as the car screamed into the parking lot. Benny doubted that was Jack's intent, no one would have missed seeing Jack Sparrow from a mile away. *Captain* Jack Sparrow, that is. With dreadlocks, goatee, and pirate leggings straight out of the Caribbean. Except this Captain Sparrow had an iPhone in his right hand, which he ferociously jabbed with a *"Where the hell have you been?"* pantomime.

Connor's car lurched to halt at a crooked angle as Keith tore open his door and made a hell-bent-for-leather dash into the back of the school, leaving everyone else behind.

What was THAT about?

Connor laughed as Keith vanished inside the building. He turned around to speak to Benny. "Well. Looks like your uncle is going to need your help. Are you going to scare anyone tonight?"

Benny could only shake his head, and Connor frowned. "You cant hide in your uncle's workshop all October. Its a holiday contra-

35

diction to work in a haunted house and, like, never scare anything. I'd give you a lesson but I've got to get to my own humble abode." Connor's *Fright Zone* was a couple miles back. Benny knew Connor would be in a hurry to get there.

"Look," Connor's voice got softer, "Don't let Scotty get you down. Last thing he'd want would be a ruined Halloween. He'd be the first one to tell you, Haunted House Connoisseurs never die."

Benny still blinked away dust from the parking lot as he monkeyed himself out of the backseat. Connor stuck his lanky head out of his window as he turned the car around for a run at the street. "If your uncle works you too hard, remember I've always got a place for you. I'll make a man of ya." Benny gave a half-hearted smile as Connor gunned his engine and disappeared down the road. Meanwhile...

What was Keith so mad about? Benny walked over to the Jack Sparrow in the parking lot, who had a look of an impending storm.

"Jack? What happened?"

Captain Sparrow's goatee scowled in utter disgust. "Darryl gutted the Redcap room."

Benny gasped. Then shivered from the primeval fear of what Keith would now be forced to do.

THREE

ZOMBIES AREN'T SUPPOSED TO run. They're slow, lumbering oafs.

But in full zombie face-paint, Keith ran the distance from the far edge of the parking lot to Darryl's office in the basement in no less than 15 seconds.

The sight of Zombie-Keith charging like a blood-drinking killer through the back corridors of the *HallO'Scream* failed to elicit any reaction whatsoever. His actors were well accustomed to seeing Keith running somewhere, and a freakish corpse was hardly out of place in this building anyway. On his way to the basement Keith passed grinning ghosts, hooded executioners, and a devil in an orange tuxedo. Keith didn't pay them any mind, for they were doing what they should be doing. Keith's target was someone else entirely.

The door down the stairs had the conceit to label itself "Darryl O'Grady: Manager." Keith shoved it open and charged into a choking cloud of cigarette smoke thicker than Halloween fog. Darryl's office had nothing but blank brick walls, hand-me-down chairs from the abandoned cafeteria, and a table full of paperwork. And Darryl, leaning over his account books like a bean-counting money grubber. The world according to Darryl O'Grady had no imagination, just overhead.

Next to Darryl hovered a petite girl in a black velvet cape with fangs and red contact lenses. This black-haired lass apparently thought she was a vampire, or at least wanted to play one on TV. However, upon seeing Keith's rotting face, the vampirette instantly wilted and ran out of the room as Keith stomped right up to Darryl.

"You couldn't even ASK, could you?"

Darryl scribbled furiously in a notebook, not even looking up.

"It was a dumb idea, Keith. And you were fraternizing with the enemy."

"Connor's our friend!"

"Your friend. Until he gives us a share of his sales, he's a competitor."

Darryl wouldn't be Darryl without miserly condescension. But Keith wasn't going to tolerate it this time.

"Connor goes with me to the trade shows because you can't be bothered to learn this business. Speaking of which, I'm putting the Redcap back. Stay out of that room."

"No, you're not. That room is occupied."

"That's right. I'm the one occupying it. Your dumb ideas are supposed to go on the second floor so we'd stop butting heads."

"They didn't want the second floor, they wanted the first."

"Who the hell is *they?*"

"Shriek Bootique. That Halloween retailer on Washington Ave—"

"I KNOW DAMN WELL what the Shriek Bootique is. Why are they harassing my house?"

"*Our* house. They volunteered to do a room for us. They're putting up a picture booth."

"Exactly what are they doing with a picture booth?"

Darryl finally looked up at Keith as if he was an idiot. Keith had seen that look too many times and forgave it less each time.

"People will pay to have their picture taken with monsters obviously. Then the Bootique gives a hard push on their gift shop. Tonight they're bringing in a school bus of little kids to fire it all off. Your room was the best place to put it all."

Keith steamed. "I am *not* pulling actors out of their stations to have a Disney photo-op! We barely have enough to run both floors as it is! I'm taking the room back."

"No, you're not. The Bootique paid us for the whole weekend, and we get a cut of every picture they take."

Keith sighed. *God help me having to put up with this.*

Darryl just huffed. "In case you didn't notice, and I know you didn't, we're 20% behind where we were last year. People want to buy moronic pictures so they can post them and brag to all their moronic friends. The booth stays." Darryl went back to his ledger. "Besides, you don't have an actor. Mike quit."

Keith gripped Darryl's desk in surprise. "MIKE QUIT?"

"His last words to me were, and I'm quoting exactly: 'Keith takes this way too seriously.' He had it with your obsessive compulsion."

Keith's eye's whirled, *That conniving backstabber...* But Darryl didn't let him finish the thought.

"Do even know how much of a perfectionist tyrant you are?" Darryl continued. "Mike hasn't been the only one to say it."

Keith couldn't deny it. Whatever. That wasn't the problem now. "Fine. I'll do the RedCap."

Darryl laughed out loud. "I bet you would! You wanted that all along didn't you? Play your own little Halloween hero, while I'm the one stressing about keeping ourselves open for another week."

Keith released the desk, but knew Darryl was right. He reeled his anger back in. "What exactly is this "gift shop" selling?"

"T-Shirts. Small toys. Cheap stuff we can mark up for $10 to $15 apiece."

T-shirts. Other houses sold them. Flimsy prints with low-quality *"I Survived the Tunnel of Terror"* and so forth. They radiated cheesy. "Direct from an Asian sweatshop, no doubt," Keith mocked.

"Whatever. We're aiming at kids now."

"Since when?"

"Since this was a kid's holiday! And don't give me that face. Here." Reaching into a cardboard box behind his desk, Darryl grabbed a handful of black shirts and threw them at Keith. "*HallO'Scream*" was in thick orange and red bold lettering, arching like a gateway of flames, with white lettering beneath it:

HALLO'SCREAM

We ARE dead people

HALLO'SCREAM

In our space, EVERYONE can hear you scream

HALLO'SCREAM

If you don't leave screaming, you won't leave at all

Keith threw the shirts back on Darryl's deck.
"Corny."
"What's your point?" Darryl's face split with an evil grin.
Keith growled. "If the funds are that bad, then you shouldn't have wasted so much petty cash on your damned robot chorus line." Darryl had almost given Keith a heart attack a month previous by showing up with several animatronic monster mannequins. Jason Voorhees, Freddy Krueger, Michael Myers. They didn't scare anyone over the age of six. "With the money you wasted on dorky movie-stars we could have hired five more actors—"
"No, we saved on hiring five more actors!" Darryl broke in. "We don't need any more overhead, we need kids to give us their money for a picture with Freddy Kruger."
"Everyone uses Krueger! Everyone you do is a celebrity yutz from the 80s! I want something that people won't recognize—"
"KEITH!" Now Darryl stood up to smack his palm against the table in frustration. "If people don't recognize it, *why* would they ever want to pay for it? " Darryl leaned forward with a mocking leer." *You* need enough money to not sleep on your nephew's couch," Darryl grinned, and Keith's frontal brain lobe flared in heat.

That's my damn business.

Darryl leaned back. "You also said you were getting that job with the Lakeview Police Department, and this year you wouldn't be around so much."

How dare he bring that up. "That....didn't pan out."

"No, but then a great deal of your life hasn't 'panned out,' now has it? What was it this time? They checked your work history and found out about the—"

"SHUT UP!"

Keith's eyes burned red as his fists curled. THAT topic was off-limits and Darryl knew it. Darryl just looked at Keith with a tiny hint of... fear, and backed down. His next words were softer.

"Keith, we need to end this year with money to burn. I've got dances and parties lined up all over town. Halloween is on a Saturday, so, if you're the Halloween genius, prove it. Give me a monster people will actually pay to see. An *American* monster. The *Haunted Hollow* is killing our word of mouth with that Headless Horseman they have running around their parking lot. Get me one of those. Or better yet make it a vampire. Everyone wants to be a vampire."

Keith's fists turned white as Darryl went back to his books.

Yes, celebrity monsters ruled Halloween. Worse, no one knew why that was moronic. There was no winning this. Except maybe...

Oh yes, he'll love this.

"You want a nice all-American Headless Horseman? All right. Maybe we can."

Now Darryl looked up with a half-smile, so Keith pounced with a sales pitch, exclaiming every syllable with an exaggerated waving of his arms, and movie-trailer punch.

"Imagine THIS horseman: A 7-foot-tall rider that carries its own sunken dead head. Its other hand carries an Indiana Jones whip made of human bone which it swings around grim reaper style. I can make its head glow white. I can make its whip glow red. I can make screeching yells to be heard a mile away."

"Now you're thinking like a businessman," Darryl smiled. "Anything from a Johnny Depp movie gets the girls, and the girls bring their boyfriends. Everyone wins."

Keith turned to open the door out of Darryl's office. In the hallway beyond, actors rushed into their places.

"Everyone wins all right," Keith said as he exited the room. "Except I wasn't describing a Johnny Depp movie. I was describing a real monster. It's called a 'Dullahan.' And it's *not* American. It's from Ireland, Mr. O'GRADY!" Keith shouted as he slammed the door with righteous fury.

FOUR

KEITH HATED PURPLE.

For a long time Purple enjoyed its proper place in the crayon box, coming out in the spring when one needed to doodle an Easter Egg or perhaps a purple people eater. But somewhere along the line it escaped Easter, bypassed St. Patrick's, and jumped right over Christmas to land in the dead center of Autumn.

Into Halloween.

Darryl's new concession stand had infested the entire HallO'Scream with purple, Purple skeletons, glow sticks, and fairy wings lay crushed underfoot in the foyer and throughout Keith's cherished pumpkin field.

"I hate purple."

Benny watched his uncle take slow strides around the foyer, out to the front door, then back again. Keith's face was back to human now, the zombie make-up washed off with nary a trace. Benny didn't have to wash up, but he always helped clean up the house. He liked it here. The inside entrance to the *HallO'Scream* was a showcase of movie posters. Representations from every era of horror movies going back a century. A big screen TV flickering over the line kept up a continual loop of the scariest scenes from those same movies. The background noise helped Benny think. Benny also wanted to talk about Scotty. His death had come too quick out of nowhere. Benny also wanted to talk to Keith about his sister, about how at night ever since she died, Benny thought he could hear... *No, I can't talk about that.*

Benny chickened out and flipped through a text on his phone. He only had one to read. You needed friends to get texts. Or a Dad that cared.

Work held over another month
Home by Xmas will call later

That's all Benny ever got out of his dad. Reason #347 why he lived with Keith. Except Keith's explosion with Darryl had rattled him. *How can I ask Keith a question without him blowing up?*

Easy. Talk about Halloween. Benny picked up a crushed plastic bottle as he caught up to Keith. "Did you mean what you said to Darryl?"

"Which part?" Keith asked as he rapidly filled a garbage bag with debris.

"The Headless Horseman ripped-off of something Irish?"

"From his severed head to the hooves of his horse." Keith replied as his hands moved from mess to mess. "The idea of a headless killer collecting dead people goes back a thousand years. Washington Irving just stole a good idea of a monster that was already there."

"You remember who wrote *Legend of Sleepy Hollow?*"

"I remember everything."

Benny believed that. Benny thought he knew a lot about Halloween, but Keith always reminded him how much he still did NOT know. *And it's not as if Keith had anything better to do. He's been unemployed for about two years, since— no, better not go there.* Benny kept on topic.

"So why doesn't anyone else know?"

Keith laughed. "Since when does anyone else know anything? A culture that can't even remember when vampires didn't sparkle?

44

And Darryl's always the last one to care. He's more greedy than ever before. Something's changed."

Benny followed the wall of the foyer, picking up gum wrappers. "So what did a 'Dullahan' do?"

"The Irish Grim Reaper," Keith answered. "If you were going to die, he'd show up at your door on a black hell-horse and throw a bucket of blood in your face, laughing through the whole thing."

"How'd he laugh without a head?"

"The Dullahan carried his head like a lantern. Irving made a few alterations to give his story a plot complication, and give Icabod something to fight for. But the pure form goes back centuries before Sleepy Hollow."

"A headless horseman who carried his own head, and poured blood on you if you were next on his death list?" Benny paused, but Keith's answer was classic Keith:

"Yep. Probably looked pretty cool." Keith picked up a pop can, ducking under the black gauze curtain separating the queue from the ticket booth. "Irish monsters didn't do anything by halves."

Benny filed all that away, and took the moment to climb around the foyer. The queue wrapped around a mouse maze of plastic chains and wooden stakes topped with dark gray skulls. Benny looked into the empty eye-sockets and lost his train of thought.

I wonder if he poured blood on Bridget when she died—

YOU WILL NOT THINK ABOUT THAT! Benny mentally slapped himself.

Don't you dare think like that again.

Benny dropped his garbage bag, mad at himself as Keith continued his meticulous scouring of his foyer. He quickly thought of another question to distract himself.

"The RedCap was Irish too?"

"Yes. Celtic."

"Was he ripped-off too?"

Keith looked up with a laugh. "If only anyone knew." Keith put down the garbage sack and waved at all the movie posters surrounding them. "Everything is a rip-off of the RedCap."

Everything? Benny considered. He had seen the RedCap suit, but he'd never really known much about it. Keith had always been too busy to ask. All this time, and Benny still didn't know what the name "Redcap" meant.

"Bland name," Benny said. Especially in an Ireland filled with "Dullahans" and "Banshees."

"Its literal," Keith replied. "They wore a red hat or bandana drenched in human blood. They lived in the darkest corners of the darkest castles and ambush any human they found." Keith's face grew into a leering smile as his enthusiasm leaked to the surface. "Murdering you with bloodthirsty delight, then wearing your blood as a trophy. The original slasher." Keith looked at Benny. "Now tell me, Mr. DVD. Who does that remind you of?"

It came to Benny immediately from his TV in the queue. Endless horror movie previews Benny had picked himself. He knew exactly who Keith was thinking of.

"You mean Leatherface."

Keith made a congratulatory "snap" with is fingers and pointed to a poster across the room advertising *Texas Chainsaw Massacre*. "A serial killer who slices up human corpses and wears a mask of human skin. Perfect modern incarnation."

Benny had seen the original Texas Chainsaw from the 70's, an honored part of the MacCools' well-stocked DVD collection. It had sequels, of course, even a remake some years back, but nothing could beat the first low budget grainy film made by amateurs with an excessive love for the genre.

"Did those guys know they were ripping off the Redcap?"

Keith shook his head. "Definitely probably not. It's just the slasher genre in general. Jason Voorhees is the same way. The speechless killer who wears a mask. And the mask is more famous than the monster, the cultural constant no matter what century we're in. Name another."

Benny's eyes wandered to the movie posters scowling from the walls. The original *Frankenstein, Evil Dead II. The Hills Have Eyes* on one side. *Dawn of the Dead, Blair Witch Project* and *Alien* filling the other. A representation of nearly every golden age of horror, from the classics to 70's schlock. And in a corner, one very curious addition. A dark silhouette of a rabbit pulling for its life from a neck snare against a cold sunset. It was a movie, a cartoon, but for Benny's money, THE scariest movie ever aimed at directly at children. 1979's *Watership Down.*

Next to that, John Carpenter's *Halloween.*

"Michael Meyers," Benny said.

"Exactly." Keith rapped his knuckles on the picture frame for the horror opus. "A psycho more famous for the rubber mask he wears. Name another."

"Hannibal Lecter."

Keith nodded. "Anyone can wear his mask and you know exactly who it's supposed to be. Even better, he's famous for eating people."

Looking around, Benny tried one more.

"Freddy Krueger."

"Not quite." Keith meandered up to the poster for *Nightmare on Elm Street.* Vicious metallic claws hung over the head of the young actress clutching her bedsheets. "He's more recognizable as an actor. Good ole Robert Englund. Not a direct descendent of the RedCap, but definitely in the gene pool. The entire graduating class of the 1980's. Monsters who are more famous for being celebrities."

"But your room, it was going to have the "Redcap" the way it used to be?"

"Pure version," Keith nodded. "Before it was watered down. Most monsters have changed so much we have no idea what they used to be. How could they? Most people don't even know where their own family immigrated from!"

Keith had nearly completed his meticulous clean-up, but his rant had a ways to go.

"We can't even remember our *own* monsters! Every generation has less monsters than the one before. Remember Frankenstein? The Mummy? When was the last time you saw either one of them? They're gone. Now there's only two monsters left. TWO."

Benny knew which two.

"Vampires and Werewolves."

"The sexy ones," Keith nodded in disgust. "But the back of our head remembers the rest." Keith waved at the diorama of posters. "A memory of what we're *supposed* to be afraid of." Keith walked over to pick up one last purple skeleton. "But we don't have monsters anymore. We have celebrities." Keith twisted the skeleton around in his hands, folding and unfolded it. "Makes you wonder what else we've forgotten, doesn't it?" Keith's good humor ran dry as he walked to the front door and looked at his lawn, which still needed an exhaustive cleaning of its own.

"Remember when Halloween was orange?"

Like a rubber band, Keith flipped the purple skeleton into the nearest garbage can.

FIVE

Orange. Benny's bedspread was orange. But lying under his orange bedspread at 2 AM, he couldn't sleep.

He knew another nightmare awaited him if he did. It bubbled in the back of his head, festering, ready to jump him like an animal. If that wasn't enough, there was another very pressing reason why Benny hadn't been getting much sleep lately...

*Step...Step...*In the hallway outside his door.

Thump Thump. Benny's heart pounded in time with the steps. Benny might have ran, might have screamed, but had the courage for neither.

Then the nightmare found him.

Looking up at a sign of orange neon, burning away with a BUZZZZ into a deserted night, Benny knew where he was.

SCARE ASYLUM.

Taylor stepped out the door. No longer wearing the Joker costume, but Benny recognized him all the same. The nightmare wouldn't let him forget.

Benny now he remembered why he hated waking up in the middle of the night.

For a half second his eyes flashed open, long enough to see that he was still in his bedroom.

Long enough to see that he wouldn't stay there.

Dead of Night. Not that Taylor was scared. He was always the last to leave, to turn off the lights and lock the door. Wind brushed him with cool fingers, branches waved at him as he passed. Taylor had a brisk walk over several blocks to get home. Alone.

Except maybe this night, Taylor was NOT alone. A black form appeared down the deserted street, a silhouette against a moon, heralded by a simple sound echoing down the street.

Clippity Clop

Taylor didn't hear a thing.

Benny could see it. A monster on four legs. A horse. With a rider.

With the heave of a steam engine it hurled itself down the street toward Taylor at a full gallop.

Benny couldn't move, couldn't help.

Why didn't Taylor see it?

Clippity Clop. Clouds of dust erupted from the monster's hooves. Sparks shattered the pavement, splashing the rider's frayed coat and torn leggings with yellow embers. The rider—

Had no head. THE RIDER HAD NO HEAD. But it carried one, a head that glowed pale white in his decomposing right hand. The left hand gripped a rusted wooden bucket.

Taylor saw nothing as the rider charged him. In one more second Taylor would be trampled under monstrous black hoofs... until the rider swerved, raised its left arm high, and dumped the contents of the bucket over Taylor's head with an ear-splitting cackle. The bucket drenched Taylor with blood. Sickly red blood soaked his hair and clothes, sticking to his face like festering glue. The black rider then continued on, his beast pounding sparks as both vanished into the night air. The wind from his passage brushed just a breeze through Taylor's hair.

Leaves rustled.

But the blood remained. Taylor never saw a thing. Just kept walking home.

Benny's legs pumped empty air. He awoke again for another half second, grasping at blankets that held him in place. His muddled mind remembered something he'd heard earlier about blood, but the nightmare claimed him again. Now he knew something he didn't before—

Taylor held a horrible fear of speed. Of cars. Of crashing.

Benny had enough consciousness to ask. "How did I know that?"

Because the nightmare knew.

GRRRRRR

Taylor stopped at the sound, coming from a darkened street beyond. What did he hear? A noise? A threat? Standing under brown trees swaying in the wind, Taylor looked and saw nothing. He gave a smirky smile. He had taken this street back home for years. Maybe someone was being a wiseguy.

Trying to scare ME, are you? Ok, wise guy. I dare you. Scare me.

Challenge accepted.

An explosion of speed as Taylor opened his mouth to scream, but impossibly beastly arms scooped him right off the sidewalk. icy wind burns his skin as the breakneck velocity plastered him to the beast. Taylor's heart pounds with terror in a horrific ride of jumping over rooftops. Taylor can't escape as his knuckles clench with blood. Taylor hates speed.

Too fast!

Blood fills his mouth as his own teeth bite his tongue. He can't get off! Yet the road ends in a brick wall. The beast doesn't stop!

STOP!

The wall fills his sight. Taylor's heart beats out of his chest.

Too fast!

TOO FAST!

Taylor screams.

CRASH!

51

Benny jumped awake with limbs flailing. His desk lamp had shattered on the floor, fallen.

Or been pushed.

His eyes wouldn't focus. The nightmare still blurred his sight, but—

Shhh.

Steps, outside his room, footsteps so quiet he shouldn't have heard them. But he did, because the steps had come from his sister's old room. But his sister was dead.

Unless she wasn't...

SHHH. Were they getting closer? Did the doorknob shiver? Were there shadows under his door? Clutching his eyes tight, he screamed with everything he had.

"GO AWAY!"

Nothing responded. Benny dared breathe as silence pressed down around him.

He grabbed his blankets and buried himself beneath them.

SIX

NOTHING IS AS DEPRESSING as a sunny day in October.

Pumpkins yellowing in the sun, plastic skeletons revealed as broken tripe made in Taiwan. Keith despised it. He preferred, no, he *demanded* cloudy days. Rip-roaring storms that swept golden leaves from a thousand trees. Autumn demanded nothing less.

But today the sun shined bright, and no matter how obscenely late Keith stayed up, he was always wide awake with the sun. Usually Benny rose just as early to stare at the TV, but today he crawled out of bed at noon as sick as a dog. Keith recognized the "bad dream" hangover when he saw one. He'd had too many of those himself.

Any more arguments with Darryl and I'll have nightmares too.

Then they got the news. Police had come to their door wanting to talk to Keith about Taylor.

"How well did you know him?"

"Do you know anyone who would hurt him?"

Keith answered their questions in curt sentences. He didn't like talking to police and had nothing to tell them. Taylor had been alive when Keith last saw him. He answered what he could, but kept looking backward to see if Benny was listening. The police eventually left and Keith relaxed, his hands unclenching the newspaper he had subconsciously twisted into a knot. He noticed what he had done and threw the paper away.

Then Keith told Benny about Taylor. Benny's eyes stared straight ahead, almost like he already knew what happened. Benny didn't say anything. Didn't do anything either, refusing to eat or talk.

That wouldn't do. Benny was his responsibility, given him by Benny's mom, Keith's sister, and Keith took that responsibility very seriously. Fortunately, Keith knew exactly what would cheer Benny up. What would any Haunted House connoisseur do to raise their spirits?

Visit a haunted house of course.

"Comb your hair and get your shoes on. We're going to see Connor."

TWO NIGHTS. TWO NIGHTMARES in a row. Benny could count the pain receptors in his head one at a time and just wanted to melt into his couch. But he couldn't go back to sleep.

Bridget hasn't left.

Female Student Killed in Car Accident, Another in Critical was the last headline Benny saw his dad read in his own home, and now that Benny was done with school, his Dad came home from his "business trips" less and less. That made Keith, his mother's brother, the closest relative he had for 1000 miles. He also had a picture of his sister, Bridget, on the coffee table in front of him. Dead since November. He had missed her every day since.

Except at night.

Then this morning he found out Taylor was dead. Found "beaten to death" in an alley behind the *Scare Asylum*. The police had told Keith. Keith had told Benny. But Benny didn't need to be told.

I dreamed it. Again.

Benny had watched hundreds of hours of monster movies. None had ever given him even a daydream, let alone a nightmare. Yet even now images of blood smeared his mind's eye. Sticky, coagulating.

Blood.

Worse, he *knew* these dreams were real. Scotty was dead. Now Taylor was dead, and Benny had seen the killer. Kind of. The headless rider was definitely a Dullahan.

Wait, how do I know that the headless rider was a Dullahan? But the answer was scarier than the question.

Because that's what it was.

But that wasn't what killed him. Another monster had done that.

In all Benny's horror-movie expertise, his mind refused to accept what monster he had seen last night. The scariest monster in the world, the monster that had killed Taylor, killed Scotty, scaring them both completely to death, was...

A horse?

SEVEN

KEITH WOULDN'T EVER ADMIT to being jealous. Nevertheless, Connor's *Fright Zone* had a location to die for.

A few miles away from the *HallO'Scream*, it may as well have been downtown itself for all the traffic he got from the freeway exit ramp. Connor had billboards everywhere, a festering ghoul holding up a mile marker announcing, "One Mile to your LAST EXIT!"

Benny thought up that line.

Off the exit, the *Fright Zone* lay in a huge sprawling field of corn, peppered with abandoned grain silos. During the day it was a family fun maze, laughing and giggling. But at night the *Fright Zone* morphed into something very scary indeed. As well it should, Connor's knowledge of old school scares was worth any other ten Halloween enthusiasts.

Which brought Keith to his friend Jack Cavanaugh. Keith invited him along on this day trip, but he hadn't expected Jack to tour the maze in costume.

As Captain Jack Sparrow.

Keith groaned as he saw the Jack that waited for them at the ticket booth, ready to practice his charms on any available young ladies they might meet. Jack smiled.

"Put on your smiley-face mate," Jack warbled in his perfect channel of Jack Sparrow. "Thar be lasses awaiting."

With a roll his eyes, Keith followed Jack into the Fright Zone. A look at Benny revealed a smile.

Good, it worked.

CONNOR HAD KNOWN JACK too long to be surprised.

"Mr. Cavanagh! Mr. MacCool actually convinced you to come out in daylight hours? Not possible."

Connor's personal office lay deep in the heart of the *Fright Zone.* Actors buzzed around them getting ready for the evening. Keith let Benny have the only other chair in a tiny workshop filled with monster making tools. Keith leaned against a wall next to Jack, who leaned into Connor's challenge with a wagging finger and a Johnny Depp-mustached smile revealing all his teeth. "No, no, no. Not *probable.*"

To Keith's relief, Benny smiled. *Glad we can both laugh for a bit. God knows Darryl is no fun back home.*

Another laugh came from the back of the office. A husky body leaned up from digging inside some cardboard boxes, coming up with a wad of ragged old costumes in both hands. Keith couldn't miss the shoulder length hair and a bright blue T-shirt emblazoned with Captain America's shield. He spoke with the extroverts smile.

"Keith, you know you can't let Jack be around the ladies after dark."

Keith laughed. "Hi, Quentin."

Quentin O'Neil was a newer friend and the consummate entrepreneur. He treated Halloween a little nonchalantly as even from ten feet away Keith could see that every single costume wadded up in Quentin's arms belonged on some spandex flashing superhero.

I guess he still hasn't found a real job. Keith thought. *I won't rub it in.*

Quentin lived in the Big City where he made a few extra bucks in the October season by dressing up as whatever was the movie-superhero Du-jour and taking money for pictures. Keith had seen him in action on the downtown plaza, and to call him "scary" was generous, but Quentin obviously had other priorities. Stuffing the superhero costumes into a duffel bag, he stepped up to shake Keith's hand as Connor went back to his work.

Connor stood above a young woman on a stool, her back to the group. Wearing a black t-shirt saying *Who Said Night is For Sleeping?* Connor's hands blurred with brushes and corpse colored skin cream, quickly transforming the woman's youthful features into something monstrous. Quentin played up the conversation with Jack at the same time.

"Well Jack, let's have a look at you," Quentin said, taking a complete view of the Sparrow ensemble. Keith smiled in anticipation of the biting criticism Quentin was famous for.

"Your hat is the wrong color, and your mascara is running. Your boots have an obvious zipper running up the side, and your dreadlocks still don't match your real hair. You are without a doubt the worst Jack Sparrow I have ever heard of."

"Ah ah," Jack swaggered another swirling finger. "But you *have* heard of me."

Jack was tall, buff, and had been Keith's indispensable man for crowd control for years, but Keith just could not stand the suit Jack insisted on wearing: The quintessential movie celebrity. Jack's job kept him at the front door, where he used his celebrity to get first look at any good-looking females that might enter. Any woman of appropriate age was treated to a pillow full of sweet talk and exchange of cell numbers. Rumor had it Jack hadn't gone home alone in any October in memory. But Jack never neglected his bouncing duties, so Keith looked the other way.

But Keith noticed Jack's eyes never looked at the one girl in this room. The one Connor worked on the chair.

"And respect, good sir, that's *Captain* Jack," Jack broke his Keith's daydreaming as he waved a hand encrusted in pirate rings in Connor's direction. "And I do believe the word you're looking for is 'parlay.' Savvy?"

Quentin smiled as he raised open palms in mock surrender, earning a laugh from Connor who paused to wave his own hand at Jack, "Funny thing about Jack Sparrow, I seem to remember him being in the very first *Nightmare on Elm Street* movie. Got killed in a geyser of blood. Keith? Tell me I'm wrong."

"You're right."

Connor smiled back to Jack. "See, Captain? You have a horror movie pedigree. Please sit down in my chair. Let me turn you into a horrific scourge and finally get that scowl off of Keith's face." Reaching across his table of overflowing jars and brushes, Connor grabbed a rubber facial appliance and held it across for Jack to touch.

Jack stepped forward with a bejeweled finger to poke the boney mass right in the eye, then brush it aside. "No, no, no. You know your problem, mate? You're far too compelled to add a delicious sense of the macabre to any delirium." Jack trilled. "Who could ever improve on a captain of my dashing features?" Jack went on. "I could never be fooled into—"

Connor spun the stool of his young female, showing her face to Jack, a roadkill of freshly flayed skin, blood oozing from her eyes.

Jack choked on his tongue. His ramble stumbled. But a half step away from losing his balance with wobble kneed Sparrow theatrics, Jack caught himself, staring at anything in the room except the bloody girl. With eyes shut, he grabbed her chair and spun the chair back around to Connor. "My apologies young lass," he whispered in her ear. "To not make your acquaintance shall be my one great regret." Jack opened his eyes and backed up towards the door.

"Let this day be your good fortune," Captain Sparrow swaggered his way to a dramatic exit. "You'll remember this day for the rest of your life as the day that you *almost* scared Captain Jack Sparrow." Then with a laugh he was outside, mingling with the other actors of the *Fright Zone*. Especially the females.

Keith laughed to himself. *Worth a try. He'd make a fantastic Gravekeeper if he'd just drop the Disney bit for two minutes. At least Benny looks better.*

AFTER A NICE SUNNY day, Benny had almost felt normal. Until Connor spun the bloody girl around.

Blood

But Jack's reaction was too humorous. Jack had no trouble making people laugh and didn't let nightmares of headless killers ruin the whole rest of his day. Benny envied that. At least until Connor spoke again.

"Benny, make sure you don't grow up like that."

Benny turned. "Like what?"

"Scared."

"Huh?"

"He's scared to death of blood you know."

Benny's mind struggled to put it together. "JACK?!?"

"Of course," Connor nodded. "Didn't you see him? He's petrified of the stuff."

Jack? Scared?

"Don't tell me your uncle never told you."

Keith kept a stolid face. "Jack doesn't need his personal life advertised."

Benny was still playing catch up. "Jack is scared of blood? But..."

"But he works in a haunted house?" Quentin laughed as he zipped up his duffel and threw it over his shoulder. "Where he shows up every night as a Johnny Depp impersonator? Why do you think he works the front door?"

The roadkill girl completed, she stepped off the stool and out the door as Connor washed his brushes in a jar of odorous cleaner that stank up his entire office. In the corner, a TV circa 1985 fizzled off and on, showing some grainy 70's movie drive-in movie called *The Legend of Boggy Creek*, a Bigfoot film if Benny remembered. Connor enjoyed Benny's brief confusion as he finished with his brushes and sat in an office chair, rolling its squeaky wheels across a bumpy wooden floor.

"Scares aren't just about what goes "boo." Connor spun his chair around his office." Its about two wires in your head that were never meant to cross. In the Civil War General Grant visited a field hospital and wigged out. For the rest of his life he ordered all his steaks to be cooked extra well-done. The slightest amount of meat juice would trigger an upchuck worth of dry heaves."

Keith knew Connor would know that. His walls were plastered with pictures of gruesome wounds. Zombies were his specialty. "But Jack? Not so sure what his crossed wires are. I think he told me about an old family dog that went bad when he was a kid."

"What's so scary about a dog?" Benny wondered.

"Anything can be scary."

Benny's mind yanked him back to his bed at 2:00, with footsteps outside his door. *Yes, anything could be scary.*

"Ask Jack. Maybe he'll tell you."

"He won't," Keith replied with utter certainty, ending the conversation. Quentin changed the subject.

"Sooooo, I took a spin through the infamous HallO'Scream last night."

Keith's face turned to shock but Quentin preempted him. "Well I can't very well tell you can I? I wanted to see the show before you have a chance to spike the rum. Your RedCap room was missing in action. Darryl O'Grady strikes again?"

Keith grunted and sat down on the available stool. "Darryl had another of his bright ideas."

"I saw," Quentin continued. "And the Shriek Bootique practices a hard sell. Wouldn't let me leave until I bought a T-shirt," prompting another shout of horror from Keith until Jack motioned him down. He reached into his cavernous duffel b ag. "Relax, t hey're a ctually funny, in a dumb Darryl sort of way." Quentin yanked a wadded up black T-shirt out of the bag and tossed it to Keith, who opened it up with a huff.

HALLO'SCREAM

Where You're the Last to Die

Benny saw Keith's eyebrows narrow into diabolic slits. "Nice shirt," was all Keith had to say.

Connor smiled as he examined the shirt over Keith's shoulder. "Darryl's just being seduced by kickbacks. He'll grow out of it."

Keith shook his head. "He's been worse this year than ever before. And speaking of which," as Keith checked his watch, "It's about time I got back to keep him from screwing up my house anymore than he already has. Quentin, I suppose you need a ride?"

"You know me too well," Quentin smiled as he walked out the door. "I swear my car will be fixed by tomorrow. I'll meet you by your Keith-mobile."

Benny checked his own watch as Quentin left with a wave. *Crud, it gets dark fast in October.* Then he shivered and caught himself remembering what had happened the last two nights, remembering two people dead, with likely another nightmare waiting to take him tonight. Benny remembered at all, and shuddered.

I can't do the Halloween bit. Not tonight.

Benny shocked himself with that. He hadn't missed a *Hal-lO'Scream* night in years! *How can I tell Keith?* Benny raised his head to Keith's inevitable chastisement.

To find Keith looking at him with a warm smile.

"Benny, you've had a rough day haven't you?"

He knows.

"Take the night off. I can handle it. Go through the Fright Zone and give me a complete report," giving Connor a wink.

Connor laughed. "Injecting a spy into my operation are you?"

Benny's relief warmed him back up. Yes, a night off is exactly what he needed. Keith let himself out the door with one last word. "We've all been working like dogs for weeks. Rest up, have a few laughs. This Halloween is going to end with a bang."

EIGHT

Benny's feet crunched gravel as he stepped outside. As he watched Keith jog to his car, Benny breathed in the evening air.

Autumn. A chilly breeze curled the ears, rustling branches and warning of the winter to come. But other images also filled his mind.

Blood.

"Not now!"

Ooops, he hadn't meant to say that out loud. Had Connor heard him? *I hope not.* Plenty of background noise echoed across the fields. Giggling guests had already formed a line for the nighttime entertainment. Benny heard squealing girls who saw the craggly old buildings and yelped in protest.

Benny smirked. *Amateurs. Nothing here is all that scary.* For one tiny moment, Benny let himself feel superior. That didn't happen very often and Benny barely knew what to do next. No matter, the illusion shattered as Benny's gaze floated over the parking lot and he saw the face he least expected.

Marcus. Still in his vampire trench coat, still with his sickly sweet smile, pushing people out of his way. He was coming in.

HERE? But he works at the Scare Asylum! He should be across town!

Oh yeah, the Scare Asylum was closed. Taylor was killed last night.

Blood. Benny clenched against the involuntary image, and with Benny's astounding luck, Marcus's eyes happened to pick that exact random moment to land right on him.

Oh no.

Oh yes. Marcus smiled that damned *Oh, look who it is* smile and Benny tensed as it all came back. *Being tripped in the hallway. Harassed in gym class. Pushed into snowdrifts.* And none of that was worse than defending himself to Bridget afterward.

"Benny! This only happens because you sit there like a whiny victim."

No, it happens because he outsizes me by an elephant. Fighting back is an invitation to getting stuffed into the nearest dumpster.

"That's an excuse."

Damn right it is! And it's a good one! Even if I stop him once, there's always a next time.

"Then stop him hard enough the first time."

Screw that. Benny ducked back inside Connor's office in a panic, where Connor stared right at him with a look of disappointment.

"OK, what did *that* guy do to you?"

Crud. Nothing got by Connor.

"Was he the guy who poured a bag of smashed potato chips over your head?" Connor continued. "Or the one who super-glued your locker shut?"

Benny scowled. "Both."

"And now he got you again."

"Huh?"

"You're hiding like a mouse in a cage. He got you *again.*"

Benny looked down.

"I suppose you'd rather be hiding in your uncle's basement painting rubber spiders, a job so monotonous that the wicked stepmother wouldn't even give it to Cinderella. And weren't you supposed to be in college this year?"

Benny sighed. Connor was right about hiding, he was rightly sick of that. So he risked a peek around the door. Marcus had vanished into the larger crowd. Benny relaxed, stepping outside again to scan the crowd in the parking lot. Keith was right. A *lot* more people came here than the *HallO'Scream*. As a full moon started to rise in the west, the line here was already humongous and only getting bigger. Everyone came here. Looking again to make sure Marcus was gone, Benny saw someone *else* he recognized...

A girl. His age. Red hair.

Oh no.

HER.

Bridget had been killed in a car crash, almost a year ago. But two people had been in the car. Bridget didn't walk away. But this girl *had*. Bridget's best friend, Kelly.

Benny hadn't been able to face her since the accident. He could barely look at her at all. She had lived when Bridget had not.

He couldn't admit that he hated her for it.

She didn't see him. She was walking down the gravel walkway to the Fright Zone's ticket booth with another girl, laughing as if nothing had happened at all a year ago. All Benny could do was seethe and slink back into Connor's office. This time he stayed there.

Connor sighed.

"OK big man. We're having a talk."

BENNY SAT DOWN AS Connor looked at him with a paternal scowl. Then Connor asked the last question Benny expected on Heaven or Earth:

"Are you worthy of your name?"

Huh?

But Connor's facial expression didn't change. "Are you worthy of your name? MacCool?"

Benny had no answer. *I'm vaguely insulted.*

"I know you've had it rough," Connor continued. "You never knew your mom, then you lost your sister a year ago. Now you'd like nothing better than to mope around in your uncle's haunted house for the next decade, right? I can't let you out of this room with that attitude. Not 'til I get real answer out of you."

Now I AM insulted. Benny didn't get to that point easily. "Only my middle name is MacCool."

"Your mother's maiden name, yes, given to you at great insistence so Keith wouldn't be the last MacCool on your Mom's side. It's not just any name you know."

Keith had gone off on rambling speeches about the great "Mac-Cool Legacy" from time to time. A classic Irish name. "So what?" Benny finally found his attitude. "What's your name?"

"Connor."

"That's your last name. O'Connor. Why don't you use your first?"

"I only need one name, so I picked this one. But you didn't get to pick yours." Connor gestured to Kelly, outside. "She was your sister's best friend right? If you want to talk her, you have to make a move."

"TALK TO HER?" Benny's voice exploded. "She lived when Bridget died! She—"

"You have a thing for her, don't you?"

Oh... Benny dropped his head. Connor exhaled.

"A quiet guy like you would have a thing about flaming red heads. Well, don't worry. It's not true what they say," Connor leaned in."The old legend says that they have no souls. But the truth is, they have one freckle for every soul that they steal."

Benny looked up in confusion, prompting a chuckle from Connor.

"Your other problem. Say something in a straight face, and you'll believe every word. Work on that, or I'll start giving you pick-up lines. Need a good ice-breaker? Just strut right up to her and say..." Connor stepped back to stare right into the eyes of snake writhing Medusa mask. "Honey, you look finer than a new set of snow tires."

Benny stared blankly and Connor laughed again. "Good! You passed the first test! You'd better. You've got quite a legacy to live up to. Especially this time of year."

Benny sat up. "Ok, I don't know about my name. If you could tell me all about it, we can have a sparkling conversation and get on with our lives."

That earned a nod from Connor. "Standing up for yourself. Good. You'll need to do that a lot to live up to MacCool dynasty. After all, they did nothing less than save the world."

"Save it from what?"

"Halloween."

Nine

HAUNTED ORGAN MUSIC REACHED Keith's ears as he stepped into the foyer of the *HallO'Scream.*

The deaths of his friends over the last two nights hung on his mind, but the show had to go on. Customers would still be waiting in line tonight and Keith had to be ready for them. Owing to Keith's fine-tuned organization, actors were already getting into position for the night's scaring. Case in point, Jack, raring to go in his full Captain Sparrow persona. Jack's job was at the entrance of the first scare hall. His area held a towering tombstone, ominously lit only by a single orange bulb in the ceiling. No one went any further without reading the inscription.

THE LAW

Jack's baritone filled the room. "My guests! We've all arrived at a very special place; lyrically, inescapably, horrifically. Here you're about to go off the edge of the map, maties. Here, there be monsters. Please let me explain a few rules of gentlemanly behavior. First I must ask, are you all willing to die for each other? GOOD! No worries then."

With a flair of gold rings, Jack pointed out each rule, one at a time:

Don't touch the creatures or haunted items.

No eating, drinking, or smoking

No pictures or video.

Anyone willingly damaging the Haunt will be escorted out and legal action taken.

Keith knew that Jack loved his captive audience. Had *THE LAW* been recited by some dullard, the eyes of the guests would glaze over. But Jack caught their attention with dreadlocks of fire and never let go. After him, who could suspect that the very next thing around the corner would be a blood spitting psychopath?

Which is exactly what the first scare always was.

"Did everyone hear all that?" Jack asked as Keith passed through, "For I will NOT be saying it again!"

Keith gave Jack a nod as he ducked behind a curtain, entering the backstage guts of the *HallO'Scream*. Elementary schools already had doors between classrooms. Keith expanded it into a network of back passages giving the actors access to any room. Turning a few corners he arrived in a singular room bustling with activity. The brain center of the *HallO'Scream*. Keith's costume lair.

Only another haunted house owner could have *any* idea of the insistent demands against Keith's time. Every Act of God was darned and determined to make sure the house never opened. Props broke. Scenery collapsed. Actors would call in sick, or not even show up at all even after swearing on a Bible that they would *(Damn Mike anyway)*, leaving Keith to juggle too many jobs with not enough bodies to fill them. And he never knew how bad it was going to be until less than an hour before opening. But in this lair Keith could handle everything. Bare lightbulbs lit a crowded room. One side held a dry erase board mapping out both floors of the house, charting the various scare rooms and actors that each one demanded. The other side had demonic masks overflowing every shelf, ghouls from nearly every horror movie ever made.

But the star of the room, the object to which everything else drew your eye toward, was a poster. E. Munch's *SCREAM*, complementing Keith's neck tattoo. It overlooked a table encrusted with desk lamps and half empty jars of theatrical makeup advertising themselves as *Witch's Cackle Green* or *Zombie Yellow*.

Conversely, one shelf had nothing but a single picture, framed, of Keith in the uniform of a police detective, holding a newly minted badge to the camera. The frame hadn't been dusted in a while.

Only five minutes after arriving, Keith already had a half-dozen monster projects in high gear including splotching a young girl's face with large globs of gooey blood. Standing beneath *SCREAM*, Keith wielded tonight's assets.

"Jeff, you're the Mad Doctor. Kim and Jesse, you handle the Roving Shades."

"That leaves only four of us in the Zombie Room," said a teenager putting on the rat-eaten musty clothes of a corpse.

"We've done it with only three."

"When you were in there, sure."

True, Keith could also fill any role in the house at a moment's notice and very often suspected his actors would call in sick just to make him prove it.

"Kennedy's coming in late. I'll be the Caged Psycho until he shows up, then I'll drop down to help you out."

Keith's show always went on. Only after every last guest was out the parking lot and down the road would Keith crawl back home and drop "dead" on his fuzzy couch around 3:30 am. Or his brother-in-law's couch at any rate. Home was where you found it. Keith's eyes fell to a pile of mail in an overstuffed corner addressed to him personally: "Payment Needed" "Final Notice." He ignored them. He had a show to produce. For example, what did Peter just do over there?

"Peter, you just put skeleton gloves on Greg."

Peter, a young teenager assisting another actor getting suited up by juggling a pair of rubber monster gloves, looked up in confusion.

"Greg's the Mad Doctor tonight," Keith clarified,hoping for a reaction, but Peter's face fell into a perfect blank. Keith pressed it. "The Mad Doctor wears Ghoul Gloves. Ghouls are alive. Skeletons are dead."

Maybe only a dozen people in the whole city could tell the difference between a ghoul and a skeleton. But Keith was one of them. Fishing through a box he found the appropriate pair and handed them to Peter while holding his frustration in check. Something always arose to make sure Keith started the night grinding teeth. What would it be tonight? He didn't want to know, but he had a thought.

Maybe it wasn't such a bright idea, after all, to let Benny have the night off.

IN THE BACK CORNER of Connor's office, the TV made quiet background noise with one of Connor's favorite movies. The Legend of Boggy Creek. A soft-spoken narrator gave creepy details about a hairy creature stalking the swamps of Arkansas in the 1950's.

"I doubt if you could find a lonelier spookier place in this country than down around Boggy Creek..."

Benny might have watched, but he knew he wasn't getting out of here until he answered Connor's insistent cross examination. Benny sat back in a comfy chair as Connor pulled up a chair to join him.

"Where did America get Halloween from?" Connor asked.

Even Benny knew that one. "Ireland."

"Sure," Connor said. "But did you know how long its been around?"

"It used to be called Samhain," Benny offered.

"You read it right but pronounced it wrong. "SOW-when."

Benny had heard it spoken that way too.

Connor continued. "A long time ago 'Samhain' ruled the Irish calendar. New Years, Thanksgiving, and Christmas all rolled into one. Every historical event depended on it. An army invades? Samhain. Demons fight a war with faeries? Samhain. The biggest Celtic holiday of the year. For a very important reason."

Dramatic pause.

"That's when the monsters came out."

Benny's ear quirked, the horror movie in the background providing appropriate ambiance: *"Drawn to civilization like a moth to flame, the creature creeps out around dusk..."*

Connor continued. "Which brings us to the biggest Irish hero of all time. And don't tell me you've never heard of him: Finn MacCool."

Finn MacCool. Benny had been bombarded by that name for as long as he could remember. His mom had had Celtic paraphernalia all over the old house, posters of rugged guys with long hair and kilts. *Not my style.*

"Keith talks about him every once in a while," Benny considered, remembering.

"I'm sure he does. Keith has something to prove," Connor countered. "Surely you know about the big failure in his life."

"He never talks about that." Which was an understatement. "He was a police detective, then up and quit. Never told me why."

"He's not living on your couch because he likes the upholstery. He lost his house and everything he'd ever saved."

And had been living in Dad's house, as a house guest, ever since, But Connor continued:

"Keith needs to bury some demons, and he is, in fact, horrified that he's not worthy of his name." Connor leaned forward, eyes swimming in storytelling. "See, Finn MacCool made a hero out of himself, on Halloween, by killing a monster. And not just any monster. The BIG one."

This'll be good, Benny thought, as Connor launched in and didnt stop.

"A couple thousand years ago, when the ancient gods were petty and cruel, Halloween was the most dangerous night of the year. Especially for the Irish kings, because each and every Samhain there was one Irish monster that would march right out of its cave, right up to the Hall of the Irish Kings and burn it to the ground. Year after year."

74

Connor reached over and grabbed a mask off his wall. Demonic. With rams horns and open mouth of gargantuan teeth. He tossed it underhand to Benny who caught it and gave it a cold hard look.

"They called it "The Burner," Connor said.

Benny examined the mask. The Burner.

"So after years and years of spending Halloween getting burned to death, the Irish kings asked for a hero to save them, and lucky for them, Finn showed up. He challenged the monster, beat the monster, and skewered it on his spear. The kings were so grateful they made him Captain of the Guard and gave him a fairy for a wife. That's your family dynasty. Surely you've watched enough of Sam and Dean Winchester to know the motto 'Saving People and Hunting Things?' Well that doesn't belong to the CW, it belongs to the MacCools. And Keith, God bless his tortured soul, is scared to death he's fallen short."

"Keith is scared?" Benny wouldn't believe that easily.

"Yes, Keith is scared," Connor repeated. "Of himself. And on Halloween the plot thickens. See, at one time Halloween had another name even besides "Samhain." A long time ago, it used to be called "Puka's Night."

That word again.

"As a good Irishmen you had to be ready for Puka's Night. And the most important thing the Irish taught their kids was to be *Scary*. You had to be scary. They built bonfires, wore costumes of every monster in their land. You wanted to be as growling and vicious as anything else out there. It kept you alive."

Connor stopped for a delicious dramatic pause.

"Scary was survival."

TEN

SCARY. KEITH INSISTED ON being scary each and every night. Just as his own co-workers insisted on conspiring against him.

Such as someone totally unclear on the concept of a haunted house. A young girl not a day over 17 sat in Keith's chair. She wore the black robe of the Cave of the Gravekeepers. Musty and torn with black leather boots and pentagram necklace, she was nearly ready to take the stage.

With the glaring exception of her makeup. The girl winced at the rotten gray face paint the Gravekeeper Room demanded. Three other girls were already sporting hollowed-out eyes and cheekbones over a gray palette, highlighted by fresh blood dripping out of their eye sockets. This girl wanted none of it. Keith had only a few nerves left to deal with it.

"Just sit back and close your eyes," Keith said. "I'm not doing anything to you that I haven't done to myself. I can get it done in eight minutes and you'll be out of this chair before you can say "Enchilada.""

The girl grimaced as a wilting violet told she had to dissect a frog in biology class. "But...I can't look like THAT," she quivered, looking at the other girls.

"You volunteered for the room," Keith said, his impatience bubbling. "You knew what you were getting into."

"But I didn't mean it like that. I can't... "

"Can't what?"

"Look ugly."

"..."

Keith's compassion exhausted proportionally with the merciless ticking of the clock on the wall. "What were you expecting for a room called 'Gravekeeper?' " He leaned in to start but the girl held up her hands. Keith sat back, exasperated. "Caroline, why did you volunteer for this room?"

"Because my friends are in it."

"You said you were tired of working the ticket booth. You wanted to be inside the house."

"And ... be with my friends."

"You can be, and *they* let me put their faces on," Keith threw a frustrated glance back towards the other girls.

"But, I didn't want to be ugly..." Caroline warbled. "I bought this sparkly eyeliner. Sequins for my eyes. See? I can put all this on, and you know." She blinked with heavy eyelashes, "Look cute."

RUMBLE. A hideous seizure cut right through the fabric of reality, rippling through nature, screaming through the universe-

And passing right over Keith's bloodshot face.

"What part of 'scary' *DON'T YOU UNDERSTAND???*"

Caroline burst into tears.

Oh, hell. Keith spun away and mentally kicked himself. Caroline's friends helped her out of the chair as Keith walked to the far corner of the room, muttering. He shouldn't get mad. He didn't want to be that kind of person.

But he was.

He motioned down the hall. "Jared! Switch places with Caroline. Caroline, I'm sorry. Don't worry about it. Help out on the 2nd floor. Any room you want."

With a silent sniff, Caroline wiped her eyes, and walked away with her friends. Keith breathed deep.

I can't keep doing that. I've lost Mike and by tomorrow even money says Caroline is gone too. I need these people. But, damn it, why do I have to explain the OBVIOUS?

"Keith!"

A teenager in a zombie suit ran into the costume room and Keith acknowledged him with a "What now?" glance.

"The front yard. Darryl! You have to see what he's doing!"

Darryl. Speaking of getting mad.

I really, REALLY, shouldn't have given Benny the night off.

PEOPLE LOVE TO SCREAM. They love to shriek in terror only to laugh about it later. Being chased by a hockey masked maniac is *fun.*

Provided of course, the hockey masked maniac actually looks scary.

Now, Keith looked at Darryl's latest "improvement" to the *HallO'Scream.* Benny's precious scarecrows in the front yard had been uprooted and tossed aside. In their place was a wooden stage. For dancing.

A squad of dancers were on the stage, dancing to *Thriller.* All female, dressed as feminized versions of 80's horror movie celebrities: Freddy Krueger, Chucky, and Jason Voorhees, trouncing around in long-leg fishnet stockings and mini-skirts, winking at the crowd with fluttering eyelashes.

As Keith watched the last shreds of Halloween self-respect go up in smoke, the crowd cheered in hysteria. It was time to confront Darryl again. Keith found him easily enough, standing with crossed arms on the front patio with a huge smile on his face. Keith walked right up to him.

"What happened to this being a kids holiday?"

Darryl grinned, "Only after the boys come out and play do the wallets start to loosen. Stand back and watch."

The cavorting bodies on stage were cheered on by the hooting audience, who looked like they were waiting in line for a bikini bar rather than a Haunted House. Keith's face burned, but Darryl horned in before Keith opened his mouth.

"Twice the crowd we got last night. This is exactly what it's about."

Keith couldn't deny the crowd was larger than he had ever seen it. The parking lot was a clog of double-parked SUVs. Feet trampled his lawn and Benny's pumpkins. Keith winced.

"Don't give me that roll of the eyes." Darryl drolled, "You'll love the costume contest."

"What costume contest?"

"Any girl that shows up in a skimpy outfit gets in for free."

The chords of *Thriller* faded out. The dancers ended in a climactic glare, then slinked off the stage to the cat-calls of the audience. In their place two vampirettes walked up to unwrap a white tarp emblazoned with silver and red rhinestone Vegas font:

Miss Sexy Halloween!

Keith inhaled, and Darryl laughed.

"97.3 is doing a live feed. You can't buy this kind of publicity."

Keith looked over the parking lot in wide-eyed alarm, seeing a stream of bare-leg genies and fairies stepping out of cars. The wind had its usual late-October bite that should have numbed limbs, yet one girl wore nothing more than underwear and an open army fatigue jacket. A radio station mobile van boomed with oversized speakers as the DJ took the stage:

"*And we're broadcasting live from this evening from the HAL-LO'SCREAM! Ladies and gentlemen, we're about to judge the sexiest women in town! Come on down for great door prizes and giveaways as we all find just the right delicious boot-TAY to scream for! The amount of skin on display will be FRIGHT-EN-ING!*"

Darryl wore his pride on his sleeve. "What's not to like?"

Keith counted to ten. "Sorry, I was just basking in the glow of this display of sophisticated class."

"What?"

"You, like, just forgot that Taylor died last night? We've known him since 5th grade."

79

Darryl snickered. "I've got it covered. I made sure all the girls are wearing black underwear." Keith blanched even as Darryl continued. "I told you not to give me that face. Taylor's loss is our gain. That crowd is *Scare Asylum* left overs. Best thing that could have happened to us. Hell, if we're really lucky, the murderer will come after us next!" Darryl sneered. Keith's fists rose and only his memory of Caroline stopped him from decking Darryl right then and there. Snarkiness took over.

"Well Darryl, if you want money that bad, maybe you can skip the middle man and just sell girls out of your car. I'd bet that's your only talent."

Darryl turned to face Keith, ire burning behind his eyes.

"You know why I didn't tell you? Cause you'd throw your crocodile tears again!" Darryl turned to the hooting crowd. "We're here for one solitary reason, that's separating those idiots from their money."

Keith watched another dance troop slink on stage, sexy nurses with too-short miniskirts and *very* red underwear. The crowd screeched all the louder. Keith stepped forward. Darryl cut him off with an angry shout.

"Fact is Keith, I get more done when you're not around to argue. So let's make a deal: DON'T argue. We agreed to equal partners remember? So shut up and do what I say."

Darryl backed up the stairs and pointed to the crowd, still hollering in lust. The vampirettes oozed through the crowd to approach Darryl on either side.

"There is your Halloween Keith. American Style. Excuse me." Darryl put an arm around each woman and strutted back up the stairs, leaving Keith to stew behind him with the dance stage. The DJ had positioned himself in the center and whipped up the crowd into a frenzy.

"*Look at these girls! Guys, it's all up to you to make this a Halloween you'll never forget! Look at what we got from the hospital today Fellas! A pair of sexy nurses who really enjoy giving sponges baths! Who wants to see them kiss?*"

Keith stomped back into his house.

ELEVEN

THE MOON PEEKED THROUGH slivers of clouds, creating silver ribbons across the horizon. Connor and Benny watched the crowds pass by the open door of the office. Haunted corn mazes tended to attract masses of girls. They entered giggling, only to get lost in the dark and exit screaming. Connor's DVD continued to provide ironic commentary for the occasion. *"It was a long night of terror...shaking in fear, freezing at every sound in the darkness."*

Then the DVD skipped, forcing Connor to stand up and bang the player. Benny kept watching the crowds as Connor spoke with his back turned, still fiddling with the player.

"How many times has Keith tried to tell you what your name meant?" Connor remarked into space.

Benny shrugged.

"Well now that you know, feeling smarter?"

Benny shrugged.

"Feeling scarier?" Connor asked right after. "Scary is in short supply these days. Keith can't do it all himself. He's fighting himself even as he's fighting a losing battle with Darryl."

Connor walked around his office to look out a window into the maze.

"Did I tell you the Police were over here earlier? Asking about Scotty and Taylor? They think it might be Halloween related."

Benny had almost forgotten about that. The killings that would not stop filling his vision.

BLOOD.

Not again. Benny pushed the imagery out with a heave. "What... what does getting mugged have to do with Halloween?" Benny asked, looking for anything else to get his mind thinking about.

"I don't think Scotty was mugged," Connor replied. "I think he was targeted."

Benny started to shiver. It wasn't that cold in here.

"Think about it," Connor said. "The best monster maker in town killed one day. Then the 'Scariest Man in the City' killed the next. The police didn't see the connection until I pointed it out."

"A Halloween serial killer?"

"Would that scare you?"

BLOOD. Benny shivered, struggling to push the image out of his eyes. Looking out a window, outside was a sea of black, lit only by tiny yellow floodlights.

"For all we know, I'm next," Connor remarked, without a shred of irony.

Benny turned back in shock. "You?! No one hates you."

"No one hated Scotty or Taylor either. But don't worry. I told you before that Haunted House Connoisseurs can't die. Nothing would make me happier than to come back as a ghost and haunt my own maze."

Benny grunted at Connor's cavalier attitude.

"Its something all us monster-makers need to consider," Connor said, especial you."

"Me?"

"I just told you, Halloween is the MacCool family holiday. The Irish National Holiday. Surely you've noticed all the last names in this town."

82

It was impossible not to notice the statues and monuments about the founding of the city in the late 1800's. O'Ryan. Kavanagh. O'Brien. The names were passed down through families who had by now lost all memory of their origins.

"Honestly, Keith couldn't have ended up doing anything else but working in a haunted house. Ireland IS Halloween. America just took what it liked and ignored the rest. We were supposed to keep it pure. Keep it scary. We didn't."

BLOOD. Benny's skin crawled as the room got even colder. He started squeezing his arms for warmth.

"We couldn't even let the great Irish holiday keep its own name," Connor continued. "Puka's Night? Gone. I wonder how the Puka would feel about that."

"What's a Puka?" Benny blurted out before he forgot to ask again.

Connor looked around the pictures on his wall.

"An Irish monster even Keith admitted would never fly in an American Haunted House." Connor pointed to a tiny picture thumb-tacked to the wall, a well-used playing card from a fantasy collectible game. "I bet he *really* hated that," he laughed.

Benny didn't think that was funny.

"Keith is the only one of us who'd even think to pull it off," Connor continued. "But in an obsessive way he's totally right."

Benny's impatience overflowed. "What was it?"

Connor finally dropped his nonchalance. "Scary."

Benny almost spoke, but he heard something, a tiny sound tickled his ears. Just on the edge of hearing.

Clippity Clop.

Benny had heard that before. Last night. In his dream. *But this isn't a dream.*

Connor apparently heard nothing, and continued. "Like Keith said last night, a Puka was the scariest Halloween monster of all time."

"What WAS IT?" Benny all but yelled, ignoring the cold, ignoring his beating heart. Connor watched, and sat down with an amused look. Connor's office all of a sudden got *really* cold.

"A Puka was..."

Damn him and his damn dramatic pauses.

"A horse. A black, fiery-eyed, muscle-bound demon of a horse."

Benny flashed back. *THE HORSE that killed Taylor...*

Clippity Clop.

Benny turned from Connor to look around seeing nothing even as the sound was got louder. Connor didn't hear a thing.

"Know what Scotty said when Keith told him he wanted a Puka in his house?" Connor asked. "His exact words were, and I quote: "What's so scary about a horse?"

Clippity Clop Benny ears throbbed, why didn't Connor hear it?

"But after what happened to Taylor, who knows?" Connor walked back to the DVD player, which had skipped again. "If I didn't know any better, I'd say someone was trying to kill all us Halloween experts off. Because in this wacky modern world, we're the only scary thing Halloween has left."

Benny gasped. *It couldn't be as simple as that.*

Clippity Clop

Connor rearranged some clutter on his shelves, his back to Benny.

CLIPPITY CLOP.

At that exact second a frozen wind blasted right through his office. Benny's minds-eye exploded in a vision, of a headless rider charging right through the room, cackling with an arctic chill.

SWOOSH

Then it was gone. Benny looked in every direction, seeing nothing. *What was that?!* He looked to Connor who was still facing the DVD player, who had apparently not noticed anything. Connor turned around.

His face covered in blood.

Benny choked.

"Don't tell me you're getting scared," Connor remarked, oblivious.

SCCCRREEEEEECCHHHH

A window exploded, blowing a thousand shards all over the room. Benny raised his hands as a monstrous wind picked him up and hurled him right out the door, which slammed shut behind him. Benny landed in a pile in the dirt outside Connor's office as the wind tornadoed into the rest of the *Fright Zone*. He yelped in terror as he found broken glass all over his face, but his voice was lost in the ice-chilled storm that shattered every window in sight. Several people screamed in pain as fog poured over everything.

"CONNOR!"

Benny fumbled through the fog, unable to see more than a foot in front of him.. He couldn't be that far away from the shack! Reaching out, he found the door and grabbed the knob.

The second he did, the vision drowned him.

Black.

He was dirty, wearing rags that barely fit. He had been digging potatoes. In a field. The sun was setting. Now his sister was calling.

Come home! Leave the Puka's Share! Leave it! COME!

Home? He had a home. In the distance, on the hill, silhouetted by the setting sun. But the sun sank so fast! He shouldn't be out here. His sister called again. In desperation.

She was afraid. Of what? The field. She was afraid of that. He was afraid of that too, of what happened after the sun went down. His sister ran to him, screaming at him.

Leave the Puka's Share! GET HOME!

Now he remembered. His field was to be feared. After dark something took the fields. They couldn't be in the fields after dark. They were his.

A cackle from the woods.

He couldn't see, the sun was almost gone. But... a form moved in the woods. Red glowing eyes a hundred yards away. The eyes saw him.

His sister reached him, grabbed him with a fierce pain and hurled him back to the cottage. Shrieking the entire time.

Don't touch the Puka's share!

Outside, a laugh split the dusk. Not human. Too fast. Too deep.

Then he saw it. Midnight black fur against the dusk sky. With red eyes. Crouching in the earth like a coiled predator, radiating Fear. Like none he had ever felt before. Fear that froze his heart.

The monster spoke to him through its eyes.

Yes. You are to be frightened of the fields. You are to be frightened of ME.

Across the field the monster leaped at him, a horse's mouth wide enough to eat him whole—

Benny fell backwards, landing in dead leaves and shattered glass. His eyes opened as the vision lingered for a moment. Screams penetrated his ears and Benny remembered where he was. Benny jumped to his feet and grabbed the doorknob to Connor's office—

Locked. *Oh no, you don't.* Benny's anger took over. *I won't take it from a freaking door!* Benny threw his body against the door. It smashed it open and Benny stumbled into the scene. White fog poured through the broken window. The TV flickered through a cracked screen, sideways on the floor. The narrator of *Boggy Creek* still chattered away:

"Next morning they would discover their dead kitten. Completely unmarked. Apparently she had just been...scared to death." The DVD player then sputtered, playing the same line over and over and over:

"scared to death..."

Benny saw Connor.

Still in his chair. Staring straight ahead. His fingers gripped the armrests with bloody knuckles locked into place. His skin stretched over his bones like a dried mummy. His eyes were locked open and his face was frozen in a silent scream.

Connor was dead.

"Must have been scared to death...BZZZ ...must have been scared to death..."

A noise behind him made Benny yelp. Someone was just outside the door. Benny turned back outside to the sound, desperate to have someone to help him—

And ran straight into Keith.

KEITH? Here? But—

No, it wasn't Keith. His smile laughed in mockery and his eyes glowed red as this NotKeith opened its mouth in a high pitched cackle as it jumped straight up into the air, landing on the roof of the shack to look down on Benny. Still laughing, it leaped off into the night. Benny followed its form as it flew far across the fields. Towards the *HallO'Scream*.

Benny stood there blindsided, remembering Connor's words:

I'd say someone was trying to kill all us Halloween experts off.

Benny ran. To Keith. With all the adrenaline he had to spend, Benny ran out of the *Fright Zone*, out into the dark fields beyond. Benny ran as hard as he could. He had to beat the Puka.

His next question came in rhythm to his footsteps: *Wait. How'd I know that was a Puka?* And it answered itself.

Because that's what it was.

As Benny vanished into the dark, behind him the broken TV still kept vigil over Connor's frozen form, its scratchy screen flickering over and over:

"Scared to death...."

"Scared to death...."

"Scared to death..."

Twelve

Fear. Fear was Keith's ally.

In the HallO'Scream, everyone had a job. Benny worked behind the scenes. Jack screened the door. Darryl counted the money.

And Keith wielded the fear.

Now he crawled on all fours through the rafters, a stalking predator, settling himself into prime scaring position. After his argument with Darryl, this would sooth him.

He heard laughter. The house had bigmouths in it. Teenagers only here because they were bored. The ticket taker had been harassed and the Grotto Mummy tripped. They were laughing AT HIS house. He'd see about that.

Contrary to rumor, Keith didn't anger easily. Keith smiled when he had good reason and got mad when he had good reason. Tonight, Keith had very good reason. Anger seethed behind his eyes, and these malcontents had volunteered to taste the sharp end of it.

Keith waited in a dark hallway. Wire bed frames circa 1970 had been upended in the hallway, bisecting and compressing so only a single person could squeeze through at a time. Feeling their way past cold springs of the metallic bed-frames, the scene lay in total darkness and had a carefully cultivated soundtrack for the experience. Dripping water.

Drip...

Drip...

CLANG!

Echoed, amplified. Industrial hammers. Metal on metal. Once every few seconds, in isolated darkness.

The malcontents had just entered. They had left the last room giggling with testosterone boasts, but now they faced utter black. They finally shut up as they entered single file, grasping for anything to get through this claustrophobic maze of cold metal.

Something waited for them.

Drip...

Drip...

Drip...

CLANG!

Groping, blind hands reached everywhere along the wall. In sensory deprivation the eyes deceive you, your retinas replay ghostly images as your brain grasps for... anything. But Keith knew exactly where they were. Their vibrations came though the metal frames and creaky floorboard that Keith knew by heart. More importantly, Keith knew where he was, on top of the frame. He was invisible in the dark, and by the time the party reached him, their senses would be screaming for any clue at all. With hesitant hands, they came through.

Keith struck.

A strobe light exploded, a buzz-saw screeched point blank at eye level, and Keith's arm of rotten flesh stretched out in the blinding flash, his face a horror of peeled disease *just inches away.*

The malcontents screamed and fell, the nightmare of gore burned into their eyes and ears as they collapsed in a heap of tangled limbs. The light went back out. The loudmouths whimpered and limped out of the metal cage on hands and knees. No one laughed now.

Yes, Darryl can ridicule Keith's ideas, but this is still Keith's house, and no one would ever laugh at his house again.

I feel better. But the afterglow evaporated fast. Nothing ever lasted as long as Keith wanted it, nothing was ever real enough. As Keith climbed off the cage, he laughed at his own hokum. A REAL haunted house? Like that was ever going to happen.

Right now it was time to see a girl about a mouse.

FIVE MINUTES LATER

"Keith, we have a problem."

"More specific?"

"A couple girls on the 2nd floor. They won't move. Too scared."

"This is a haunted house, Phil. They're *supposed* to be scared."

"Not like that."

"Like what?"

"Well, they're hiding in the corner behind the Lady in Wight."

"The Lady in Wight doesn't scare anyone. It just stands there."

"That's not what scared them."

"So what did? The Robots?"

"No."

"The Mad Ghoul?"

"No."

"WHAT?"

"A rat."

"We gutted the Rat Room for the Tarot Card Room."

"Not a rat room. A rat. Four legs and tail. One ran right in front of the girls, and they freaked out."

" ....."

"I'm just saying."

"Two girls go into a haunted house with zombies and chain-saws... and they flipped out because they saw a rat?"

"I guess it looked real."

For God's sake...

"What do we do with them?"

"The rats? Keep 'em. They're good ambiance. No, never mind. Health Inspector would eat us alive."

"Not the rat, the girls."

90

"Escort 'em out. Sounds like they've had enough."

"Who'll do that?"

"Me, obviously," Keith had reached his last level of exasperation. "We can't spare anyone else. It's my job to fill in for actors, to make sure the house opens on time, and to save helpless guests who naively wonder why they get scared in a haunted house." Doing a quick wash of his face, Keith put on his leather jacket and headed up the stairs.

I'll bring Jack with me. Keith thought. *He can talk the girls down, I'm seriously not in the mood right now.* Keith side-stepped through a secret door and made his way upstairs.

That had better have been one scary rat.

THIRTEEN

BENNY RAN.

Only a pale moon illuminated the dark field. He had run at full speed out of the *Fright Zone*, shivering at screams echoing through the air behind him. He hadn't thought about the best route to get back to the *HallO'Scream*. Benny knew better than to come this way, but in his haste...

He should have been there by now!

Should have, in the daylight. But at night any sound rolled across the empty land like thunder. Were those the screams of the *Fright Zone* behind him? Or the *HallO'Scream* ahead? He had no time for this! He needed to warn Keith now! Benny ran until he collapsed in the dirt, hands on his knees, wheezing. *Keep going darn it. Move!* He had to. He—

CRUNCH.

What was that? The sound of dry grass being stepped on. As a cold wind whistled in his ear, Benny looked around but saw nothing but a dark horizon.

CRUNCH

And a large dark shape. Benny's breath seized as his heart stopped in his chest as he lurched back to his feet. It was—

CRUNCH

A horse. A thick-legged barrel-chested black horse. Tail twirling, ears quivering. Just standing there like a dumb animal.

Staring right at him.

Benny stared back. A chill up his spine wouldn't let him look away. Everything about the horse looked normal, but ... *I'm getting out of here.* Benny shifted to walk away, not daring to even blink as the horse continued to stare at him. Benny thought he knew which way to go, he just had to walk a few steps and he could leave this horse behind.

A horse that now opened its mouth into a diabolically sadistic *GRIN*.

Its eyes inflamed into a phosphorescent red, illuminating the field in a glow of hate. Benny's breath caught again as viscous growl escaped the vicious mouth of sharpened teeth. Benny had no time to blink as the black monster charged him and hit with the force of a pile-driver. Benny flipped high in the air, his nose full with the stench of horse fur as he went head over heels and fell headfirst into a dry irrigation canal, landing in an aching heap on damp rocks.

Ow. Benny's bones rattled in agony as he settled into the damp mud of the canal bottom. He hurt all over, but...

Get out of this hole! Clawing at mud and sharp rocks, fighting pain pulsing through his legs, Benny heaved himself back into the field. The horse was gone. Benny stumbled around, working some last twinges of pain out of his legs as he looked everywhere in panic. Yes, the horse had left, and he was alone again in the dark field.

Why didn't it kill me? The answer came as Benny realized that the fall had turned him around, every sense of direction had been lost in the dark. Not only couldn't he find the *HallO'Scream*, he couldn't even get out of this field! Benny turned every which way as off in the distance he heard the cackle of a hysterical horse. *Laughing at him.* Terror tangled the bottom of his stomach. *It wants me lost!* Benny never screamed, that attracted attention and attention attracted trouble. But out here he finally let loose.

"AAUUUAGHGHGH!"

No one heard him.

You're not going to find Keith in time! Benny's panic rose again as his fatigue returned, and he almost dropped to his knees. *And he's going to die.*

Then something moved behind him.

Not again. Benny spun around, too desperate to be scared. He peered into the dark. The clouds painted everything a ghostly silver. A slight mist wafted on the night air.

Something walked through it.

A girl.

A teenager with long brown wavy hair, a transparent wisp of a form. After being attacked by a musclebound horse, Benny thought he had expected anything.

Anything except a ghost.

Time slowed as she approached. He could only look at this apparition. Flickering silver, silent as the grave. Benny tried but couldn't see her face even as she raised a finger and pointed towards one horizon, behind him.

Then the wind blew her away.

Benny breathed with a choke. What had he seen? He didn't have time to ask, as looking, there *was* a tiny light in the direction she had pointed. *That must be the HallO'Scream. Is it?* Benny had only a moment to decide, but trusted his gut.

She wanted me to find it.

Who?

Benny could only think of one person. But he couldn't stop to take in the implications. Focusing on the light in the distance, he ran.

THE 2ND FLOOR OF the *HallO'Scream* was under perpetual revision, as Darryl would "improve" it whenever he felt like it, forcing Keith to then fix what had just been screwed up. A never-ending battle.

The Upper Hallway for example, where a trio of Hollywood Horror monsters were placed in random locations like so many Disney animatronics. Freddy Krueger, Jason Voorhees, Michael Meyers. Darryl hadn't even bothered to hide them behind curtains. They just stood there, moving in jerky predictability. In House of Horrors Wax Museum in Hollywood, Keith noted the figures were scary precisely because they didn't move. But these? Dumb toys made in China, robot versions of exactly what Darryl had dancing outside. Why Darryl thought anything that danced on the lawn downstairs would then be any kind of scary up here was anyone's guess.

But as Keith never got tired of saying, *His half* of the house was scary.

Just ask these two girls clutching each other in the corner behind the Lady in Wight, just a skeleton in a wedding dress under a black-light at the end of the hall. They weren't alone. A mother and her child huddled with them. No one had told him that.

Keith and Jack approached them slowly. Keith hadn't run this house for years only to give a couple of already panic-stricken girls an aneurysm. Introducing himself, he coaxed them out of the corner by stomping his feet to prove the four-legged terror was gone. Taking them to the nearest emergency exit would mean walking down the 2nd floor Hall.

The ten-year old boy was in tears, full blown water-works. He gasped in such heaving sobs that Keith worried for his lack of air. All the actors were under orders to tone it down whenever a ten-year-old was in sight, but one of his actors had apparently screwed up big time. Keith would see about that. But first things first. Keith knelt on one knee and placed an arm on the boy's shoulder. *Maybe I am in a good mood after all.*

"Easy there partner. A little too rough for ya?"

The heaving sobs continued. The boy needed a little reassurance. Keith had ample experience in that. For starters, he got the little boy to look him in the eye. Unsure of what to make of a frazzle-haired Keith, the little boy looked up between tears.

Keith smiled, "Listen up big guy, I've got a little trick to share with you. I'm not scared of monsters. You wanna know why?"

Big blue eyes, red with tears stared up at Keith. Pulling him closer, Keith spoke with an absolute straight face.

"Because they are scared of ME."

The boy flinched with a surprised smile.

"Growl for me."

The kid just stared, dumbfounded. Keith kept up.

"We can be scary too. We can be the scariest thing of all, so if they ever scare you too bad, you just scare them right back. Grrrrr."

Mild grinning.

"They can't scare us because *we are* scary. Ever wonder why Haunted House workers can stand to work here? Hmmm? Because we get to scare the monsters back! That's how little boys have been fighting back for a thousand years. We scare them *back*. Got it?"

The little boy still gulped in aftershocks, but now looked with steady eyes. He smiled and reached for his mother. Keith sent him off with a "Remember. GRRR. We are the scary ones!"

The boy and his mother walked down the stairs to the emergency exit, leaving Keith alone with Jack, and the girls still in the corner.

"Who is responsible for *THAT*?" Keith demanded. But there weren't any actors in this corner of the house. Just the robots. *So who... never mind.* Keith turned his attention to the two girls. And recognized a face.

Her.

Oh my God, that's... The one in the car with Bridget.

She was here.

Thank God Benny isn't.

Keith coughed, fumbling for a moment. "Um, Kelly isn't it?" He barely remembered the name. Dressed in sparkly girly jeans, with a blue pull-over hoodie, Kelly held her eyes down and said nothing.

96

The other girl with Kelly had a lot to say. "Don't leave us here!"

Kelly's friend wore a black velvet ensemble with black fingernail polish, totally inappropriate for a haunted house. More like she thought this was a night club and she was the guest of honor. However she had been obviously outclassed by whatever rat had scurried across the floor. *Guess they don't teach you how to be scary in vampire school.*

Keith held out hands to pull them out of the corner. "We'll get you out of here. What's your name?"

"Jenna. My name is Jenna. Take us out!" she yelped.

Now Keith remembered her. Jenna had hung out with Bridget once or twice. Keith assured her. "You don't have to go anywhere you don't want to go. We can get you out of here in a flash."

Kelly finally looked up at Keith, glancing around like a lost sheep, "Is Benny here with you?"

That surprised him. Keith gaped for a second. *Put the emotional baggage away.* "No, just me and my associate. His name is Jack. He'll lead you to the door down the hall."

"But that's where the man was!" Jenna pointed.

Whoa. Keith froze. "A man? I thought this was about a mouse."

"That was first," Jenna said, still pointing. "Then someone grabbed us!"

"A man jumped out," Kelly confirmed, nodding.

Keith turned to Jack with a whisper. "No one is supposed to be in this hall."

*Supposed to be...*clicked in Keith's mind. He leaned up to Jack, "One of *them.*" Jack nodded in instant understanding. Offering his frilly Captain Sparrow hands to the shivering girls, Jack led them down the hall out of sight. Leaving Keith alone.

One of them. Some people take haunted houses the wrong way. Shady weirdos who buy a ticket and then "forget" to exit, hiding in shadows to do a little scaring of their own whenever young ladies walk by. Keith had zero tolerance for that. Whoever it was, he was not getting out of here alive.

But where were they hiding? Keith knew every nail in this house. He peered down the gloomy hallway. *Which of these things does not belong?*

He saw it instantly, and jumped. A black curtain hid a cast member tunnel, a curtain sticking out too far. Tensing his muscles, Keith dove into it and impacted a body. Bear-hugging the squirming form under the curtains, Keith raised his fist in glee. *Oh, did you ever pick the wrong house! I'm gonna beat you to a mother-loving—*

The curtain collapsed, leaving Keith holding only an empty sheet. A mocking laugh split the air as a black shadow ran down the hallway. Keith swore and ran down the corridor hot on the intruder's heels. Keith barely saw the form that ducked into another hidden door.

How'd he know that was there? Keith pounded through the door to see the intruder already out another one. He pursued...

...into the west hallway, almost running over a gaggle of screaming girls who thought his mad thrust through the service door was all part of the act. He saw the intruder dive through another door—

Into the back hallway under the attic. The figure flew through the last door and slammed it behind him. One more door and—

GOT HIM! That's a dead end!

Keith's hand hit the door and ran full speed right into—

VERTIGO

No up. No Down.

A phantasmagoria of laughing ghosts. Poking him, spinning him around.

Keith MacCool flew on by! Ran too close, and is the last to die!

Keith stumbled, lost and bewildered by the sudden panorama of ghosts stretching around him. Keith spun, twisted. *What the hell?* Keith didn't know where he was, what had happened, but in the middle of vortex of cackling ghosts and phantoms... he saw the intruder, standing right there with his back turned. With ferocious anger Keith pushed away every irrelevant wraith and grabbed the figure with both hands, spinning it around to see who is was...

He saw his own face. Bulging red eyes whirling with spiraling magic. A face of pure terror and hate.

Keith's doppelganger slapped him across the face and wrapped a huge hand around his neck, yanking him off his feet. This person was HUGE! Eight feet tall. Ten. Twelve. Keith's hands grasped his throat as he struggled to free himself. Eyes of demonic fire stared him down.

You say you're not afraid. It held Keith's eyes with its own fiery gaze. Red flame bored into Keith's skull.

You LIE!

The NotKeith lifted a struggling Keith far over a swirling vortex of spirits that howled with delight.

Live your lie. And perish!

With a high-pitched cackling laugh, it dropped Keith into the Vortex. Keith fell with an undignified shriek. The whirlpool of spinning ghosts spun him faster and faster, laughing with squeals until Keith thought his blood would spin right out of his ears.

SLAM

Keith *oommphed* onto a hard wooden floor. Claustrophobic tight corridor, plaster walls covered in Gothic chains and black curtains. The *HallO'Scream*. 2nd Floor. He'd recognize this anywhere.

Except he didn't. The floor was the wrong color. The walls were darker. Colder. Way too much fog, with real candles on the wall.

Real candles?

Something moved right in front of him. Lifting up his throbbing head Keith saw the pedestals of one of Darryl's robots. Michael Myers. Blue coveralls, white mask, and clunky boots. Keith saw the boots *step off* the pedestal to thunk down on the hard floor.

A meaty hand grabbed Keith by the neck and pulled him high into the air again. Keith's eyes bugged out of his skull as a six-foot plus homicidal killer with white rubber mask started choking him with thick hands. *Real eyes inside the mask.*

As the living breathing Michael Myers squeezed Keith's neck, Keith remembered something totally inappropriate for the situation.

Well, I did wish for a haunted house that was actually real.
Be careful what you...
Oh, never mind.

FOURTEEN

THE VOICE OF BENNY'S sister whispered in his exhausted ears as he wheezed, running until he couldn't feel his legs. Finally the Hal-lO'Scream came into shape, a silhouette glowing as an oasis of orange as the old school rose above him like a medieval fortress. Lungs burning Benny made it to the front yard.

Is that a dance floor?

Legs turning to jelly, Benny lurched up the steps to the front door. He could save Keith—

Until he got caught against the line of people waiting in the queue. Benny flailed like a twig in an ocean. Squeezing through the mass, he bumped the cell phone of an angry teenager who outsized him by at least 12 inches and 75 pounds. Benny's eyes blinked in a hundred flashbacks of bullies, towering over him.

You dont have time to be scared!

"Sorry. Sorry," Benny said as he squirmed around the crowd, succeeding only in fumbling into the back of someone else. A girl, seemingly waiting in line alone.

A girl? In line alone?

Benny didn't have time to consider the rarity of the occurrence as she turned around, about the same height as Benny, wearing black shorts and a black T-shirt advertising *Bigfoot doesn't believe in you either*. She looked Benny over with curiosity as he tried to shimmy past. She looked familiar.

"Hello Benny."

Gulp! Who is this person? Benny couldn't place her and now wasn't the time, so he burbled out the only words that made past his mouth.

"Errr hello, Nice to see you again, I've gotta go save my uncle," and ducked away before his embarrassment could register.

Finally he made it far enough to yank open a door to backstage. At the ticket booth a long-haired girl with Catwoman ears paused from counting a handful of $5 bills to look as he ran down the tight corridor, running straight into an evil butler holding a severed head on a silver platter, gawking at him with angry eyes.

"Watch it little man! Do that again and you'll get stepped on!"

Benny had no time to apologize. What was this guy's name? Clifton? "Where's Keith?" Benny all but yelled.

"Headed for the 2nd floor with Jack."

Benny aimed for the closest secret door to the main house, but Clifton grabbed him by the collar and pulled him back.

"You want Keith to skin you alive? Look before you run out into the show!" Clifton held Benny firm, watching some guests walk by. Only then did he release Benny through the door into the scare hall. "Don't screw up out there," Clifton frowned as the door shut behind Benny in a perfect seal, and he took a moment to get oriented. The *HallO'Scream* flowed in full swing, sounds of music and monsters wafted in the foggy air.

Where would Keith be? Benny ran up a stairwell to the 2nd floor. The floor wrapped around divided rooms and switchbacks. Benny knew he wouldn't find Keith unless he actually ran over him. Benny ran down the hall.

"KEITH!" he yelled down a dark corridor lit only by flickering LED candles. Nothing responded. Only old grainy photographs lined the walls, glowing under the candle light, photographs of Halloween, circa 1900. Still wheezing, Benny stopped and looked at the closest picture. A little boy, no more than eight, standing on his darkened wooden porch wearing a crusty paper-mache skull and stuffed long-johns, making a fat, pudgy skeleton. The boy just stared into the camera from a hundred years ago, trapped under sepia brown. So very old. *This kid is probably dead and buried.* It gave Benny the creeps.

"Ever play skin the cat? Hehehehehehe."

Benny leaped in surprise at the voice, only to get mad at himself. He knew better. Freddy Krueger, Darryl's new robot, twisted like a lethargic Pirate of the Caribbean beside him, a monotone laugh buzzed out from somewhere around his mid-section. Two more robots were somewhere down the hall, waiting in robotic stupidity for anyone to bump into them. Benny left Krueger behind and kept moving around another corner. He yelled one last time:

"KEITH!" Benny really not knowing what he expected to happen with that desperate ploy.

He *certainly* didn't expect the thudding laugh of a demon to ripple the air itself.

WuHAHAHAHAHAHHAAHHA.

What. The. Hell???

The laugh rippled the air itself. Benny spun around eyes wide, looking for source.

HAHAHAHAHAHAAHAHA.

Benny found it.

A funnel of white fog blasted down the hall at 100 mph, a freight train of billowing gray ripping the air as a hurricane. Benny barely had time to gasp for breath as the cyclone scooped him up and hurled him down the hall like a rag in the wind. For precious seconds Benny couldn't do anything but spin, until—

THUMP.

Benny landed in a heap on the floor, legs throbbing, back groaning as the fog continued its barrel run down the corridor, then vanished. Benny gritted his teeth with the pain of his fall. But he didn't feel the pain. He was too mad for that.

That's twice! Two times now he'd been thrown around in barely a half hour! *Who the hell is doing this?* Benny didn't know what had happened.

But he knew what being bullied felt like.

His hands formed fists, but there was nothing to do about it. No one was left to get mad at as everything lay silent around him. As chilly tendrils of fog prickled his skin, he swallowed his fury and climbed to his feet.

And saw nothing. Nothing lay in this hall except the smudgy glow of flickering candles lining the walls.

Benny looked again. *Those are real candles.*

REAL? Benny moved towards the glow, trying not to trip over his own feet that he couldn't see in the gloom. *Who put a real candle in here?* Benny reached out to grab the nearest one. *It'll start a fir—*

Out of the fog, a hand grabbed *him*.

Benny yelped as a pair of meaty arms plucked him right off his feet. Benny instinctively thrashed, but a hand went over his eyes by a form a foot taller and at least a hundred pounds heavier. He could feel himself being carried away at a run, and dropped in a heap on a floor. Spotlights blasted Benny in a room of vibrant color, thick lights of disgusting fluorescent red, yellow, and purple, hitting him from every side. A huge form stood above him. Laughing like a circus ringmaster.

"Give a welcome to our new contestant!"

Gruff hands lurched Benny to his feet. Stumbling for balance, Benny saw a man wearing the over-embroidered tuxedo of a showman, an *orange* tuxedo of crushed velvet with a green frilly vest, like a refugee from a 19th century circus. With blue hair styled into demon horns and a two-faced smile straight from the Devil's mirror.

"It's time to play everyone's favorite game, GRAVE PERIL!"

Applause.

Applause? Benny's eyes had adjusted now. He was in a triangular room bathed in sickeningly fluorescent neon light. The walls

104

were nightmare murals of psychedelic opium color under black lights, each holding an ugly green door built in the center, labeled "1," "2", and "3." A huge sign hanging from the ceiling flashed "Will You Bet Your Life?"

Benny stood in the middle of center stage with a laughing game show host. The Game Show room, second floor. Benny knew this place, he had painted those doors himself! Except, he didn't remember putting in all these lights, and the Ringmaster was supposed to be played by an extrovert young man named Garrett. This was definitely *not* Garrett.

The Ringmaster shoved a microphone in Benny's face, with a leer. "You ready to play young man? You ready to bet your life???" Applause. From a thousand people. "But first things first! We have one other contestant to finish!" With a twirl of coattails, the Ringmaster danced to a corner of the triangular room where a bright yellow spotlight suddenly appeared, blasted down on a—

Man strapped into an electric chair. Eyes bugged out, scared for his very life. The Ringmaster bent over with the microphone.

"Next question! Listen carefully!" The host smiled with demonic glee. "If you live at the end of a One-Way Dead-End street, how did you get there?"

The host stuck the microphone right into the face of the terrified man, who could do nothing but...

"Errrrr...."

"WRONG!" The Ringmaster shouted with a haughty leer. The unseen crowd booed as the lights turned a very ugly red, and the Ringmaster yanked down on a metal lever next to the chair.

BBBBZZZZZZZZZZZZZZZZZZZZZZZZ

Visible arcs of electricity coiled over the victim in the chair, broiling him in convulsions. He thrashed as his eyes curled up backward into the top of his head. With a laugh the Ringmaster pushed the lever back and kicked the body, the smoking, cooked body. Benny gasped. *That's not supposed to do that! The electric chair is just jumper cables hooked to some batteries! It cant—*

105

It could. Fire slowly consumed the man's shirt, leaving charred flesh underneath. He was very dead. Very *real*.

So was everything in this room.

The Ringmaster turned back to Benny. Benny gulped.

FIFTEEN

MICHAEL MYERS. BLUE COVERALLS. White mask.

Keith recognized every inch of this monster, even as it strangled him.

Keith kicked empty air as his vision blackened, but his last few seconds of consciousness didn't allow him the luxury of wondering why he was here, why he was being attacked.

And why his own Haunted House had inexplicably become a living, breathing thing, trying to kill him. Keith didn't care why. This was HIS house, and finding strength from rip-roaring fury he'd be damned if he died here. He looked at his attacker, saw furious eyes burning out of the mask as Myers squeezed and squeezed. But Keith had played Michael Myers, many times. He knew exactly what the weakness was. Keith couldn't reach the floor, but he could reach the mask.

Grabbing the pasty plastic with two hands, Keith spun it backwards around Myers' head.

Blinded, Myers dropped Keith instantly as ham-handed fingers tried to fix his mask. Keith landed on his feet. He gasped for breath, but he had to act now. For Myers had stepped precariously close to the back stairs...

Keith gave Myers a double-fisted body slam in the chest. Myers toppled over backwards, tripping over his feet as he fell down the stairs, bouncing his head at least twice on the way down.

Keith finally caught his breath as he peered into the dark. *Whatever that was, I better make sure it's dead.* But Keith couldn't see through the fog. He almost climbed down the stairs to check the body, but behind him down the hall he heard something else, an unmistakable voice.

Benny?

BENNY FROZE PETRIFIED AS the orange-suited game show host approached him again. The Ringmaster smiled with pointy teeth as his slicked hair sparkled under the obnoxious lights. Smoke from the dead man in the electric chair wafted into his eyes and he brushed it away.

"That makes me weep. Not Really! HAHAHAHAHA!"

Benny would have run, but there was nowhere to go. This claustrophobic room had no exit! Just three walls, and a very demented host.

"Now it's your turn young man. But we all know what happens if he gets it wrong, right folks?" the Ringmaster crooned to the crowd that wasn't there, but a crowd that cheered as a trapdoor flopped open at Benny's right foot, releasing scorching flame and brimstone that filled the room with hot stingy smoke. The door snapped shut with an ominous clang as the Ringmaster let loose with a cackle straight from the Stygian depths.

"No worries! No worries!" the host placed an orange velvet arm over Benny's shoulder. "I'm suuuuure you'll get it. Wont he folks?" More applause out of nowhere. Benny looked around but saw nothing but the three walls with the three numbered doors coated in obnoxious fluorescent paint. Door # 3 glowed in red, door #2 had sickly green, and door #1 pulsed in ugly yellow, literally shaking as if something banged it in furious anger from the other side.

"IT'S TIME!" The Ringmaster shoved the microphone into his face, and asked his question with eyes full of Machiavellian sparkles. "If... you are in a car going the speed of light and you turn your lights on, will they do anything?"

What the hell? But that was point of this room, to get the guests all flustered and disoriented. However right here, as to that question, Benny actually did know the answer.

"Yes."

Keith had clued him in once. Keith loved to play the Ringmaster.

This Ringmaster didn't lose a blink, stepping backwards in a over-pompous "Yooooooouuu'rrrrrreeeeee... "

At least Benny thought he knew the answer...

"CORRECT!"

Sparkling disco lights spun everywhere as confetti fell from the ceiling and the crowd cheered.

"You now advance to the Escape Round!" the Ringmaster roared with a twirl. He waved around the room and bent over in a bow. "Pick a door. Number one? Number two? Or Number three?"

Thank God. Benny didn't know why this place had gone real and he didn't care. He had to find Keith! One of the doors would get him out, the others had... surprises. One problem, Keith changed the numbers every night, and Door #1 kept shivering. *I'm staying away from that one.* As for the way out? There was no way to know. Benny guessed.

"Two"

"He chose Number Two ladies and gentlemen!" shouted the Ringmaster with carnival flair. "It's all yours! Open it up and receive your prize!"

Benny gulped and just flung the door open. Either he picked right or he didn't. Either the door would lead to a hallway, or—

Freddy Krueger leered at him from behind the door. The robot, alive, like everything else. Krugerbot shoved Benny to the ground as it stepped into the room. His razor claws reached up into a theatrical pose to slice Benny into several bloody pieces as the Ringmaster cackled with sadistic glee.

SIXTEEN

WITH KRUEGERBOT LORDING OVER him with bloodlust in his eyes, Benny scrambled on all fours to get away.

"I'm sorry, did that scaaaare you?" The Ringmaster sneered. "GOOD!"

Benny couldn't move fast enough, and there was nowhere to go anyway. He closed his eyes as Kruegerbot's blades, glittering in the disgusting fluorescence, came swiping down.

Keith caught them, jumping inside their reach.

Catching the lashing arm in a lock, Keith sent his right fist squarely into Krugerbot's red sweater. Krugerbot went limp and Keith dropped the body to the floor, His moldy hat fell off and rolled over to the feet of the Ringmaster.

He was mad.

"NO HELP FROM THE AUDIENCE!" His face twisted into gargoyle contempt at Keith. "I'm afraid YOU, disreputable sir, have been disquali—"

Keith kicked the Ringmaster in the gut, sending his orange-velvet in a flop into the electric chair. Keith jumped over and yanked the lever down.

BUUUZZZZZZZZZZZZZZZZZZZZZZZ

As the Ringmaster sizzled, Benny looked at his uncle with awe. For most people, the idea of being inside a real haunted house would be alarming, but Keith came from a different mold. The sort who had collected Fangoria Magazine since the age of ten and saw his first R-rated horror movie at nine. Keith was the one man in the world who would never be afraid of this.

How'd he get in here anyway?

Door #3, obviously. It hung wide open, revealing a large dark hallway ahead, thick with fog. Keith must have been on the other side. Now Keith looked at the sizzling pile on the electric chair, then kicked Krueger's floppy body, making sure he was down.

"I hate celebrities."

Benny had had enough. *Screw this.* He ran through Door #3. There was a secret door to backstage right down that hall! His hands palmed the walls, reaching for the hidden handle to get them out of here...

Only to find out that there *was no* secret door! Just a solid wall! *Crud.* He turned back around to Keith, who still stood inside the sizzling set of Grave Peril.

"What do we do now?"

"Survive." Keith was dead serious. Joining Benny in the hall, he also looked for the exit, finding nothing. The implications hit Benny with finality.

"We have to walk through the whole thing don't we? All the way to the end!"

Keith considered, looking ahead down the dark hall, now the only way to go, and smiled. "Consider this dismaying observation. This chamber has no windows and no doors, which offers us a chilling challenge...to find a way out!"

Benny scowled at Keith's macabre humor. *How can Keith quote the Haunted Mansion?* Benny freaked at what awaited them. Every room, all real... "Krueger! That means all the robots—"

"Yes" Keith said again, gesturing down the hall. Benny followed to see where Michael Myers' pedestal was supposed to be. Empty.

111

Oh no. Benny looked ahead in horrid expectation, to the next pedestal he knew was right there—

Jason Voorhees was gone too.

Benny backed up, his panic rising as he swished fog out of his eyes. All of a sudden he was aware of a host of sounds coming from every direction. A hollow moan from somewhere down a lost hall ahead of them... Heavy footsteps thunking with brute force on the first floor beneath them. Benny's heart thumped in his throat.

"Easy." Keith put his hand on his shoulder. "We didn't survive ten years of meandering through every haunted house in five states just to get killed in our own. Let's just see what happens."

Of course, there's always my way, as the Mansion would say. Keith was right, they couldn't be afraid of their own house.

SMASH

Benny nearly jumped out of his shoes. He spun expecting a hideous death—only to see Jack Sparrow stumble out of the fog. Benny actually laughed at himself, catching his breath at the sight of Jack running to join them. *He's already got two girls for the evening. Thank God. If Jack has control here, we'll all be OK.* Then the two girls stepped close enough to be seen.

"Kelly?"

It popped out before Benny could stop himself. And to his horror Benny stood face to face with the girl who had killed his sister.

SEVENTEEN

KEITH DEALT WITH FANTASY all the time, he practically lived there. It took a lot more than a real-live haunted house to unhinge him. After conferring with Jack to make sure the girls were OK, he had enough irony to ask Benny with a straight face, "I take it something happened at Connor's?"

What Benny told him, however, about Connor, the *Fright Zone*, and Keith's doppelganger, definitely pushed some buttons.

Taylor died last night. Scotty was killed the night before. And now, Connor. Three Halloween enthusiasts. Despite being in an impossible situation, Keith accepted the impossible.

"Its killing all of us. One at a time."

Live your lie. And perish! Said his doppelganger, before dropping him in here.

We'll see about that.

"Us?" asked Benny, interrupting his thoughts.

"The Halloween experts. Now it's my turn."

The girls just clutched each other. "How do we get out of here?" cried Jenna with streaks of black mascara laden tears.

"We don't," Jack replied (without a trace of Captain Sparrow accent). "All the exits are gone."

"Not all of them," Keith said, pointing down the black corridor that invoked dark claustrophobia.

Of course I'll have to lead the way. Jack can hold the rear and keep everyone moving. First thing down that hall is— Hold. *The girls had seen a rat?*

Two half-buried memories barged into Keith's thoughts.

One, of Darryl walking into the Grave Peril Room a few weeks ago with a Wal-Mart shopping bag. A bag filled with something plastic, tiny, and furry.

Two, when he kicked the Ringmaster, he noticed Door #1 had been shaking.

Keith turned around with a groan, peaking to look back into Grave Peril, just in time to see Door #1 explode right off its hinges with a flood of rats. Rats. A whole freaking floor's worth of rats. Climbing over the ruined door, clawing each other in a pile of ragged claws and tails.

Seeing several hundred pairs of beady eyes fixate on the party in hunger, Keith damned Darryl all to hell.

"MOVE!"

They ran plunging into the silver fog, the hallway stretched out to impossible lengths even as the hundreds of squeaks swarmed behind them. Running at full speed, they finally found pale yellow light piercing a crack under a door, a heavy thick wood that Keith yanked open with a single pull. Benny and the girls ran in first, then Keith, with Jack grabbing an inner iron ring and slamming the door against the tsunami of rats only feet away. The rats hit the door with a muffled thump. The door vibrated with a thousand hyper frantic scratches from the other side.

Keith watched the door even as his mind raced with his next move. The *HallO'Scream* had two stories, with the guests starting on the second floor and working their way down. Keith and company just left Grave Peril, meaning they still had serious danger before they even got off this floor! In fact now they were in the hallway with—

Kelly screamed as Jenna put a foot into a bottomless pit.

It was only supposed to be an illusion of an empty hole, but Jenna's foot dropped into dead space! Keith jumped to catch both girls from falling down into cavernous depths. In the stumbling, Keith kicked a crushed pop can down into the dark, its clanking echoing a mile down.

Geesh.

Only a skinny path next to a flat wall let everyone squeeze by. Jack and the girls went first, Keith and Benny went across last, back-flattened against the wall as they shimmied past the bottomless hole. The girls awaited them on the other side, still shivering from the barely averted disaster. Keith knew had to get control of this.

Now what room are we in? Past the game show, through the switchbacks, past the pit, that would put us right into...

Keith's eyebrows twitched. With a sigh, he opened the curtain behind the girls.

Spiders. Five hundred of them.

Hell. Five thousand. Fifty thousand. Benny would be the one to know, he had personally painted every last one. Glowing spiderwebs stretched across every surface of the Web Room. A living carpet of hairy legs. The girls inhaled in a prelude to a squeal as Keith darted in front to give them a shield, then looked at Benny in silent agreement of what to do.

"Hold your breath and walk slowly. You see the way out over there on the left."

Keith went first, making it across in five quick steps to brush a few cobwebs out of his hair. The rest followed one at a time, mostly in silence until Jack bounded through in his gargantuan pirate boots. The *crunches* were sickening, but everyone was through, waiting around the corner where a sickening green glow lay just beyond. Keith looked ahead to the glow, then behind at the spiders behind him. They quivered and shivered.

115

Then as a single carpet, following them out the door.

"HELL!" Everyone took off yet again.

KELLY. HERE.

Benny's first reaction shamed him. *Not fair to think she killed Bridget. She was just in the same car.*

But Benny still couldn't look at her, especially with the rats and spiders demanding his attention. But after escaping the spider room, Kelly looked up at *him,* checking herself with frantic swipes for stowaway spiders and mouthing a silent, "Thank You."

Benny didn't want to be mad at her. Her red curly hair fell to her shoulders. Her face had a few freckles.

Just like the last time I saw her.

Except the encroaching spiders ruined the moment. With thousands of little legs closing in, Benny did the last thing he expected, grabbing Kelly by the wrist, and took off into the next room, Jenna fell in behind.

What happened to the rule about monsters having to stay in their area? Benny thought. *No one told the spiders. But they won't catch us. The next room only has a—*

A green glow, a single deathly green light bulb illuminating an open refrigerator filled with body parts, shelves full of bubbling multicolored liquids. An electrical spark arced between two metal poles. The Mad Scientist room. Every haunted house needs one. Except this one had a repugnant odor. Clouds of yellow noxious gas bubbled from concoctions on the lab table, and the operating table in the middle of the room had a corpse on it, with pus oozing out—

Beside Benny, Jenna gasped. "What is this place?"

As the hallway behind them continued to fill with a squiggling mass of spider legs, Benny lead the girls into the room, staying far clear of anything that boiled or bubbled. Eyeballs on the shelf *followed* them as they walked past.

It looks about as I remember, except this room should have a—

116

A frazzle-haired ghoul with bloodshot eyes and a bloody lab coat ripped aside a black curtain, firing up a pair of hedge-clippers with a gurgling scream.

Oh, yeah. There's a monster in here.

A REAL monster. A frightening mutation of a white gorilla and Dr. Frankenstein. Facial lacerations dripping purple ichor as a forked tongue threw sizzling spittle between knife-edged teeth.

Jenna's eyes went wide as she shrieked "A vampire!"

The stupidity of which cut through Benny's hesitation. *No, that is NOT a vampire. It's a freaking ghoul.* But this wasn't the time for that. Benny's mind turned the whole scene to slow motion. There was a lot to think about. Real monster, in a real haunted house. What do you do?

You could run back, try against hope to get to the front door. *Which isn't there.*

Try to run forward? Hope to outrun the monster and hope he can't leave his area? *He'll run us to ground and eat us.* Try as he might, as time sped back up, Benny couldn't think of a third option.

Fortunately Keith did. He flew across the room, sending the monster in a flail of lanky limbs into the back wall with a flying Tae Kwon Doe jump kick in the sternum. Keith didn't wait for it to get up as he grabbed the operating table with the corpse on it and shoved it into the ghoul, pinning it to the wall with an *oomph*. The ghoul hissed in pain as sharpened teeth bit at the air.

Good lord. Benny retreated from the altercation, only then noticing Kelly was still holding him, shivering, and remembering that 10000 spiders now fully engorged the hallway behind them and were moving in. Benny only had thirty seconds, tops, to escape this dead end.

Keith didn't need that long. He slammed the table into the ghoul again, doubling the monster over as Jack grabbed the ghoul by his bloody lab coat and threw him to the floor. Keith grabbed a flailing corner of the bloody lab coat and wrapped it around the ghouls head in three quick twists, then pushed him hard into the open refrigerator. Jack slammed the door and held it shut. For a precious moment, the only sound was the bubbling of the laboratory elixirs. Benny exhaled.

Whoa. That was pretty cool.

Jenna looked like the proverbial deer in the headlights, but high pitched squeal from the spider-infested hallway broke her out of it.

Spiders don't squeal.

This one did. Bright yellow skull on his carapace, fully a foot across. Eyes and mandibles creeping in all directions. It skittered right into the room and touched Kelly's leg with a long hairy leg of its own, earning a scream that would have shattered any window for 50 yards.

Escape! But this room was still a dead end. Unless that's exactly what Keith wanted everyone to believe. Leaving Jack holding the fridge, Keith ran to the far wall and ripped away a bloody curtain, revealing a dark hole going down. A slide to the next level.

Keith waved Benny over to him to go first. Benny turned to Kelly as the fridge, started to bang from within. "We have to get in."

The girls gave head-shaking chorus of "No's."

The ghoul in the refrigerator jolted under Jack's muscles, and Keith put on his angry face. "Ladies, do you think there's an escalator behind a shelf? That's the way out!" The giant yellow spider skittered farther into the room with hundreds of its smaller friends started filling the wall. "Benny show them!"

Benny knew the slide was the only way out. He turned to grab the girls, only to see Kelly's eyes frozen on the giant spider with the yellow skull. *His* spider. He had painted the freaking thing, and he'd be damned to see it eat Kelly now. Scooping up the ghoul's dropped hedge clippers, he ran right over and—

Impaled it. Skewered it right to the floor. The spider squealed and collapsed. Dead.

Holding the clippers in a death grip, Benny stared at what he'd done. Time ticked by in heartbeats as he turned back to the girls. Jenna's mouth was wide open. But Kelly was looking at him. Their eyes met.

I did that to protect her. The heartbeats continued as they took in each other's eyes.

"WILL YOU GET IN NOW?" Keith all but screamed. "Or do you need to get a room?" Grabbing Jenna by the shoulders Keith picked her up and pushed her in the slide feet first. Her scream lasted ten seconds as she fell away into the dark. Benny's lull broke as the Spiders engulfed the green lightbulb, darkening the room. He ran to the slide, climbed in, and looked right at Kelly. "Follow right after me. You have to." Kelly nodded and Benny pushed himself down.

Into Darkness. The rush of the falling. Claustrophobia. Panic.

You're falling down a hole.

YOU'RE GOING TO CRASH! THERES NOTHING AT THE BOTTOM!

Benny landed on a pile of soft mattresses, glowing under a small orange light.

Real house. Real mattress.

Benny untangled his arms and legs. Jenna whimpered beside him, startled by his landing and unable to get her footing. Benny helped her up and yelled up the shaft.

"IT'S SAFE!"

He heard rustling above him as everyone else came down, anchored by Keith with what Benny could tell was a running leap to avoid both a floor full of spiders and an enraged ghoul still trapped in a fridge. *We made it.* Then Benny remembered where they were. His spine irresistibly shivered. They still had an entire floor to go.

A ghostly moan echoed through the tight hallway. The rest of the *HallO'Scream* awaited them.

119

EIGHTEEN

FEELING HIS WAY WITH bare hands through the utter black of the Dark Maze, Benny finally had time to think about the events of the last 2 hours. He avoided it.

One advantage of the Maze was that it had no monster in it. But what had been a minor crawl through 30 feet had expanded into an endless black eternity of wall after wall. Benny shuffled behind the girls who tip-toed ahead of him, their fear getting contagious.

How far could this go? The halls went left, right, doubled-back, then straight for what seemed like a hundred yards only to switch back. The girls had the advantage of blissful ignorance, having no idea how far the maze was supposed to be. But Benny knew they should have been out long ago. *The maze can't last forever, can it?*

"Benny? Are you there?"

The voice was soft-spoken, barely a whisper, afraid to make any noise in this endless quiet. But right next to him. Female.

Kelly.

Benny tensed, unsure of what to do. *Well, maybe I should answer her.*

"I'm... right here." Fumbled words for a fumbled search.

"Are you OK?"

She was asking him? "Sure. I guess." Best he could do at the moment. Then several seconds too late, "Are you OK?"

"Yes. Is this for real?"

Was it? Benny couldn't see Kelly, he couldn't even see his own hands grasping the wall. Her voice just floated in this total darkness, disembodied. Benny couldn't handle girls even if he could see them. "I... uh... Just keep walking. We have to get out sooner or later."

"You're not scared?"

"Not really." Benny was. Not that he would tell her that.

"But...I can't see anything."

"Just close your eyes."

"What?"

"Close your eyes," Benny repeated as his hands pulled him down the midnight hallway. "It's easier if you can't see what you can't see."

Silence for a bit. Benny almost thought Kelly had abandoned him until:

"I haven't seen you in a while."

"You still can't see me," Benny said without thinking, immediately regretting it, but Kelly laughed, immediately putting him at ease.

"I've been asking around for you," she whispered.

"You have?" Benny's confusion was obvious. Heck of a first conversation. Benny didn't have the gift of gab that God gave an Irish toad.

"Will we be OK?" Kelly asked with a whispered squeak.

"Just keep doing what Keith does. He knows what to do."

"I know."

Huh?

"Stop." Keith spoke with authority. Benny reached out and found his Uncle ahead of him as his other arm reached into Kelly. Turning around he got nothing but got a mouthful of hair. Blowing it out, he caught a whiff of lavender...

"Shhhh," Keith went, followed by shuffling of feet as Keith apparently twisted around a corner, a corner with...red light behind it? *Thank God.* But what room was it?

"Girls, huddle," came Keith's smooth voice, betraying no emotion. Benny and Jack and the girls all pressed together, now visible with the meager light bleeding around the corner as black shapeless masses. Benny could finally see Kelly in the red gloom, but Keith demanded everyone's attention.

"You're not going to like this, not one bit. But either we do this or go die of old age back in that maze."

Outside the maze the walls narrowed into single file, and then shrunk into a tight little crawl space, like a coal chute, lit only by a faint red glow. The only way forward.

Benny looked at the dark hole in the wall and shuddered. Fog still wafted around them, pushed by a breeze that whispered in his ears. He thought he heard a faint heartbeat . .

"Give me your coat." Keith said to Jenna. It wasn't a request. Jenna blinked, but yielded and handed over a black vinyl goth jacket. Keith shook it out and held it before him as he stared into the tunnel, and tentatively placed one knee inside.

"When I yell, crawl through here as fast as you can. Don't stop. Don't fidget. The tunnel's only about 20 feet. Go right over the coat. Whatever you hear, do not touch the coat." The girls nodded and Keith looked to Jack, "Pick up the rear," and then crawled into the red tunnel. Ben heard the shuffling of Keith's hands and knees against the stone floor for several feet. Then silence. The whispering breeze turned arctic, pushing the girls into a huddle. Benny shivered as he looked for Keith in the dark crawlspace.

Where'd he go? There's only one way out, and Keith couldn't go through without passing over the—

Benny gasped as he remembered why Keith needed the coat.

"Come through!" reverberated Keith's voice from the far side of the tunnel. The girls fought chattering teeth, but fell to their knees and entered the crawlspace. Benny followed, hearing minor yelps from the girls as they bumped their heads on the hard ceiling. The cramped space made slow progress.

Jenna stopped, clogging the tunnel. "Why's my coat spread out on the floor?"

"CRAWL OVER IT!" bellowed Keith from the far end. The girls rustled through all the faster, not wanting another yell. Benny was next. He put a hand on a coat...

THUNK.

From below. Below the coat.

THUNK THUNK.

"Keep moving!" Keith bellowed.

THUNK SCRAPE SCRAPE.

The girls hurried as the floor thundered and shook beneath them. As Benny crawled after them, something beneath him pounded with enough force to actually knock him a few inches off balance. Flailing an arm to catch his equilibrium, he dislodged a corner of the coat, revealing clear Plexiglas underneath.

Don't look at it.

POUND.

A frantic desperation of thundering strikes hit against the floor. Ahead he saw the shadows of Kelly exiting the tunnel. *Catch up!* Benny started to cross the coat. The small corner was still exposed, with plexiglass underneath. Benny couldn't help himself. He looked down.

A rotting black eyeball pressed against the other side of the glass.

Benny pulled away the coat entirely—

A decomposing face mashed against the transparent barrier, gnawing at the smooth surface. Seeing Benny, the fiend flew into hysterics, pounding the flimsy barrier. The tunnel was so low the corpse was almost face to face to Benny as b+oney fingers scraped against the glass. The mouth licked with a swollen gray tongue.

Licking the glass.

Benny tore out of the tunnel, landing in a heap on the other side. Keith picked him up as Jack came out behind him, breathing hard, coat in hand. He gave it back to Jenna, who sniffed it before she put it back on. At Keith's motion the group continued down a tight corridor of cold, hard brick. Benny looked for Kelly, she looked afraid, shivering in the chill. Moving to follow Benny, she passed close enough to pass the slightest whisper.

"You were brave."

Benny tripped at the sound of her voice, but quickly recovered, for even now another cackling screech rippled from the hallway far ahead. They weren't out of this yet.

Only later did it occur to Benny that Keith had crawled through that tight tunnel, nose to nose over that decaying face, without ever uttering a sound.

NINETEEN

THEY GOT TO THE CORPSE CATACOMBS before Benny realized they hadn't run into any other guests. Was it just the five of them stuck in here? *Apparently it only wants us.* Benny followed as Keith ducked into musty tunnels, kicking wooden supports that creaked with the strain of a real abandoned mine. With real corpses. And real bats.

After that, the Hall of Jack O'Lanterns. A long single-file cave with dozens of carved pumpkins staring down from every side. Silhouettes of sinister faces with flickering eyes and teeth threw shadows on every wall. Just staring. But not a face had been altered. Benny ought to know, he had carved them all. The party passed through without a word, the jack O'lanterns measuring their progress, following them with orange eyes.

Somewhere in the tunnels they entered a labyrinth cave. As they bumped their heads on the rocky ceiling, something growled out of the shadows. Everyone stopped, hearing nothing but the *drip drip* of water on the rocks, echoing through endless caves. Keith held the party back and stepped around a corner. Everything left in silence until a huge *CRASH* made everyone scream. But Keith came

125

back around. "That one won't be bothering us." Benny forgot what was down here. He didn't want to remember.

Finally, a crawlspace let them crawl out of the tunnels into a regular cement hallway. Into a hall of mirrors. Strobe lights were supposed to go off to blind you with a hundred reflections of... yourself. Scary enough. Except now the mirrors weren't reflecting just light. Jenna looked into one right as the light flashed—

Her own skull sneered back, open-mouthed death.

Benny was certain the girls didn't want to see anything in here. He ran as Keith pushed everyone through fast. Benny's heart thumped with the exertion. Until he stopped he didn't realize that he was hearing *another* heart, thumping faintly through the floor itself:

Tha Thump. Tha Thump.

Keith halted, making the universal *silence* gesture with his finger and mouth. They entered a corridor bracketed by skull candles dripping blood red wax down their faces. Keith peeked his head around the next corner, where a dull blue glow came from somewhere beyond. Beside him hung a sign on the wall, partially shredded, dripping with green ooze. *Biohazard.* Benny knew where they were.

"Damn."

Keith nodded to Jack and mouthed without speaking: "Zombie Room."

Other rooms came and went, but never this one. The Zombie Room was always open no matter what else in the house went empty. Keith saw to that personally. Now he rubbed his hands and adjusted his jacket.

"This is going to be exciting."

EXCITING?

"Hold arms. We cant run until I find the way out. Don't break your grip or..." he shrugged.

Benny didn't know how he would have ended that sentence either, but Keith continued.

"We'll have a few seconds to find the door before it starts. Just make sure your shoes are tied."

"Before *what* starts?" squeaked Kelly. Keith didn't answer, just led everyone around the corner.

Into the color blue. A cold arctic blue from lights in a low ceiling, highlighted by fluorescent red goop pouring down the walls and pooling on the floor. The glow didn't reveal much, just a skinny room with narrow walls and hard cement. Pillars down the middle were plastered with *Biohazard* signs, around which were bodies wrapped in sheets on tables spaced evenly along the walls.

A morgue.

As they entered, an eerie wind brushed their hair. Moving one creeping step at a time, the party passed silent unmoving bodies on either side. The wind fluttered the sheets and blew ripped shreds of fabric across the floor.

"Stop." Keith said after they were several yards in. He turned around in a whisper. "It's going to start. You're going to get only seconds to run for the door. It's got to be somewhere down at the end."

The girls held each other, not looking ready to run anywhere. The breeze gusted. Jenna arose out of her frozen stupor long enough to risk a nervous giggle.

"Why... Why do you call this the Zombie Room?"

Why indeed.

LIGHT LIGHT LIGHT.

Strobe lights blasted their eyes from point blank range, turning Benny's eyes into spots. Grabbing for anything, he caught Kelly's hand. For an instant his vision cleared to see her face. Smooth. Innocent.

The next instant he saw rotting faces reach for her from behind. Festering with decay, mouths sputtering black blood and screaming through broken teeth. They came from every side

"RUN!" Keith hurled the girls towards the far end. But they were blinded by strobes which left glowing splotches in the eyes. The strobes caught the zombies in ghastly slow-mo, bony arms waving without sense, feet stomping but never hitting the ground. Benny gasped at them with a stupefaction that threatened nausea. They were huge! Dripping in gore, spitting blood, these were born of Keith's fanaticism to be *The* Scariest House in Town.

127

Seemed like a good idea at the time.

Benny saw a blur of Sparrow frill as Jack plowed ahead, shoving shoulders first and knocking several zombies down. The girls ran in clumsy starts with Benny pushing from behind, trying to watch every zombie at once.

Maybe the zombies won't grab us. They can't bite. Can they?

They could. A rotten hand reached to yank out a tuff of Jenna's hair by the roots. Another arm wrapped around Kelly's neck and a mouth full of razor teeth moved to chomp down.

Benny didn't think as he planted his fist in the monster's face, sending mushy gore everywhere. He was not going to die in here. He grabbed both girls by the arms and all but hurled them towards the back wall. He saw the door now. It came and went in alternating splotches as the strobe assault continued.

Keith didn't wait for the door to reappear. With a quick one-two skip and front kick, he dislocated a zombie's kneecap, tripping it and a pile of zombies right behind. Another spin sent his elbow into a mushy face, sending gore everywhere and sending more zombies to the floor.

Snarling, they all got back up. They didn't feel any pain, they were zombies.

Jack reached the door, wrenching it open and pushed the girls through, but decrepit hands seized Jack's dreadlocks and yanked him backwards back into the mess of bodies. A rotten mouth spewed steaming orange puke onto Jack's chest, eating through his Sparrow jacket like acid. With a shout of anger Jack ripped off his smoking clothes and decked the zombie into the hoard. Keith jumped in to help, but more claws ripped at them all.

A slash on Keith's forehead. A rip on Jack's hand.

Blood started to pour as a mouth of teeth opened up for a huge bite out of Keith's neck. Benny turned around to help—until he saw the look on Keith's face.

Furious. This was HIS house!

Black blood sprayed as Keith sank a fist into a pudgy face. He wrenched the arm of another backwards and a spinning roundhouse kick sent broken teeth across the room. Meanwhile Jack's strength propelled several bodies into the air to land like broken dolls on the floor.

Keith doesn't feel pain either. Benny knew Keith had had years of hand-to-hand combat courses, but he'd never seen it used. Keith's arms and legs snapped out in practiced precision to snap bones, crack necks.

Finally they'd pushed the monsters back far enough to let Keith and Jack make a b-line for the door. Keith slammed the door on top of several rotting arms, splattering blood over the walls. Jack joined in and slammed the door again and again against the blocking arms. Chunks of flesh and gristle spattered into the air, causing shrieks from the girls who were ten feet back. With each slam the number of arms pulled back in howls, until the last one retreated in incensed rage and the door slammed shut. Keith and Jack braced the door shut with their shoulders, both breathing heavy. Underneath the door they saw the flashing light of the strobes switch off, returning the room to the soft blue glow, awaiting its next victim. Benny looked himself over. He bled from his ear, having no idea when that happened. Jack's sleeve was torn from shoulder to wrist, exposing a bloody gash. Keith had numerous scrapes on his arms and a massive bruise on his neck, and the girls seemed to have escaped with only mussed air, with Jenna nursing a bleeding scalp. Leaning against the door, everyone just exhaled.

Two seconds of rest, please.

A high pitched scream.

Everyone spun in every direction looking for the headless monstrosity that must certainly be about to eat them all. They saw nothing but Jenna, looking embarrassed.

"It's... there was... Well. I thought I saw another rat."

Keith's face turned a furious red. Jack just laughed to himself. Even Benny smirked.

Certain people have no business going inside a haunted house, Benny thought.

—going inside a Haunted house. Keith thought.

He stewed. He'd been amazed that the girls had made it this far. But now, a door. Nothing to be surprised about, except this door was solid wood, covered in branches and pine needles. Keith tried to open the door without touching the sap that dripped down in a river from the ceiling, and failed miserably. Keith shook his hand in an aggravated fit and wiped the gunk on the walls.

"Where is this?" Jack asked behind him. Jack had been taking care of himself so far. His Sparrow suit suffered severely, but Jack's bravado kept at full power. Good, Keith might need his help.

"The Midnight Forest."

Jack shuffled. "Is this the one where you put the—"

"Yes," Keith answered without looking. *This is exactly where I put...it.*

Keith turned to the girls "My advice is to look at your feet and just follow the path. It won't follow you out."

Jenna's voice only came out in between chokes. "What won't follow us out?"

"Better that you don't know," Keith said, and flicked open the door before she could argue.

Trees. A huge forest grove, crowding overhead in a thick canopy. Owls hooted and crickets sang with the songs of the deep woodland. Keith barely hid his awe. This was no "room." It was an honest to real forest! He could see the stars above them. *Good God that's a cool effect.* Then it hit Keith, there was no door. Anywhere.

"Crud."

Keith moved the party in with baited steps, stepping on dry leaves. Winged insects fluttered around a leafy darkness as far as the eye could see in any direction. Keith had watched enough Dr. Who to appreciate the concept of "bigger on the inside," but experiencing it in person flared another brand of vertigo entirely. *Agoraphobia.* Having nowhere to run because there was everywhere to run. The brain went queasy and took the stomach with it.

"What's out here?" asked Jenna.

Keith actually smiled. The girls, bless them, didn't know that they were still supposed to be "indoors."

"Only what we take with us," Keith said, scowling at his own bad humor. "Err...nothing, if we find the door," he added quickly. Which was true enough, even when bumbling through prickly pine trees as high as telephone poles, until—

An open clearing, bathed in moonlight. With one single large gnarly tree, very dead. Conspicuously out in the open.

With a desiccated corpse swinging from a noose on an extended branch.

Finally! Keith's impatience yelled. *What's that doing over there? It's supposed to be— Never mind. The door is right past it. Or should be.*

"Should be" was the best Keith could do under the circumstances. He admitted that any sane person would be rip-roaring scared. But fact was... this just too gosh darn cool. After a lifetime of disappointment in haunted houses (too short, too cheesy), the irrational part of him didn't want this one to end. But his doppelganger had warned him. *Live your lie, AND PERISH!*

Keith suddenly found a memory, from a time long past, that chose this exact moment to surface.

Stop. You're not allowed to remember that. Keith wouldn't remember that, not ever again. Keith pushed it down. He didn't have time. The clearing awaited with the hanged man, swinging in the forest breeze. The path went right under him. Keith turned around to the girls with a face allowing no argument.

An owl hooted.

"You girls need to go first."

Kelly and Jenna displayed faces agape with shock. They were absolutely *not* going first.

"What's that thing going to do?"

"Nothing if you go first."

The girls stared at the swinging corpse. So old, mummified skin flaking off in the breeze, covered with pine needles as if it had been there for a 100 years. Maybe here, it had been.

"Ladies, I guarantee nothing will get you, but only if you go first. Look, you can see the way out from here. See?" Keith motioned everyone to stand as close to the treeline as they would squeeze, and serendipitously positioned himself behind the Kelly and Jenna, who had leaned in.

Keith sighed. "You'll thank me for this later," and shoved them into the clearing.

The girls stumbled several steps and fell in a heap under the hanged man. Face to face with it, they screamed and screamed until... nothing happened. Nothing at all. With teary eyes they looked in all directions until it was blatantly obvious that nothing was coming out to eat them.

Hated to do that, and they'll hate me for doing it, Keith thought. *But I couldn't let them take this one.* "Girls? See the door in that tree? Run to it please."

Dirty, embarrassed, the girls fumbled over their feet as they bumbled out of the clearing, confused by the whole thing. Keith looked across the clearing. "Nothing" was exactly what he had expected to happen. It's just one of those things. Haunted house monsters never attack the *first* person in line.

Keith was now the second.

The original effect, in the "real" world, was a Pepper's Ghost illusion, where the corpse was a distraction hiding a projector that blasted a screaming specter on a sheet of plexiglass, making a transparent forest ghost that screamed at point blank range.

Then the corpse would grab you.

But this wasn't the real world anymore. What would happen? Would it scare Keith? *Not in a million years. Not in MY house.* Keith entered the clearing and walked right up to the tree.

Nothing happened. Yet.

Taking advantage, Keith waved Jack and Benny on past to catch up with the girls. Keith stayed behind to make sure nothing jumped out until everyone was safely past. Then he was alone in the clearing.

Still nothing happened.

What was the gimmick here? What was supposed to happen? Keith knew he should leave, knew his first job was to protect Benny. There was no reason to stay here.

But he wasn't going to be bullied out of his own house.

Looking up at the tree, he spoke proud to whatever listened.

"I dare you. Scare me."

Maybe a snarling ghost would fly right through him. Maybe the tree itself would come alive and grab him. Or maybe the ground would even open up wide and swallow him whole. Keith expected all of that and more.

What he *didn't* expect was a voice behind him.

"Help me."

A little girl's voice. Keith looked behind the tree, seeing a ragged little girl in a dirty white nighty, long black hair hiding her face. Small and helpless. Very much dead.

To many people such a sight was the scariest thing in the whole world. Keith just thought *What the hell?* Out of the corner of his eye he caught Jack waving with frantic arms, his expression betraying a fear for Keith's life. Keith turned to walk out of the clearing.

"I'm lost!" A squeaky voice, pleading. "Help me!"

Keith didn't stop, this had turned into yet another disappointment. Pity.

"You lied to me."

Keith faltered. *That wasn't the voice of a little girl. It almost sounded like...*

He turned around.

The girl was gone. Just the swinging corpse remained, turning in a slow spin so Keith could finally see its face. It was supposed to be a dead male. This was a female. An older woman in a business suit, a broken neck flopping in the noose an unnatural angle. Blood gushing from a bullet hole in her forehead.

Pointing a finger at him in furious anger.

133

"You lied!"

Keith looked at her face and— blanched.

Not that. Not her...

"YOU LIED!"

Keith knew he had to get away. He didn't. He couldn't move as the woman exploded in a shriek that rattled every branch in the forest, blasting out of the noose as a monstrous skeletal corpse taking up the entire sky, swooping down to dive bomb Keith's frozen body. He had only two seconds to think.

Not this. NOT NOW! He ran, like a scared rabbit, his dignity trampled under the leaves. He reached the door with a frantic gasp as the specter swooshed over his head and into the night.

"YOU LIIIIEEE!"

Her scream echoed in his ears as Keith threw himself across the threshold onto a brick floor, he hit the ground gasping for air and eyes squeezed shut. *I won't let that come back. I won't.*

Silence.

Finally, Keith looked up. Everyone was staring at him. Jack reached down to help him up.

"You OK? What was that?"

Something I'll never tell you. Keith stumbled to his feet, resuming his place in the front. "Something... I didn't expect," Keith answered, regaining his composure. But looking ahead at the corridor that awaited, Keith finally...

Shivered.

YOU LIE!

Keith pushed the memory out of his head. He couldn't let that in, he had to save some strength for the end. The worst was yet to come.

Every house had a grand finale.

TWENTY

THE END. THE HOUSE all but announced it as Keith led the way through black brick walls that squeezed closer and closer together. They were forced to walk single file even as the ceiling dropped lower, but Benny noticed even more than that.

The whispering is getting louder.

The wind had been a whispering in everyone's ears throughout this experience, but now Benny could hear something new. A heartbeat.

Tha Thump. Tha thump.

A hairpin turn revealed another mocking hallway, dull torches on the walls threw flickering shadows everywhere. Then...

POUND.

Kelly gripped Benny's hand. "What's that?" Benny honestly didn't know. The *HallO'Scream* wasn't supposed to have a Grand Finale ever since Darryl had gutted it for the purple concession stand.

POUND. The stark brick walls rattled as Benny yelped. *What was that?* He didn't want to find out even as the heartbeat got louder.

THA THUMP THA THUMP

Benny tensed. *It's go on or stay in here forever.* They walked down the last hallway, and there it was.

That's not the concession stand.

He saw a room of gray misshapen brick walls with a cracked stone ceiling. Torches and smoldering orange embers in fire pits dotted the walls and floor. Chains swung from the rafters, holding various body parts still dripping with fresh blood, swaying in the breeze.

A dungeon.

Benny held his breath as Keith led them in with cautious steps. No danger. Yet. Nothing ever attacks you going *into* a room, and the dull orange light was enough to reveal the exit, another passage in the far wall. Would they make it?

No. The glow also revealed the huge form blocking the exit. Benny's jaw dropped as he saw coveralls and hockey Mask. The mask alone told you who it was.

Jason Voorhees.

Well, he had to be somewhere.

Keith pulled everyone into the heart of the room. Benny knew they couldn't dare get caught in a choke-point as only in the open did they have a chance to run around him. Benny saw Keith's brow furrow as he formulated a plan, but then the torches flared with a blinding crackle, revealing the movie monster from head to toe. It wore the quintessential hockey mask, but the rest was ... wrong. Its joints were in the wrong places, the limbs too long.

And why is there a bloody rag on its head?

Benny looked to Keith, and for the first time since landing in this horror, saw Keith's eyes shock open.

"That's not Jason," Keith said.

No. It wasn't.

A clawed hand reached up to tear the mask from its face. The constricting coveralls bulged, then ripped apart, revealing thin arms, scraggly muscles of deceptive strength. Red skin.

The naked creature was taller than Keith, underfed skin stretching over bony knees and elbows pockmarked as old red leather. Black hair frazzled out in all directions, emphasizing a flat pug nose and large pointed ears that stuck out on both sides. Around its neck was a necklace—made of human fingers. An impossibly gnarled fist clenched a medieval pike with a jagged forked point, and it wore... boots of metal. Boots that drew sparks with each *POUND* on the floor. Its mouth opened to reveal layers of serrated teeth dripping with saliva. It stared at them with black dull eyes of hate.

Benny knew what it was. He had seen Keith create this monster. The *original* monster. The red rag tied in sloppy knots around its head. Red with blood.

A RedCap.

Benny swallowed and couldn't move. Literally couldn't. For at that precise moment as Keith threw himself in front of the monster to get the girls out of danger, Benny saw —with perfect clarity— a headless rider galloping *through* them with a cackling laugh and phantasmal force that left spots in his eyes. When his vision cleared, Benny saw the result.

Jack's face. Covered in blood.

THA THUMP.

THE REDCAP SCREAMED IN guttural hate, slamming the jagged pike into the floor with a shower of crackling sparks. That was his gimmick. Every finale needs an earth-shaker and 99 times out of a 100 it's a chainsaw. Keith wanted number 100. He got it.

God that's cool. But Keith couldn't ogle or he'd see the pike from the inside out. "Benny!" he pointed, and Benny took off with a girl in each hand. After so many girls in so many Haunted Houses, Benny would know how to get the girls out of here.

Good, because the RedCap charged, shoving its sharpened fork forward with a cascade of sparks. Keith dove inside its range. He couldn't let anyone else do this, only he knew what to do.

Only Keith knew that the shaft could be safely grabbed past the first 8 inches.

Keith grabbed the shaft and shoved the point of the pike into the stone wall, creating a cascade of ricocheting sparks that flew into Kelly's hair. As she screamed and flailed with her hands to brush them out, Keith pushed all his strength to wedge the pike into a corner so the red-leather monster couldn't lift it for another swing. Except the monster pivoted its whole body and with a monstrous howl picked up the pike—with Keith still on it, and hurled him across the room. Sparks showered the floor and ceiling, popping the stringy hair of the monster with static electricity. Muscles rippled through his skinny arms as he raised the pike for another swing, a swing Keith knew he couldn't let the monster take. He now realized he had made this monster too strong.

But because Keith had created it, he could also destroy it.

Keith hurled himself under the pike's reach and tackled the red creature directly, knocking it on its knees. Jack jumped from the other side to punch it squarely in its repulsive pudgy face as Keith sent a punch into its gut. Howling, the creature loosened one hand from his spear to backhand Jack across the face, then dug five clawed fingers into Keith's chest, drawing blood. Before Keith felt the pain, a mouthful of bloody teeth clamped down on his shoulder, piercing down into soft flesh. Keith roared in pain, but didn't disentangle himself.

Hold on! He couldn't let the monster go, couldn't let it use its superior strength. So he struck back in white knuckle desperation. Fists, elbows, and a knee into a red-leather gut. Fast nasty fighting. He had to hurt the RedCap and hurt it bad. He did. The creature howled, giving Keith a chance to kick one of its stinking feet into a pit of sizzling embers. As red flesh sizzled the creature screamed and loosened his grip on the pike. Keith looped an arm around it and heaved it across the room.

Having had enough, the RedCap responded with two pile-driving arms into Keith. Overwhelming strength smashed Keith to the ground as two gangly hands squeezed around his neck. Keith saw stars as he choked on the gurgling vomit smell of the monster.

Jack had recovered enough to smash the RedCap over its head with its own pike, then wrapping one of the hanging chains around its neck. The RedCap threw Jack off with a backhand across the face, but it gave Keith the chance to roll away gasping for air as the creature locked its teeth into a frilly Jack Sparrow arm. In the spitting sparks and burning torchlight, Keith took a long cold look at his creation.

The RedCap would kill him and Jack both. A natural-born slasher without pity or fear. Knew the only way to stop it was to kill it.

That's why when it looked from Jack back to him, Keith beckoned with both hands. Fixing its blank black eyes on Keith, the lanky red monster moved to jump him again.

Keith jumped it first. Hurting, gasping, and not entirely sure if he was not seeing double, Keith twisted himself atop the RedCap's stinking back, wrapping an arm around its neck and hanging on for his life. The monster bucked like a bronco, its head turning *all the way around* to hurl a black gritted gaze eye to eye with Keith, but it couldn't break Keith's grip. Not missing the chance, Keith poked it straight in its eyes, earning an enraged scream as the fiend dislocated several vertebrae and finally threw Keith off.

And Keith swiped the blood-soaked bandana off its head.

Keith *ooffffed* on the floor, bandana in hand. With a yelp, the creature reached to its head in a frantic grab for the disgusting red cloth. Gasped...

And fell over dead.

The monster in a heap at his feet, Keith picked Jack off the floor, wincing in pain, and examined the bloody cloth in his hand.

Monsters can be grisly, but nothing is invincible. A Redcap takes its name from its headwear. The cap is more famous than the monster. The RedCap's weakness.

Take the cap off, and the monster dies.

No one knows more about Halloween monsters than Keith.

No one.

TWENTY-ONE

BENNY DIDN'T WANT TO leave Keith, but Keith had trusted him to get the girls out of there. So he ran around the perimeter of the room like he had done with cowering females so many times before. Past the smoky air he saw the door on the other side.

Get to the door! That's all they had to do! *RUN!* Showers of electrical sparks flew over their heads as Benny pushed into the tunnel beyond. A spinning tunnel, black velvet tube spinning 360 degrees over the guests as they ran down a skinny catwalk surrounded by a twirling kaleidoscope. Keith insisted on having it be the only way out of the Grand Finale. People lost their balance stumbled, and fell. Many people got nauseous. Keith could walk down without missing a step.

Benny couldn't, and colors now spun in a hallucinogenic frenzy. Strobes of lightning only revealed the exit in intermittent flashes. So far way... and getting farther. The spinning walls thwarted everyone's balance as they stumbled with every step. There was no up, no down and every time the lights went off, the door disappeared.

Benny dragged the girls to their feet and ran. He couldn't let the tunnel stop him, nor could he let the ghosts that now shot out of the walls. Ghastly faces cackled in a cyclone, laughing at the foolish mortals in the world that wouldn't stop spinning. The girls tripped over every leg possible. They fell, got up, and fell again. The tunnel didn't want them to escape. Dark shadows rose above Benny, laughing as large as any tormentor from school. Every single one with Marcus's face.

But he could reach the door. Grabbing the girls in a double bear hug, Benny lunged, smashing the door open. Everyone landed in a heap of dirt.

They were out.

Cold. Quiet. Soft.

Benny hugged the ground as he just breathed the night air. Cool against his skin. He dared breathe a sigh of relief. The girls rustled in pain on either side on him, touching bruises. Could he just stay down for a moment? He didn't want to get up.

Then he heard giggling. Benny inhaled and lifted his head up in inhaled apprehension, fearful of what he'd see.

Magnificent desolation. In every direction.

Blasted earth, dying trees. Field after field of dead crooked corn stalks, a windswept field that stretched off into the horizon. There were no houses, no lights. Anywhere Benny looked he saw nothing but a dead world. A ferocious wind blasted him in the face with a thunderclap, then scoured across the landscape to spin up dust clouds. Dust that took form.

Ghosts.

Adults, children. Transparent forms fading in and out as they swirled around the fields. They locked in on Benny and the girls with mouths open in silent screams, floating over to cluster around them. Benny knew they hadn't escaped anything, but he hadn't any strength left to do anything about it. He tried pushing himself up off the ground but nothing happened, and started to panic. Who'd get them out of *this?*

"That's it, I'm sick of this," Jenna said, as she picked *Benny* up and ran. Benny wasn't going to argue.

But where to go? The only path went into the corn fields surrounding them. Benny found his footing and ran with Jenna and Kelly in the rear even as ghosts screamed around them. Sharp yellow stalks pricked their arms as the path constricted farther into the field, becoming obscured with ghastly thick fog. *Same fog I saw at Connor's,* eventually blinding everyone, forcing them to stop as they struggled to see anything more than a foot ahead.

Benny in fact did see something. A pair of fiery red eyes pierced the fog, staring them down. Benny, Kelly, and Jenna all stared, still panting for breath.

And the eyes spoke to them.

Yes you will be frightened of the fields.
You will be frightened of ME.

Benny couldn't move. There was nowhere to run anyway as the fog parted and a shadow stepped out, floating across the earth on two feet, then slinking over the ground on all fours as a boneless beast. But the head stayed the same.

A horse.

A black horse, mane whipping in the wind, staring at them with eyes of red flame. The same horse stalking Benny's waking dreams these last few days. Jenna inhaled for a second, then relaxed with an incredulous gaze. Benny looked at her new strength, deducing her experience in the *HallO'Scream* had finally inoculated her.

"What's so scary about a horse?" She asked.

The horse grinned with a mouth of jagged teeth, then fixed its eyes directly on her.

And it wasn't a horse anymore. Rippling with black magic, the bones and muscle rearranged into something else. Glowing red eyes bored right into Jenna, and she inhaled for a scream that never came as she beheld the new monster in front of her. A rat. A vicious black mangy-furred bipedal rat with a mouth of a thousand teeth, opening wide in a demonic hiss.

Benny saw Jenna freeze solid, staring in catatonic terror. Her face turned red as blood vessels broke under the surface. Her mouth opened in a hideous contortion as blood appeared in the corners of her eyes and dripped down.

As Benny watched, Jenna's eyes rolled back into her head, her throat gurgled, and her skin stretched over thin bones. Jenna collapsed in the dust with a thud, dead.

A screech echoed across the fields as the red glowing eyes oriented on him and Benny knew it was *HIS* turn. Black magic rippled again and the monster wasn't a rat anymore. Benny gazed and gasped. He had never told anyone what scared him, not even Keith. Never told him about the creeks in the old house, the footsteps in the dead of night, the sounds from his sister's bedroom...

He had never told Keith the *real* reason he obsessively labored at the *HallO'Scream* every night, instead of going home. And now under a sky of swirling nightmare, Benny stood face to face with it.

His dead sister.

She floated towards him inches above the crushed earth in a flowing dress of white. Her face under a veil, her hands reaching toward him. Her heart, thumping away in a ghostly red glow.

Tha Thump.

Benny's blood curdled. Before his bloodshot eyes, the apparition mutated, the white dress blackening to charred ash, the arms drying into wrinkled bones. And her face, mouthing gnashing teeth. But the heart remained.

Tha Thump.

Tha Thump.

Benny couldn't move. And looking at the desiccated rotting corpse of his sister, reaching for him with arms of chewed flesh, Benny knew he could never move again.

KEITH RAN DOWN THE spinning tunnel without a blink with Jack tumbling behind him. Keith ignored everything until he reached the door and shoved it open.

Into Ghostland. The sky churned with angry clouds, ghostly forms of men and women whirling on the air currents.

I know where we are. But he had to find Benny. He found him and the girls far ahead in a field that stretched to the horizon. Keith ran, tearing through the corn, getting slashed by a thousand dead husks, feeling none of them.

"BENNY!"

Benny didn't answer. Keith finally almost reached him—and stopped cold. He saw Jenna, in a heap on the ground, saw Benny frozen stiff next to her. And he saw the dead sister, his niece, wretched, corrupted, grasping for Benny with flaky dead flesh.

Then Keith saw the monstrosity.

It turned its flaming eyes toward him. The monster saw through him, saw everything he was, and its form took on another shape.

Live your lie. Keith MacCool. Live it.

Keith's breath caught. His eyes screamed. He couldn't look away. It wouldn't let him.

LIVE IT AND PERISH.

Keith, who had fought a house full of vicious monsters now faced something he couldn't face. Keith now heard the scariest sound in the world.

>*CLICK*<

Twenty-Two

CLICK
Keith stifled a scream in the back of his throat. He wouldn't scream. He just squeezed his eyes shut with clenched fists. The monster laughed above him. Keith couldn't move. His mind locked onto one moment. Replaying it. Over and over.

>CLICK<

A simple sound. But in the worst possible place.

Behind you.

>CLICK<

Darkened room. Late at night. That's your job. Police Detective. Hostage situation. You're the only thing between a woman's life and a meth head with a trigger. You're alone. It's up to you. So move to save the woman...

>CLICK<.

A gun trigger. Behind your ear. Exactly where you should have looked before you moved. But you didn't.

Keith MacCool almost saved the woman.

Keith MacCool almost did everything right.

>CLICK<

Keith made a mistake. A mistake is temporary.

Death is permanent.

>CLICK<

Keith knew the sound. He had heard it in his nightmares for years. Ever since...

Keith's vision blurred. He fell to his knees, tearing bleeding fingernails into the crusty dirt. Trapped inside one terrible moment.

Until Jack came crashing through the corn. Keith could barely lift his head to see the monster fix its burning red eyes on the preposterous form of Captain Jack Sparrow. Jack ran right into the monster before he even knew it was there, meeting its red eyes, freezing in place.

The monster changed again. Black limbs elongated, stretching into some four-legged beast. A dog, a gargantuan dog as tall as a small man. Patchy shaggy hair, blood-shot eyes betraying disease, raging from infection, and every square inch of its fur drenched in blood. With a saliva spewing snarl, it jumped on Jack, who raised his arms in a scream as the beast knocked him to the ground.

Blood. So much blood. Blood spilled over Jack's hands, pored over his head, seeped into every corner of his Sparrow costume. Jack flailed under the disgusting monster, writhing as blood covered him, screaming as rancid teeth snapped right in his face.

Keith watched, helpless. *An old dog Jack had as a boy. A sick, bloody dog...*

No one knew what had scarred Jack's psyche. But the beast knew. It knew how to ransack every corner of any mind. Then it scared you, to death. Through splotches of vision, Keith watched his friend die.

Jack thrashed and screamed. The clouds gusted with heaving billows as Jack, his face and body drenched in red, shrieked and writhed, and broke. Jack's eyes rolled back in his head, as his skin desiccated, aged and stretched right in front of Keith. Dead.

The dog dropped him with a puff of dust into the dirt. It turned back to Benny.

Not Benny! Keith seized his muscles, but couldn't move. His mind couldn't break out. Benny would die.

Then so would he.

>CLICK<

THE FOOTSTEPS IN THE *hall...*

The rustling of frayed cloth...

Rotted arms with grizzled flesh...

Benny stared into the black sunken eyes of his dead sister, coming for him. Coming for him in a land churning with ghosts, soaring all around the scene in moans and cackles.

Jenna was dead. Jack was dead. Watching his dead sister, he felt his heart skip a beat, and again Benny knew he was next. He almost let it happen.

Something wouldn't let it. Appearing as a whisper of a wind, right beside him, yet another ghost appeared. This wasn't a corpse, but the perfect image of a young girl.

His REAL sister, standing at his side.

KEITH SAW IT TOO. He didn't know what it was ... until he saw a flickering face.

Bridget.

Her ghost now stood between them and the burning eyes of the monster. Raising two transparent hands, she shoved the corpse-Bridget backwards into the corn, where it exploded into dust.

For a moment there was only the sound of the wind.

Then a roar of anger broke the silence as the beast reformed, rising to a monstrous height over Benny and his ghostly sister, the ghost that now turned her face to meet Keith's eyes. Then she vanished.

But Keith could move.

Not because he wasn't afraid, but because he was. But this fear freed him. A fear that demanded that he GET UP! With a desperate hurl Keith jumped and tackled Benny, pushing him into the dirt and covering him with his own body. The monster roared but Keith didn't let go. He didn't dare.

The monster laughed and Keith looked up. It stood right over him, eyes of red flame boring into him. And speaking to him.

You know what YOU'RE afraid of.

>CLICK<

Keith clutched Benny as the black mass changed its form again. Taking the form of...

A woman?

A dead rotting corpse, the one from the hangman's noose. Raising a crooked boney finger with gray skin that flaked off with every motion, and pointed like the shot of an arrow right at Keith.

Your fault.

Keith squeezed his eyes.

YOUR FAULT!

Keith refused to look as the rotting woman screamed with rage. *YOUR FAULT!*

Every part of Keith wanted to knuckle under, but he couldn't abandon his nephew. Keith was scared, but not of the monster. Keith feared something FAR worse.

A dead Benny.

He feared that more than a monster from Hell itself. Enough to stare right into the red swirling eyes of the corpse and remember his greatest strength.

You can't scare me. I AM scary!

He shouted back with everything he had.

"I AM SCARY!"

The corpse responded with a shriek of anger. Keith wrapped his arms tighter around his nephew as the ferocious roar rang in his ears. The monster changed form again and Keith saw at last what it really was. An elongated head holding a pair of emblazoned eyes. Black muscles rippling with strength that revealed a creature seven feet tall. Two humanoid legs, but long arms impossibly out of proportion that dug into the dirt before him, crouching on all fours, the power of its body tensing with every heave of air as it bored its burning eyes into Keith. The horse's head opened a mouth wider than any real animal could ever dare, revealing jagged teeth with sharpened points. A thick mane of black hair writhing in the air like serpents. The two-legged horse smiled with a demonic grin as it smothered the back of Keith's mind with terror. Keith held its gaze. Terrified, but resolute.

You can't scare ME. Keith's heart thumped out of his sternum. His eyes watered, his teeth started to bleed, but he wouldn't move off of Benny. He wouldn't fail this time. He *wouldn't.*

We ARE scary!

The monster-horse screeched with frustrated anger, then dug two legs into the dirt at impossible angles and leaped high in the air, off into the clouds. Gone.

Ghostland went with it. The clouds and ghosts were all wiped away as chalk dust in a gale. A ripple over the fields and it all swept away. Nothing remained.

Keith blinked for a moment as he decompressed, daring to think it was over. Finally seeing the stars above, he actually smiled. Were they back in mortal land? Around him he heard the sounds of the city and people. They must be back!

But... was that dawn on the horizon? What time was it? How long had they been in there? With great pain, Keith pulled his tortured body up and around see behind him, and saw the *HallO'Scream.*

Burning.

Flames pouring out the brick windows on the 2nd floor, fire trucks blurred the air with lights and water. Keith moved to get up but collapsed in exhaustion. His house had to wait, Benny was more important, and he was still breathing. Kelly had fallen over but seemed to be OK.

Jenna wasn't. Her body had frozen, her skin stretched over muscles that split with the strain, eyes rolled up into the back of her head. Jack wasn't either. Other than ground in grime and minor wounds, he was clean. The "blood" was gone. But his body was contorted. Bent. Dead.

Both of them were dead. They had been killed by the most terrifying monster that wasn't supposed to exist outside of Halloween's Irish homeland.

A Puka.

Somewhere Else

Benny dreamed. About his sister.

"There's a dance at the school this weekend."
I'm sure you'll have fun Bridget.
"Can't you go? You'll never make friends watching TV all day."
No one asked me.
"Benny, you can ask them."
Humph.
"My friends are starting to wonder if we're really related."
Your friends don't like me.
"I know one who does. She wants me to introduce her to you."
Don't YOU DARE!
"No, I suppose that would involve you actually speaking to another human being."
You hoarded all the genes for plucky outgoing self-awareness. All that was left for me was the brooding cynicism. All I need is it getting around that my sister finds dates for her pitiful brother.
"It's either me or the love fairy. You've never even kissed a girl, have you?"
SHUT UP!
"Talk to a girl and get busy."
The graffiti in the gym bathroom says you've been too busy. What would Mom say?
"That's none of your damn business! And be nice. I'm the only immediate family you have left."

That night, there were no footsteps in the hall.

153

TWENTY-THREE

BENNY WOKE WITH A CHOKE, sitting up in a tangle of blankets on the couch. *Where am I?* In his father's house, the living room. Gray daylight from the bay window told him it was well into the afternoon.

Benny twisted out of his blankets and saw Keith standing at the front door, already awake. Or maybe he had never gone to bed at all. He was talking to a police officer, but Keith had never looked like *that*. Hands clenched, eyes red. He never liked talking to police. *They're probably asking about Jack.*

The police officer left. Benny watched the patrol car drive away as Keith walked back inside, resting an arm on Benny's couch. Benny moved to join him, groaning as he found bruises he didn't remember getting, and as he remembered parts of last night he didn't want to remember.

Jack. Jenna.

Benny hadn't seen death before. Not even his sister's. But last night, he saw her ghost. He had to know what Keith had seen, but saw Keith already looking at him, and asking HIM a question.

"What did you see last night?"

Benny's mind struggled at first, *I don't even remember coming home last night.* But he knew what Keith meant, and it spilled out.

"I saw Bridget."

Keith didn't laugh. He nodded. "I saw her too."

Benny believed him.

"I saw her twice," Benny continues. "First time, she was dead."

An image barged into Benny's mind. *A corpse reaching for him.*

"No." Keith said. "That was something else. Something trying to kill you. Using your worst fear to do it."

And the other Bridget saved me.

"Puka."

Keith gave a silent nod and Benny continued. "That's what... Connor told me."

"Connor," Keith looked away. "The police say he died in a 'tornado.' But you saw it, didn't you?"

Benny nodded. He'd seen more than that. *The Dullahan. Marking them both with blood.* Benny wobbled over the big bay window seeing a steel-gray sky cast a gloom over every tree in view. *Bridget's dead face* shoved itself into his eyes again, and he wanted to shove his face back into the sofa cushions.

"What was it?" Benny asked in frustration. "What happened to us?!"

Keith's voice went even, smooth, as if looking through an encyclopedia in his head. "Wherever we were, it wasn't here," Keith looked Benny in the eye. "We were in Ghostland."

"Ghostland?"

"The Other Side. The Irish called the border between here and there 'The Veil.' The Veil can merge the worlds of life and death together and catch helpless mortals in-between. Like us."

The Ringmaster, the Zombies, the Field of ghosts. Did what Keith said actually explain all that?

"The whole HallO'Scream, going crazy... Did that really happen?"

"Yes. You have the bruises to prove it. It was a practical joke at our expense. Our house merging with the Other Side. Courtesy of a Puka."

"The horse."

"The horse," Keith repeated, dead serious. "A shapeshifter. A monster so scary it used to have all Halloween named after it"

"Puka's Night. Connor told me that too."

Keith nodded. "In old Ireland it was the last night of hoarding their crops for the winter. But the Irish never kept everything they grew. They didn't dare. They always left something behind in the fields. The 'Puka's Share.' A bribe. A payoff. To leave them alone. In their minds, he *was* Halloween."

Benny's mind replayed Connor's last words. A Puka. A horse. *Yes, they CAN be scary.*

"And this monster has taken an interest in us," Keith continued. "It killed Connor, and Taylor and Scotty. It almost got us last night."

Bridget. Decayed and rotting filled Benny's eyes. He jumped up and paced, desperately thinking about anything else as Keith turned to him.

"We were supposed to die there," Keith said.

We would have if Bridget hadn't been there. She came to help. The real her.

Benny shifted his weight and groaned with even more bruises. He saw that Keith didn't look any better. What had Keith seen, last night in the cornfield? What else happened?

"Why did the night pass so fast?"

Keith fingered a pen he found on a table. "The Other Side isn't meant for Mortals. Time passes differently. But we survived. This time."

"THIS TIME?"

"The closer we get to Samhain, the weaker *The Veil* gets. What happened last night isn't the worst part."

Benny knew this was where the other shoe would drop.

"The worst part is wondering when they're going to do it *again*."

AGAIN? "But it's not Halloween yet! Today's only the 30th—"

"Old school Samhain lasted three days. The last three days of the year. October 31st was their New Years Eve. Last night was only the first. We still have two to go. It's going to happen again."

157

I can't go through that again. Benny now had a lot to think about. Monsters were real. Denizens of The Other Side could pop over to this side, making a little mini-Ghostland in mortal time wherever they wanted.

And Bridget is out there. Benny's breath caught and he held his chest, nearly hyperventilating. Keith moved close, reassuring him. "Last night wasn't the first time you saw Bridget, was it?" Benny lowered his head in embarrassment. Keith continued. "How long?"

"Almost a year," Benny said softly.

"Since she died," Keith replied, softly.

"I...couldn't tell anyone. They'd..." Benny thought of the whole year wasted, time he could have spent telling Keith. But tell him WHAT?

"They'd lock you up. But now you know."

"About the Puka?"

"About your Classic Irish Name."

My name? "Bensel?"

"MacCool."

"Connor told me about Finn MacCool...but that's not us."

"Isn't it?"

"I didn't know any of this! I never even heard of a Puka before last night!"

"No one has. What does anyone know about Halloween? We gave it a cute little name and made it a cute little kid's holiday. Puka's Night has been dumbed down into something unrecognizable, even as we drown ourselves in celebrity monsters and pretend they're scary. Even the Puka couldn't escape Hollywood. He has a movie too."

"He does?"

Keith nodded. "God help us, a Disney movie. *Darby O'Gill and the Little People.* Sean Connery was even in it. It also had a Dullahan and leprechauns. I hope to God we get out of this without having to endure any of them."

Benny grimaced.

"But that's all we get. A Disney movie from the 50's." Keith continued. "So imagine, what if someone time-traveled from Celtic Halloween to now and saw what Halloween is today? They wouldn't recognize a damned thing. No one even knows how much has gone wrong." Keith looked at Benny directly. "Except us."

"Why would it bother us here? Ireland is an ocean away!"

"What's an ocean when you can just jump across Ghostland? I bet these monsters can jump in anywhere, *especially* here, where a million Irish ran to escape a potato famine. Darn near a fifth of their whole freaking population. I don't know if this is specific to us. We definitely don't know everything that's going on yet. Who knows how many Irish families came here? Maybe the monsters followed."

"Where?"

"A furry monster in the darkened woods. A specter of your old grandfather in a darkened room. We've always lived next to monsters, we just never minded. Pushed out by new religions, they hid wherever they could. Leprechauns weren't always short, you know."

"Huh?"

"The ancient monsters fed off of belief. So, if the people stopped believing, the monsters lost their power. They shrank. Fairies, brownies, leprechauns, all shrank because the old Celts found new things to believe in. Eventually, with no one left to remember them, they just withered up and died."

"Except..." Keith mused, "What if they *didn't* die? Maybe they just curled up in a dark hole and went to sleep. And maybe there they stayed for a very long while."

Keith's eyes looked back into time.

"Except sleep rejuvenates too. Fast forward a millennium or two, and maybe they wake up, wake up with more strength than they've had in a good long time. Enough strength to be their old selves again, at least for a while. Long enough to get people scared of them again. After all, after they wake up, look at what they find."

"Sparkling vampires," Benny said. *Everyone knows to make fun of them.*

"Exactly. A long time to wait, but it was worth it. The old traditions are gone. Halloween is now the first shopping day of Christmas. So the monsters see their holiday ripe for the taking, and..."

Benny stopped breathing at the dramatic pause.

"Maybe they want it back."

Benny felt a creep up his spine.

"And your sister has been trying to warn you for a year."

Benny's eyes blurred with rapid-fire sights of spirits. The image of his dead sister filled his mind...

CRASH.

Benny gasped as a lamp fell off a coffee table, bumped by something moving. From behind the couch, behind where Benny had been catatonic all day, Kelly raised a frazzled head of red hair. She held a blanket around herself like a shawl.

Benny nearly swallowed his tongue.

"Sorry," Kelly murmured with down-turned eyes and shy voice. "I...I couldn't go home. There's no one there. Jenna was my ride. I had... nowhere..."

Benny's eyes whirled to Keith, who nodded at him with a whisper.

"Couldn't leave her out there."

Benny gulped. This was the first time he'd ever had a sleepover with a girl. And Kelly was, in fact, a girl. Mop of curly red hair, green eyes peeking out from a tear-streaked face. Benny couldn't stop looking at that face...

STOP IT! He yelled at himself. He had just enough presence of mind to pull his blankets off the couch and offer the cushions to Kelly. With hand gestures that is, as his speaking ability had chosen that moment to short-circuit. Kelly sat down in a heap. From the kitchen Keith brought her a glass of cranberry juice.

"Do you have anyone you can tell? About Jenna?" Keith asked. Benny wished he had thought to ask that. But Kelly just shook her head.

"Her parents are out of town... We were having a night out. I lost my keys in the tunnel."

"You can stay with us for awhile."

It shocked Benny to hear that, especially when he realized that he was the one who said it. Kelly just mumbled a tiny thank you into the bowels of her blanket. Then it *really* hit Benny—

I've just invited a girl to stay in my house.

Kelly peered out of the blanket, and for a perfect moment, engulfed him in perfect green eyes. Benny forgot where he was.

All this time, had it really been that easy? Why shouldn't it be easy?

"Keith, I guess we can go back. We can find the keys."

"We won't."

"They're in the tunnel."

"We won't get inside the HallO'Scream."

"Why?"

Keith's face usually held emotion like a stone. But Benny knew him long enough to see feelings surging under the skin. Keith hadn't told him everything yet. Something was wrong.

Keith looked right at him.

"There IS no HallO'Scream."

TWENTY-FOUR

KEITH'S HAUNTED HOUSE STARED at him in a gutted ruin.

The Fire had been extinguished before it got to the 1st floor or caused any structural damage. But the rooms, costumes, scenery, of the 2nd floor were all ash, leaving an outside brick facade that looked every bit like a singed skull. Scorch marks licked up out of every window as flakes of ash fluttered in the breeze. The very air stunk of burnt plastic. Several years of Keith's life up in smoke.

Keith just stood there staring at it in his parking lot. None of this was the worst of it.

Jack had died only 50 yards from here. The monster in the cornfield had killed him, and all his other friends too.

Keith knew anger very well, he had plenty of it with room to spare. But what he never showed was guilt. Guilt led to regret. Regret led to self-doubt. Self-doubt led to panic...

Focus damn it.

Keith didn't get scared. At least he never admitted to it.

But he was now. Jitters sent tremors up his hand, reaching his elbow. Keith's body releasing the pent-up fear where no one could see it as the events from the night before played before his eyes.

The dead woman. Blaming him.

Don't lose it. Don't... His eyes squeezed against images that would not leave. He couldn't get scared. He wouldn't allow it!

You did what you could. You can't blame yourself. Not for her, and not for your dead friends.

"KEITH!"

The voice shocked Keith out of his stupor. Blinking back tears of pain, he saw someone approaching, making thick crunches in the gravel. A tall, confident form wearing jeans and a blue T-shirt advertising *Marvel's Avengers*.

"Quentin?"

Nice to know I have a few friends left. Keith thought as Quentin ran over from his car.

"Geesh, are you even OK?" Quentin pumped Keith's hand in hearty welcome. "Thank God you're here. This is all over the news but they never said if you made it!"

"I'm... fine," was all Keith could utter at the moment.

"Something happened to both you and Connor? On the *same night*? Is someone out to kill all the haunted house owners or what?"

Keith looked up quickly, then caught himself. "I...don't know what happened to Connor."

"He was found dead in his office, or what was left of it. Several of his buildings collapsed. Just like that. You?"

"Firemen said everyone got out. I've found all my actors. They're all safe, except..."

"I saw about Jack. Sorry, man." Keith looked up. "Any idea what started it?"

Actually, I do have an idea, not that you'd believe it. What AM I going to tell people about last night? Keith adopted a poker face. Best to stick with the news story for now. "One of our robots got vandalized. Started an electrical fire."

163

"Is that the story?" remarked Quentin, prompting a surprised face from Keith. "The police are screaming arson. Think about it, you and Connor and Taylor, *and* Scotty? It's got to be some psycho! Everyone's freaking out, calling it the Halloween Killer. Police are asking everyone to close everything this year."

"They're doing what?"

"Closing all the houses. No one is arguing either. They're doing it as far away as Lewiston. The Freak Farm put out a tweet this morning. They've canceled the rest of the year."

"That far away?"

"Not just them. All the spook alleys at the university. And the Statutory. The HorrorCrux. The Tabernacle of Terror. They all posted the same thing. They're all outta here 'til next year."

"That's... every house f or 100 miles." *Good Lord.* Keith's mind wandered as he processed it. *Every house on this whole side of the state is gone.* Keith's vision jolted back. *That's what they wanted all along. To gut the houses.* His eyes swung to what was left of the HallO'Scream. *Or kill everyone who ran them.*

Keith's mind whirled back to full speed. There were other Halloween events, would they be targeted? *Who else?*

Quentin answered that question for him. "There's a few holdouts. Like Darryl. The Trick-or-Treat at the Mall tonight."

Oh brother. "Yep, that sounds like Darryl." Darryl's big party was another tentacle of his Halloween empire. *It was tonight?* "He's crazy."

"He's greedy," said Quentin, earning a look from Keith. Quentin laughed. "Darryl's never been an easy man to work with. I know."

Yes, Quentin likely did. Darryl had had more than his share of fall-outs with more than his share of people. "I was just hoping to survive this year without another blow-up, but now..." Keith said, watching the lingering smoke.

Quentin was quiet for a moment, until Keith noticed he was examining Keith's mosaic of bruises. "You sure you OK?"

I can't possibly tell him: "Oh, by the way, there's a giant super scary horse on the loose that killing all the Haunted House Owners?" This is going to get even more ridiculous before it gets better.

164

Keith's head started to hurt. He needed to think—but with a *SCREEEECH* of tires and spinning gravel, a car spun to a stop in the parking lot, and Keith knew he wasn't going to get any time to think about anything.

Speak of the Devil. Keith didn't have to look up to see Darryl's face, fire-breathing with anger. He leaped out of his car with its "ENVY ME" vanity plates, and charged Keith, ready and able to eat someone alive.

I am soooo not in the mood for him.

Quentin politely backed away as Darryl walked right up to Keith's face.

"What did YOU DO??"

"ME?" Yes, that was Darryl for you. Only this time, Keith didn't have to tolerate it. There was nothing left to lose, and Keith stepped right into Darryl point blank. "What the Hell were *you* doing? Eyeballing your dancers? I was actually in there saving people!"

Darryl was unimpressed. "You were? Really? ALL FREAK-ING NIGHT?"

I was in there alright. I'm not about to tell Darryl I was sucked into a supernatural ghostland. But I'm not letting him get away with this. "Guess what Darryl! They're saying this was started by your damn robots! I told you they were shoddy! And I had fire extinguishers in every hall! Why didn't anyone use them?"

A direct point, which Darryl completely ignored. His eyes glossed over in prejudicial hate, supremely confident of his own infallibility. "I had the Shriek Bootique begging to double its concession space, and give us a 30% cut for the rest of the weekend! We'd have made up our losses for this year in a night. Who *cares* if it's scary or not?!"

Typical Darryl, counting the money. Keith stared him down. "I'm fine by the way. I'm so glad you took the time to ask," Keith finished with a sarcastic sneer. "But you? You couldn't be bothered to notice the school burning down right behind you?"

Darryl hesitated, and Keith hoped he'd actually penetrated Darryl's unflappable superiority complex, but Darryl was never one to admit fault on anything.

"Such as not noticing an old school was burning down while you were *in it*," Darryl mocked. Keith had to admit he was right about that. "What were you doing in there?"

"Someone has to be in there," Keith shouted. "Can you imagine what would happen if a malcontent vandalized one of your robots? I mean, it might start a fire."

Darryl blinked at that, so Keith kept going. "For some reason we were shorthanded and I had to pick up the slack!" Keith yelled with a red face. "So how was your little skin contest? Got damn good publicity did you? Got the radio station live coverage of this place burning to the ground?!" Keith jabbed a finger at the burned shell. "Maybe if you'd kept more people inside, kept people at their stations we could have stopped this before it started! Answer me! Why didn't anyone put out the fire?"

"There was no one on the 2nd Floor. I pulled them out."

"After the fire?" Keith asked, looking to the scorched shell of his house.

"Before. I needed crowd control for the radio station."

Red spots flashed in front of Keith's eyes as that last statement processed through a weary brain. Keith turned back around slowly.

"You did ...what?"

"I cleared the 2nd floor. We don't need anyone up there anyway."

"You...pulled out ...every actor on the 2nd floor?"

"A half dozen refused, saying they wouldn't leave without hearing from you. So I fired them."

Keith's face squinted into a rare form: righteous indignation. His cheeks started to flare red, "You fired a half-dozen actors..."

"You weren't around, and I needed them outside. They wouldn't go."

"They work for me."

"For *us*. It's half my house." With a devious smile.

Keith's vision went red as he finally had had enough. Had it with the undermining, the condescension, and the continual sabotage of HIS hard effort.

"No."

"What do you mean, no?"

"It's not *half* anything. It's mine. My house. My business. And we're over." Darryl blinked, finally getting it before Keith said it:

"They're not fired. *You* are."

Anything remotely funny drained from Darryl's face. He leaned in close. "You can't do anything without my bankroll. Without me it's over."

"Yes, but it will be mine."

Darryl's seriousness turned into red splotches. "What can you do?"

Keith stood up straight. "I don't know. But I do know I've had it with you."

He looked Darryl straight in the eye.

"Get the hell out of here."

TWENTY-FIVE

KEITH DIDN'T EVEN BLINK as gravel from Darryl's squealing tires flew across the parking lot. Beside him, Quentin covered his eyes and coughed from the dust.

I'd totally forgotten that Quentin was still here, he saw the whole thing. God, as if I had any reputation left.

But as Keith's blood-pressure returned to normal levels, Quentin spoke very softly, while looking at the smoking remains of the HallO'Scream. "I know that was hard. You and Darryl go a ways back."

Keith stared off into space. "Darryl's not the same person anymore. He... he really hasn't been my friend for a long time. He's been worse this year than ever before."

"Know what's going on with him?"

"No. Like he just wakes up wondering how he can start an argument."

You don't make it easy on him."

Keith stiffened. "*Me?*"

Quentin shifted balance."You both feed each others weaknesses. Darryl has to be king of whatever hill he's on, and you have a fanatical hatred of worthless people. The two of you never should have lasted this long."

Keith's mind flashed back to childhood days, elementary school. The friends goofing around in the sandbox during recess. Simpler fun from a simpler time. For a few precious moments his tension vanished. "A few years back I needed help, and he had it. But he took the favor and pushed."

And I wish I knew what's gotten into his head lately.

"Well, seems like now you need even more help." Keith noticed Quentin now averting his eyes from the *HallO'Scream*, as if he knew even watching it would embarrass Keith. "Halloween's tomorrow. Have a plan?"

"Not a one."

"And after that?"

"Even less."

It finally hit Keith. Halloween was almost over. The holidays were about to come barreling in, with nothing for him do for several months except stare out the window of Benny's TV room.

Quentin stepped up, cautiously. "Do, uh, do you need any money?"

"NO!" Keith exploded in anger, immediately regretting it. *That's right, my friends taking pity on their poor broke friend who sleeps on his brother-in-law's couch.*

Quentin nodded at Keith's obvious guilty face.

"You might take this as a sign. An opportunity. You could always go back to your first career," Quentin offered.

>CLICK<

"No."

Keith opened his eyes. He didn't remember closing them.

"Sorry," Keith said. "Its just... too soon. With everything that's happened." Keith sighed. Quentin nodded. *Bless his heart, he's too nice for his own good. Even when I yell at him. I'm just so damned tired of...everything.*

"I don't know what I'm going to do," Keith finally said, offered his humility to Quentin. "For right now I'm just going to try to survive Halloween."

"Always a good idea," Quentin smiled. "Maybe you can visit the Big City tonight. I'd love to have your help on the streets."

"You're doing the full court press tonight?"

"Nothing but," Quentin said. "The people of this city deserve a better class of superhero, and I'm going to give them one."

"Which suit are you going to wear?"

"All of them."

Quentin offered Keith a hand, after which he turned back around and walked to his car.

DARRYL TERRIFIED BENNY. HE always had. An aura of *confrontation* just oozed off of him. Even in the ruin of a destroyed business and several dead friends, Darryl still had the audacity to walk right up and blame Keith to his face. Benny never could have stood up to that withering assault.

Fortunately, Keith ate confrontation for breakfast. Benny exhaled when Darryl's car finally spun out of sight. He didn't want Darryl anywhere near here. He just wanted to see the *HallO'Scream*. He and Kelly had been walking the perimeter of the police tape, just looking at the mess. Too much. Too fast. Monsters aren't supposed to be real. Friends aren't supposed to die.

And you're not supposed to be haunted by your dead sister.

Nightmarish visions of dead Bridget swum through his eyes, followed by Jack whose death he had been front and center for. Benny shivered, not wanting to remember he walked through the *Hallo'Scream's* waterlogged queue, desperate to fill his mind with anything.

"You spent every Halloween here, didn't you?"

Kelly had spoken. Benny just nodded.

"Every Halloween since Keith opened the place up?" she asked.

Benny nodded again.

"Weren't you ever sad?"

Sad? "I like it here!" He said before he could stop himself. Kelly continued.

"But, well, maybe this is a good thing. You can go have fun now. You never went to the Halloween parties."

"I didn't want to go."

"Bridget did."

"She had more friends than me."

"Bridget had friends all over the city," Kelly said. "A different party every weekend. You never wondered what you were missing?"

"I never had any friends in the city." *I never had any friends, period.* "Keith needed me here."

"And you liked being here more than you liked people."

Benny squirmed. Kelly was looking at him real weird. The thrill of being next to a girl had worn off. He pulled away to walk back to Keith—

"I'm sorry. I didn't want to make you mad."

Benny halted and sighed.

"You can hold my hand if you want," Kelly said softly, next to him. Without waiting for an answer, Kelly gripped his hand. "I hope I didn't scare you away. I...just can't be alone now. And you look so much like... *her.* You know."

"People could tell we were related from across a crowded room."

"Do you know what happened last night?" she asked with a lithe voice.

"Keith thinks he does. But it's too weird for me."

"I can't believe he lived through last night. So many others died."

"Keith is too mad to get killed."

"Is he?" Kelly's hand felt smooth in his own. "I know he's had a bad history."

How does she know what happened to him? Maybe Bridget told her.

"I hope he can survive tonight," she whispered.

Say what? Benny stopped, and Kelly drew back slightly alarmed, as she reconsidered her words.

"Well I mean...it can't be over yet, can it? That thing is still out there. What if, what if it tries again?"

171

Benny started moving again, still holding Kelly's hand. "That's what Keith said."

"It was, wasn't it? Who will it kill this time?" Kelly asked.

Awfully blunt way to put it. But Benny couldn't help thinking about the answer. How had Keith described the problem, people are too ignorant of Halloween?

Who is ignorant of old Halloween?

Benny walked down the stairs to the front lawn with Kelly right beside him. Benny's eyes caught Quentin walking to his car. The sun was going down. Orange clouds spent their last rays over a smoldering wreck of the *HallO'Scream,* stretching into streaks of red across the horizon. Benny couldn't believe the day was over already. Where'd it go? *Easy,* Benny thought, *You spent half your day comatose on your couch, and the rest moping in your Mountain Dew about the death of the HallO'Scream.*

Standing under the darkening sky, he looked at his front lawn of delicately carved pumpkins, now smashed and broken. What was he going to do now? He'd always spent Halloween in a haunted house. Alone.

I'm not alone. I have Kelly.

Who at that moment, gripped his hand even tighter.

An evening breeze seemed to suck the rest of the warmth away. *Oh well. Connor would say Finn MacCool wouldn't mind a little cold,* as the wind chilled past his ear.

Except that wasn't the wind. Benny's gaze went up to the blackened second story of the *HallO'Scream.* Inside one of the blown out windows—

Bridget was staring at him.

And Benny was somewhere else.

Finn MacCool was cold.

Even with the furs. The Night had arrived.

But he had chosen to do this, to follow this path to the end. His destination lay beyond the hills, beyond the woods, in the Hall of the Irish Kings.

Finn MacCool, with braided hair and leather tunic, had sworn to complete a task. Sworn to kill a monster, and had to brave the terrors of the Night to do it. He heard their moans. Heard their shrieks of freedom as the Veil fell and they tasted mortal air. His mortal flesh quivered. If they caught him, they would kill him.

But first, they had to catch him.

White fog spread through the trees like a smothering blanket. Pulling a cloak of animal skin around his shoulders, Finn MacCool walked the path into the woods.

Benny snapped out of the vision.

Bridget!? In the window? She—

Was gone. Nothing there but broken glass. The sky above lost its color and turned the gray of ordinary dusk. Keith was over there, with Quentin still walking to his car. None of them had seen a thing.

Another dream. Just like the last two nights, except now Benny had seen it with his eyes wide open. *Because Bridget had been here.* That thought shook him so much, he didn't notice that Kelly was looking right at him. But Benny felt the ripple through the air, and the Vision took him again.

This time it wasn't Finn MacCool.

The white ghost appeared only as a ripple in the air. If you didn't look, you wouldn't see it.

But it saw you.

The horseman leaped out of shadows, propelled by the muscle of a monstrous beast that snorted fire, shrieking down the road on a horse that shed sparks with every gallop. The rider's cape whipped back against the sky as his right hand held a glowing lantern. Except it wasn't a lantern. It was the horseman's own rotting head. The head laughed, a hysterical laugh that could never come from the mouth of a living man.

The Dullahan.

The Headless Rider galloped right into the front yard of the Hall'O'Scream. Benny's eyes widened at the sight of a horse pounding its way through the gravel. The very breeze froze in time around the spirit, not daring to rouse its attention. The birds stopped. The crickets halted.

Benny's eyes froze on the Herald of Death. It was going to run him down.

Until, the Headless rider jumped over Benny entirely. Fiery hooves sailed over his head as the maniacal laugh cut the air. The horse landed an impossible distance away, in the fields beyond the HallO'Scream, and stopped. The severed head turned to regard Benny with yellow eyes, and with gruesome mockery, smiled.

Then vanished.

Benny collapsed in the crunchy gravel, darn near dragging Kelly down with him. He landed hard and scored his hands with a dozen abrasions. He silently cursed himself as he looked in every direction. *Was that—* Then Benny met Keith's eyes, seeing them with just as much shock as his own. Perception shot between them—

Keith saw that too.

Another c*runch* in the gravel made Benny glance over to Quentin's car as it made a leisurely turn out of the parking lot. Quentin honked, then poked his head through his window as he drove by arm held high, waving to Keith.

His face drenched with blood.

Quentin, oblivious, honked his horn as he hit the gas. Within seconds he was just a blur down the country road.

Benny knew Quentin was going to die. *It's not just the haunted house owners.*

And the sun set.

KEITH SAW BRIDGET IN the window.

She looks so much like Benny.

Then the vision took him. A slow-motion blur, highlighted by the angry red sunset behind him, with the Dullahan thundering into view.

Dullahan. He hadn't seen it yet, but a headless shrieking rider could scarcely be anything else. It sailed over his head with a cackle...

And the world restarted. No one else had seen a thing. Not Kelly, not—

Benny. He'd seen it too, and Keith saw Quentin.

Blood.

It's going to happen again. But Quentin had already sped out in a roar of squealing tires. It was too late for Keith to even yell as the sun gave up its last, and a ripple in the air announced what he already knew. *The Puka is already here.*

In a grove of trees across the street, something rustled in the field. All Keith saw was a blur of black shadow with glowing eyes of red that found Keith, catching his sight in a red tunnel of screams. For the second time in 24 hours, Keith shuddered.

Then it was gone. After Quentin.

No! Keith didn't know what he was doing, he only knew that Quentin wasn't dead yet, and that if he just stood here and let Quentin die, he'd hate himself forever. Keith saw Benny already running to Keith's black Chevy Nova with Kelly in the rear.

Kelly? Well, we can't just leave her here. Keith dove into his car, seeing Benny take the backseat and bracing his arms. Kelly huddled beside him with her hands over her eyes and Keith took off hell-bent-for-leather. A ferocious charge through fields of grass disappeared into five lane thoroughfares amidst a sea of asphalt and extremely orange traffic lights. The glow of the Big City rose above them, towering pillars of concrete and steel, skeletal fingers reaching up and up, dazzling with yellow light. Keith heard the horsey laugh echoing through his car windows. The Puka was waiting for him here.

Keith didn't care.

TWENTY-SIX

KEITH ALWAYS DROVE LIKE a man possessed, even when he wasn't possessed.

Quentin's head start had been enough to get him past several red lights and out of sight. Keith had an excellent idea where Quentin was going, but slow-poke drivers blocked Keith's offensive driving at every turn, prompting profane outbursts. Squeezing the steering wheel in anger he took an illegal left turn down a wrong way street into the suburbs. This got Keith out of traffic, but gave him an in-his-face reminder of why he hated Halloween weekend in the Big City. Front lawns lay adorned with gigantic inflatable purple spiders, strings of purple lights, and endless dummies of dead witches smashed flat against trees.

It would get worse the further Keith went. Quentin was a street performer, a sidewalk artist. He'd go where the people were, with couples who could be pegged for an impulse buy. Keith knew just such a place that Quentin couldn't refuse.

The Puka knew it too.

>CLICK<

NO!

176

Keith felt the presence on his mind. In every shadow the twilight curled into the shape of his form. Keith's eyes caught the black shadow sneering at them from a high rooftop, the wind whipping his black haired mane into a demonic frenzy.

>CLICK<

NOT NOW!

A howl rippled through the air, reaching Keith's ears even through the windows of the car, causing him to grit his teeth and shiver in his seat. It was waiting for him. It wanted them there with Quentin. Wanted them to watch him die.

Keith drove anyway.

A city's worth of lights blasted him from every direction, blinding him as he wove through traffic in a kaleidoscope of color. Keith's fingers went white on the steering wheel as he cut through a fast-food parking lot, then through a neighboring strip-mall, banging his bumpers at every dip. More lights drowned his vision, swirling in a drunken orgy in front of his eyes: Green.

Yellow.

Red.

CRASH

Keith woke up. The front end of his car smashed against a lamppost. Steam from the radiator curled up from under the crumpled hood. Keith pounded his dashboard in fury, but looking up he found what he was looking for: spotlights. They illuminated a shopping zone with a Pottery Barn, Starbucks, and Chinese Eatery. All dwarfed by a massive 21 Theater Movie Expo. The heart of modern civilization, and tonight, it hosted a 5k Run. And not just any 5k, but a zombie chase. Hundreds of people clogged a central plaza with a big "START/FINISH" line. They mingled with runners and snapped pictures with abandon. Squeezing out of his car window, Keith took two seconds to see if Benny was OK, then he rounded the corner and entered the fray.

Runners were everywhere. Another person might have thought that dozens of zombies running through the streets would have put some people off. Except hardly anyone attended a zombie run actually dressed as a zombie. Oh, a few here and there were wearing fake blood applied with the grace of a blind-folded gorilla, but far more common were Batman and Captain America, waving at the cheering populace. Then came anything else the Wal-Mart Clearance aisle could provide: Cowboys. Toga clad ancient Romans. Captain Picard. If they even bothered to dress up at all, as the vast majority showed up in t-shirts and jeans. Keith almost cursed them all until, as he ran over sidewalks clogged with cheering bystanders, he caught a glimpse of exactly what he was looking for. Quentin would want to be center stage. And the best place would be...

There. The Finish line. Standing on ladders to get above the crowd, every single 5k official attended in a full-blown clown outfit, of poofy cotton candy hair, red nose, and floppy shoes. They directed runners under a seven foot high inflatable arch, with purple and yellow streamers. Speakers loudly played the theme song to *The Munsters* as another Batman jogged by with Thor close behind. Keith ignored them as he beelined through the packed crowd of gawkers. An October breeze rushed through the theater neon, forcing several Catwomen to huddle together for warmth, wrapping each other with far too flimsy black superhero capes, their barely-there costumes having no business out in this chill. They shivered, but it wasn't the cold.

It's here.

>CLICK<

Keith blocked it out, clenched his fists until nails bit into his palms. He stood in the center of the mob. Red and blue lasers danced on the asphalt, projected on the street from windows high above. Monolithic buildings reached into the sky. Visions of neon raced across a silver moon...

>CLICK<

NOT NOW, DAMN IT! Keith forced his eyes to focus. Where was Quentin? He could be dead already!

No, that wouldn't be any fun. It wants me to see my friends die. And Benny.

BENNY? Keith suddenly remembered that he ran all this way without Benny. Was he still—?

Yes, Benny had kept pace right behind him, with Kelly at his side holding his hand. Seeing Benny safe kept Keith's vision grounded for one precious moment.

Long enough to look right at Quentin.

Across the street, in the Plaza courtyard next to a fountain. Hamming it up for pics as Spiderman, the costume Keith saw him borrow from Connor yesterday. The superhero suit was the perfect uniform for any exhibitionist show-off.

And it worked. Couples and laughing families all crowded around the superheroes finishing the 5K. Quentin worked the crowd like a pro, striking action hero webslinger poses between two giggling teenagers, who squealed with joy as they took selfies. The crowd donated crumpled bills to a red/blue Spiderman candy bucket labeled "Tip Jar." One of them wrapped two arms around Quentin's head and gave him a full kiss, straight through his mask. No one saw the mask had blood on it.

No one but Keith. Even he suppressed a gag. *HOW COULD THEY NOT SEE THAT? Never mind.* Through the blinding lights and ear-bleeding noise, Keith ran for Quentin.

He never made it.

The city, the crowd, and the lights all stretched into an endless tunnel. Keith saw nothing but Quentin laughing with a family at the far end. So far away. Then the black hit him.

TWENTY-SEVEN

BENNY'S FLIGHT IN KEITH'S car had been a blur of swirly lights which had nothing to do with Keith's suicidal driving. His vision kept blurring with Bridget filling his mind's eye. *Wearing the white shirt and green jacket she had died in.*

Kelly gripped his hand, and Benny jerked back to reality. Kelly huddled next to him, eyes frozen shut in fear from Keith's near-death maneuvers. Her nails bit into Benny's palms. Prompting a flood of memories, and guilt.

Kelly didn't have anything to do with Bridget's death. It was a screw-up who ran a red light. I don't want to blame Kelly. Odd thing to think of right at the moment, while chasing a raging killer of a monster that's murdered three people right in front of you.

CRASH

Benny's teeth rattled as his head impacted the side window. Keith had crashed the car cock-eyed against the cement foundation of a lamppost. Benny rubbed his head as Keith growled, tore open his door and ran, leaving Benny to remember what happened before his head exploded.

Quentin. Right. They were here to grab Quentin before something happened to him.

But...Before what happened? Benny was alone with Kelly now. *Errr, should I follow Keith?* Benny wasn't sure, until Kelly took charge, pulling him out of the car and towards the teeming crowds.

"Come on. We can't leave your uncle all alone out there," she said with a smile, green eyes glittering with the reflection of street lights. "Something bad might happen to him," and before Benny could think, she pulled him into the wilds of the city.

Benny looked for Keith as he tore ahead, earning rude looks as he broke the path with all the grace of an elephant in a pottery store. Benny merely had to follow the wake while keeping an eye on Keith, who was now far ahead. All Benny could see was the back of Keith's jacket and towering bodies.

Then Quentin. Perched on a fountain.

Spiderman? Of course, that's Quentin. That fountain is the perfect place for him too. Looks like he's made a barrel's worth of money already. Not very scary though.

Odd thought. Or not. As when Benny looked again, he saw Quentin wasn't alone.

Bridget stood behind him.

A flickering image in a store-front window on the other side of the fountain and Benny's senses came back just long enough to remember that Quentin was going to die. Then Bridget's eyes exploded with light, and Benny was somewhere else.

Finn MacCool gripped the animal skin tightly around him as he walked the forest path. His skin crawled as the murmuring of the trees halted. Owls ceased and crickets froze in an utter silence reserved only for the darkest midnight.

They were here.

A scream just out of sight. A mortal man burst out of the trees a hundred paces ahead. Lost and bleeding and in utter terror for his life. On this night he would be. Finn almost ran for him, to give him some chance for survival even at the expense of his own safety. But before Finn could move—they sprang.

181

Skeletal arms on wisps of fog found the terrorized man. Razor claws raked his body as ghastly faces swirled around him, pulling him off the ground, even as he screamed and screamed and—

Gone.

The man had been taken so fast Finn barely had time to blink. Finn would be next.

No, Finn wouldn't let himself be taken and instead stepped boldly into view. Bracing himself, Finn MacCool walked directly into the fog wrapped in his animal skin and face painted as a hollow-skinned skull, eyes frozen forward in a blank mask.

Wispy faces peered at him. Ghostly hands blindly reached, but drew back.

But nothing touched him.

Finn kept his gaze beyond the mist as he walked past the spectral faces with reaching fingers. The spirits watched but never touched, as the fog passed, lost into the dark of the woods. The sky revealed the stars above as Finn eased off the animal skin and breathed out, his first breath since entering the fog.

Survival lay in fright. To survive the Horde one must hide under their own image. Finn's hands touched the ash over his face, ensuring his mask remained. More of the Night awaited and the path stretched long ahead of him.

But he would not be taken.

Benny blinked under the bright lights of the big city. Bridget was gone. Spiderman stood directly ahead, delighting his paying customers with laughs and hugs.

Survival lay in fright.

In a flash Benny knew what awaited Quentin. He almost ran to him, but Kelly pulled him away.

"He'll get what he deserves. Let your uncle save him. We can leave."

Leave? "But Keith is—"

Kelly stepped directly into his gaze, forcing her ghastly bright green eyes into his own and Benny couldn't look away. "I have some friends waiting for us." Kelly gripped his hand and pulled him away.

Benny looked back. *Keith will wonder where we went...* But the thought died as Kelly kept tugging, yanked him deep into the night lights. Where was he going again? Where was Keith? He wanted to go with Kelly. Go see her... friends? "Who? I don't know anyone out here."

Kelly's voice carried laughter. "It's Halloween isn't it? We're going to go to a party."

"I've never been invited to—"

"You're invited to this one." Kelly whispered to him, "I've seen to it."

Kelly's breath tickled him, dimming his vision as she led him out of the Plaza, past the shops surrounding the theater and into the jungle of monolith buildings. Benny got so preoccupied he almost didn't notice the—

WHOOSH.

A massive wind blasted him from behind, nearly blowing him to the ground. Kelly steadied him before he fell. Benny looked back in shock, blinking dust out of his eyes.

"What was that?" he asked, looking back to Kelly.

"Nothing at all," she said. Holding his hand in a vice grip, Kelly pulled Benny away.

Five seconds later, he had forgotten all about whatever it was.

KEITH LAY ENCASED IN *black.* The crowd around him, so solid a moment ago, were now blurred more as shadows than substance, colorless and silent. Keith knew why.

The Veil merged again, just like last night. I'm seeing Mortal Land from the Other Side.

Keith tried to run but could only wobble like a fly in amber. Stopping to focus through the black, Keith saw Quentin.

And saw the Puka rising behind him.

Keith struggled as the black furred equine-humanoid with eyes of fire rose high above the fountain, blackening Quentin with its shadow, a shadow no one saw.

Except Quentin. He had been taking a selfie with a couple of teenagers, but now he looked up and saw... *something* standing on the fountain, something that towered over him like a tombstone and invaded his mind looking for his fears. Such as into the nightmares of a child.

Suffocation. Quentin was afraid of suffocation.

Falling into a river on a summer's day, he'd swallowed enough water to nearly kill him. He'd never enter the water again.

Quentin had a single second to gape before the equine creature poured its fiery gaze right into him. Its black body rippled and rearranged its shape into the form of a boy. A very large boy, seven-feet tall. Quentin's older brother. The Puka barreled back on both legs and heaved itself into Quentin, dunking him in the fountain behind him. Keith, trapped on the *Other Side*, couldn't do a thing except watch, watch as Quentin's brother stuffed him under the water. Keith thrashed against his prison, but Quentin never even had a chance to scream.

"Just a little fun," his brother would always say. And that's what this was, fun.

Fun to push Quentin into the water.

Fun to watch him squirm.

Until Quentin went limp, and his brother pulled him up in shock, but by then it was too late. Quentin had felt it. Felt the terror of helplessness. The horror of submersion.

The panic of feeling his brain shut down.

Now Quentin felt it again, and again. And again.

Keith kicked and squirmed getting nothing but vertigo as his legs pumped quicksand. Then it all vanished. The real world rippled back into place and Keith fell to the ground. He was back in Mortal land.

With Quentin dead in the fountain.

A girl shrieked. Screams cut the air as everyone saw a contorted Spiderman face down in the fountain. They hadn't seen anything except a ripple in the air. Keith's mind thought it out: on the other side of *The Veil* time ran however it pleased, and anything on the other side was but a shadow here, unless it wanted you to see. Now there was nothing but one high-pitched cackling horse laugh echoing through the streets, the same laugh Keith had heard last night.

Keith moved to Quentin, pushing away the gawkers.

He never had a chance. But why? Keith thought. Scotty, Taylor, and Connor had all been Haunted House owners and actors. Quentin wasn't one of them, he'd been just an innocent.

Unless...

Scotty and Connor, they were killed *because* they were scary.

Quentin was killed because he *wasn't.*

Keith whirled with understanding to face Benny, to tell him—

"I know where it's going next."

Except Benny wasn't there. Keith jumped to his full height in a panic as he scanned every direction, but the crowd blocked his sight as it surged even closer to see the dead Spiderman in the fountain. *Rubbernecking like lemmings,* Keith thought, disgusted even as he turned frantic. He had to find Benny! He jumped to the lip of the fountain to see over the crowd—

THERE he was! Almost out the Plaza and disappearing fast, going against the flow of traffic, pulling out of sight quickly. With Kelly in the lead. *What did she think she was doing?*

Keith jumped through the crowd in a single bound, pointing arms ahead to slice through the unwanted masses. He closed the distance before Benny could vanish around a corner, and when Benny was an arm's reach away Keith's hand whipped out for Benny's hoodie—

WHOOSH

A *Force* scooped him right off the sidewalk as a massive wind stole his breath, propelling him backwards past buildings and people in a warp-field blur. The force spun him upside down and then straight up. Blood rushed to Keith's forehead as his eyes went white and he penetrated the clouds. He yelped as he found himself at least a mile in the air! For a moment, Keith just hung there high above the city, seeing the entire panorama beneath him, a thousand pinpoints of light moving along the streets. Life.

But up here, Death. The clouds parted to reveal whirling red eyes in a churning icy wind. Wind roared around Keith as the eyes formed into a head with a whipping mane of serrated black hair. A demonic horse. Laughing at him.

Then Keith fell.

The lights of the ground rushed to meet him. His eyes squeezed against the winds blasting his face. He bit his tongue as nausea threatened to take him. But there wasn't time for even that as the ground came up to hit him.

Twenty-Eight

Benny let Kelly lead him under the towering structures of the Big City. The sidewalk went through a grassy park where dull street-lights cast long shadows. "Know where we're going?" Kelly pointed. "To a friend's place just right over there."

Benny looked across the park, upward to an apartment tower on the other side, stretching up at least 10 floors. Several balconies ringing the edge were alive with laughing people with beers in hand. Kelly led him into the foyer then into the elevator, pressing one of the upper floors. Kelly held Benny's hand all the way up, squeezing occasionally. The elevator speakers were tinny, several decades too old, playing "*Time Warp*," courtesy of the *Rocky Horror Picture Show.*

When the doors opened Kelly led him down the hall, stopping at a door *thrumming* with heavy bass. A cheesy dollar-store Dracula doll was hanging from a nail. "We're here," Kelly smiled, and rang the bell.

A vampire answered. Or at least it was someone with far too much vampire on the brain: Slicked hair, blood-red contact lenses, mirrored by a mouth full of pointy canines. The tall form looked at Benny like a bug to be squashed, but Kelly's grip wouldn't let Benny inch away as the vampire saw Kelly and opened the door wide. Benny got pulled into a dimly lit environment of cigarette smoke and bad music. Benny finally collected enough courage to ask.

"What is this?"

"A Halloween party, of course."

A party. With people in it. Benny shivered. The most he knew about a Halloween party is that he had never been to one. Benny's eyes hadn't adjusted to the dark yet, but this party had obviously started early. Illuminated only by scented candles, the modest apartment had several teenagers lounging on couches, freely consuming any number of alcoholic beverages. Benny coughed several times from a thick murk of cigarette smoke amongst other aromas. A pack of leather-jacketed girls passed smokes among them with humorless faces. Industrial music thudded from speakers in the back, next to a wide-open balcony door, which let in the evening chill.

Benny's nerves demanded retreat from so many people looking straight at him.

"I...I'm not ready."

Kelly laughed, with that soothing soft voice. "Of course you are. Why would you say that?"

"I...need a costume." Only Halloween fanatics like Benny had the recurring nightmare of being caught on October 31st without a costume. It usually struck Benny around mid-August, even if his last several Halloweens had been spent in the bowels of the *HallO'Scream*. He couldn't be here and started to turn around. Once out the door, no one would remember he had ever been here.

Kelly pulled him back with surprising strength. "Why would you need a costume? Hardly anyone else has one." Indeed, other than the vampires, and a girl with black fuzzy cat ears, no one had bothered to dress in any kind of Halloween attire. "Dressing up is for little kids, Benny, and for people too pathetic to not know they're not a little kid."

Benny hadn't thought of it that way.

"You're safe here," Kelly continued. "These are my friends."

Her friends? Yes, Benny recognized several from school. They recognized him too. *Oh no, don't look at me, don't...*

Kelly's hand brushed against his back. "Easy, they're just curious. We'll be gone soon."

"We're not staying here?"

"We're just here to change. The real fun is somewhere else."

Something about the word "friends." Benny didn't like that, not at all, and anger swelled behind his eyes.

"You don't mind that I have other friends, do you?" Kelly asked, as if she had been reading his mind. "I have lots of friends. Here's one!"

A girl in black nylons, black cutoffs, and ratty black T-shirt bounced up, giving Kelly a hug of welcome. Benny's anger fell a bit, but another emotion remained, something he'd never felt before. Jealousy.

"Benny, this is Sarah. You'll like her, she's wearing a costume."

Benny frowned. *That was a costume?*

"I'm a vampire!" She said in a bubbly voice.

Benny looked at her, incredulous. "You are?"

Sarah opened a mouth to show ridiculous plastic fangs, then spun back around to her friends. Kelly laughed and led Benny deeper into the crowded living room. Everyone else hung around in cliques of two or three. Kelly sat him down on a chair in a corner, then sat beside him.

"Don't you like it here?"

Benny didn't want to be negative, but ...

"I don't like vampires."

Kelly laughed. "But everyone wants to be a vampire!"

I don't, Benny wanted to say, but instead he just looked around, fidgeting with his hands. "So, what do we do?"

"Oh the usual," Kelly replied. "Watch scary movies and drink. But stay here for a second. I need to go change. I've been wearing this since yesterday, remember?" and before Benny could blink Kelly was off, leaving him alone.

The TV flashed with a slasher movie. Benny recognized it immediately as *Dracula*. Not the Bela Lugosi version from 1931. Not the

189

Christopher Lee version from 1958. Not even the Keanu Reeves version from 1992. This was *Dracula Reborn*, circa 2012. 20% on Rotten Tomatoes. 3.2 rating on IMDB. No one was watching it, rather staring at iPhones. Benny just sat there, alone, looking no one in the eye. Whenever someone looked at him, he looked back to the TV.

Drinking. Smoking. iPhones. His first Halloween party. He fidgeted with his hands again.

"Making friends?" Benny looked up and Kelly was back...in a new outfit. Benny's eyes popped out. Gone were the conservative blue-jeans and green pull-over. Kelly now sported a black leather miniskirt with black nylons, a midriff exposing t-shirt tied very tight around her chest, all under a black Levi jacket. Her eyes had been attacked by a bottle of 80's mascara, and her hair woven with black dreadlock extensions.

But it was the T-shirt that caught Benny's attention. And not just because of how it...stretched, over Kelly's form. It was from the *HallO'Scream*.

HALLO'SCREAM

A Dollar For a Scare.
A Nickel for your Soul.

That was vaguely risque'. Benny frowned.

"Where'd you get that? I thought they all burned up in the fire."

"Darryl gave it to me weeks ago. Who do you think gave him the idea in the first place?"

"The T-shirts were *your* idea?" He'd never seen Kelly around the house before.

"I have lots of friends. Come on," Kelly picked up Benny off his lonely chair and led him to the kitchen counter, to a stack of red solo cups filled with what was obviously beer. Kelly picked up a cup and offered it to him. Beer? He didn't like beer. Keith would guzzle it on occasion, but was there a single person here of legal drinking age? Benny sure as heck wasn't. He'd better not.

"Drink. We're here to have fun."

Fun. Benny would like that. Maybe he should drink it.

No. Something wouldn't let him. Something pressed on his mind. Then, there she was: a rippled form, a lazy mist in the cool air.

Bridget?

Benny locked his eyes on her, but she couldn't solidify. She had only a shaken ghost body. Her mouth moved. Was she trying to say something? Every failed word made the next one even more desperate. Benny stared—

Kelly gripped him, making Bridget disappeared with a breath of wind. Benny forgot where he was, seeing nothing but the flickering TV. A masked maniac waving a bloody blade around.

Kelly held up the beer again.

"You're with me, young MacCool," she smiled with vivid green eyes.

"*Drink*," she demanded.

Benny did.

TWENTY-NINE

*S*PLASH

Keith landed headfirst into a bottomless hole of cold dark water.

BREATHE!

Falling deeper, Keith looked up to see one tiny point of light, getting smaller. With a surge he pumped his legs up, aiming for the light. Between the fall and the water, his eyes went blurry as his was heart about to rupture. If he didn't find the top soon...

GASP.

He broke the surface with a heave, flailing out of the oversized puddle, grabbing the edge and gasping for his first full breath since before he reached for Benny. All of that was incidental next to the pain of impact in his chest. And ribs. And arms. He did nothing but just breathe for a solid ten seconds, arms over the edge of the water. Finally he got up, wincing at rocks slicing into his hands as he found purchase to pull himself out of...

...a pothole?

Upon testing it, he found it was only six inches deep. A cackling animal laugh echo through the air as Keith looked up and scowled, wringing himself out as best he could. Where was he? As things came into focus, all Keith could see was a massive block of brick, glowing yellow around the edges. No sound except the wind.

No, he heard music. Tinny. Hollow. The kind you hear in big box store parking lots.

Oh no.

Keith ran towards the black mass, now recognizing it as the back of a monstrous building. The music droned from speakers under dull lights illuminating a parking lot, blaring away a perfectly torturous version of *The Addams Family.*

Keith had landed in a strip mall. The FAR side of town, miles away from where he had just been. Keith looked around, seeing nothing but an endless river of American-neon lining the route back to downtown proper. Even if he ran, Benny's last known location was an hour away.

Keith growled. He knew whatever brought him here wanted a big laugh at his expense. This wasn't just any strip mall. This place had something special right there under the purple light.

The Shriek Bootique.

Darryl's partner in Halloween crime. The doors were wide open. Even now everything directed one's eye-line to outrageously large inflatable pumpkins on either side of the entrance. And inside pink poofy wigs. Pink spider rings. Pink sippy straws, in the shape of a skull.

Keith hated pink nearly as much as he hated purple.

People walked out of the doors, apparently oblivious that a man had just fallen out of the sky and sank fifty feet into a six-inch pothole. From overhead *The Addams Family* wound down, with *Flying Purple Eater* quickly taking over. Keith knew that if he remained much longer he'd be treated to *Ghostbusters, Monster Mash,* and the theme to *The X Files.* In that order. He wasn't setting one foot inside that store. Nor was he just going to stand here like a dummy waiting for something to happen. The street back into downtown was obvious enough. Keith sighed and made a jog for it. He just might find Benny before—

"Whoa. That dude is baked!"

193

Keith spun at the sound of a quartet approaching him through the lot.

"You OK, dude? Looks like you just crawled out of the sewer," said a tall twenty-something young man, dark hair cut short, just a hint of a goatee, dressed in dirty jeans and wrinkly shirt, and blasted out of his mind. The reek of alcohol hit Keith from ten feet away. Keith recognized the type, the perpetual weekend drunk, who spent every Saturday guzzling himself into a bragging stupor. He came from the direction of several parked cars in a nest of music and laughing. A tail-gate party of sorts.

94er's. Keith groaned, remembering a very old epithet to a very old disaster. In Anaheim, California, Halloween of 1994, Disneyland promised that anyone who showed up in a Halloween costume before 8:30 am would be granted free admission. Problem was, Disneyland's front gate got clogged with hordes of holiday freeloaders. "I'm dressed as a teenager!" or "I'm dressed as a redneck!" The same mold created these drunken yutzes in front of him, apathetic whores whose only use for the holiday was to get plastered. Keith despised them and turned back to downtown.

"Hey Buddy hold up!" The man ran the remaining distance and stuck himself right in Keith's face. "I knew that was you! Saw you on TV! You're that guy who burned down his ghost house!"

Oh hell. So that's what's gotten out. This idiot didn't seem the kind of intellectual who could even operate a TV, let alone watch the news. The man would be forgettable... if not for his company. A veritable harem of women, the prototypical blond, brunette, and redhead, all giggling at absolutely everything they saw. The exertion of their laughing must have kept them warm for Keith honestly couldn't see what else could have. Their mini-skirts ended mid-thigh exposing bare leg to mid-calf, where cowboy boots took over. Their arms were in long, lacy sleeves, too flimsy to be at all functional against the Autumn chill.

One of them in particular demanded his gaze. Flawless pearl skin with deep eyelashes about an inch long. A tightly wound t-shirt contained a well-toned body belonging to either a decathlon runner or the prize of Hugh Hefner's Grotto, wearing black and orange striped stockings that Keith usually assigned to cornyville, but he had to admit that they looked good now. Oh, boy, did those legs go up. But the t-shirt?

A cartoon witch sitting on a broom, flying over a crescent moon.

"You must have been really screwed up last night, right?" The guy's laugh broke Keith's gaze. "Oh well. No big loss. The girls forced me through your spook alley last week, and it sucked! Who would be stupid enough to be scared of that?"

Keith caught himself before he gave the bigmouth a fist in his teeth. This wasn't the time or place.

"Name is Aiden," the man said. "Listen man, you're famous! Hang out for a sec!" Aiden fumbled for his android while the girls were already sticking their heads on Keith's shoulder for quick selfies, giggling all the way to social media.

I'm a celebrity? Is burning down your own house all it takes these days? Maybe I should have gutted the second floor years ago.

But "hang out?" That wasn't going to happen. Keith tried to turn around to escape when Aiden put his hand on his shoulder pulled him back.

"Come with us!" Aiden said again. "The ladies need to do some shopping before we hit the big party."

The woman with the witch t-shirt looked right at Keith and gave him a wink that would have set fire to an entire row of church pews. *As if, little girl.* But the sultry blond pressed against him, blocking his escape. Keith gave her outfit another look.

The witch costume had always been about feminine empowerment. The Wicked Witch of the West, for example, was her own boss and dared anyone to get in her way. But the modern witch wasn't wicked anymore. It was Reese Witherspoon, when her character in a forgotten movie held up a sexy dress in front of her friends and pronounced "No, it's not slutty. Its fun." As if the 21st century knew the difference.

These girls didn't. In picking a costume about female empowerment, they were living proof of the Halloween Law of Physics: Scantily clad women had an immunity to the cold. As long as a group of under-dressed girls had enough fabric all together to cover any one of them, the entire group could withstand anything up to an October flash frost. Keith had seen it firsthand.

Meanwhile Aiden still wouldn't shut up. "Hey, I know! We're running in there to buy a skull mask. You can sign it for me! The Halloween guy who burned his house down!" Aiden grabbed his arm, pulling him into the doors of the Shriek Bootique, and that's where Keith drew the line, yanking his arm from Aiden's clutches, instantly drawing a look of semi-anger. Aiden wasn't used to being told, "No." Well, he'd bloody well hear it tonight.

"No. I'm not going in there."

"Why not?"

"Because it's a cesspool of plastic banality." Hoping to put this meeting to bed, Keith groaned as Aiden's eyes only glassed over. God save me from the monosyllabic. Fine. Time for the big speech.

"You don't want to buy a mask."

Aiden vehemently disagreed. "You BET I DO!"

"No, you don't. Masks are the worst choice for a Halloween costume."

Not just "not a good idea," but "worst." The word carried an implied insult. Keith saw the insult hit with a wrinkling of the guy's eyes. Good. That means Keith had his attention. So he laid in.

"Follow along. You want a mask. Whatever. Except you're going to a party, lots of beer, lots of friends who are going to talk your ear off whether they have anything smart to say or not. And that's whenever you're not pouring cups of cheap beer down your throat. Right?

"So, let's walk through the whole night. You buy the mask, but you don't put it on yet. How can you drive? So you hold it in your lap as you drive to the party, only putting it on in the driveway for the whole 90 seconds it takes you to walk to the front door and ring the bell.

"What happens then? You walk in, get a big cheer, then you take the mask off to drink that beer. Then you'll start talking. Then you keep drinking. All the while holding the mask under your arm know-

196

ing you can't put it back on, because if you did then you couldn't drink or talk.

"So that's where the mask stays. Under your arm. For four hours.

"So, the end result is, you spent $50 on a skull mask which you're going to wear for about a minute and a half, and then throw in your bedroom closet, assuming you didn't lose it in the bathroom or under a seat-cushion to be lost forever. Congratulations."

Aiden blinked. He didn't seem to have the attention span of a 13 year-old, but money gets everyone's attention.

"Any of this sound like a bad memory from last year?" Keith wrapped up.

"Well...I...err..." Aiden stammered a bit, then grabbed one of the girls. "I think I'll buy something else tonight, thanks man."

"Oh no, thank you." Keith said with a pound of sarcasm. *Idiot.*

The group entered the pompous doors of the Shriek Bootique, and Keith could finally get away. He turned to run when the girl in the witch t-shirt gave him one last sneaky smile before she disappeared inside. Keith didn't know what that was about, and didn't care. He took off.

Keith had to run a hundred yards just to get to the street, jogging around several inconveniently placed fast food establishments. When he reached the sidewalk he saw dozens of stoplights running into the horizon, blinking over and over again. Keith sighed. Hell of a long way.

That's when the fog rolled in around his feet.

Keith stopped. Where was this coming from? He turned around and saw. It was coming right out of the open door of the Shriek Bootique, followed by a ripple in the air, as if Nature was losing its breath. Something was crossing *The Veil* again.

Crud.

Keith had nowhere to run. Wisps of fog wrapped themselves around Keith like so many octopus tentacles and yanked him into the air. Still nauseous from his last ride, Keith's stomach twisted in knots as he flew upside down and backward back through the parking lot—

Through the doors of the Shriek Bootique.

Keith scrambled to find any handhold before the fog pulled him deep into the store. The refrain of *Ghostbusters* infected his ears as he passed the threshold. His hands scratched asphalt as the front doors slammed in front of him, a slam of finality resounding across the parking lot.

No one noticed.

THIRTY

FROM THE APARTMENT BALCONY, Benny could look down on a great swath of downtown. He was on his second beer.

The streets were crowded with party-goers, left-overs from the 5k, and little kids.

Kids ran right under him on the sidewalk below. A three foot tall Optimus Prime with a Mickey-Mouse candy bucket. Then a giggling Iron Man, stuffing his face with an extremely messy Hershey bar.

The vampire/goth crowd in the dark apartment continued their smoking and drinking. Then more smoking, then chitter chatter about God knew what. They also passed around a wine bottle with some red liquid in it, which looked a lot like...blood?

These guys can't be that dumb, to actually be drinking real bl— Benny realized with Kelly right here, he really ought to be talking rather than thinking. He still didn't think Kelly was right about this being a kids holiday. But didn't want to argue either. To say Benny didn't like conversation was an understatement's understatement. But he had to say something.

Kelly beat him to it. Dressed as she was, Benny would have expected her to say almost anything.

"Why do you like Halloween?"

Except that. Benny choked on a sip of beer. But oddly enough, his speech center loosened up. Beer *was* called "liquid courage," after all.

"It's one of the only things I've ever liked."

"You miss trick or treating?" she asked.

"I trick or treated longer than... all the way into high school. No one ever told me I wasn't supposed to."

"And your uncle just cheered you on, didn't he? Letting you look stupid."

"Yes," Benny couldn't disagree.

"Halloween has a habit of doing that to you. Remember 9th grade?"

"You remember that!?"

"Don't you?"

"First day of school, teacher asks everyone in class to name their favorite ride at Disneyland. Every male, and I do mean every one of them, all had the exact same answer. Space Mountain."

"Except you."

"Except me. I had the idealistic naivete to answer honestly." Angry heat burned the alcohol inside Benny, from an old memory he didn't like one damn bit. "I said 'Haunted Mansion,' and got laughed at for it."

Kelly leaned in. "Don't be hard on yourself. You had to be honest for who you are."

"And who am I exactly?"

Kelly laughed. "Silly. You're the big Irish hero MacCool. The Classic Irish name."

Now heat really rose through Benny's skin. "How come everyone knows my family name better than I do?"

"You know exactly why. Look at that movie," Kelly gestured to the TV set. "You know exactly what it is and when it was made, right?"

Benny looked away, embarrassed.

"Now look at that girl over there with the cat ears," Benny did and Kelly continued. "You had three classes with her last year."

Benny choked on his beer again. *I DID?*

"Do you know her name?" Kelly asked.

Benny did not. He looked right at the girl, but... nothing.

Wait, he did recognize her, from the *HallO'Scream* last night. He'd bumped into her while looking her Keith, and she had called him by name. Now she wore plastic kitty ears atop a weave of black hair, with a T-shirt announcing *Keep Calm and Carry on My Wayward Son*, with pentagram from *Supernatural* at the top.

"She knows your name."

She does? Benny looked at her again. Brown hair. Petite. *Who was that, dammit?* He gave up.

"She did her senior project on Clan MacCool. She probably knows more about your family than you do."

Now Benny was annoyed. But then his school could have had Katy Perry and he wouldn't have known.

"She even knows your name is spelled wrong."

"What?"

Kelly pulled over a napkin and wrote with a black pen pulled from somewhere, "Your ancestor's name was "Fionne MacCumhaill," she said, spelling it out. "Finn MacCool is just the English corruption, passed down to you."

"Mac..." Benny asked, peering at the napkin in the gloom.

"Cumhaill," Kelly finished for him, pronouncing it "KOO-wull."

Benny considered. *The visions... of Finn a thousand years ago.*

Kelly interrupted his memories. "She researched everything about him. Even about how Halloween is supposedly based on Satanic Druids."

"That's revisionist bull!" Benny yelled. "That was a deliberate hatchet job by religious bullies out to make the Celts look stupid, to justify pigeon-holing them as—"

"EASY!" Kelly patted his hand. "I just wanted to see you finally get angry."

"You *wanted* to see me mad?"

"Only to see if it was possible. You said, like, maybe ten complete sentences in all of high school. I just wanted to see. I mean, you never acted in the HallO'Scream."

Benny didn't like where that was heading. "Putting myself on display is just a humiliation waiting to happen."

"You're right," she whispered, leaning in close to pull his gaze to the surrounding crowd of vampires Corny fangs and polished fingernails as far as the eye could see. "There's the other side, the show-offs. They'd die if they didn't hear everyday how pretty they are."

Pretty? Benny couldn't argue with that adjective. Benny had seen a lot of Halloweens, and one thing he had never seen was an ugly vampire. From the balcony, Benny could see some of the party had migrated down to the sidewalk, with a collection of drinking "vampires" hanging on the front steps of the building. Some of them grabbed a female passerby and almost sank fake plastic teeth into her neck. The woman tore away screaming, the "vampires" congratulating themselves with laughs.

Those idiots are going to get their fake plastic teeth- and their real ones- kicked in if they keep that up.

"Funny, if you think vampires are supposed to be monsters," Kelly broke in. "The toughest monster we have."

Yes, the morons downstairs notwithstanding, vampires were supposed to be the toughest monster in the world. Even *World's Deadliest Warrior* had a face-off between Vampires and Zombies just to prove it. Vampires won, looking good doing it.

"Well, they don't look very scary to me," Kelly remarked.

"No, they don't," Benny said as he leaned back.

Kelly leaned back in her dreadlocks and miniskirt. "That's what's changed. Why aren't monsters ugly?"

Benny knew exactly why. "We hate ugly."

"Exactly!" Kelly gestured to the "vampires," young women in short-dresses and eyeliner. "You hate ugly so much you won't even inflict it on your worst enemies. Some things are *supposed* to be ugly. To remind you to be afraid of them."

Benny looked around. This crowd certainly wasn't ugly. Pretty faces everywhere, with alcohol clearly getting to their heads. Even as Benny watched, a table full of girls opened their plastic-fanged mouths to pretend to *hisssss* at each other, Dracula style. Benny watched, embarrassed. *What the hell are they doing?*

"Look," Kelly said as some of the guys dropped by the girls and *HISSSS* right back at them. "Everyone wants to be a vampire."

"I don't! Anyone who picks vampire as their favorite monster is an illiterate newb. Too brain dead to even know how many choices they're ignoring"

Kelly cocked an eyebrow, "So what would you pick?"

Benny was slightly embarrassed by his outburst. "I wouldn't."

"Because you don't think you're strong enough?"

Benny looked away. A buzz entered his ears and wouldn't go away. A pressure that gripped him whenever he felt Kelly's hand against his own. Kelly whispered again.

"But you *can* be strong. You were last night."

Last night. Already only a blurry dream. A haunted house that came alive? Did that really happen?

"You never told me why you weren't afraid," Kelly continued.

"Of the Dark Maze?"

"Of everything."

"It's no big deal."

"That *was* a big deal! You got me through it! And you're supposed to be the shy one."

Cigarette smoke wafted into Benny's eyes from elsewhere in the room. He angrily tried to wave it away. *Is all that really all that goes on in these parties? Empty cigarette cartons and vampire pantomime?* But he knew how to answer Kelly.

"So this is a vampire party?"

"Yes."

"Ever watch *Buffy the Vampire Slayer*?"

Benny smiled as he finally caught Kelly in a blink. Yes, he did occasionally say something clever.

"Buffy once had a Halloween episode where everyone who bought a costume from a certain costume shop was magically changed into their costume. People in pirate suits became pirates, demon masks became demons, and everything started rampaging." He looked Kelly in the eye, in rare confidence. "Well last night I kept remembering that episode, and how the answer to the monster rampage was ridiculously easy, but no one ever thought of it," Benny smiled as Kelly paid rapt attention. "What the heroes should have done is gone straight to that evil costume shop, and picked out the strongest costume it had, like a superhero. Then the magic would turn them into that superhero, and they could sweep the streets and save the day. Last night, I kept hoping the same chance might be given to us."

Kelly laughed. "Sneaky. I never would have thought of that," and Benny smiled, proud of himself. "But that raises a *very* good question," Kelly spoke softly, leaning in. "What costume would the great descendant of Finn MacCool have picked? What do you really want to be young MacCool? Hero, or monster?"

Benny didn't have an answer, except, "Keith asks me that all the time."

Keith! His face popped into Benny's mind with a flash. *Where's Keith? I need to—*

DING DONG.

"Oh goodie!" Kelly nearly jumped and applauded. "That's the last person we were waiting for!" She ran to the door, and Benny forgot what he'd been thinking about.

"Come here!" Benny barely heard Kelly yell for him over the synthesized drudge music. "Here's someone you just have to meet!"

Benny looked over. People blocked his view, but snippets of the new arrival's voice seemed familiar. From school maybe. Kelly reached through and pulled him to the door. "Look who's here."

A black-trench-coated figure peeled himself out of a dark collection of laughing friends to eyeball him with a malicious laugh.

CRUD.

All of Benny's new-found courage evaporated as Marcus looked down on him with mocking eyes, "Well look who it is. Funny finding you here, Benny."

THIRTY-ONE

FEELING RETURNED TO KEITH'S limbs as he fumbled out from under a pile plastic debris. He kicked enough out of the way to stand, and when his eyes finally focused...

Fiber optic pumpkins. Werewolf wallpaper. Inside the Shriek Bootique thick white fog even now twirled around row after row of consumerist cheese. Mannequins guarded every corner, sporting costumes of Disney princesses, cavemen, and even Hermione Granger. You couldn't miss this was a Halloween store if you were stone blind.

Keith preferred to do all of his Halloween shopping online, and wouldn't come in a place like this except under physical duress.

Or dragged in backwards by your feet.

Finding his way to his feet with a curse, Keith looked for the entrance. He wasn't going to stay in here one damn minute. He ran straight to the front doors and shoved, finding them solid as a rock. No getting out this way. Only then did it finally penetrate Keith's consciousness that there wasn't anyone else in the store.

Wait a cold second... Aiden had just come in here! There were people everywhere!

Not anymore. Keith was alone. No matter. If Keith couldn't get out the front, he could find the back. Making a beeline through some aisles he looked to the back of store, only— There was no "back" to the store! Walls stretched into infinity. Keith ran at a fast clip, but the far end never got closer no matter how many aisles he passed. As he pushed deeper into the store, each aisle conveniently labeled where he was, in golden lettering on a purple background: Roaring 20's. Hippy 60's. Disco 70's. Teen. None got him to the exit. After running for what had to have been at least a 500 yards, Keith stopped, out of breath. Trapped in his own pocket of Ironic Hell.

Meanwhile, Benny was God knows where.

"Damn it, LET ME OUT!"

Silence. Except for the electronic jittering of a shelf full of bobble-head mummies singing *Purple People Eater* two aisles down.

And movement to his left. Keith spun towards whatever awaited him, only to see himself. In a mirror. Dirty. Wet. Utterly frazzled. *I look ugly as hell.* But that wasn't the scary part.

That would be when his mirror image shot a pointed finger right at Keith and started laughed hysterically.

Keith jumped out of his skin, tripping over a stand-up display of Styrofoam tombstones. Made in China. DAMN YOU! Keith's attitude came back as he charged right at Not-Keith in the mirror—

It was gone.

A shrieking laugh behind him apparently found that hilarious.

HAHAHAHAHAHAHA

Keith's anger settled in for a long stay. Kicking debris out of the way, he spun around with righteous fury—

To see an entire wall laughing at him, of masks. Skulls. Demons. Clowns. Basketball heads. Celebrities and politicians. All laughing their heads off. Literally. Weirding out Keith was no small accomplishment, but a wall full of living breathing Halloween masks laughing themselves silly definitely did the job. Especially when the rest of the store joined in. Including more damned robots. A headless butler. A hanging spiderweb mummy and zombie baby. Even the Captain America mannequin. Every last one heaved back in a huge belly-laugh at Keith's expense. Keith growled. He was NOT hanging around for this, and ran into the next aisle. This one had—

An endless trove of HallO'Scream merchandise. Plastic glasses and purple rubber skeletons. Keith gawked until something black fell over his eyes, he grabbed it off in a white fury.

It was a T-shirt.

HALLO'SCREAM

If MacCool dies before he can wake,
His name is a lie and his courage fake!

"SCREW YOURSELF!" Keith yelled as he threw the shirt away, hitting another full length mirror.

Which didn't have his reflection.

Where Keith should be standing lay just a huge empty aisle. Keith grabbed his head with both hands to make sure he was still there. He was, just not in the mirror.

Aiden and his harem were.

Right there on the other side of the glass, walking down the aisles of the Shriek Bootique walked Aiden and the three women. Keith pounded on the mirror but they made no sign of hearing him. Aiden hung in the back as the girls giggled about fluorescent green wigs and sparkly blue nail polish. The scene didn't change for a minute, leaving Keith almost bored enough to leave. Except—

"Hey, where's Catelyn?" one of the other girls asked in a squeaky voice coming through the mirror. One girl was gone. The harem looked around for only a second before deciding to carry on. Keith hadn't seen her leave either, but his heart dropped as he guessed what was happening.

"Hey, where's Heather?" Aiden asked, suddenly noticing he was now missing not one, but *two* girls. His dull eyes scanned the store, seeing nothing.

Only one girl left, the one with the Witch-on-a-Broom T-Shirt. She wrapped an arm around Aiden. "She'll be around. Come over here," she soothed as she led Aiden away.

And looked right at Keith with a wicked smile.

Keith pounded the mirror in fury, knowing what this was about. On cue the image vanished as the mirror rippled, changing scenes, and Keith could see Catelyn again. Turning a corner, she got lost in the maze every bit as much as Keith. Running from corner to corner, she collapsed in tears. Utterly alone in a cavernous horror. Until a shadow fell over her. With the flaring mane of a horse...

Keith pounded the picture as it vanished again. The image returned with the second girl, Heather, as she admired a big poofy Mad-Hatter hat with turquoise pom-poms. She was a little rough with it—and the hat apparently agreed, opening up into a huge gaping mouth, sucking up/devoured Heather into its depths a single bite. The hat landed on the floor with a plop. Heather never even had time to scream.

The mirror rippled one last time. Back to Aiden and the witch. By the men's costume aisle. "Undead Zombie." "Roman Toga." "Kylo Ren."

"Pick one," said the witch, sparkly eyelashes fluttering.

Aiden grunted. "For what?"

"To play with me."

"I don't need any of these to play with you," Aiden leered, reaching his arm around her neck, reaching in for the obvious prelude to a french kiss. The witch intercepted his arm, bringing his hand to her mouth, lips puckering for a kiss on his palm.

"You've got to be more fun to play with me, little man. You have to be *scary*." She pulled him over to a costume labeled "Horse." Aiden laughed with the absurdity of it.

"What's so scary about a horse?"

Oh hell.

HEHEHEHEHHEHEHE

The infuriating laughter filled the entire store just as the mirror went blank.

And Keith saw through Aiden's eyes.

One man. Callused hands from a lifetime working under the sun in Irish fields. Endless rows next to a dilapidated cottage. Every fool is so scared of the fields, deserting them when the sun went down. Crying about "Leaving the Share!"

Nonsense! He'd make sure he got what he had earned. There's nothing out here.

There was, but Keith could voice no warning to the man who now wore Aiden's face.

The man walked his field as his wife wailed like a pitiful woman. She was always wailing about leaving The Share. Well, no more. He would take it ALL. He reached into the earth and collected more crop the wife had abandoned. He'd give it to no man or no beast. It was his.

Keith saw what the man couldn't.

The shape floated across the earth. It made not a sound as its legs gripped the earth, stalking, its black form all but invisible as the dying orange gave way to the deep blue of dusk. The hills fell invisible, surrounding the mortals below. Such fragile mortals.

The chirp of the crickets ceased. The songbirds fell silent. But the stubborn man comprehended nothing. His mind of dirt gave no place for appeasing greedy spirits. He'd give them nothing. Let them come.

They did.

Keith fought against the vision, fought to yell something to the man, Aiden, trapped in another time and place in self-imposed ignorance. But Keith saw the beast. Elongated in a snout with a black mane whipping in the evening wind. A horse, with the supernatural power of the faerie.

The Puka.

And the Puka rules the fields.

Black fur blended into black sky. Rippling muscles clenched in power. Eyes of the thickest red burned right into Aiden's back, radiating ghostly hate. If this money-headed mortal wouldn't give respect with his Share, he'd give it with his life.

Keith broke free for only a moment, and shouted, the only warning he had:

"AIDEN!"

Aiden spun around as he remembered, for the briefest second, who he was.

He looking for the way out, far too late. For now he saw it, a beast that couldn't exist. A horse that opened a mouth like a crocodile, exposing rows upon rows of serrated reptilian teeth.

Aiden hated reptiles. And as the teeth sliced his skin, he screamed and—

"LEAVE HIM ALONE, DAMN YOU!" Keith was back, looking at the mirror. He couldn't stop it, but he could smash it. In a rage he lifted the mirror over his head and shattered on the floor into a hundred pieces.

HEHEHEHEHEHEHHE

"Screw yourself!" Keith ran down an aisle. He didn't care which one. It happened to be labeled *Superhero.* Someone was there! At the end of the aisle, Keith saw a figure with his back turned. Keith ran to him, daring to hope he might get out of here, but when he got closer he noticed the figure wore a yellow unitard and red cape. The man turned around— Not-Keith, glaring behind a red cowl and glowing eyes. Laughing his head off. Keith tripped on his heels and retreated backward.

Into *History,* running into Not-Keith in a black cowboy duster and hat, cocking a Winchester repeater. *WHOOPS* . Keith took one more turn—

Down into *1980's,* into a hair-metal rock band, screaming into amplifiers. The overhead lights of the Shriek Bootique shattered with sparks and ear-splitting guitar feedback. Not-Keith shredded an axe with Gene Simmons hair and death-rock make-up. Looking at Keith, he turned his head straight up and spit a geyser of steaming blood into the air. Droplets of oozing red fell all over everything, burning sizzling holes in whatever it touched: shelves, linoleum. Keith's leather jacket.

YEOW. Keith pulled himself down a side row right before a gigantic red blob burned a humongous smoking hole exactly where he stood moments before.

One more aisle revealed only gaudy lights highlighting a be-speckled billboard advertisement: *Everyone Wants To Be A Vampire!*

Keith swore.

HEHEHEHEHEHHEHE

The laughter followed Keith, until he just dropped to the floor. *This definitely isn't working.* He now heard nothing except flapping. Looking up he saw rubber bats tethered to the ceiling on long bits of string, flapping their wings mindlessly in endless circles.

Just like me.

Keith looked around for anything that could pretend to get him out of here, finding only pathetic plastic scythes, foam rubber swords, and row after row of "Witch Sparkle Nail Polish." He gave up. From the rafters, fog settled around Keith, filling the aisles until it obscured the whole of everything.

Keith MacCool as a Spider's Fly!

Got trapped by a witch and was the Last to Die! HEHEHEHEHEEHE

That was new! The voice chilled Keith's blood, a *witch's* cackle if he ever heard one. Keith quickly found the source. A nearby aisle labeled—

Sexy.

And that's what walked out of it. Aiden's witch in a black-velvet bodice, walking toward him with the strut of a runway supermodel. She smiled as she saw him, her voice carrying on an air of incense and jasmine.

"Keith MacCool, so tireless."

Oh no, he wasn't falling for that!

"Always running. You need rest."

But, Keith had to admit he was kind of tired. He hadn't had a lick of sleep for two days. The witch raised her arms in an embracing gesture, and Keith felt his eyelids droop—

No! Keith was NOT going to hang around to see how this ended. Turning on his heel he dashed down another aisle—smashing right into another robot. A green wicked witch.

With Catelyn's face, contorted into a scream of abject terror. Frozen in plastic.

Keith didn't remember screaming. But he ran back the way he came, bumbling into a shelf of Halloween hologram pictures. He had a few in the *HallO'Scream*. But not one of these.

Not one with Heather in it.

One view showed just her, unmoving, blank expression inside the Shriek Bootique, empty aisles behind her. The other view had her clawing the frame, in psychotic desperation to get out. With a horse-headed monstrosity rising over her shoulder.

Keith.

Freaked. And fell over.

Why them? I didn't even know them!

Keith managed to find his feet one last time, and ran straight into the witch. Eyelashes born of spiderwebs locked Keith in. "So tired."

So easy to get lost in those eyes, eyes of swimming green. He caught himself yawning...

"Sleep brave MacCool. Sleep and take your reward."

Keith's eyes felt way too heavy, he needed a bed. His legs dissolved out from under him as he stumbled to all fours. So sleepy, yes. A nap would be nice.

"Sleep Heir of MacCool and receive your reward."

Keith's eyes closed.

"Your *eternal* reward."

Thirty-Two

FEAR IS SO EASY.

Fear of being trapped. Fear of being alone. Especially with a bully in the room. Oh yes, *life* is the scariest terror of them all.

Marcus looked down on Benny with eyes of demonic delight. He always looked down. Benny was too damn short. Caught in a strange place, all he could do was freeze.

Marcus laughed. "Someone is up past their bedtime!"

Oh no. Marcus was...

Drunk.

Marcus grabbed Benny's cup from his hand, spilling beer all over the floor and Benny's arm. Marcus smirked as he guzzled it, then spit it against the wall. "Who gave you this sewer water?"

Too many people laughed.

"So why aren't you trying to scare anyone tonight? That's right, your uncle got so flaming psycho that he burned down his own house! I hope the insurance pays off. *After* the law gets through with him."

Benny couldn't move. He didn't dare.

"Where is he anyway? Off drinking himself into a hole?"

NOW, Benny's anger flared up. Without thinking about what the hell he was doing, he stepped forward—

"Uh oh, looks like I hurt your widdle feelings."

Oh crud, did I just do what I thought I did?

"Trying to scare me? Well, this I have to see. Come on, scare me."

Benny froze again, Marcus just pushed in closer, swaying in his alcohol haze.

"I said, scare me! Or can't you do anything without your uncle holding your hand? SCARE ME!" Marcus latched onto Benny's neck and forced him backwards, dragging his feet to the balcony, pushing him right up against the railing, so hard the metal poked his flesh in excruciating bites.

"Are you scary yet, little man? Are you SCARY?"

Sheer muscle lifted Benny off his feet, tilting him over the railings edge."Well how about this, are YOU scared yet?" Benny squirmed in fright as his arms clamped onto Marcus's hand, in panic about falling and a LONG drop below.

He wouldn't do it. He wouldn't!

Helplessness. Benny hated it.

"Are you SCARY YET?"

HATED IT.

Suddenly Benny's feet found the balcony again, and he opened his eyes to see Marcus being pulled away by a couple of other bulky friends who weren't quite so inebriated. Marcus stumbled into the party, laughing all the way. He'd already forgotten.

"I'm sorry Benny," Kelly said while reaching an arm around him. "I forgot the two of you had a history."

Benny saw Marcus grab another beer. The vampire wannabes pushed out cigarettes and filed to the door. Kelly reached for Benny's hand and led him out as well.

Wait, we're following that lunatic? Benny couldn't go with him! He had to get back home and—

"Peace," Kelly's voice soothed his raging mind, evaporating his fear. "We have to follow. And believe me, you want to go where we're going."

Benny believed her, her touch extinguishing his anger. Finding his feet, he followed her down some stairs and out into the busy streets, still full of squealing party-goers.

Benny noticed some of the party goers peeling off to go their own ways. His eyes caught the girl Kelly had pointed out walking the other way. His eyes followed, Kelly pulled him with the majority hung together, who walked in a loose pack down the brightly lit sidewalks of the Big City. Benny hung back, as far back as he could, letting Marcus get a large lead. He didn't want to be anywhere near him. Kelly spoke.

"You've known him a long time?"

OF COURSE I DO. He wanted to yell, but couldn't, not at Kelly.

"He was a friend from..." *No he certainly was not a friend.* "I knew him at school."

"You don't like him do you?"

"Why the hell should I?" That came out with none of Benny's careful self-editing, he didn't care. "I had to avoid him everyday for about four years! Even after the funeral last year, everyone else left me alone. Not him."

"What did he do?"

"You just SAW!" Yelling was easy when Marcus wasn't staring at him. *Sure, I'm real freaking brave when he's not around.* Benny ground his teeth as unwilling memories surfaced, memories he'd rather bury with the rest of his adolescence: Getting tripped in the hallway, having books ripped out of his hands.

And never...ever...being brave enough to do anything about it.

"I'm sorry. I forgot."

One tiny voice in Benny's head said *"Lie."* But he forgot a second later as Kelly's continued.

"Why does he do that?"

Benny knew the answer to that. "Because he's a horse's ass. Because he's fulfilling self-esteem issues. At least that's what all the teachers said, while just sitting back and watching him do it. And because of the easiest reason of them all," Benny let himself have a dramatic pause. "Because I can't stop him."

215

Kelly laughed, which wasn't at all what Benny expected. "Sorry," she giggled. "It's just that's the longest sentence I've ever heard you say. You talk more when you're mad."

"What?"

"You can talk to people like a regular person when you're mad. It lifts your repression."

"That's...well, I just never had anything to say."

"Sure you did. You want to talk about everything, but you're too afraid of being judged. Anger lets you forget that. You're a lot happier when you're mad."

"I'm happier when I'm not being harassed."

"Maybe. But have you ever asked yourself a very important Halloween question?"

"What question is 'very important?'"

Kelly looked upward to the cloudy sky. "Why, exactly, do the dead hate the living?"

Benny turned away from burning holes in Marcus's back to look at Kelly in incomprehension. "Say what?"

"Why do the dead hate the living?"

Benny shrugged with exasperation. "I have no damn idea."

"Yes you do. They're jealous."

Jealous?

"Jealous," Kelly took Benny's hand to her face. "Of breathing. Touching. Feeling. The living have the gift of sensations. The dead don't. It makes them mad. Spiteful. Especially after what they see mortals wasting it, like drowning themselves in numbing alcohol, or staring at a smart phone for 16 hours a day. Why would anyone throw away a chance to feel? The core problem is simple as it is true," Kelly adopted a look of conscious introspection. "Life is wasted on the living."

Life is wasted on the living. Benny could see the point there.

"And you're doing it now."

Benny almost got mad at that, and Kelly stopped them both on the sidewalk. "FEEL, Benny. Let it out. All of it. Every emotion

216

you've ever bottled up. You've held it in too long and only suffocated. Let yourself feel."

"Feel what?"

"Get mad!"

Kelly framed his face with her hands, and gently turned him. "Look." Benny followed her gaze and saw the spotlights not far ahead. The vampire entourage had cut through a residential area and now approached more lights.

The Mall. That's where they were going. Even from here, Benny could see a line up of cars entering the parking lot, hear the giggles of a hundred kids as they ran towards the front doors with strollers and candy-buckets.

"Now look at that." Kelly said, turning Benny's head again to a nearby lawn.

A lawn of pumpkins. Dozens, covering every square foot up to the door. A graveyard's worth of creepy glowing pumpkins eyes bathed the entire two story house in a coddling orange glow. Obviously the home of a Halloween fanatic, on par with Keith on his best day.

"There's a hundred hours of work sitting there," Kelly said.

At least. Benny could only get the *HallO'Scream* yard completed after drafting a dozen or more of the actors in a single several hour splurge of effort. This yard was impressive.

"Wouldn't it be fun to just smash them?"

"What?"

"You hate them. I know you do. Don't lie to yourself."

Hate them. Benny never thought of it that way, but as he thought of it, each and every carving night was pulling teeth to get it done. Truth be told, he was darn sick of the whole thing.

"Smash them."

Smash them? Sure he hated the work. But he couldn't. All the effort put into this yard. All the...

"You had pumpkins too didn't you? And someone smashed them last night. Smashed YOUR pumpkins. But not these. How fair is that? Just once, wouldn't you like to scream how unfair it all is? GET MAD!"

Yes, he was mad. Seething mad, and Kelly's voice spurred him on.

"Take revenge for a wasted life, Benny."

Benny felt it. Anger. Rage. Yes, smashing them would be fun. Exactly what he wanted to do! He stepped forward—

Bridget filled his vision.

>SLAP<

Then she was gone.

"Wake up!"

Kelly had...slapped him? He should be hurt, but instead, Benny's thoughts clogged between the real and the imagined. *Did I see Bridget again? And what was she trying to say? She tries to talk but—*

>SLAP<

Benny's sight returned to Kelly, in his face, furious. Her green-eyes stared right into him. "You can't leave until I say! Until the end! SMASH THEM!" Vision after vision propelled through his mind's eye, a thousand inspirations of a thousand ways to smash pumpkins. BUST them.

"Til the very end, young MacCool," Kelly crooned.

When Benny's eyes cleared a line of pumpkins lay crushed behind him. He had stomped a path through them and now stood in the middle of the yard. He had no memory of getting there. But now that he was, dozens of glowing orange faces mocked him from every point of the yard.

And every single one had Darryl's face on it. He *hated* that.

He stared in vindictive fury at the closest pumpkin.

And smashed it.

Then he smashed some more.

"YES!"

His foot hit like a sledgehammer. His heel punched through face after face. It didn't hurt. None of it hurt. In fact it felt good.

Out of the corner of his eye, he saw Kelly laughing with delight, and then Kelly pointed to the Mall.

There was a great deal to hate at the Mall.

THIRTY-THREE

KEITH YELPED WITH A searing shock of PAIN as if some lunatic was jabbing his left palm with a pocketknife. Keith looked down to see—his palm being jabbed with a pocketknife. His pocketknife. He jammed his palm again.

OWWWWW.

THAT woke him up. Keith jumped away from the witch in howling pain. His eyes cleared as fingernails sharp enough to slice his neck open grazed his flesh. Keith tripped over piles of Halloween junk as he floundered backwards. The witch winked at him with amorous green-eyes, eyes that made him so tired...

OWWWWWW His knife found its way into his palm again. The point broke the skin, drawing blood. "STOP THAT!" But he couldn't very well get mad at himself. He was saving his own life. For that was no Sexy Witch.

Well, not sexy anyway. For every time Keith felt the pain, she changed. Pearly white skin turned green and warty. Marble fingers turned crooked and craggly. The velvet mini-skirt and corset morphed into a rotted cloak full of holes and musk. Ridiculous bent nose and chin, and utterly ugly. Enough to make even Keith gag. No easy feat.

Neither was jabbing himself with a blade, but if he lost the pain she'd cloud his mind again and he'd be finished. She wanted him asleep. To feed on him. If Keith let her touch him, he'd be dead before he hit the floor.

The Irish witch. The Hag.

She was so close now, her face of beauty now revolting, emetic. Black teeth snarled as she reached with a clawed finger. Keith had only two seconds. If you don't want a witch to touch you, what do you do?

You touch her first. Keith's fist went straight into her repulsive face. Soggy flesh gave way, and the "woman" sprawled all over the floor.

Hags are only carrion eaters, attacking the weak. They have no power against physical pain. Especially after Keith picked up a broken mannequin of a feminized Thor and smashed the Hag over the head with it five or six times. He only stopped when she was a broken huddle on the floor. Some tiny part of Keith's conscience rebelled over hitting a woman. But that wasn't a woman, that was a predator. Keith stared at the form with a victorious, if exhausted, smile.

"Halloween is not only getting too commercial, it's getting too dangerous."

Keith walked around the aisles with a laugh, yelling at nothing in particular.

"Know why that wasn't going to work? Listen." Keith waved around. "Know what I don't hear? I don't hear maniacal laughter of a severed head. I don't hear the clippity clop of the Dullahan. Know what that means? The Dullahan hasn't marked me! And until he does, I have a Get-Out-of-Death-Free Card."

Keith kicked the witches prone body. " Bleh. You don't know what scary is, and never did. People might be aroused by you," he said as he started to stalk off.

"But they fear *me*."

Keith looked around the store. It was silent. Good. He'd get out while he could. Turning on his heel, Keith ran down an aisle.

HEHEHEHEHE

He ran right back into the wall of masks, still laughing like idiots.

HEHEHEHEHEHE

Screw those guys, I'm finding the front door again. The endless maze of stretched into infinity, but Keith was not going to die here. He wouldn't let himself. He ran, looking for the door. And turning a corner, suddenly there it was, sitting at the end of a long row, a mocking promise of escape. Keith looked for a moment, thinking.

It won't let me go that easy.

Rumble

I hate being right all the time.

Something else was here. Behind him. Sighing, Keith turned around.

Another mask? No. The hag? No.

It was ...a black shadow rising out of the floor. Glowing red orbs morphed into eyes as arms elongated and legs twisted into hooves. A Head split into a ghastly grin that grew an oversized muzzle, rising impossibly tall.

Keith knew he had to run, get away. But he wouldn't let himself. Every instinct froze him to the spot as the Puka arose.

Seven feet tall. Standing on back legs, an equine head atop a humanoid frame in an insane cross of man and horse. Black mane whipping like a thousand snakes. Arms ending in clawed hands that gouged out divots in the linoleum as it pushed itself up to its full height. A horse with a heaving chest and swirling red eyes glaring down on Keith like an insect. Opening its mouth in a grotesque mockery of a smile.

Keith watched every quiver. Red energy swirled as it flashed a ghastly horse's grin, and Keith now knew how foolish a mortal he was.

Yes, it would scare Keith. Scare him to death.

Run.

As if.

RUN. The door is right there!

HAHAHAHAHAHAHA

The wall of Living Masks again had another jolly jeer at Keith's expense, laughing at the mortal too dumb to run for his life.

RUN YOU IDIOT.

Yes, that's what it wanted. It wanted Halloween expert extraordinaire Keith MacCool to run for his life. So it could chase him down. Yes, it would enjoy that a great deal.

HEHEHEHHEHE

Screw it.

Keith ran to the door. Bracing his shoulder, he hurled himself at full speed, fully expecting the door to bounce him back to the floor in exquisite pain.

SMASH

It opened.

Keith flew with a tripping sprawl into the parking lot, landing on hands and knees and pain from a thousand cuts. A godawful mocking laugh announced his victory.

HEHEHEHEHEHEHE

TOO LATE! Keith was out and he was staying out! All he had to do now was get over to—the city?

Keith stared in shock at what lay outside the door. The city was gone.

Skeletal storefronts had long since collapsed into decay. A dusty wind scoured a desolate landscape of rusted cars and crumbling buildings. Churning dark clouds reached down to the horizon as far as Keith could see. Just a twilight world of cold, cold gray.

Dead.

He hadn't escaped anything. He was still over the Veil, and the hunt had just begun. And he was the hunted. Keith's eyes opened at a new sound echoing through the towering tombs of steel.

Clippity Clop

Ah. There's *the Dullahan.* Right on time.

"Gulp."

Thirty-Four

KEITH RAN, TRAPPED AGAIN in the *Other Side.*

Broken skyscrapers rose like monoliths above him in this world of the dead. Half-dead at any rate, for illuminated signs still flickered above store fronts, betraying a hideous sense of humor as they mocked the dead world around them:

Scary Queen, Taco Hell, and *Chick Freak-A* ringed the parking lot, and it became more macabre the farther away Keith ran. *Dead Robin, Cemetery 21 Real Estate, Bloodbath and Beyond,* and *Upchuck-O-Rama* lined the broken road in the distance.

If he hadn't had been in such a hurry to find any way out, Keith's corny meter might have overloaded. *Home Despot,* next to the pizza place called...*Little Seizures?*

HEY! That's going too far!

Mocking laughter hit his ears. Something apparently thought that was an absolutely hilarious name. Well, screw em.

If they couldn't kill me in my own haunted house, they sure as hell wont get me here either. I haven't lived this long to die from a bad pun.

But unceasing winds buffeted him as Keith passed blocks of desolation. Running accomplished nothing more than wearing him out. How did one escape an entire city? Maybe one didn't. When Keith ran around the corner of an *El Pollo Muerto,* he saw that he wasn't alone.

Ghosts. Flickering images of people, wandering through devastation in a ghastly parody of life. Very much dead. Keith ran right into a pack of them and froze, anticipating danger. He found it when the closest ghost pulled up his head and stared right into him.

Jack.

Captain Sparrow formed from a wind-blown vapor. Pointy hat, fake dreadlocks. Dead hands covered in rings—

Reaching for Keith.

Keith fell backwards over a crumbling sidewalk. Jack's ghost stumbled toward him in a wayward lurch, hands open as if to grab him. His transparent mouth opened in a gaping maw that couldn't close. Keith's heart pumped as he crawled on all fours until he got enough distance to stand up and get away.

You're not Jack! Running off, Keith made a turn down another other equally dusty street. Another figure materialized to block him—

In a Spiderman outfit.

Keith ducked under Quentin's red and blue flopping arm and kept running. He didn't know if an immaterial ghost could even grab him in the first place, but had no intention of finding out. He wasn't going to stop and ask.

For out of every corner, more ghosts came.

Connor.

Taylor.

Scotty.

Not just one. Dozens, hundreds with the same face, all forming out of the fog mouthing a single phrase over and over:

Your fault.

Keith's heart skipped as he desperately avoided a minefield of groping hands. He didn't do this! They had been killed by a homicidal Irish horse that got its jollies from hunting mortals!

It's all another show. They can't get you.

224

>CLICK<

Or could they. Surrounded by the dead, Keith saw one more face, a face he'd tried to bury but now exploded into his sight. He couldn't run from it, couldn't hide from it. One horrible image of a woman's face.

>CLICK<

His eyes blurred.

Keith 's arrival had brought him straight into a hostage situation. A WOMAN in a hostage situation, with a gun to her head. Keith has his gun trained on her attacker. He'll save her. He'll stop this idiot right here and now.

Except he failed to check the corner before entering the store. He didn't see who was hiding there.

Didn't see them put the gun behind his ear. But he didn't know that was going to happen. Yet

>CLICK<

Keith never got scared, but it had all been a show. One he'd put on for years. All to hide one little memory. Intruding on his dreams.

And the Puka knew exactly what it was.

SLAM.

Keith's fist blasted the door open with his police badge in one hand and his gun in the other. There was the meth head creep at the counter. Arm wrapped around a frantic female. Gun pointed at her head. Keith already had his gun pointed at him.

You've got this. He won't do anything, not yet. Just step slowly into the room. You know it's clear.

The woman met Keith's eyes with wide-eyed fear. And an unspoken plea, from her eyes to his.

Save me... She screamed with her eyes. Only her eyes...

With his eyes, Keith promised the woman she'd be safe. He could save her. There was only one idiot, face-twisted in desperation, backed into a corner. Keith had him. Just don't shock him. Keith drew a breath, readied his muscles, and—

>CLICK<

Behind his ear. From the corner. The place he'd forgotten to check
>CLICK<

RIGHT BEHIND HIM! Another meth head! A misfire! RIGHT BE-
HIND HIM

Keith chokes.

And fires.

Shots. Keith feels the bite of a bullet. And falls. His vision blacks out.

When he opens his eyes, both suspects are dead.

So is the hostage. Bullet through the head. Her eyes are still open.
STARING RIGHT THROUGH HIM
>CLICK<

That sound follows him into his dreams. Pursues him in waking
hallucinations.

He hides in his house, it follows him.

He quits his job, it follows him.

He buries himself under fake scares and a hundred costumes, but
Keith MacCool sees that woman's face in his dreams every night for the
rest of his life.
>CLICK<
>CLICK<
>CLICK<

Keith's eyes flashed with hundreds of faces reaching for him.

But he saw only one.

A decayed corpse of an angry woman in a business suit, with a
gunshot through her face, raising a deathly pale arm to point right
at him.

YOUR FAULT She shrieks. YOUR FAULT!

Yes, in this world, Keith was the hunted.

And he had been caught.

Clippity Clop

THIRTY-FIVE

HALLOWEEN HAD TAKEN OVER the Mall.

No one could miss it with the humongous inflatable pumpkins on the roof that were visible for miles. Huge spotlights spun over the clouds above, the universal sign for *This Is The Place To Be*.

Benny approached the doors with Kelly at his side. Kids pressed against them on every side, candy bags flailing in the air and dragging helpless parents behind them. A little Dracula no older than eight ran by, followed by a little girl with pink fairy wings. Little toddler boys dressed in full body monkey-suits ran screaming into the mall's central concourse, toward a towering Jack Skellington with a huge bowl of candy who handed bite-sized Butterfinger bars to the squealing mass.

Chocolate. Jolly Ranchers. Peanut Butter Cups. Lines of screaming kids ran from store to store with Mickey Mouse, Spiderman, or Incredible Hulk buckets, all amassing a stash of sweet treasure that would either be rationed out until mid-December, or gorged in a stupendous feast while watching scary movies on basic cable. Oh yes, Halloween was here.

Any other Halloween, Benny would have taken a moment to catalog the costumes. But this time blood burned in his face and he stomped through it all. He was going to scour this whole place store by store.

He was going to find Marcus. This time he wanted to.

Benny reached the center concourse escalator to the 2nd floor and headed up. He bumped other people. He didn't care. Then Kelly motioned to his left, where a black coated form revealed itself at the top of the escalator. A prissy vampire, pushing everyone aside like he was the master of all he surveyed. Benny hated that. A hundred other times Benny had ducked around corners whenever he caught sight of Marcus. This time Kelly stood next to him, her soft breath filling his ear. "Remember how you *want* to feel."

Benny remembered anger all too easily.

"You *want* to be furious."

Yes, Benny did. Benny stood straight. Marcus saw him and laughed, still intoxicated. Perhaps even more so. Benny hated that too.

From behind Marcus stepped a peroxide blonde, dressed in black lace corset and short-shorts, more appropriate to a Victoria Secret runway than a shopping mall. Her smile betrayed a vacuum behind her eyes. Benny recognized her from school, one of the perpetually vain who would never suffer the indignity of wearing the same outfit twice in a single school year. She once called him "Little Benny."

Benny *really* hated that. But he didn't move yet. He let Marcus stand right in his face. With a smirk, Marcus turned his eyes to Kelly. *He wouldn't!*

He would.

"Kelly, you didn't tell me that *this* was your date tonight!" Marcus looked to Benny and back to Kelly again. "He must have had quite a wad of life savings to buy an hour with you."

Benny's vision starting to blur, like watching a movie, but he didn't move yet. Marcus wasn't even warmed up.

"Or is this a prelude to pity-sex?"

Kelly's face fell into a shocked pout. Benny seethed. His back rose, his legs strengthened beneath him. For the first time in his life, he could stare at Marcus eye to eye. Anger filled him. He relished it. Stoked it.

But Marcus had to exercise petty alpha-male dominance one last time.

"Well that's what I would expect. It looks like it took five girl-friends to squish you into that outfit. Yet from what I read in the boy's bathroom, it only takes a single beer to get you out of it."

Now.

Are you scary?

No, Benny was much worse.

His fist went straight into Marcus's teeth, who stumbled backward with an arm on the nearby railing. Benny's fist then entered his gut and Marcus fell to his knees in pain. Benny stood over him, vindictiveness tinting his face a deep crimson. Marcus cupped his face and looked up in shock.

POW

Another fist crunched into Marcus's eye socket like a cement brick. Marcus collapsed and rolled over to the side, letting loose a howl as his hands covered his head.

KICK straight to the gut, and Marcus shut up. Benny didn't stop.

KICK

Shocked exclamations from the crowd, only now noticing.

KICK

Marcus curled up, hands bloody.

KICK KICK

Marcus's blood puddled the floor.

KICK

Someone cried for Benny to stop as he'd reduced Marcus to a bloody pile on the floor of the Food Court with legs kicking frantically to gain escape. Benny kept on him, kicking. Marcus screamed with every impact, flailing around as Benny kept hitting him, laughing as he did so.

He liked it.

STOP!

A single voice stopped Benny cold. A voice he knew as well as his own.

"Bridget?"

*Where is she? Is she...*She wasn't there

Marcus was. Bleeding on the floor. Benny looked. *I did that.*

Bridget stopped me.

Several friends picked Marcus up by the shoulders and led him nearby into the restroom. Benny followed Marcus's broken form all the way in, then he looked at the crowd surrounding him. They stared at him in horror, but also in awe.

He liked that.

Kelly then reached for him as the crowd filtered off, careful not to make eye contact. Kelly pulled his hand close, and looked at him. Or perhaps, looked *through* him. "Look at you, Benny. You've become a monster."

She pulled him deeper into the mall, her laugh echoing off the walls.

Thirty-Six

CLICK

The sound.

>CLICK<

That horrible sound. BANGING in his ears. Over and over.

>CLICK<

>CLICK<

>CLICK<

Keith ran. Through a ruined storefront, through a pile of cars standing on their ends. From all sides reached thousands of corpse-faced ghosts. Each one wearing the face of someone Keith had let die. In the churning gray sky above him, a thousand more faces peered through the mists.

The Other Side held no secrets. Death hides nothing from anyone. Keith's pain lay bare before them, and here, they would kill him with it.

Live your lie and perish!

Keith's life had been a lie for a long time, a lie to his family, his friends, and himself. The *Other Side* had a special fate for liars. Keith knew what unspeakable terrors stalked this place. Now, a vicious scream rippled the lifeless gray of this dead city, something was coming.

Coming for him.

Keith knew exactly what it would be.

The Other Side held all the dead of the year, but some never passed on. Some of the most vile were trapped here for eternity as punishment for a life of wanton cruelty. The Irish held a special fear of them, now Keith saw them approaching through parted clouds. Keith could only describe it as a cascade of black water. Of black ghosts. With white eyes. Flowing as a single, screaming, howling mass of contorted forms of diabolical semi-animal,shapes with too many joints, too many limbs. A ghastly warping of man and beast mirroring the tortured soul. The mass flowed like black ink into the dead city, drenching the ruins in a sickly *funk* of spirits too corrupted to ever pass beyond.

Keith's memory involuntarily coughed up the mood:

By the prickling of my thumbs, something wicked this way comes.

These were the *Sluagh,* and they were coming for Keith.

Clippity Clop The air rang with a psychopathic laugh and the sound of horses hooves striking pavement. The Dullahan approached.

Keith didn't care anymore, and stopped running. Ghostland was a fitting place for a Halloween connoisseur to die. Misty faces leered down from the clouds and laughed with voice of howling wind.

LIVE YOUR LIE AND PERISH! One last time, the faces of the dead revealed themselves. Going backward in time. All the deaths Keith could have prevented.

Aiden. *Fitting, the most recent to die.*

Quentin. *Spiderman suit now tattered and frayed with decay.*

Jack. *Smile now corrupted into Jacob Marley despair.*

Connor. *Goatee ratted and rotten.*

Taylor. *Still wearing the psycho clown outfit*

Scotty. *He hadn't seen him in a while, pity to see him like this.*

Keith dreaded to see what came next. He *knew* what would be next. But he couldn't look away.

Bridget.

Dressed as she was that very day she died. Small frame, long hair, almost Benny's exact size and shape. Keith couldn't have saved her, but she would always be a broken promise made to Benny and Bridget's mother, his sister, on her deathbed a promise to protect his niece and nephew. He failed.

Keith fixed on the transparent form of Bridget, a ghost trapped here since her death, waiting to pass on with Halloween. That would be soon enough. He'd go with her. She looked at him, sadly.

Clippity Clop

Just get it over with. Keith's vision clouded as he nearly gave up.

Until Keith saw one more ghost.

Exhausted, Keith pulled everything to focus on one last spirit. It formed before him, another dead soul from the last year. Bridget was... NOT the last one? *Who else was there? Who else had died even before Bridget?* Keith took a long, hard look as the last ghost formed before him.

And looked. And looked.

An electric shock jolted his failing body. The face, the form. There was no mistaking it and the implications pummeled him. One after the other.

Oh no.

The animal howl rattled broken windows across the dead city. The *Sluagh* were coming.

Get up. FOR GODS SAKE GET UP!

Keith hurled his body down the street and pushed against all the pain. He had to get out! He was the only one who knew!

Knew that Benny was going to die. Tonight.

And Keith was the only one who could save him. He would. Even if it killed Keith trying.

Clippity Clop

THIRTY-SEVEN

KEITH STUMBLED OVER THE broken landscape, barely visible in the twilight. Ghostland's clouds broiled above him, spinning far too low and spinning apart faster than one could watch.

Keith didn't watch. He was listening to the screeches. They got closer with every howl. A shriek no human could ever make, born of a wild-animal in the throes of death. The *sluagh* were the holy terrors of man's subconscious, and they knew Keith was here. They could smell his mortal stench and would rip it from him in bloody shreds.

Keith took one moment to look in the direction of the screams, cataloging the scene just as a hundred haunted houses before. The smell of the air, the grit of the ground. The dark shadows stretching to touch him. He knew exactly how long he had to live.

Live was exactly what he was going to do. Keith had gone through far too much to die now. That movie poster from his beloved *HallOScream* flittered across his mind's eye, the one Benny loved. *Watership Down*. Such a delicious tag line:

"Prince with a thousand enemies. If they catch you, they will kill you. But first, they have to catch you."

234

Keith caught glimpses in the distance of a black river. Inside the undulating mass were human forms contorted into inhuman, vicious beasts of misshapen claws and cloven hooves. Awe inspiring.

But they weren't going to catch him. Keith knew where to go. Though the streets, past the ghostly crowds, Keith backtracked all the way to the end, then around a corner and there it was. The Shriek Bootique. This time he ran in willingly, not turning back even as animalistic cries rippled the air behind him. Any lingering ghosts scattered, vanishing back to whatever dark corner that spawned them. Keith passed the threshold, thick into the Money Changers in the Halloween Shrine.

HEHEHEHEHEHEE The Wall of Masks welcomed him back.

Yes. Freaking hilarious, especially if I don't find what I need in time.

Instead of even pretending to keep track of where he was, Keith ran right back into the maze, knowing full well it would lock him away yet again.

Fluorescent colors assaulted his eyes as he charged into the infinity of aisles.

How much time did he have exactly? The *Sluagh* were approaching, but not here yet. He had maybe five minutes before they caught him. Time pressure, just the way Keith liked it. He stopped in the perfect aisle of plastic Halloween tripe, and smiled.

Didn't anyone realize that he had the advantage here? All he needed was right in front of him. Anything the Halloween fanatic could ever want. Keith started grabbing.

A big block of gravestone styrofoam. Keith swiped it.

Big bottles of nail polish remover. Stuffed into pockets.

Couple of black tablecloths, XXX large. Folded around an arm...

Leather belt. Bottle of black Zombie Blood and a big orange candy bowl. *Thank God something is orange around here.*

Keith grabbed a few more seemingly unrelated items until both arms were full, and then dashed for the farthest corner the endless aisles could provide. Hurling his pile to the ground he whipped out his pocketknife and got to work. Pulverizing one gravestone into tiny chunks, he then dropped those chunks into the candy bowl followed by the contents of five bottles of nail polish remover, which melted the styrofoam into a sloppy goop. Keith poured the black zombie blood on top of that.

Then smeared the whole mess all over his face.

It stung, but he expected that. Keith tuned out the store, the screaming, and the mocking laughter. With the pair of scissors and a face of encrusting goop, he got to work, humming his ringtone.

As the moon climbs high over dead oak tree
Spooks arrive for the midnight spree
Creepy creeps with eerie eyes start to shriek and harmonize
Grim Grinning Ghosts come out to socialize.

Five minutes? Hell. He once ruined his whole life in only five seconds.

The Sluagh poured through the City of the Dead. The darkness had opened for them, revealing the way so very close to the mortals. The mortal stench filled them with bloodlust, and now they knew one lay near. They smelled his flesh. Caught the scent of his blood. They were going to feed. Tonight.

The prey lay so near...

Something moved, beyond the crumbling edifices. Succulent flesh, hiding a bright soul within?

Yes. A body moved into their view. Primal urges drove them to FEED and the swarm of the Sluagh rushed to catch it—

And recoiled.

A figure of corrupted flesh, held in tattered robes, limping with a wrecked body, its rotten form encrusted with putrefaction. This was indeed a mortal, but one already taken, festered and black.

The wretched limbs of the Sluagh reached towards the corrupted body, daring to touch the ruin of decay... But it saw them and lifting its own desiccated finger towards them in dead memory.

Unlife.

Worse even than the limbo of the sluagh, locked inside a corpse's shell with its own madness, too foolish to know that gray death had already claimed it. A mindless mockery of life. A grave-monger.

And tasteless poison to the sluagh. They must go further to taste blood, further toward the mortal light.

There the small mortal souls will be.

They turned their cursed backs on the corrupted creature and left it to its fate. Behind them the Unlife shivered, reaching out in confusion in a pathetic cry for help. But the Sluagh seared ahead. They forgot the putrefied fool as the unlife hung its head and trudged off, letting the Sluagh leave it far behind.

Alone.

But after ten steps, the Unlife turned around and followed the sluagh with eyes that were now VERY aware.

THIRTY-EIGHT

BLOODLUST INFLAMED BENNY'S HEART.

The thrill of beating Marcus filled his mind's eye as he stood on the mall's 2nd floor balcony overlooking the concourse below, gripping the railing with white knuckles. Strength. This is what it felt like. He would take as much as he could get.

Except a chill had just formed in his gut. His adrenaline started to evaporate, bringing dizziness and blurry—

Kelly grasped his hand, and the strength returned. With an odd ...flavor. But the fire roared up again and Benny forgot about it. Kelly's vampire friends bumbled around him, hissing, scraping claws on the handrail overlooking the balcony. They obviously thought way too much of themselves, and—

Did that one just BITE that woman's wrist? Yeap. Drawing blood, which the "vampire" eagerly licked up.

Their elevator isn't going to the top floor.

Benny's fiery temper contrasted starkly to the innocent scene below. From here he had a commanding view of the mass of trick-or-treaters. Dinosaurs, Batman, ballerinas running from store to store.

Usually Benny would be nice, usually he liked Halloween at the mall. Now he didn't, and said so.

"I hate this place."

Benny focused on one family across the way. The father wore a particular face Benny had seen on his own dad, the face begging to get away from such inconvenient holiday rituals. His own father had never taken him out trick-or-treating, and this man clearly projected his inner contempt. *"Why do I have to be here?"*

Another family crossed paths with the first, a zombie family in doctor and nurse getup, wearing blue surgical scrubs ripped into zombie-wear. They led two kids, a boy and a girl of grade school age who growled with zombie faces at the store keepers passing out candy, earning a few smiles in return.

Except Benny saw how the rest of the parents were keeping just a *slight* distance, glancing at them with disdain.

Who are these freaks? Stay away from me.

One family. ONE family was scary, out of the entire mall. "Heaven forbid someone show up to a Halloween event actually wearing a Halloween costume."

Kelly leaned far over the balcony railing, joining his view over the expanse. Benny could feel her smooth smile, even without looking. "Yes, it's not the holiday it used to be. Can you imagine seeing all these children in old Ireland? Halloween *used to be* the night you kept your children hidden away. Now it's backwards, the children leading the parents."

Benny would have answered, but ...his vision started to blur again. Where did his strength go? Now he could barely keep himself balanced.

Kelly gripped his hand and steadied him, even as his heart raced faster and faster.

Like my heart can't keep up, Benny thought. *Like the last time I gave blood.*

Kelly's grip came stronger. "We're almost done. We're here to see something special," Kelly pointed a finger below. Speakers were being turned on around a stage and the lights dimmed. The

239

crowd gathered as they knew something was going to happen. Fog machines poured sickly fog all over the stage as a THRUM rattled the speakers. Benny recognized the tune immediately, perhaps *the* most overplayed Halloween melodies in world history: Michael Jackson's *Thriller.*

The show began, the fog parting to reveal the Monsterette Dancers from 97.3. FM, same as last night. Female Jason and Freddy, except this time, in a mall, their costumes properly covered them. The crowd applauded with the dancers. Pictures flashed into the fog, making a spooky spectacle in the low light.

Benny had seen it before and was unamused. *Thriller* had been overcooked for a long time. Kelly giggled. "They're not scary either, are they?"

"They wouldn't know where to start," Benny responded as the dancers and milling crowd got harder and harder to focus on. Parents. Children. So many children. Out at night.

"And they're not ugly either," Kelly said, easing up to Benny, her voice now the only thing piercing his glaze "But something ugly IS going to happen. Tonight."

Benny's eyes gleamed as he looked down. The cold in his core flared for a moment, stronger than ever before Kelly's grip washed it away again. But he was getting colder, from the inside out...

Just listen to her voice, that's all you have to do.

>POP<

Benny blinked as a flash hit him in the eyes and for a brief moment, he remembered enough to ask: *Why was he in a mall? Where was Keith?* And he felt so horribly nauseous, a wad of wiggling black *funk* settling in his gut. He turned around in dizziness, looking for balance, when his eyes fell to a dark window of a closed store and he saw his reflection in the glass, staring at him.

The ghost of Bridget stood next to him.

Screaming.

Benny fell over the railing, visions of Bridget spinning through his head.

KEITH TRUDGED WITH A hunched back and crooked limp for a solid five minutes before he dared break character, the black robe dragging behind him.

Mixing Styrofoam with professional cleaners made a goopy slime that hardened in minutes. It stung like the blazes but with some blood and artistic license it became a mask of decayed petrification. Keith used it in the off-season for Paramedic training. His "robe" was a simple double "T" shape cut into a black tablecloth with a hole for his head. Throw a belt around it and instant Gravekeeper Creeper. All with common household products. George Lucas had done it for less when he mass-produced Tusken Raiders for filming Star Wars in Tunisia in the 70's.

Now Keith followed the *Sluagh*. If they could get out of this dead land then so could he. Keeping a safe distance, Keith followed them right out of the Shriek Bootique and into the city. This time, as Keith saw images of people, real people, pale shimmers, not quite there. Glimpses of the real world.

I'm seeing humans from a ghost's point of view. The mergings keep getting stronger.

The shrieking *Sluagh* poured through the streets in their black surge of contorted limbs. Keith followed in their wake, finding that in this Ghostland his thoughts carried him along almost as if he was a ghost himself. It took only minutes to fly past miles that would have taken an hour or more as a mortal. More flickering images of real humans appeared, and Keith could feel a vibration in the air, a *HUM* from ahead, calling the *Sluagh* forward as if called by a siren song.

There's another cross-over coming, another portal is going to open, they can feel it.

Keith didn't know where he was just yet. Fog swirled around the whole area, obscuring it. Except for the sounds of children.

The laughter of children. *That's right. There's Trick or Treating at the mall.*

The mall.

Even now, appearing in the pale reflections from mortal land, Keith saw toddlers in superhero outfits, running along in grinning joy. The *sluagh* sensed them too, pushing faster with the promise of fresh blood lying beyond.

They wouldn't dare, but Keith already knew, *Yes they would.* These were Celtic monsters, and what did he say earlier? *I know where it's going next.* The vapors of the *Sluagh* steered towards laughing and bustling crowds, getting more visible the closer they got to the portal ahead. And never far behind was—

Clippity-Clop

Over the horizon, the charging steed of the Dullahan sent sparks up in huge fireworks, galloping as fast as four ghostly legs could take him.

Toward the mall.

Toward the kids.

Keith growled. He *really* hated being right all the time.

THIRTY-NINE

Bᴇɴɴʏ Fᴇʟʟ ɪɴᴛᴏ Hɪꜱ sisters eyes, falling down a hill.

Finn MacCool crashed down a hill into a gully at the bottom. Branches lashed his skin into red welts. His own fault for not watching the path, but the journey exhausted him.

A scream had distracted him. A woman, in the trees, waving a torch high above her in fanatical desperation.

THE SLUAGH COME!

Finn's eyes widened. He had stayed out too long. With a bound he joined the woman in a flight over a crooked path he never would have seen, leading Finn to a thatched cottage in a lonely clearing. Adults and children worked outside in feverish panic.

Children outside? Tonight?

They approach!

Two men, another woman, and a gaggle of children gasped up in fright.

The skulls! CARVE THE SKULLS!

The family worked with all haste. Calloused hands held dirty bulbs from the harvest. White and gray. Finn grabbed one, whipping out a blade and carving into the bulb.

But from the road, shrieks.

THEY'RE HERE! HIDE THE CHILDREN! A grizzled uncle wrapped up every child and hurried them into the cottage, down into the cellar. The Night was no place for children.

Finn's blade returned to his bulb to gouge out two holes and a mouth. Eyes in a skull. The face of death. Carved skulls ringed the cottage, guarding the sides, the windows, and the door. The family placed burning animal fat inside every skull. The ugly skulls radiated with scowls of challenge, protecting the family.

Just in time. For THEY had arrived.

Benny gasped and opened his eyes wide. He caught his breath as he absorbed the vision, and as Bridget's eyes found him again.

Kelly yanked back on his hoodie, keeping him from a fall to the concourse but screaming in anger. She reached for Benny's face—

Bridget grabbed him first and wouldn't let go.

The moan of a thousand voices rose with the wind. A thousand desolate souls returned for one last Night to claw the living Earth. The family ran to the cellar, hiding in its depths even as the noise rumbled above them.

But Finn stayed just a little longer. He had to see what awaited, see if he held the bravery. The family yelled to join them from within the cottage. He would, but first he drew his own cloak around him and presented his own face of death.

Good, for they were here.

A thick fog flowed out of the trees, its wispy tendrils crawled across the clearing and surrounded the cottage. Sunken eyes stared blindly as hands reached to scrape the very air. NOW Finn retreated into the darkened home, bolting the door behind him. But he peered outside through the cracks, watching.

The Sluagh couldn't follow. The eyes of the skulls repelled them, so many eyes of golden flame that never blinked, denying their passage. But the hoard circled the cottage, testing every entry—

Finding one left carelessly open. An unguarded window. A cry of triumph as a pale face pressed through it—

A filthy boy appeared next to Finn and shoved another flaming skull into his hands. Finn all but threw it into the window, pressing back against the intruder. The tortured soul retreated back into the fog...

Baleful screams filled the air, screams of pain unsatiated and thirst unquenched. Their hungry WANT pressed through the walls of the home onto the family, who gripped each other shivering. But the hoard could not enter.

So with lonely moan, the hoard moved on.

After a minutes passing, Finn opened the door to the cottage in a silent creak and peered into the now empty Night. The family followed with baited footsteps, but the sluagh were gone, with nothing but the hooting of distant creatures.

The children were safe. Especially the little boy who had given Finn the last skull.

Finn gave his thanks to the family, then set out to find the road again.

Benny fell backwards, his back screaming in pain against the hard tile. His breath wouldn't come, he couldn't gasp fast enough!

Kelly was there. Benny's eyes cleared, and he could see the mall, the *Thriller* dancers. The kids. Benny's blurry mind barely had enough wit to register that it had all of a sudden gotten very foggy inside the Mall.

Kelly picked him up. "Awake, young man."

Benny looked around as he found his feet. The fog had moved across the skylights, bringing a chill that sunk to the bone. The families wrapped their coats around themselves as the fog enveloped everything, settling into a phantasmagorical whirlpool highlighted by the strobe lights.

Just like last night, thought Benny, as the whirlpool grew to take up the whole stage and Benny's eyes widened. In response, Kelly just gave a full cackling laugh. Had Benny still had full use of his mental facilities, he might have called it evil.

"Was that painful, young MacCool? Of course it was. That's what means to live, sensations. The unliving crave them, and just as you gave me your anger. It was intoxicating for both of us."

Benny's eyes drooped again as his pain overtook him. His strength had disappeared for good this time, and wasn't coming back. Kelly held him up to whisper in his ear.

"Now the children will give me *fear*. We're going to remind this brave new world why you shouldn't bring your children out at night." Kelly said with a smile.

"It will be delicious."

Benny watched as the whirlpool opened up, revealing the desolation of the *Other Side*.

With creatures inside.

FORTY

THE LIGHTS IN THE mall courtyard flickered once, twice. Then went out entirely into total darkness, even the emergency lights. The swirling portal on stage cast a pale glow over the entire assemblage.

"Cooooool," a nameless kid said. The bright lights of the food court had robbed the patrons of their night vision and people tripped over each other, yelping. The *Thriller* dancers stumbled over each other and stopped to look around. It was just another part of the show, wasn't it?

Benny should have been more concerned. But he hadn't been in his right mind since last night and was so ghastly tired. Kelly however was more vibrant and energetic than ever. "Watch young Mac-Cool." Kelly's excitement radiated off of her. "Watch!"

The glowing vortex spun faster, mesmerizing the audience as ghastly dark shadows appeared in the fog, contorted beings of ghoulish stature that could never be mistaken for human. Benny struggled to see over the railing as the wrinkle in space grew, becoming so large it filled up the entire length of the dance stage. Benny's mind whirled with possibilities as shapes started forming in the gray.

There are monsters in there! We need to escape! But he couldn't speak, couldn't move, and could barely even manage a simple thought.

What would come out first?

He got his answer as a black shadow filled the void, the mangled form of an impossibly tall creature. Arms raised, the angry silhouette charged the portal as a horrific apparition. Someone in the crowd screamed, some even running as the black form filled up the entire whirlpool as an impossibly huge phantom. Benny didn't dare blink as excitement filled him. *What was it?* What ghastly Halloween horror would it be? HE HAD TO SEE!

The form jumped through, and Benny saw—

One single figure. Quite human. Clothed in an unexciting dirty black robe. Benny drew back, confused.

Well that was anticlimactic.

The black-robed figure ran right into the stumbling *Thriller* dancers, who still did not know what had happened to their stage. The creature held up hands to apologize, exposing hideously scarred skin. The dancers screamed as the audience cheered, thinking it was still part of the show. Benny knew better. His trained eyes saw what the rest did not. That was *not* a robe.

It was a tablecloth.

Worn by a very dirty mortal. His face looked like roadkill three weeks dead, but it was a mortal. Benny frowned. Beside him Kelly had a different reaction, gasping in shock and...*anger? What was the matter?* Benny's eyes came in and out of fuzziness, but he'd know a modified Star Wars Tusken Raider costume anywhere. That couldn't be...

Keith?

But he didn't look long at the robed figure, for in the rippling of the portal, something else was on its way out.

Something big.

KEITH'S BLOOD BUBBLED AS he approached the portal. Hearing the scream of a hundred moaning ghosts, Keith took a big heave and jumped over the threshold right into—

The mall.

The prickly chill of the *Other Side* vanished as Keith took a deep breath of luxurious air (albeit mixed with way too much smoke machine fog), then fumbled in nausea but he had no time for an accident. Outrunning the *Sluagh* had been no easy task, but he managed it by making the *Other Side* respond to his will, propelling him faster than possible.

Now he bumbled into the middle of some dance stage, and lost precious seconds as his eyes refocused. People were staring at him, as if he were either a psychopath or escapee from the hospital morgue, or both. Keith just raised a ghoulish hand and waved. It was the day before Halloween, people expected weirdos to be walking around. God, Keith loved this Holiday. Behind him, The Veil howled as the blasted landscape of the other side came into view, a huge panoramic of dead trees and dead land.

And the swarm of the *Sluagh,* charging the portal, shrieking in anticipation of the feast of mortal flesh on the other side. Their stench of *unnatural* radiated out from the portal, making several people gag, but everyone was too stupid to leave. The parents and children all just stood there gawking, and Keith all but shouted at them. They were all going to die, right here, and they didn't even know it.

Clippity Clop

The hoof-beats of the approaching Dullahan shook the very stage beneath him. Either Keith stopped this now, or no one would. He spun around to face the huge glowing portal, just in time to see the *Sluagh* pour into the portal with bloodthirsty lust. Only Keith stood in their way.

He didn't move. Keith just watched, cataloging the scene, just like any other haunted house.

Modern monsters were just revisions of old memories, such slashers and witches evolving with the centuries, but always the same essence at their core. The *Sluagh* were no different, a tale retold in a thousand scary stories about the Monster Under the Bed or a Boogeyman in the darkened woods. Every strength, every weakness.

Keith was the first thing they saw as they penetrated mortal land. He faced them as an unflinching presence, hand raised in a classic STOP. Keith didn't move, didn't so much as blink as the wails of a thousand souls poured out of the Veil. Keith stood as a pillar in a maelstrom, buffeted by a storm of screams. The *Sluagh* pushed. The delectable children were *so close!* Howls of hunger pained all the louder as they tried to surge forward.

But their path was blocked by Keith. They screamed against him. Keith didn't move, he pushed *back*. Staring into their glowing white eyes, he could read their primitive thoughts: *He'll run! Mortals always run!* That was their mistake.

Keith never ran.

As a Haunted House Connoisseur, Keith had quickly caught onto a huge assumption in houses everywhere. All the monsters based their actions on the convenient premise that the guests will run away, away from the loud noise, away from the scary monster.

Keith never ran away. He'd plant his feet right there and dare the monster to pounce on him. Keith would even occasionally sneak in a collapsible Star Wars light saber and keep it hidden right until the chainsaw maniac leaped out. Then he'd whip it out in shining angelic justice and charge the maniac head on. Nine times out of ten the monster tripped and ran away backwards, with Keith laughing all the way. Whenever he found a monster that held his ground, Keith offered him a job at the *HallO'Scream* on the spot.

They expect you to run.

Keith did not run. Not in anyone's haunted house, and certainly not here. The hurricane fury of the *Other Side* blasted with gale force winds, pushing the scattered parents and children to panic. But Keith didn't move, and the Sluagh couldn't cross. Keith stared right into their eyes with the unblinking glare of a Haunted House Connoisseur, and dared them to step one stinking rotting foot into mortal land. In response they howled louder with screams that cracked windows and brought blood to the eyes. But Keith stood with arm raised.

YOU AREN'T CROSSING.

The sluagh screamed and screamed and...

Keith's body buffeted the wind rich with decaying musk. But he didn't move. The howls blasted around him as anger poured over Keith like red flame. But Keith did not move. The Sluagh couldn't cross.

And then, the Sluagh...blinked.

Parting like water before Moses, they scattered, wailing back into the twilight of the *Other Side*, taking the wind and dust with them. The portal rippled... and then vanished.

Keith finally dropped his arm in exhaustion. But then he had that nagging feeling he had forgotten something.

Clippity Clop

Oh no.

The Dullahan galloped across Keith's vision in the musty smother of *horse,* charging into the courtyard and costumed children. The sheer atmospheric blast threw Keith to the floor, but he forced his head to stay up, forced his eyes into the apparition as it galloped around the courtyard, sideways against the storefronts ringing the assembled parents and children. Then it charged through the crowd directly, laughing like a lunatic with every step.

Watch it. WATCH IT! Keith screamed to himself as he scanned every face, every mortal form it touched.

Then with one last laugh the rider vanished. Disappearing through a wall with a puff of mist. Gone. Keith scoured every face in the courtyard. Every parent. Every child. He had to know!

No blood. Anywhere.

For the first time in God knows how many hours, Keith exhaled. But he had someone to find. Turning in every direction he scanned the mall, knowing exactly what to look for. If the *Sluagh* came here, then so would—

There. Second floor balcony. Kelly. Their eyes met, her face a ripple of surprise, frustration, and anger. In that moment of eye contact, Keith made certain his message got across with no ambiguity.

I know what you are.

251

But then Keith saw Benny, being held by Kelly like a possession. But Benny looked...sick. Eyes glazed over, barely able to hold himself up. Keith's breath stuck in his throat.

No, Benny didn't look sick.

He looked like a bucket of blood had been poured over him.

FORTY-ONE

BENNY! KEITH CHOKED ON his own breath.

Not him! He can't!

Kelly sneered as she pulled Benny away into the crowd, getting lost with the rush of parents and kids. Keith moved to follow but got blocked by a dumb crowd still gawking at him. People still didn't know whether to applaud or scream. Keith almost screamed in their face. The Veil could open again at any time! All these idiots had to get out. So Keith made the choice for them, jumping off the stage to the nearest wall, reaching for—

"WHAT IN THE HELL ARE YOU DOING?!?"

Keith spun at the voice.

Darryl.

Running across the concourse with eyes shooting pitchforks, mad as all Hell. Of course this dance stage was his own Darryl O'Grady Exclusive Production, and Keith had just belly-flopped into the middle of it.

Sorry Darryl. We'll just make up your lost 20% next year.

Keith turned back to the wall where, with his black-robed elbow, he smashed the plastic cover over an ominous red button and pulled the fire alarm. White strobes went off. Sirens blazed. Finally the crowd scattered as parents scooped up kids and fled. The Thriller dancers blundered around for a moment, being stopped by a couple of wide-eyed teens. "Cool effects man!" But the courtyard finally emptied.

Keith ran toward Benny's last known location, peeling off his gory face and dirty robe as he went. He knew Benny was somewhere on the second floor. Keith pounded through the rapidly emptying mall, jumping over planters and kiosks, finding himself going against the flow of traffic as the mob of panicked parents were insistent on going the other way. Keith found himself stalled no matter which way he went.

There's a dozen exits out of a mall! Why does every lemming always pick the same one?

Not everyone, apparently, as Kelly had been aiming for a seldom used hall which exited into the upper parking lot. Now Keith saw Kelly a level above him, Benny at her side along with a dozen or so black-wearing goths that Keith could have recognized as vampire wannabes from a time-zone away. Kelly either didn't notice Keith or didn't care, but if he could get to some stairs he could get ahead of her. The running parents disagreed.

Get out of my way!

Pushing past one last clog of toddlers, Keith finally saw stairs to the second level. There were precious few people left in this section. If he vaulted up the stairs he could catch Kelly now! Keith pushed his endurance, aimed for the stairs with a leap, and—

POW

A punch in the gut sent Keith him sprawling all over the mall tile. Keith's chest heaved with loss of air as instinct pulled him back on his feet, only to be knocked down again. Keith's eyes shot around looking for his attacker. Where? That wasn't a witch or a monster or anything. It was—

Darryl, standing above Keith's heaving form wearing a black suit like a wannabe G-man, grabbing Keith's collar with a white-knuckle hand.

"Are you out of your damned mind?!?"

Mad as the 8th level of Hell.

"Are you really stupid enough to do what you just did? Tell me I didn't just see you throw your life away on a dance stage! Tell me!"

Two musclebound bouncers with no smiles manhandled Keith to his feet. He didn't resist yet, still trying to get air back into his lungs. Grunting, Keith saw Kelly pass the stairs and go out of sight towards the exit. Darryl had real lousy timing, his face burning with red anger.

"You're Bone-dork crazy! Losing the HallO'Scream was so bad? You had to throw on another monkey suit and jump on a dance stage to beg for attention like the mentally arrested lunatic you are?"

Keith twisted in the grip of two burly bouncers. I'm not even going to bother telling him what's going on. If I'm lucky he'd only throw me in a rubber room.

"Sorry old pal," Keith began with a wink. "I figured your Thriller could use some spice."

Darryl just snorted. "Keith, whatever stupidity brought you here, I'm glad. You're giving me the pleasure of putting you where you should have been years ago. If you're lucky you'll only get the psych ward."

Keith tested the grips of the bouncers, and smiled. These guys only knew enough to get themselves in trouble. Keith positioned his feet beneath him.

"You know, maybe I'm real glad you're here," Darryl said. "I get to tell you some good news personally. I get to impale it with a pitchfork to make it stick." He gestured to the bouncers to keep him still. "Can I tell you? We're going to salvage the HallO'Scream. A clean-up crew will be there in the morning. Going to throw out all your crud and make it into a dance floor. This is where you ask me what the hell you think I'm doing? But you've skipped that part so I'll tell you.

"I bought the HallO'Scream. It was never yours in the first place remember? Your brother-in-law held the title. Well he was aghast when he heard of the fire. When I told him about it anyway. He was mad that you couldn't be bothered to tell him. And when he learned how bad a loss it was...I made an offer and he accepted. It's mine now, and I'm now doing whatever I damn well please."

Darryl's naked spite was so thick it couldn't be cut with a lightsaber. Darryl had always treated his friends with scorched earth intolerance, but this was malevolent, and he wasn't done yet.

"Tomorrow we're having an even bigger party downtown," Darryl continued. "The biggest, baddest, most debauchery-ridden Halloween party this city has ever seen. $20 cover charge, and people will pay it. I am going to make so much filthy stinking money that I'll never have to share a business with any idiot ever again. You're welcome to come by. Oh wait. You're not."

Darryl has drank the Kool-Aid. Keith looked deep into the eyes of his former friend and didn't recognize a thing. A strange funk clung to him, something dank and vile. High above him in the skylights a sickening swirl of the clouds formed, growing more chaotic, more angry with each vindictive snarl out of Darryl's mouth, and getting lower...

Clippity Clop

Keith tensed just as Darryl delivered the coup de grace. "Hold him. I'm calling Security." Darryl flipped out his phone as rough hands started dragging Keith back. Keith gritted his teeth and set his weight. The bouncers were strong, but Keith was no stranger to pain. Neither to receiving it nor inflicting it.

Keith spoke as soon as Darryl's back was turned, "Darryl?" Keith asked as Darryl turned back around with impatience. "You know those times when I'm too tired to talk and you're too tired to listen and we both just blow up in an irrecoverable point of no return with physical violence?" Darryl stared at him in incomprehension as Keith smiled.

"This is one of those times."

Keith put a jumping front kick right into Darryl's nose.

Darryl flopped to the ground in a spray of his own blood as Keith spun a one-two backward kick in the shin of one of the bouncers and a back fist to the nose. That pushed him back for a second while the other bouncer continued forward out of momentum, separating the two of them long enough for Keith to wrap two hands around the other guys wrist and wrenching it backwards, winding the man's entire arm around his back. Done correctly the pressure points hurt like the blazes.

When you sink your knee into a gut at the same time, it's excruciating.

As one bouncer fell in a gasp holding his arm, the first one had recovered from Keith's sneak attack and threw two meaty hands at him. Which of course left his knees exposed again, which Keith kicked out from under him. The man fell to his knees and Keith struck an open palm flat against his nose, making sure the man fell down and stayed down. He did. As for the other one, Keith grabbed his head by the hair with one hand and gave him a full punch to the face with his other, flopping him with a poof into a nearby planter.

Keith took a moment to give Darryl's writhing form a parting glance. "Sorry, I do believe that permanently ends our partnership," he said, and took off full speed up the stairs to the second floor, three steps at a time.

Benny was gone.

Everyone was gone. The hall stood totally empty and still except for some glass doors that slowly drifted shut. Keith ran through them and into the parking lot outside.

This part of the mall lot lay on an incline, the parking lot dropping down to the more populated areas below. Up here, on the far end, there was no one. No parked cars, no milling people. Just Keith.

Clippity Clop.

That too. Keith didn't want to know where that was coming from. He heard commotion behind him, someone coming out of the mall, but didn't look at that either. Maybe it was Darryl's knuckle draggers, but Keith had already put the parking lot behind him, leaping towards a chain link fence separating the mall property from the undeveloped land beyond. Open fields with movement in them. Keith could see tiny figures moving deep into the fields. There was nothing that way but abandoned farmland and dead trees. *Why the hell would she take them out there?* Didn't matter, that's where Benny was so Keith went there too. Keith's feet hit bare earth as he ran towards the figures, away from the mall's ambient light. The darkness stretched around him, the noise of the city being pulled away from him in a blur as the clouds moved faster and the wind breathed harder, pulling Keith deeper and deeper into pure black, with only a single moon staring down on him.

Living within an arms reach of a light switch breeds laziness. One doesn't remember what black is like, true black that reveals how much the light hides from you, a black that paradoxically lets you see farther than the light ever could. The dome of the sky soared unfathomable miles above Keith, a vast ocean of empty so deep that it drowns mere mortals in panic, as they finally see exactly how far away they are from anything. After the sensory assault of living haunted houses, walls of laugh masks, and a crayon box overload of ghosts at the mall, Keith had to stop and just look at the sky. Milky ribbons of clouds highlighted by a silver moon.

A moon which cast shadows moving all around him. Blurry figures that vanished when Keith looked directly at them. Ghosts. Keith could feel them as a pressure against his soul, as a black stench that wouldn't go away. The Veil was whisper thin, the *Other Side* was bleeding through.

Clippity Clop.

The Veil would drop again. Keith could feel it and he had to get Benny out of here before it did. His face was already bloody.

Don't think about that! Keith didn't think he would panic, he wouldn't dare. Not even when he was attacked by a black figure jumping out of the dead grass, snarling with claws that raked Keith's neck.

That's no ghost! But Keith had no time to argue as the black shadow pounced on him, squeezing its legs around Keith's midsection and pummeling his face with strikes from clawed hands. *WHAT THE HELL?* But Keith's muscle-memory took over, years of martial arts training had him grabbing a wrist before the next attack landed, twisted the hand the wrong way and driving the attacker to the grass in pain. Keith sent his other hand directly into the assailants head and his right foot in a cut-kick into its gut for good measure. The form gurgled and collapsed face-first into the grass, heaving. Keith bent down to get a good look at whatever-it-was, his eyes finally adjusted to the moonlight. He saw this wasn't any vicious saber-toothed beast from Celtic legend.

It was a weak, skinny teenager. Pasty pale. Dressed entirely in black with dyed hair and phony plastic fangs. A vampire.

"Are you serious?" Keith said to the night. But a vampire was exactly what this was. A half dead one, judging by its malnutrition.

CRUNCH.

It wasn't alone. Silhouetted against the darkness, Keith saw himself surrounded by four more, circling him like vultures, heaving with exaggerated breath of wild animals. In the moonlight, Keith could see ivory fangs inside the growling mouths.

They really think they're vampires. Good God.

But Keith couldn't stop to save them. He already survived a dead city of ghosts, an attack by bloodthirsty spirits, and a consumerist living hell. He would not be delayed by any of these losers.

Clippity Clop

Especially now.

The clouds above him spun faster and faster, eating the horizon under a thick fog. Keith looked upward to see angry broiling thunderheads, pushed on the heels of an icy autumn wind howling through the field. Inside the gusts, Keith could hear voices, moans. Time was nearly up.

Clippity Clop

The vampires growled as they stepped into Keith's range.

"I *really* hope you idiots are here to start a fight," Keith said as he cracked his knuckles and the figures sprang.

FORTY-TWO

BENNY COULD BARELY KEEP his eyes open as Kelly pulled him through the running crowd. Panicked people shoved him from all sides, but he felt nothing. His limbs were slowly going numb. The crowd soon disappeared as Kelly took him out a back entrance of the mall. The newly-developed mall lay on the outskirts of the city, opening up to the empty acreage of the black beyond. Mountains peeked up as silhouettes in the distance and Benny saw stars twinkling between streamers of clouds, streaking the sky in moonlight silver.

Like the streaks of spirits...

Kelly pulled him along. Members of her vampire horde bumped him as they ran beside her, but he barely noticed. He just wanted to lie down and sleep, for long, long time. *Why are we going so fast? And—*

"Was that Keith back there?" Benny barely had the strength to ask. Kelly slowed only for a half-second to answer him in gritted frustration.

"Yes."

"Why can't we—"

"Your uncle is pushing me faster than I wanted. He just won't lay down and die. I was saving this for tomorrow, but out here will do. Perfectly."

Hate. Benny could feel Kelly's radiating hate like a burning sun. But she said nothing more as several members of the vampire party ran ahead in various directions into the field. Ahead Benny could see even *more* vampires, laughing, sloshing, ignorant masses with mussy hair and perfectly corny fangs. A whole crowd of them.

"They're here for me, young MacCumhaill," Kelly said as if she could read his mind. Kelly pulled him through the crowd and up a pile of broken concrete in the middle of nowhere, an abandoned public works station perhaps. Kelly climbed to the top of the jagged chunks, keeping Benny close to her side. The vampires stayed below. *We're alone up here.*

No, Benny wasn't alone. Benny could see wispy figures. Ghosts, pronounced against the black field below them. Benny could feel them coming through the fields. His strength barely let him stand, but the sight fascinated him, dozens of flickering figures just walking along. So many ghosts, in all directions. *The Other Side is bleeding through.*

One of them looked right at him. Bridget. At the bottom of the pile.

She reached for Benny in desperation, pleading for him with her eyes. Benny stepped toward the reflection of his sister, seeing her as a shiny object in a sea of black. Her mouth moved. *She's trying to speak.* Bridget's form was so clear that Benny could almost lip-read her. Three words. Saying them over and over.

Last To Die

What...?

Benny almost had enough of his will left to grasp her, but Bridget's form gave a silent scream as an unseen wind ripped her away, and Kelly stepped into his vision.

"No Benny, your sister is too late." Kelly held his head in soft hands, viewing the dead masses around him. "A long time ago, a MacCumhaill took this night away from me. But now he's gone."

261

Benny could barely understand her. Her face lay at the end of a long tunnel that took every effort to see the end of.

"And you're only a pale jest of what he was."

Benny's vision returned, revealing a solitary figure in a black-leather jacket running across the field. Towards him.

"Yes, Benny, that's your uncle. He's come here to save you with the same mule-headed arrogance of your ancestor of old. I never guessed that sensation would be so delectable."

Benny watched his uncle get closer, eyes widening when Keith got dog-piled under a storm of Kelly's vampires. Kelly laughed. "Yes, my friends wished to be monsters. Wished to sacrifice their grace for transparent power. That's how shallow your 'Halloween' is."

Benny's eyesight blurred as the *pressure* of the Veil closed in on them all. It pressed into the space behind his eyes, forcing them closed in pain.

POP

Benny's eyes opened to see Kelly, for the first time. Her form lay cloaked in a gray mass of charcoal smoke, shrouding her in wispy tendrils. The tendrils reached across the field and were embedded the chests of every vampire, beating in tune with their heart, sucking energy away. Into Kelly.

Benny looked down into his own chest, to see a smoky tendril embedded there as well, leading to the mass surrounding Kelly.

Feeding her.

Kelly followed his line of sight and spoke.

"And you're the tastiest one of them all."

SEVERAL BODIES SMASHED KEITH from multiple directions, snarling with extended fangs and excruciating corniness. Keith almost fell over under the weight of it all, except—

These guys couldn't bite their way out of a bag of Cheetos.

As an arm lashed outward to slice Keith's face, he side-stepped it, grabbing the wrist and yanking the rest of the body over his outstretched leg. The "vampire" tripped over the ground, taking another wannabe with him. From the other side, two hands shot out to strangle Keith, who countered by smashing the flat of his palm against the attacker's nose. Blood flew liberally as Keith kicked the knee of another attacker behind him, and connected a punch into the eye of a black shadow to his front.

All four attackers now lay on the ground, silently. No groans or yelps of agony, just heaps of vampire cliché. Keith surveyed the mass of maximum corny overload, kneeling down to see skinny, lily white boys with pockmarked skin and protruding ribs. All were totally unresponsive.

These guys are all half dead.

Keith knew why, but also knew he couldn't help them. He was here for Benny. He was out here somewhere with Kelly, and Kelly would be—

Staring at him.

Kelly stood on the pile of broken concrete holding Benny. More 'vampires' stood around her, completely blank-eyed. The wind picked up, billowing dust across the field. Kelly's hair blew in a flurry of green dreadlocks. Keith might have found it fascinating except, ghosts started rising, clouds started spinning faster, and the invokable *PUSH* on Keith's middle ear told him all too loud that he was out of time.

Clippity Clop.

Kelly spoke first.

"Worthless shells. You have no more sympathy for them than I do, no more than you give yourself."

Live your lie and perish! flashed into Keith's head. He pushed against it. He was getting Benny out of here, and didn't care to respond to anything Kelly said. He stepped forward, but had to YELP as something sharp dug into his ankle, which Keith jerked away to see one of the vampires crawling for him. His eyes were blank as midnight, and—

God they look even thinner. As the broken vampires clambered to their feet, Keith blanched. They *were* getting thinner! Muscle dis-

263

appeared as their bodies emaciated before his eyes, showing bones pushing against malnourished skin.

Their bodies are burning up, consuming themselves.

As Keith watched, brows mutated into demonic points, creating faces of vicious hatred. Fangs and ears grew to preposterous lengths as the *Nosferatu* face took hold, the face of mindless hunger betraying no higher thought. These were what vampires were supposed to look like, and they were not pretty.

Keith looked to Benny, who looked every bit as blank-eyed. Kelly laughed even as the wind started to howl in fury.

"Yes, they got exactly what they wished for. Have you earned any less, Elder MacCumhaill? A mortal who wishes he were dead can commit no greater sin!" Kelly almost had to scream to be heard over the wind.

Keith just stared back. "Maybe I don't want to die just yet."

Kelly laughed. "Don't you know where you are? These are the fields, MacCumhaill. The Puka rules the fields! And the Puka demands tribute!"

>CLICK<

Keith stumbled, looking around. He saw it just out of the fog between him and Benny, a whipping mane of hair surrounding an elongated head and red eyes. Keith felt the Puka bore through his head. He knew he couldn't stand up to it again. Kelly saw his pain and jeered.

"I give him YOU!"

>CLICK<

Not this time! Keith couldn't succumb! He wouldn't. He had but one moment to gasp before *black* pressed on his soul as the realms merged so much stronger than ever before. Nothing would stop it this time.

CLIPPITY CLOP

CLIPPITY—

Keith felt the rush as the headless rider charged through the field. The Dullahan rode a wave of gray mist, bowling through the field with the power of a steam engine, smashing grass, dislodging rocks that flew into everyone's eyes, laughing hysterically as it passed by. Keith didn't need bother to look who had been marked, the vampires now all sported faces of fresh dripping red.

Just like Benny.

Above them all, the bubbling clouds burst open to release the *sluagh*, pouring out as a flood of screaming black inky phantoms. Their shrieks merged into a single *howl* as the mass spiraled down to the open field, a vortex of screams and white glowing eyes.

Keith ran to Benny.

>*CLICK*<

The Puka wouldn't let him get there. Out of the mist, SHE formed again. A decrepit corpse of gray skin stretched over crackling bones. Her ferocious yellow eyes locked him down with the accusation of the grave, where Keith had unwittingly put her.

>*CLICK*<

Pain. The shattering of ones skull as a bullet penetrates the bone. Keith had been grinding his teeth in that nightmare night after night.

>*CLICK*<

Driven from his career, driven into a huddle on his brother-in-law's couch, Keith had hid from anything that carried the memory.

>*CLICK*<

Keith's head swirled with images of gun flashes, especially the one behind his ear-

>*CLICK*<

No. If I die, Benny dies too.

>*CLICK*<

HELL NO! Keith kept running even as the vampires surged around him and the flesh-rending *Sluagh* dove upon him. He would not crack!

LIVE YOUR LIE.

Not this time. It took the threat of his nephew's demise for Keith to finally admit his lie. Keith was a coward. Terrified of failure. Failure had ruined his whole life.

But it wouldn't ruin tonight.

A dead Benny scared him even more than failure. Keith filled his mind with Benny's bloody face from the mall, the face marking him for death. Keith filled the image with every emotion he could summon, making his Mind's Eye so vivid that it brought tears to his eyes.

One fear blocked the other. The Puka couldn't touch him.

With a roar of emotion Keith screamed, a blast of fear so great that it ripped open the *Other Side* itself, tearing his Scream tattoo off his neck as a living breathing manifestation, and blasting the Puka right in its demonic eyes.

It hurt.

A howl of pain raged Keith's ears as the Puka fell back into the fog. Keith couldn't wait to see if it came back. He would be damned if he just sat here drooling like an idiot as his nephew died. Keith ran for him.

Just as the tsunami of *Sluagh* hit the vampires.

VAMPIRES. THAT'S ALL BENNY had time to think before the cloud bank exploded into a black wave of demon-ghosts.

The "Vampires," now grotesque mutations with pointy ears, knobby chins and gnarly hands, hissed at the ghosts with challenge and fury. Vampires were the champions of bloodthirsty strength! As the *sluagh* charged them, they raised their clawed hands to strike—

And were torn to pieces.

An ocean of *Sluagh* smothered the wannabes like sand castles in a tide. Bloody body parts flew through the air as the spirits wove around the field in a constriction of screams. Watching the massacre from his prime position, Benny could see Kelly waving her arms over the field as the broken corpses released their spirits and ghosts of the vampires floated upward, mouthing silent screams. Wreathed in a black aura, Kelly grabbed the closest ghost by the ankle and pulled the writhing spirit toward her.

She consumed it.

The blue flicker of the ghost faded into a sickly green before Kelly's black aura completely absorbed it. Her face glowed with delight as she leaned into Benny, filling the air with lavender scent.

"Life molds death." She took his face in her hands and pulled him close. "Life's final purpose is to die. So now imagine all the life of the MacCumhaill clan, trapped in one frail little form."

Surrounded by a hundred screaming phantoms howling for blood, all Benny could see were Kelly's luminous green eyes. "Imagine what I can achieve when I mold you. When ..." Kelly's face reached up to his—and she kissed him. A full lip lock with tongue. She then pulled back with a leer in her eye.

"When you are the LAST TO DIE!"

Kelly pushed Benny off the stones into the fog of death below.

KEITH SCREAMED AS KELLY hurled Benny over the side.

Benny hit the ground with a wet thud, surrounded by the still constricting circle of *Sluagh*. Keith was close but a thousand greedy eyes were closer, shrieking as they saw him leave Kelly's protection. Keith didn't know how to get Benny out of here, he didn't even know how he could save himself.

You're going to fail again. AGAIN!

But he did know that he sure as hell was not going to watch his nephew die right in front of him. Eating the distance to Benny in seconds, he looped an arm around Benny's chest and scooped him up, still running, hopefully in the direction with the fewest monsters. Behind him the phantoms shrieked with anger and closed in. If he could just break out of the fog—

He wouldn't. The *sluagh* surrounded him. In his mad dash he stepped on the bodies of the shattered vampires, their spirits still rising from them. The Veil had stretched further into mortal land than ever before. Keith ran, but Benny didn't help, squirming with incoherence under his arm. He was....reaching for Kelly?

"We can't leave..." Benny's eyes were wide.

Kelly is still attached to him! Keith screamed to himself. Only one way to break it. Keith twisted Benny's face in a free hand to lock their eyes together.

"THAT'S NOT KELLY!"

One more ghost materialized right in front of them.

And time stopped.

Keith and Benny stood in the eye of the storm.

With Bridget.

Benny's sister moved between them and the Sluagh. Still holding Benny tight, Keith saw another form appeared beside her, a human form. Keith had seen this other one before. In the dead city.

Kelly.

A flickering ghost of Kelly, still wearing the ratty Levi jacket she wore when Bridget crashed last year, the crash that Kelly had survived.

Except if she hadn't.

Her ghost stood in front of all of them. Keith saw Benny's eyes snap open. He knew. Bridget died in that crash.

Kelly had died too.

Ghost-Kelly raised her arm of ghostly white and pointed across the field at the Other-Kelly, the Kelly who had been watching Benny for a year and now all of sudden wormed her way into his life right just in time for Halloween. The Kelly who had brought him here tonight.

Time started again.

The shrieks of Not-Kelly blasted pulses through the fog.

"Kill the MacCool!"

A hundred tortured forms of *sluagh* turned their eyes on a single uncle and a nephew. But Keith didn't see them, he saw Bridget, saw her ghost lift a single finger to a rip in the fog.

A portal.

In front of them, a swirling mass of clouds opened up. Through it Keith saw the magnificent desolation of the *Other Side* that he had escaped only an hour before. Around him the outstretched claws of

268

the *sluagh* shined as sickles in black water, seconds from drowning him. He could never escape by going back.

So he escaped forward.

Keith hurled himself and Benny into the portal. The instant he did a hurricane gale caught Keith and Benny both, sweeping them up and away. Not-Kelly shrieked in anger, but couldn't follow as the portal closed in her face immediately behind Keith. His own sight was then lost entirely as the winds pulled him faster into the desolate realm, the wind screaming in his ears-

YOU DON'T BELONG HERE!

The dead world spun without purpose or direction, assaulting with nausea and vertigo. There is no up. No down. No land.

NO MORTAL BELONGS HERE!

Falling.

Keith hit the ground in a cloud of dust, Benny next to him. They were under a cold blue twilight sky, with cold dirt beneath them. There were no people. No monsters either. But every tingle through Keith's body told him he absolutely *did not belong here.*

But they were here.

Keith had just trapped himself and his nephew on the *Other Side.*

Unconsciousness took them both.

Somewhere Else

The sun went down on the third day. Finn stared at a sunset stained with filthy orange.

Mother Earth screamed as the Veil was torn open yet again.

From beyond a small vale, the cries of death reached his ears. A funeral, a father being laid to rest. But the families' eye's shifted in fear around the woods. They knew what night this was. The Sunset stretched into purple, and a howl rumbled through the dark woods.

The family retreated, making no sound as they stepped back to small homes where gourds already burned with eyes of flame. Whispering to themselves, Finn heard one phrase dared not spoken aloud.

"Last to die."

The sun sunk behind the mountain as the people hid behind their locked doors. Finn knew he shouldn't stay, but the grave, the father...

Moved.

An arm of silky smoke arose from the loose earth, rising into an apparition with the face of the father. Finn watched as The Last to Die took his place.

Samhain could now conclude.

"Benny! Where do you think you're going?"

Midnight movie.

"What in god's name is playing on Thanksgiving night?"

"Dark City. The Directors Cut."

"..."

In honor of Black Friday.

"Expecting to meet a lot of girls there?"

I expect to have fun without cracking under the pressure of exchanging phony social pleasantries. Besides, my hermit nature precludes me from getting any communicable disease.

"Dad wants you to meet people."

If Dad cared, he'd pretend he actually lived here.

"You're parroting Keith again."

Keith actually asks me what I want to do, instead of making domineering demands.

"Can't you get any friends your own age?"

What do you care? Aren't you a Black Friday lemming? Who waits in line at midnight to buy jeans? You give me a double standard and I'll choke you with it.

"I'm only driving Kelly somewhere."

Well, don't get in a wreck. That would be a crying shame.

FORTY-THREE

BENNY GASPED FOR HIS life, his eyes opening against cold dirt. His fingers dug into dust clods as he pushed himself up with the caution of the grave.

Where am I?

His only answer was an overcast sky with angry blue streaks, a fantastic churning of violent thunder funnels that formed in thick silence, then spinning away into wisps.

Benny found himself in the plain of a dead valley, amidst roots of scraggly trees pushing themselves out of the dead earth. No color of any kind, and even Benny's own hands looked...gray. A pale murk clung to the entire landscape. A chill breeze created tiny dust devils, wisps that spun before dying in whispering mutters. The breeze carried voices right at the edge of hearing, but in no language from Benny's world.

Because Benny wasn't in *Benny's* world.

A *buzz* pushed against his consciousness. The whole panorama oppressed him, racing his heart as the clouds hurled violently above him.

Tha Thump Tha Thump

273

Benny's gaze lost itself in the undulating storm clouds, inducing vertigo and chest pumping nausea.

Tha Thump Tha thump

An angry purple twirl spun itself out of nothing right above his head. Twisting tendrils powered by hurricane winds pressed Benny back against the cold clods of Earth. The tendrils formed into teeth. A mouth. Fangs.

Tha Thump Tha thump.

The fangs parted in vicious promise of pain, morphing into a figure of a skull with Kelly's face. A skull that would consume him.

Close your eyes! Benny flipped to the ground and squeezed his eyes against the clouds coming for him, his heart threatening to blow up inside his chest.

STOP!

Stop.

Tha Thump.

A heart. Benny's heart, starting back up. He opened his eyes and spit out a flick of dirt as he turned himself back over. The fangs were gone. Benny could hear his own thoughts again, and remembered it all. The vampires, the field.

The smoky tendril embedded in his chest! Benny frantically tore his shirt up to feel his skin beneath. It was gone.

But Kelly had almost killed him.

That's when the shadow fell over him. Benny almost ran, but it came into focus, and he relaxed.

Keith.

"WHAT DO YOU REMEMBER?" Keith asked.

How long had it been since he had seen Keith? *Seems like days.* His memory of last night came as a smudge of someone else's voice. He almost had trouble remembering who Keith was.

She had tried to block him out. Make me forget. So what did Benny remember? In the churning twilight, Benny relived the previous night, every ghastly piece of it: the mall, Marcus, the blazing fury, then the exhaustion, his life almost drained out.

"Everything."

Keith helped him up. When they touched a dust devil ringed about their feet, catching the earth and spinning specks of dirt high that expanded into a gaping mouth with arms that reached for the both of them... before collapsing in a puff of dust. Benny swallowed. He had every reason to be unnerved. He had almost entered this place last night. Permanently. Benny ached as life slowly reentered cold limbs. *Feels like my body is starting back up.*

"Don't move too fast," Keith said. "You're only running on half a tank."

More dust devils spun off around them. In the distance, twisters the size of mountains roared with ferocious anger, spinning themselves into nothing only to reappear over and over. But that wasn't the interesting part. Keith stood beside him as a vortex spun up very close to them, creating shapes, merging forms. "Keep looking," Keith said, "You know exactly what that is."

Benny's eyes widened, "That's..."

"A ghost," Keith finished.

A ghost, an honest to God ghost. Out of the swirling dust it formed a pale-white spectral form, with blank white eyes that stared right through them. Odd that after being chased by vampires and trapped inside his own haunted house, Benny would now shudder over seeing a mere ghost, but... *This one is real.*

The ghost spun itself away as more appeared, taking transparent forms all around them. The more that appeared, the more substantial they became. Benny could make out clothes, and cars? Buildings? Hazy after-reflections, like very old movies, visible only in the dust kicked up by their whirlwinds:

A woman, mid 30's, dressed in a modern business suit. Couldn't tell the color as she drifted in and out of sight as she walked across their path. She didn't look up at either Benny or Keith, didn't seem to notice anything at all, talking on what appeared to be a cell phone. She appeared to step *down*, must have been off a curb.

Then looked up as a car struck her out of nowhere. Her body shattered into motes of dust, leaving behind only the wind whispering in their ears. Benny gawked, but understood.

"The hit and run last week... by the mall." He recognized her from school. She had been a volunteer.

"The mom who got killed," Keith finished.

Another image spun up. A trio of boys wearing football jerseys in the back of a pickup, hooting and hollering away with a beer in every hand. The pickup was a specter of ghostly noise, spinning through the dirt in obvious drunken abandon.

Before crashing into an unseen obstacle, throwing the teenagers in back to the hard pavement. Two of them cried out. One didn't.

"The DUI. Riverbend football game," Keith said as the pickup and two other boys vanished, leaving the unmoving one on the ground for few seconds longer until the wind picked up and blew the image away like so much chalk dust. And more images appeared, one after another.

An old man in bed surrounded by his family.

A burglar being shot in a home invasion.

An accident victim in an ER.

The end of life. Recorded here. Stored where the ghosts lived forever. But none of them betrayed any awareness of Keith or Benny. They appeared, then disappeared leaving Keith and Benny alone with the wind.

Ghostland.

Keith took a slow spin, categorizing the panorama with his encyclopedic memory. "The Irish Other Side." Benny looked confused, so Keith couldn't resist. "Well, what you were expecting? A line of Irish step dancers?"

Benny scowled, looking around. "So where is our world?"

"On the 'other' Other side."

"How do we get back?"

"This exact second, we don't want to. Kelly and her cast of thousands are back there waiting for us."

Screaming spirits, clawing, screeching. Benny shivered with revulsion. No, they couldn't go back the way they came. "But won't they find us here? They've pulled us here before, the HallO'Scream—"

"Was only a tiny pocket of this universe, shaped to their desire. This time someone *else* opened the Veil. We're in a time and place of our own choosing. Real Ghostland, not their funhouse version. They have no idea where we could have landed, and this is a big world, getting bigger the closer we get to Halloween. No, I don't think they'll find us for a good long time."

Benny breathed easier. Keith's confidence was contagious. Meanwhile, more ghosts fluttered by. Benny tried to count but then saw specific faces and sucked in his breath.

"These people, they're ours. I mean, I know them."

There, fluttering by...

Jack. Still in his Sparrow outfit.

Then Connor. Dumb smile on his face.

And Quentin. As Spiderman, bringing flashbacks to Benny's eyes. He felt Keith's steady hand on his shoulder.

"Everyone who died in the last year. They're all here, waiting to move on. From one Halloween to the next."

Every death for a year. Benny started getting dizzy from the swirling scenes. How many people die in an average American city in a year? How many crime victims? How many accidents? How many did death claim in a year?

Clippity clop

Oh no. Horse hooves came over the horizon and Benny spun around in a panic, eyes-wide to catch an undead horse running hell bent for leather through the valley, spurred by a rider carrying a screaming head in his hand. The Dullahan approached, and... disappeared over the ridge, rippling like a mirage. Off to mark the next "accident." This time Benny's queasiness didn't go away.

"He can't get us." Keith said, following the Dullahan. "We're already here."

Benny exhaled and just took a moment. In the gray light he looked at himself and realized he looked like he had crawled a mile on his hands and knees: ravaged hair, disheveled clothes, scratched and torn skin.

"He marked me."

"Yes, he did."

"So why did he just ride off? I'm supposed to die! Supposed to..."

"Cross to the Other Side? But you did. You're across it now."

Benny gripped his hands in front of his face, staring off into the dead land, "I'm across, but..."

"You're not dead? Well it certainly would have made the crossing easier. But you were marked to cross over, and you did. No one ever said that you had to *die* to do it."

That made a perverse amount of sense.

"I wish I had thought of it, but it wasn't my idea," Keith said. "It was hers."

Benny looked up. *Hers?*

Then it hit him. *Accidents in the last year. Oh no. He couldn't face that.*

Too late. Benny's eyes caught another dust devil expanding into another spent life. He hadn't been there when it happened, but he knew exactly what it was.

The death of his sister.

Oh lord no. In a bath of gray dust, the scene played out right in front of him.

A blue sedan, driving to the mall.

Inside: Bridget and Kelly, laughing about whatever girls laugh about. Bridget in the driver's seat. Good driver. She had never been in an accident.

She is going to be.

The car takes a simple left turn— and is smashed by a red pickup running the red light. Crunched metal spins end over end, stopping in a heap of jagged metal. The pickup is also a catastrophic ruin.

People run to the car in futile rescue... But Bridget...Bridget was already gone. Benny knew beyond any doubt. So sudden, no chance for pain. That relieved him. Now from the twisted heap, her form arose. Not her body, which remained imprisoned in a pretzel of metal.

This was her ghost.

A pale transparent wisp of a form, looking at the scene around her. She knew what she was, fluttered above the scurrying crowd, an invisible presence watching the mortals free her shattered body.

Then another form rose from the wreck, a form which Benny recognized all too well. Benny had wondered how Kelly had survived when Bridget had died. So simple now.

She hadn't. No one had survived the crash. No one at all.

As a spirit of pure white, Kelly's spirit joined Bridget's as the Veil opened behind them. They understood they had no more place in mortal land, and floated toward the portal.

Until something came out *of it.*

A black robed shadow shot out of the Veil with a howl of triumph. A spirit of sickening darkness, radiating black essence that repulsed Kelly and Bridget. This was no ghost.

This was a theft.

The black shadow screeched as it circled the wreck of the car, its substance fouled the very air and made the rescue workers shiver with a chill. Then the form slipped inside the car, smothering one of the bodies in blackest smut.

A body which now breathed in a shuddering gasp.

Kelly lived. Her broken, bloodied form entered an ambulance which sped away with whirling lights. Inside, she just managed to smile...

Leaving the ghosts behind. The Veil still flickered, but they didn't enter. They couldn't. Not now. The wispy forms of Bridget and Kelly rose above the wreckage of jabbering mortals and floating up and away. Benny knew the direction Bridget took.

She went home.

And Benny would have his first dream of his dead sister that very night.

POP. Benny collapsed.

Kelly. For the entire year, all the times he'd watched her across the hall, across the room. He spoke, shuddering.

"Kelly never made it out of the car."

"No," Keith answered. "But something made it *into* the car. Something just waiting for a chance to bust across the boundary, but someone needed to die to open the door."

"How did you know?"

Keith breathed in, remembering. "They pulled me in here again when I tried to chase after you. I saw every ghost from the last year. ALL of them." Keith stiffened.

"Kelly."

"Yes," Keith got serious. "Kelly's ghost. She's here. She's been here as long as Bridget has. The "Kelly" we left behind is something else, something that's been stalking us for a year. Ever since..."

"Since..." Benny repeated, and around them the landscape dissolved, with another scene taking its place. Many others, a hundred images all layered on top of each other, a whirlwind history of the last year.

Kelly's year.

Benny saw her in the hospital, then going home, going to school, meeting with friends. He saw more than just her, he saw beneath her skin, saw a *black* wriggling through her veins, a black that corrupted every one she touched, leaving behind invisible tendrils that drained them of their will and strength.

Benny saw Kelly with friends at school, friends who then got sick for weeks at a time.

Benny saw her weaving her way into the vampire troop, consorting with them at midnight beer binges, leaving behind pulsing *funk* inside each of their auras. And then...

"Darryl," Keith muttered. Yes, Kelly had infected Darryl. Almost from the beginning, at a forgotten meeting last spring. "That explains more than I wanted. His rampant greed makes more sense now," Keith continued. Kelly had gone after Darryl considerably. The black funk on his aura was wild and nauseating, sending an invisible tentacle back to Kelly over the magic of the *Other Side*, feeding off of Darryl's greed and anger. "He never had a chance," Keith was almost sentimental as the images caught up with present time and spun themselves away.

"Why him?" Benny asked.

"To drive a wedge between us I imagine, and because she could. Just in time for Halloween."

Benny watched the last images drift away into the distance. Now he had nothing but his thoughts of the last few days, of everyone who had died. And his sister. The frustration of it all finally blasted out.

"What did we do to deserve all this?" Benny nearly yelled.

Keith shrugged. "We're MacCools. Saviors of Halloween. And looks like we're going to save it again."

Benny frowned. Trapped in a world of ghosts with no sun, no light, and a hundred thousand salivating monsters just waiting to eat them alive, Benny did not share his overoptimistic appraisal of the situation.

"Why us? There must a million MacCools in the world!"

"Maybe they're all dead too," Keith said. "How would we know? You can't even get your Dad to call you on the phone, so what would we know about a 3rd cousin 3000 miles away?"

Benny considered as Keith continued.

"Maybe we're not the first. Maybe she's already killed God knows how many," Keith slowed. "And we're just the first ones who survived the first round."

"Survived so far," Benny remarked as more aches throbbed through him. *I can't face anyone like this.*

"It's not us against the world," Keith said, seeing Benny's pain. "We have help. This is as much her idea as mine." Keith pointed over Benny's shoulder.

Bridget stood behind him, watching.

The fear seized Benny's heart again as he fought for control. *It's your sister. You shouldn't be afraid of her.* But he *was* afraid. The way her mouth opened but couldn't speak, the way her eyes just pleaded, it had scared him for days. But now...Benny had time to look at her, just look, and see her for what she was. This wasn't a creaking floor in a darkened empty house. This was his sister.

And he missed her.

The fear faded, and he could finally grieve. He could never be scared of her again. Staring at each other, the wispy ghost of Bridget...smiled. Then turned, waving for Benny and Keith to follow.

"She wants to show us something." Even as Keith's words left his mouth, more spirits appeared, shuffling through the horizon, end to end.

"Is she showing us the way out?" Benny asked.

"Not yet. No hurry."

"No hurry?"

Keith gestured towards the road. "Trust your sister. She brought us here."

Benny looked down the way. The cold field eventually gave way to a road of sorts, flanked by dead trees with skeletal branches the swayed in the chill wind. Benny walked after his sister.

The ghosts followed.

FORTY-FOUR

TIME MEANT NOTHING IN this land of the dead. Purple clouds churned in silence as ghostly images flickered in the periphery. They made Benny's skin prickle. Even more curious, even after walking for a while, Benny felt no pain, no hunger, no thirst. *But then in this place, who did?*

Scratch that, he did feel something. Anger. Endless walking gave him plenty of time to get mad. About Kelly. The landscape didn't care one way or another. The dust devils had ceased, giving way to rolling fog in fields of dead grass. Every once in a while a foggy tendril took a humanoid shape before being whisked away by the wind. Bridget still led the way. Benny was lost in thought until—

"The ghosts are getting older," Keith remarked. Benny noticed the same thing. The phantoms appeared in clothes from decades past. Cars and trucks also aged, turning into relics from the 1930's, the Halloween of old. Kids dressed as raggedy scarecrows, eyes peaking out from burlap sacks. Others wore masks of cats and witches, misshapen from lumpy paper mache'.

"I've seen this before," Benny said.

"My photos on the 2nd floor. Told you they were creepy," Keith replied, with a smile.

Yes, that particular candle-lit hallway always gave Benny the creeps, now he saw those old kids running through old streets, laughing under a quiet harvest sky. They had made their costumes with whatever was lying around, old sheets, old bags. Labors of love. As fast as they appeared, more history overtook them, cars giving way to horse-drawn wagons, cities disappearing into rural cottages. *The history of the world.* Benny watched as much as the dusty images appeared disappeared faster than he could see.

"They're forming behind us," Keith announced, prompting a start from Benny as he turned around to look, seeing nothing behind them.

"Where?"

Keith kept his eyes on the sunset. "Keep looking."

Benny looked again at the road vanishing into twilight behind them. Two opposing ranges of mountains rose up to either side, their peaks merging into the churning clouds and shadows.

Wait, the shadows...*they were moving.*

Not just one shadow, but hundreds of ghostly figures, merged into a single shadowy mass. Benny turning back around.

"How long have they been there?"

"For a while now. They're slowly gaining on us."

"Then walk faster."

"They're not here for us. Look."

Ahead the road was about to crest a hill. The landscape gave way to sloping hills. And nestled inside them:

"A house."

No, a *cottage.* A rustic one-room cottage, and another, and another. An entire village rising out of the dust, built of crude wood and stone from centuries past, just as transparent as the ghosts who occupied it. A ghost town. Literally.

"Keep your cool, they're moving in."

The shadows formed into dark ghostly figures, getting clearer the closer they became. Keith pulled Benny aside, off the beaten

284

path into grasses as the shadowy figures undulated towards them. "Give them the road."

Benny clenched, but Bridget caught his eyes and Keith spoke for her. "We're safe, they're just going home."

Safe. Benny tensed as the ghosts passed through them with only brushes of cold. These weren't Dark Side specters, these were regular people, living, working. As they flowed into their ghostly village they took up axes, folded linen, rustled children around in their families. Benny saw they wore tunics, leather pants as if they came from 1000 years ago. Which Benny supposed they did. Each ghost had an entire lifetime on which to draw, and acted out every memory of their lives.

Maybe memories were the only thing of value in this place. Memories about a life well spent. Like Kelly said, it's about sensations. Using it while you have it.

But the village vanished in the wind, leaving only the hills. Keith moved back to the empty road, "They were thicker that time."

Benny had an idea why. "Maybe the longer we're here, the more we're capable of seeing. Maybe the more they want us to see." As they continued to follow Bridget down the road, more images appeared, more families, more lives played out like an old video tape that didn't know anyone was watching. It was hard to think of them as ghosts anymore, the people now had flesh in their cheeks, color in their hair, and the air began to carry the sounds of life, of people laughing and loving as the seasons turned around them. The images now caught winter changing to spring then to summer. But even through these illusions, Benny could still feel the tingle of autumn.

It's always autumn here. And they're still getting thicker.

The flurry of activity made that all the more blatant. A close-up of a particular time:

The Harvest, the bounty of the year. The families collected it in the fields, then brought it home where the hearth fires were stoked and the people gathered. Everyone helped at this most special time of the year.

Until night fell. Then the laughter stopped. Glances peered away from their homes across the hills and woods. Children stayed close to parents as every face now traced the path of the sun, dying in the west. *They're afraid.* But they had a purpose. Every family had a pile of gray roots, strange vegetables that they attacked with knives, carving them into hollow forms with faces. Families sat together carving face after face.

No. They're carving skulls.

Dozens of skulls, in front of every door and window even as the sun continued to sink and the sky turned from a loving blue to a sickly black. One by one, the families carried out burning animal fat from their home fire and dropped them in the skulls. Every family now held guard. Guarding against...

"It's the end of Autumn," Keith said to the silent air. "You know what night it is."

Yes, Benny did. So did the people, who now disappeared into their homes. Benny watched as they locked themselves behind wood and stone. Children were hustled away, rushed inside, leaving the only flickering eyes of skulls to stare across an empty land. Keith looked...excited?

"I wonder how real they'll be this time."

Benny gulped as the wind blew across the quiet village and the sun finally set. He knew he didn't have long to wait, he could hear them already. Whisperings, carried on the wind from far down the road, carried along with wisps of dirt that spun... like footsteps. Trees groaned as the wind blew ever fiercer in protest. As the sky darkened, Benny took a step closer, he wanted to see. So did Keith, who stepped with him, eyes equally wide.

"They're here."

Yes, they were. Gravestones shivered as hazy apparitions of smoke rose from the earth, dark shadows with burning eyes. Benny gaped at a hundred incarnations of death, shuffling out of every corner of man's world, dragging their feet, opening broken jaws to mouth their names in life. Sightless, noiseless, they lumbered with toes that never quite touched the ground, lumbered toward to the village, their old life.

Benny stared right at this hoard of the dead and couldn't look away. Keith didn't move either.

"We can watch," Keith whispered. "This is just a memory." Benny was anything but convinced. The horde stretched down the road farther than he could see. They couldn't just stand here! They—

"Stand and watch. You're not alone," Keith gestured to Bridget, who again graced Benny with a smile. *Safe,* and Benny stayed.

The horde was then upon them, passing through with a pale white shudder on their way to the outskirts of the town. Benny saw Keith eying the horde with his wide-eyed artist's fascination. Did he see a smile?

"I wouldn't miss this for all the ghosts of the Greenwich Village Halloween Parade."

Keith moved closer as the horde entered the village. Phantom hands brushed against shutters and opened gates. Blind eyes gawked for mortal life, inside the cottages. Nothing stopped them.

Except the Jack O'Lanterns.

The eyes of fire burned against the horde, denying them entrance. Wispy hands reached out to the unblinking skulls and tried to touch, but pulled back. Nothing could enter where the skulls guarded. The horde searched past doors, past the shuttered windows. All were blocked by glowing faces. Benny peered closely, finding that in this Land of the Dead, he could see the Jack O'Lanterns as the phantoms did:

Blazing faces of terror with snapping teeth, scowling and growling into the faces of the horde. The horde fears them.

The horde disappeared, defeated. Benny watched with wide eyes, remembering.

Scary is survival. Connor told me that.

Then Benny heard scatterings inside the cottages. Doors opened with fearful eyes, peering into the evening. One by one, the families stepped out in their world again. They were safe.

But still terrified. Benny heard whispering, muttering. Something else was left. What were they still afraid of? From a father and mother holding a little boy, Benny heard it. The mother had whispered into the boy's ear. *"Last to die."* The horde had *not* left, instead they had surrounded the cemetery, where smoky reflections reached out of their graves to flow into the ranks of the Horde. But all sightless eyes eventually fixed on but one grave in the entire yard.

A freshly interned body.

Benny watched Keith move closer. Benny hesitated to follow, until he felt the warmth of Bridget behind him. *I can't be hurt here.*

The grave opened.

Long bony arms of transparent white floated out, wearing parched skin like a mummified corpse's. Tatters of a white burial robe flowed from gawky limbs. White scraggly hair floated about its head as if drenched in static electricity. With outstretched arms, the ghost mummy took its place at the front of the horde. As a single mass the swarm moved out of a graveyard back onto the road. Benny and Keith were left alone as behind them they heard more rustling from the villagers checking Jack O'Lanterns in a fevered rush before hurrying back inside. Benny saw the same mother he had heard before, and heard her words before she pulled her family behind a door and locked it.

The Ankou.

"Ankou." Benny repeated it, and saw Bridget's transparent form staring at him, mouthing the three words again. *"Last to Die."*

Last to Die.

That's what Kelly tried to do to me last night. Benny shivered at the memory of being smothered by screaming ghosts. Then Keith was next to him, hands on his shoulders. Benny watched the Ankou disappear, then spoke, "I haven't heard of anything like that before."

"Hardly anyone has," Keith replied. "It's too old, goes too far back. I'm not even sure that's the right name for it. But the Celts knew about him. Samhain wasn't just the last day of their year, it was about death stalking them. Literally, Death walked the roads."

Benny was still shaking out shivers. "I thought that was the Dullahan," *Severed head cackling while charging you down under a dead horse.* Benny had seen too much of that monster already.

"The Dullahan only marks you," Keith continued. "Then he leaves. But *after* you die it's the problem of the next monster up the food chain. That guy," Keith did a backwards thumb point at the disappearing monster fog. "And he was the creepiest monster of them all." Keith stepped away. "Because it could very well be you."

Me.

"Whoever died last in a community before Samhain," Keith continued. "The last dead sucker on Samhain would find his soul hijacked, stolen by whatever supernatural force turns the hands of time and opens the Veil in the first place. Corrupted into ghostly servitude. It was his burden to collect everyone else who had died that year, and then march them off to the afterlife. The Ankou."

Bits of twirling fog still hovered around the graveyard. *That's creepy.* The cold wind caught Benny and chilled him all over again. Bridget lowered her eyes. And Benny's anger roared to the surface again.

"Why does she hate us that bad? Kelly? Why'd she want to do that to me?"

"I have a feeling it's because of our famous relative."

"Finn MacCool."

"The man himself. That's why we're here, why Bridget is giving us this grand tour. Not to ask if you've worthy of your name, but to tell you why you *should* be." Keith looked to Bridget. Bridget looked back, eyes bright. The scene vanished. Gravestones, village, all evaporated into smoke around them, leaving just the road and the hills.

"But it's not Halloween yet. If I died last night, I wouldn't have been the last to die."

"She likely controls the Dulluhan, she could make sure you would have been the last."

"Does she control it?"

"You want to find out the hard way?"

No, Benny didn't. *Still, something to think about.*

Meanwhile the horde had entered another village. The fog of spirits crested a near hill and crept down towards the flickering fires of mortal life. People were there, preparing.

Fascinated, Benny almost didn't notice his feet stumbling beneath him as he bumped into a young boy. The boy's hands, feet, and face smeared with the dirt and grime of a life on the farm. He gave a shout of alarm as he pushed Benny away and ran away. Benny thought nothing for a second, then it hit him.

He had touched the boy. They were real. The shadows were fully formed now.

Down the road the boy shouted into the village and pointing up the road. At his cry the townspeople dropped everything and hustled off, grabbing children as they went. Benny and Keith followed as the horde flowed into the heart of the village scraping at every door. Only houses with the carved skulls turned them away, the faces of flame scowling in challenge.

All of them, except one.

One wispy specter stopped at a path to a cottage. A carved skull stared back leering with pointed teeth. The specter looked at the skull- but didn't leave. Instead it...changed. Becoming softer, less monstrous.

Human.

The ghostly humanoid took a step and walked right past the skull, right up to the door of the cottage. Benny inhaled. "It didn't stop him! It—"

"Can't keep a man out of his own house," Keith said.

His own house. *He had lived there, and was returning home.* With transparent legs the humanoid took slow steps towards the door. The shutters were closed, the door undoubtedly barred, but he was coming home.

And he was expected. Peering closer at this particular cottage, Benny saw a plate set at the front step, laden with bread and tiny cakes. The ghost reached the door and almost moved to knock, but the wind blew his hair and shifted his eyes, letting him see the offering at his feet. Reaching down he grabbed a cake which instantly turned ghostly white at his touch. Holding it in both hands as a delicate prize, an unseen wind floated him back into the horde of apparitions.

Through the shutters of the cottage, Ben saw someone furtively peeking at the offering plate at the front door. Keith leaned down to whisper in Benny's ear:

"Trick or treat."

Before a handful of other homes the scene repeated itself, with ghosts floating out of the pack to fixate on a single dwelling. An old woman. A young girl of marriage age. A man of the fields. They all flowed to their cottages and reached with transparent hands for the offering at the front steps. Food. Drink. Tokens. Taking a portion they disappeared back into the flowing mass of the horde which moved ever onward out of the village. Many spirits moved on.

Many did not. Over every cobble-stoned path, behind every tree, and covering every inch of mortal domain, skeletal hands scoured and searched, looking for mortal warmth. Spectral mouths released howls that chilled the marrow in Benny's bones. The creatures of the night shrieked in ravenous delight in their freedom.

Until a door opened, and a single man came out. Benny watched him, fearing for his life, until remembering *this is only history.* The man pulled out furs, furs sown into a hood and sleeves. The man put it on. He was putting on animal skin.

No. He was putting on a costume.

A fur cape covered his body. Black ash smeared his face, around his eyes and under his cheekbones, resembling a skull.

Another door opened, revealing another young man wearing a long well-weathered and frayed robe, sewn together from a pile of black rags. He had also blackened his face to give the appearance of death. Then another door, and another. Throughout the village, people emerged, stepping boldly into the road, in costumes. They hid themselves under hoods, under masks made of ripped cloth. The entire village assembled in the street, with turnips carved into ferocious skulls thrust out in front of them.

The howling horde saw them, and a hundred grisly arms horned in on the mortal flesh. Benny widened his eyes in terror as skeletal hands groped outward to seize a feast—

The village roared in their face, screaming in challenge. The spectral hands of the horde stopped in mid-air, quivering. Benny stared, unbelieving, until he felt the presence of Bridget next to him. Her own pale arm touched his own, sending a jolt through his entire upper half.

Benny could now see through the eyes of a ghost, and could see the people as the horde saw them:

Eyes of Jack O'Lanterns growling in anger.
Animal faces snarling in ferocious challenge.
Dead skulls that chomped dead air with rotten teeth.
Blurry forms of fright that didn't run.

The horde wavered. Sightless eyes could not focus. Wisps of ghostly hands reached forward in confusion. The costumed people shouted again, shouting in the eyes of the horde as maniacal skulls of pale death, angry and terrible.

And the horde retreated.

They're scaring the horde away, thought Benny in wonder as the people kept pushing forward, pushing the horde further back until they flew out of the village entirely. Flowing into the woods, the horde evaporated into mist.

The people screamed in victory. This was their home, and they would defend it.

They returned to their homes, passing torches to everyone's hearth as they went, sharing their fire. Benny watched every moment. They had saved themselves with *scary*. Fighting the scares by being even scarier. Beating the monsters at their own game.

Benny turned to Keith, whose eyes gleamed in serene satisfaction. "As if anyone would dare try to tell me ever again that scary doesn't matter," and Benny actually laughed.

"They're not done yet."

Benny looked far off and saw that it wasn't just this one village, but beyond entire congregations of people were marching. Far in the distance he saw an entire migration climbing the hills. What was that on top? A fire?

"They're coming together as a community. That was the final weapon."

Atop the hills, fires burned high. Towers of flame extending higher than the clouds, sending spirals of orange embers across the valley below. Around them people danced, sang, and held fire in their hands, daring the Night to come get them. Benny knew it wouldn't. Keith touched his shoulder.

"I think Bridget thinks we're ready now."

"For what?"

"The biggest Halloween story there is. Can you see behind us?"

Benny turned to Bridget. As he did, the fires, the village, and the valley all melted away. The world gave way to an even earlier point in time, further back than Benny had even heard of. Bricks gave way to huts. The woods grew thick around them. How far back were they now? Benny looked to Bridget and back to the hills, not seeing anything.

"Look on top of the hill." Keith pointed into the black.

Benny saw a figure. Stepping down and walking towards them. It was a very old image, a man with shoulder-length black hair, wearing leather tunic and jerkins. He had his own filthy animal cloak, stained with the muck of days and days of travel through infested wood and rain. He carried a sword and spear strapped to a muscular back, with a face stained with ash to walk the Night unmolested. He'd obviously been walking a long way.

It smacked Benny. *Him.*

"We're ALL the way back," Keith finished his thought. "Back to him."

The quintessential Irish hero. Bridget had been feeding him with images of the man for days now.

Finn MacCool stepped into view, and Benny gaped. He was so short.

293

"*That's* Finn MacCool? But..."

"You're taller than he is."

Benny was taller than Finn. He knew people were chronically shorter back in the day, but in this old world, Benny would have been a goliath.

If the figure saw either Keith or Benny, he paid no heed. Indeed, how could he? He'd been dead for thousands of years. *Which is why I can see him now,* Benny realized. *Here in this ghostland, everything dead lives again.* Here Finn MacCool's shadow lived one last time, to finish his story for his descendants. As the road to perpetual twilight stretched out in front of them, Benny MacCool Bensel watched every move of his ancestor. The last story Benny needed to see.

The Grand Finale.

FORTY-FIVE

I**T WAS ALWAYS DUSK.**

Streaming clouds above Keith and Benny churned with reds and grays pushed by silent winds. Benny kept one eye on the horizon and the other on his ghostly sister, keeping pace beside them as an incongruous apparition in blue jeans and curly hair. Benny's third eye, if he had one, was on Finn MacCool, walking with grim determination to his destiny. He was only another phantom, but realer than anything Benny had seen so far.

They passed more villages along the road, spaced between rolling hills and dead trees. These were only slabs of rock piled with loose earth, bare huts with an open hole in the thatched roof for a chimney. This was so old Benny wouldn't have believed it. Finn walked through them with a face carved in righteous fury.

These cottages had been torched.

Blackened houses dotted the path, standing only as skeletal fire pits. Lost in a raging inferno of flame, burned. Inside, lay bones contorted in agony. Finn hung his head, and whispered an oath to the fallen. Let them be at rest.

They weren't. Even now ghosts hovered over their charred bodies, burnt in life and now black in death. They whispered but a single word over and over.

"Burner."

Finn had no comfort to give them, and could only gauge the monstrous appetite of the Burner. His stench lay thick in the ash, claiming this place in the death of his victims. Finn would claim it back. He would find the Burner, and put an end to him. Finn gave the dead one last respectful look, then moved on.

Soon now.

Benny watched from a fair distance, not knowing if he should get closer. Bridget put a ghostly arm on his shoulder, gently moving him closer. Finn had moved on, into some woods beyond.

"How far does he have to go?" Benny asked.

"He's real close," Keith said. "But he's got a few more things to do along the way. I think this next part will be especially interesting."

"What does that mean?"

Keith just motioned.

Finn knew he neared the Hall of the Kings. These woods would not impede him. Nothing here but—

Voices.

Finn stopped with his spear at the ready. But it wasn't a threat. It was a lyrical melody. Soft on the ears, pleasing. He couldn't help but yearn for the source.

The dead heard it too, lost souls wandering through the wood with nowhere to go until the voice opened their eyes. They flowed through the trees like water down a hill as Finn followed them, running through a thicket of prickly bush, toward the sound of a running stream.

There, a small pond fed by a creek. Trees soared high above like the pillars of an ancient chapel. The twilight sun barely reached here, letting only a few trickles of sunlight bounce along the water's surface, creating rings of light. High in the trees, birds sang the song of sunset.

At the water's edge, a form of female beauty such as Finn had never seen. A lithe form wrapped in a white dress revealing skin the color of pearls and hair so red it might burst aflame even as Finn's eyes beheld it. Her face turned away, facing the opposite glade as the dead flowed toward her.

Finn's footsteps broke the silence. The woman dispelled the spirits around her and turned to behold Finn with eyes as green as emeralds. A face of supple cheeks, tiny nose, fairy beauty. She had been singing as Finn entered the glade, but now stopped and spoke.

"Brave son of Clan MacCumhaill. You have traveled so far to challenge death at the hands of the Burner. Has it not been far enough? Have you not given already? Remain here. Let me offer my serenity."

Finn took a step forward, and the green eyes flared with lustful hunger.

"I offer you eternal rest."

Benny choked. He did that a lot. He'd known that face for years. "That's Kelly!"

Even as a ghostly replay it could be no one else. Benny felt Bridget beside him, soothing his surprise and anger. Keith came to his other side, the only solid form amidst a sea of phantoms.

"Yes and no," he said. "That's her face only because that's how we know her now. Finn probably saw some other face entirely."

"But the spirit inside..."

"Her, yes."

Benny stood fast and scoured the face of the female figure. Squinting through the flickering light, he could see an aura around this woman, the *black* aura that he'd seen earlier when it had escaped the *Other Side* and entered a wrecked car.

The lithe woman rose from the bank of the pond and raised her hands to Finn, approaching him with slow steps.

Finn braced his weapon... and, yet, felt only peace. The voices in his ear promised him rest with the dying of the day. The woman reached her hands up to caress his shoulders. Her swirling green eyes met his and wouldn't let him go, even as she began to drag him backward and her feet entered the water.

Exactly where Finn should never go.

A dagger flashed and sliced the woman across her marble face. A scream shattered the peace of the glade as she clutched her face, blood dripping through her fingers. Finn backed up to the shore, dagger at the ready. He knew exactly what this bewitching beauty was, seeking to corrupt the hearts of brave men.

The Leananshee.

Leananshee. The name meant nothing to Benny. Keith reminded him.

"Shee. As in *Banshee*. A distant relative, but this one is a predator. She steals souls of the weak. The name literally means 'Love Fairy.'"

Connor's face appeared in Benny's memory with brutal clarity.

"*Red haired girls have one freckle for every soul they steal.*" And now she wanted Finn's.

"She's a spirit, or a monster?" Benny asked.

"She's old. That's all I know," Keith said. "So old that none of the legends agree with each other anymore. The name Leenan might even be a modern form of the old word 'Lilith,' the first Succubus."

"A *what?*"

"Something way past your pay grade. She's a leech."

A leech. Benny thought. *She eats emotions. That's why I got so tired. She was feeding on me.*

Keith followed his line of thought with a grimace "A Leananshee was the Irish..." He hesitated, not wanting to foul his mouth with the corny word.

"Vampire."

The screech of the red-haired siren rattled the branches of the glade. Blood from her face sizzled into black steam as it dripped into the water.

Finn knew too many mortals that had been reduced to a plundered shell by the love spirit's voracious appetite. A plague on mankind's temptations, she left entire graveyards of young men in her wake. She now screamed between bleeding fists as her face stained with red ichor.

"The sluagh will feast on the marrow of your bones!"

With an evil leer, she reached up one of the many floating spirits, inviting one to touch her hand. When one returned her touch...It vanished, sucked into her body with one moment of stark raving terror. The Leehan's eyes closed in pleasure, and as Finn's eyes beheld, the jagged scar healed, her face once again a porcelain beauty.

More spirits came to her call, daring to touch the slender hand, and were also absorbed. Barely a scream of fright heralded recognition of their fate. She would eat many this day.

Benny looked on in horror.

The ghosts. *Kelly was EATING them.*

And the Burner gave her all the lost souls she could consume.

Finn watched with every weapon at the ready. She was a danger, but had no power that was not given to her freely. He would not be taken. But she was not alone. Far beyond the trees, the first howl of the Night drifted on the twilight air. Finn scanned the woods. He could not stay. Keeping his eyes on the female, he backed out of the glade. Her anger only grew.

"The Night approaches foolish man! I'll live to dance on your grave tonight! You will never survive the Burner! NEVER!"

Finn heard growling behind him, and spun to see a black form penetrate the woods, a shadow on four legs with a horse's head. Stalking like a feline predator, its lips peeled back to reveal jagged teeth that smiled. The puka tensed to attack.

"Stop!" The woman held up a hand. "Let the fool pass. Let the Burner render his bones." She turned to MacCool. "Time might come that you will wish for a peaceful death by my hand, brave mortal." She started toward him, walking on the water. "Not too late. Take my hand and all is forgiven."

Finn stepped back, keeping his dagger between himself and both the woman and Puka, which still stalked him at spear's reach, keeping pace on all fours. The leananshee scowled...and leaped upon him in a roar of hatred. Red hair flared out in serrated points to slice flesh as her white dress exploded out in bat wings, reaching to suffocate Mac-Cool in a black mass—

Finn's blade slashed out again, drawing another scream. The wings flew off into the twilight, leaving a voice...

"The Burner is here! And tonight he'll burn YOU!" The shadow flashed through the trees. Gone. Finn looked for the Puka. Gone as well, with his mistress. Finn was alone with the wind.

Or not. A fierce roar of a ferocious beast rumbled through the glade, shaking a whimper of ash off the dead trees.

Finn had found his enemy.

Benny just... watched.

Kelly. Bridget had been trying to warn him ever since her death. Now Bridget stood next to him. Benny looked down. Keith spoke softly.

"You didn't know."

"Yes I did." Benny said. *I knew being scared of my own sister was stupid, and I did it anyway.* "I should have told you Bridget was still around."

"Even I would have told you to go back to bed. No, you did what you do. Never apologize for that."

"Maybe I should."

"Don't say that either. What scares you is your own business. You at least had a ghost to scare you speechless. Your Dad has even less. Why do you think he's never home?"

Benny followed the logic. "He goes on business trips because he's scared?"

"Horrified. It has to do with a movie that scared your Dad senseless."

"Dad hasn't watched a movie with me in his life."

"He watched the one with Will Smith."

Will Smith...actor, singer. Benny ran through his movies in his head... "*I Am Legend? Independence Day? Hancock?*" Earning a "No" from Keith on each one until he gave it up.

"The Pursuit of Happyness."

The Pursuit of... "That's not a horror movie," Benny said.

"Its not? A dad loses his home, gets arrested before the biggest job interview of his life, and has to hide his homeless little boy in-

300

side a subway men's room because he loses every drop of money he had to the IRS?"

Keith leaned in, all humor frozen off his face.

"Some people would consider that the most horrifying terror out of the Devil's 9th Hell."

For the first time, Benny recognized the hidden pain behind Keith's eyes. *Keith sleeps on my couch.*

"Your dad never comes home because he's certain if he stops running for even a lunch-break, that's exactly what's going to happen to him," Keith continued. "And you."

Benny shuddered as Keith backed up, his demeanor returning.

"So we're getting you out of here and kicking Kelly out."

"Can we?"

Keith snorted "She sure as hell thinks so! That's why she's been trying to kill us! Think about it, she has to!" Keith raised his arms and spun around the whole scenic panorama of Ghostland, eyes wide in that fanatical gleam that arose whenever a new scare brainstormed itself.

"Breathe this in! What does this feel like to you?"

Feel like? Was Keith a juggler short of a circus? But Benny took a moment. Scares coming from every side. The shuffling ghosts, the whispering wind, the fog induced vertigo...

"It feels like a haunted house." Benny said. "This whole *Other Side* is one big haunted house."

"Exactly!" Keith jumped with excitement. "A rip-roaring haunted house! That what haunted houses are: a memory of this place. One of those gosh-darn cultural memories fighting to surface from deep in our hind-brain. A memory of what we're *supposed* to be afraid of when the Veil drops entirely, and what would happen if the real monsters ever got out again."

Benny thought that made sense. All the classic monsters were just modern molds of the Irish ones. Slashers = RedCap. Headless Horsemen = Dullahan. Monsters so old no one even remembered them anymore. The haunted house was the same concept, on a macro level.

Keith waved at the sky. "That's why she had to kill us! Taylor! Scotty! Connor! We're the only ones who want Halloween as scary as we can get it." Keith pointed at every ghost he saw. "Worse, we're not scared of it!"

He was right. Scotty and Connor pushed scary as ferociously as Keith ever did. *That's why Kelly killed them.* Benny knew the simple logic, something only a Halloween fanatic would ever even think to say: "Those who deal in monsters cannot be afraid of them."

Keith nodded. "We're exactly the ones it had to stop."

Benny looked back at the vanished images of Kelly, then to Finn, who had returned to the road. Benny moved after him, turning around to Keith on a half-step. Straighter, taller than he had stood in a long time.

"Let's see who stops who," Benny said.

Keith grinned.

FORTY-SIX

THERE WAS NO DOUBT where Finn was going. All Keith and Benny had to do was follow the black corpses. Scorched, screaming.

Finn MacCool started to run. Hands on his weapons, he ran up the road at a speed that should have left Benny gasping after a block. Fortunately, the visions moved for them and Benny never tired.

Neither did Finn.

FLAMES.

The only remnants of the village were the billowing ashes left behind. People had lived here, but no longer. One could follow the Burner's path from the smoking footprints, footprints large enough for a mortal to get lost within. This was indeed a monster, and it was near.

A scream, from far beyond the village. Something shrieked in terror as the Burner stalked yet more mortal life.

No more. It ended tonight.

Benny rushed to keep up as the image of MacCool ran through orange embers floating on the air. Finn brushed them aside the flames got even fiercer. This man feared nothing.

The woods grew thicker as the chase grew desperate. The Hall of the Kings lay just beyond the forest. Finn had arrived!

But so had the monster. Finn could not allow it to get any nearer. Around him scorched branches and ash ridden corpses dotted the ground. Ghosts arose from the bodies, seeking Finn, but any claw that dared to touch him only earned a slice of his sword. Finn faced the closest spirit and dared it to touch him again. It did not. The spirits fled in a hot gust and Finn turned back to the path.

Suddenly the ash ended. Finn saw living trees that reached high into the twilight sky. The Burner hadn't been here yet. Finn had outpaced it, seeing in front of him a proud wooden castle. The Hall of the Irish Kings, the seat of mortal power. Set on a cobblestone path leading up a man-made mound, surrounded by rings of gray stones set in green earth. Stones set for a calendar, for protection.

Only they could protect against nothing this night. Mists whispered voices into mortal ears as the Burner approached.

Finn MacCool stood on the steps of the Hall, surveying an approaching inferno. The forest cried with every step the Burner took, disturbed spirits scattered as they fled the beast who now roared with pleasure as it saw its goal. A massive form pressed through the thick wood, silhouetted against the conflagration. It stepped into the clearing and Finn finally beheld his enemy.

Twice the height of any living man. Coarse body hair blew wildly in the heat of the flame. Four-toed feet matched four-fingered hands with knuckles that oozed stinking ichor. Its eyes radiated the red flame that filled the woods behind it, its feral muzzle like that of a wild beast with broken canine teeth that sizzled with waves of heat.

Finn grasped his spear in two hands as the Beast approached, fixing beady eyes upon him. Its wicked jaws opened in a blast of fire, baking the cobblestone path and cracking the stones under the inferno. Flaming ash pelted Finn as the Burner moved to swat him as an insect.

Finn held his spear tightly, but didn't move. The spirits of Samhain swirled around them both, howling, fearing the one and mourning the other. The Burner growled as it stepped up the green mound. This would end tonight.

Finn MacCool had met his destiny.

Flames singed the air around Benny. The fire couldn't hurt him, he hoped, but the superheated air was lot hotter than he had ever felt before...

Scorching flames from the lungs of a blast furnace scorched the stone and stairs of the hall, where Finn stood in defiance.

It never touched him as he ducked under the flame and charged the Beast directly. The Beast, so certain that mortals would run in terror before him— never even saw Finn until his spear impaled the Beast straight in the abdomen.

A ROAR of pain opened the sky as The Beast coughed on his own flame. A meaty paw swatted the mortal, hurling him and his weapon across the cobblestone ground. The spear flung end over end, spraying droplets of liquid fire. Finn rolled with the throw and ended up on his feet. Dripping blood from the Beast's wound melted holes in the ground even as it expanded his bellowing chest for yet another blast.

Finn had the spear back in his hand and examined his enemy. This Beast was exactly that. It possessed no soul. But Finn was a man. HIS was the right to be here and he wouldn't surrender that right, even as a searing hurricane of flame engulfed him.

He never felt a thing.

This was mortal land. Spirits were the intruders and had only the power mortals foolishly gave them. Finn gave this one nothing even as the flames smothered him. Nothing could ever hurt him here. HIS was the right!

No. Benny's was the right! The fire, the mound, the Hall, the vision drowned Benny's senses. It wasn't just history anymore, Benny knew Finn's mind. Shared it.

Benny inhaled as the maelstrom overwhelmed the feeling of his own body, and his breath started heaving in tune with Finn.

The Burner howled in anger as Finn stood defiant. This wasn't how it was! Mortals were meant to die as they always did! Samhain after Samhain he had burned so many! But the Burner had never en-

countered such a mortal. His selfish existence allowed for no idea what to do if a mortal refused to die for him!

The Burner knew fear. If one mortal could resist him, then they all could. The Night might never take any mortal ever again.

In its confusion, Finn attacked. His spear spiraled through the smoke and impaled the Burner in the chest. A geyser of liquid flame spurted across the steps of the Hall. The Burner's scream toppled the towers set to watch the Hall. It brought blood to Finn's ears.

No. To Benny's.

Benny's ears rang with pain, his hands flying to block out the animalistic scream, coming back covered in blood. *HIS* ears bled. *HIS* muscles burned.

Benny was Finn MacCool. Seeing through Finn's eyes, heaving with his strength. And as Finn MacCool, he ran the distance down the steps of the Hall, and drew his sword. He was in this fight, and Benny knew that he would win.

So did the Burner. It ran. Digging clawed feet into the earth, the Burner powered its body to the safety of the trees. It had to escape!

Finn/Benny wouldn't let it. He intercepted the beast in mid-stride, wrapping a hand into the beast's mangy hide and hurling himself to the beast's back. His other hand raised high with a sword and impaled a hairy shoulder, smearing himself in a steam of black blood. The Burner shrieked even as it kept running, but Finn's grip held, and the sword came down again. The beast ran faster in instinctual panic- and the sword came down again.

And again. And again.

Finn/Benny's body was drenched in black ichor from the monster. The rotten stench made him gag, but there was too much monster to miss as he sliced over and over, and this monster had killed so many.

Thick branches cracked against the Burner's head as panicked pain drove him faster and faster. But Finn/Benny wouldn't let go. The Beast screamed and the spirits answered, pouring out of every dark shadow of the forest to snap at Finn/Benny with snarling skulls, chilling his flesh with spectral hands in vain attempts to release the Burn-

er. A hundred wails of a hundred wraiths filled the air, but of fear. They feared the MacCool.

Finn/Benny just struck at the beast all the harder. Finn/Benny knew this was the secret, of how mortal men would survive this Night for the next thousand years, by being every bit as fearsome as the beasts were. Every bit as scary.

The Burner bounded down rocky hills, plunged into a rushing river. It ran across land, rock, and green, desperate to escape the pain. But Finn/Benny held on with hair glued to his face and eyes stinging with blood. The air filled with the stench of fear.

And finally, death. The Burner collapsed, hitting the ground with a heaving bellow. Finn/Benny held its broken body and gasped for breath under the cold night sky, not letting go until a tuff of hair pulled out from the roots. He fell off the bleeding corpse and lifted his head to behold the scene.

The horde surrounded him. A thousand spirits with a thousand blank eyes of death, all beholding Finn/Benny MacCool drenched in the lifeblood of his enemy. MacCool's eyes beheld each spirit in return, and with a scream of challenge he threw the mass of hair at the horde.

Another scream answered from behind the horde. Not of a monster, but of a man. Finn/Benny saw a man step forth into the clearing, and he wasn't alone, a hundred mortals stepped out with him into the clearing. Faces painted with ash, bodies covered in dark cloaks, they thrust carved skulls in the air. They had hidden from the Burner, hid from Samhain, but no longer. They had come to see the corpse of their tormentor, to see they could never be tormented again. Again they screamed their challenge and advanced on the horde.

The horde saw them all, saw glowing eyes they couldn't explain, monstrous forms that wouldn't cower before them. So they fled, falling into the ground, drifting away on the wind.

Mortals won the Night. Won Samhain, and they wouldn't give it up for a long, long time.

The field emptied as the people returned to hearth and home, and Finn/Benny dared rest. His journey had been long and could finally rest.

No. Something remained. One last touch of dark smudged his muddled mind. Turning around Finn/Benny found the broken form of the Leananshee staring at him. Her body wrinkled, aged, weak. But staring with green eyes of vindictive fury. Finn/Benny looked at her and snorted. The Leanan's strength had vanished with the mortal ascension. She could do nothing and she knew it. But her eyes promised a threat. No matter how many eons she would have to wait, she would get her revenge. But now Finn/Benny stared her down as the Veil opened and swallowed her into a pocket of night.

She wouldn't be back for a long time.

Sitting in the grass Finn/Benny felt the night wind on their back. A chilling gust propelled a spiral of flaming embers high into the sky, under the sea of stars.

Stars...

Benny's eyes opened. He was on the ground, looking up at the stars. Bridget leaned over him, smiling. Benny sat up...

Finn, the village, the burning, all faded away, lost in a cloud of dust. Ghostland returned. The howling spirit filled land of the dead. Keith picked him up as Benny tried to focus.

"How..."

"You remembered your name. Always a plus. What did that feel like?"

What *did* that feel like? Benny considered, and felt... a lot better. He had strength, like what Kelly had slipped him with to beat-up Marcus, but his own.

"That was a rush."

"Maybe I should be jealous," Keith remarked. "But now Finn thinks the MacCools have one more Halloween to save."

The ground finally stopped spinning and Benny took control of his head. "Save Halloween? From Kelly? Her vampires are dead. What does she have left?"

"She ate her vampires to give her power. But Kelly wants a whole lot more, and has a whole Monster Manual's worth of bloodthirsty Celtic killers who want some too. They've been waiting for this kind of Halloween for a long time."

"The kind full of ignoramus idiots who think purple cat ears count as a scary Halloween costume."

"Exactly."

"She's going to eat the entire city."

"Yep."

"How can we save them when can't even get out wherever this place is?"

"Can't we? Look."

Benny looked up expecting to see the churning hurricane clouds above, only to find them gone! The entire purple/gray sky had grown into a sharp orange, with the first stars of evening peeking through. *Wait, Ghostland didn't have stars!* But the real world did. Benny felt the tingling pressure as the landscape blurred. Beyond the trees and hills twinkled hazy images of buildings, people. Flickering in and out, but getting stronger as the orange sky got brighter. Two worlds, merging. Mortal land, coming back.

"Weren't we supposed to be trapped here?" Benny asked, still looking up.

"We were, for a time. But Ghostland, the Ever After, Nevernever, whatever one decided to call it, the two sides are only separated by a flimsy Veil. And on one special night of the year, the Veil drops."

Even as Keith spoke, the city wrinkled back into existence around them. Benny blinked at trees, cars, and people. He could even see the sun, how long since he had seen the Sun? Felt like a week. Benny's mind caught up with him.

"And that night is tonight," Keith finished with satisfaction as the ground melted away to show green grass under Benny's feet. The date clicked in Benny's head, today was...

"You knew we could get back the whole time?"

Keith shrugged. "That's the whole point of Samhain. Once a year ghosts get to go home again. And if the ghosts can cross over, so can we."

Benny watched a thick curtain of *blur* crawl across the landscape, engulfing the *Other Side,* changing gray to color, exchanging dark for light.

"And I have no intention of missing it," Keith exclaimed. "It's Halloween, Benny MacCool. Time to get home."

And with a suck of pressure, the Veil passed over them. Tickle in the stomach. Quiver up the spine. And the Other World just...dissolved, melted like snow under a hot sun.

Then...

BREATHE! Benny's lungs opened to suck in an ocean. Even if the air carried the musk of garbage and car exhaust, it was real. Benny found himself on his back in luscious cold grass. Trees rose above him, tinted orange by an autumn sunset. Just out of sight he heard running water with giggling teenagers milling around. Benny sat up, looking for his bearings—

"The Greenbelt," Keith said, sitting next to him. "We're back in the City."

The Big City's concession to wholesome family picnic areas included a large park running right down the middle, hugging the river that bisected downtown. It was quite popular, with over three miles of jogging lanes, Frisbee golf, and simple luxurious greenery. Keith and Benny had been plopped down right in the middle of it.

But they weren't alone. The cheers of a nearby crowd prove something huge was going on right behind a clump of trees, something loud, obnoxious, and using far too many spinning lasers. Getting to his feet, Benny walked slowly to the trees and peeked around.

A party. Benny could see most of the noise coming from a custom painted van emblazoned with *97.3 The Rage!* Black speakers blasted out techno music as huge laser projectors bracketed a brightly lit stage on a platform of overturned straw bales. Several portable spotlights created a perimeter a hundred yards wide containing a drunken village's worth of party-goers, swigging alcohol freely.

But Benny's gaze went to the DJ, standing atop the stage addressing the crowd, dressed as a severely overweight Tony Stark. The DJ swaggered with a cordless microphone, pumping his fist to get cheers from the audience massed in front. Wearing Stark Industries sunglasses, his phony smile was three feet wide.

"Ladies and gentlemen! If you're ready for the Costume Contest Finale, give me a scream!"

The crowd roared.

"Let's see our finalists!"

Standing on the stage of hay-bales, several costumed party-goers stepped out to a variety of cheers. Benny watched each one, categorizing them all in seconds:

Male: Giant wizard with a goofy fake beard, wearing a blue robe with gold sequined stars and pointy hat.

Female: Black faery wings, lingerie, and black bobble antennae. Bare legs of course, and a mile of midriff.

Male: Werewolf. Flannel long sleeve shirt with fake fur sticking out of several rips. This wolf wore a cheesy rubber mask with a big goofy grin and red cartoon tongue.

Female: Little Red Riding Hood, holding the "leash" of the werewolf. The "hood" in this case being the majority of her costume, being a severely short skirt and pearl white halter-top. At least her red-leather boots came up past her knees.

And finally an obviously very drunk male, stumbling up wearing a T-shirt that said "This IS my Halloween costume."

Still slightly wobbly from the transition, Benny leaned on a nearby tree for support. Keith stepped up beside him as they both took a good long look at modern Halloween in the American Big City.

Benny spoke first.

"We're in a lot of trouble, aren't we?"

FORTY-SEVEN

BENNY WALKED INTO THE party, getting a better look at the crowd and the stage, noting how many of the patrons hadn't bothered to dress up in anything. Most had just wandered in with the clothes on their backs. Benny grimaced even as he expected nothing better, just as he knew exactly how the costume contest was going to end.

More contestants had stepped up. A Superman with fake muscles and a woman in Supergirl lingerie; a sexy pirate in a ripped bodice; a man in a toga. Benny scowled again, until something extraordinary entered the light. He stood wide-eyed at a beautifully intricate zombie cyborg with cybernetic implants. Its chest held an exposed heart that actually "beat" from an internal red blinker, hand-crafted. The 31st Century Ghoul (for lack of the better name) trudged into view in a decaying creeper's robe, and upon reaching center stage palmed a button in his hand to pump green glow-juice through several surgical tubes in his brain, earning an "oooohhh" from the crowd. The ghoul stayed in character the whole time, hunched over, snarling, crooked arms flailing at the crowd.

315

Benny saw Keith go wide-eyed at the cyborg as well. No easy feat. But after the ghoul one last entry stepped onto the hay bales, someone who needed no introduction.

Dracula. No, not that one. This was a twenty-something girl wearing a red velvet miniskirt with leather go-go boots, a form-fitting black bodice, and a beehive hairdo. With spinning flair the girl revealed her face to the crowd, a face drowned under about a pound of red lipstick and eyeliner.

If Benny wasn't still weak in the knees, he would have face-palmed.

The DJ strutted over behind the girl in the red cape. "Who votes for Little Red Riding Hood!" receiving a thunderous drunken cat-call from the crowd. Next, he held the microphone over the cyborg. "Who votes for this...iPhone monster?" earning another cheer and actual applause. The Ghoul lapped it up, growling at the crowd with a mouth of sharped teeth and spitting up blood. *How the hell did he do that?* Benny thought as the crowd yelled in approval, and Benny held a grain of hope. The ghoul might, just might, actually win.

Until Benny saw Little Red Riding Hood standing to the Ghoul's left. She was holding back, letting the ghoul have his moment, but only one moment. Taking a step forward she locked eyes with Dracula, who winked back. Jumping to center stage, Riding Hood grabbed Dracula with two arms and lip-locked her. Full tongue in full view of everyone. The resulting *ROAR* was primal, dirty, and disgusting as the entire party came to its feet in a sustained standing ovation.

"We have our winners!"

The DJ laughed as he mockingly hugged both women, milking the audience of every last juvenile scream. The girls got their prize money, laughing as they jumped off the stage. The Cyborg Ghoul shuffled off in the other direction, dejected, and dropping character to disappear back into the parking lot.

"Clap for the illustrious winners," Keith droned as Benny stood beside him, mouth agape.

"That was... That..."

"Was how we lobotomized ourselves," Keith answered for him, seething. "Take a mental picture of that and hold onto it forever. It's exactly how stupid we've let this holiday get."

Yes, it is, Benny thought amongst the *boom boom* of techno music that accompanied these shindigs. *Bridget never would have stooped that low. She—* Benny inhaled as he finally realized something was missing. "Bridget! Where is she?" Benny's eyes shot around. "She didn't cross over!"

Keith nodded. "She can't. Not yet."

"But we did!"

"We're mortal. We belong here, we were able to come through before the Veil dropped completely. See, there's still a bit of sun left."

Yes, just a sliver of sun remained, bright enough to cast long shadows, darkness creeping over everything the sun abandoned.

Bridget's still there. Benny's heart raced from being so close to his sister, then being separated so fast. *I wanted more time.*

As usual, Keith read his mind. "Bridget will get back, and a whole lot more is coming with her. Right now we have a chance to stop this before it starts."

Keith was right. Benny pushed it out of his mind to get his bearings. Greenbelt, by the river, in downtown. They had entered the *Other Side* miles away from here, escaping Kelly at the Mall the night before.

Benny shivered. "You want to find Kelly."

Keith nodded. "I do. And she'll be exactly in the dead center of this dumbed-down mass of testosterone. There's no one left now who even pretends to know what Halloween is supposed to be. She killed everyone else who did."

Benny's guts quivered. *She's tried to kill both of us already.* The excitement of seeing ancient Halloween through the eyes of Finn Mac-Cool had evaporated, leaving Benny feeling just like...Benny, small, perpetually underweight Benny. *Sure, we're the MacCools, but...*

"Does it have to be us?"

"You think we can call the Ghostbusters?" Keith asked with frustration. "Monster Hunter International? Harry Dresden? Its not like

Sam and Dean Winchester are on 911. Do you see a 1967 Chevy Impala hurtling down the street to save the day? Because I sure don't."

Benny considered. No, no one here would have the foggiest idea what to do. It was up to them.

"It's us or no one," Keith repeated, and moved into the Halloween party crowd, into Darryl's intractable consumer empire. Benny saw Darryl's fingerprints covering everything:

Glow-stick vendors, carnival booths, and an actor dressed as The Terminator posing for pictures and taking money. He wasn't alone, all the 80's slashers were back. Leatherface, with skin mask and leaf-blower, posed for pictures with a trio of giggling girls. Michael Myers slinked around some party goers in his white mask and blue coveralls, arms wrapped around several loud-mouthed boys who were taking turns pretending to be strangled for the photographer. Jason Voorhees jumped up and down in ridiculous "gotcha" poses to flashing cameras. Dracula walked throughout, at one point doing a break-dance spin on the dance floor, prompted by an impromptu dare by the DJ. In the middle of a photo shoot, some wobbling girl with two left feet stepped on Dracula's right foot, eliciting a howl of pain and vicious yell. "Those vere my Bruno Maglis!"

How many actors did Darryl hire? Benny kept seeing more: Jack Skellington, a *very* sexified Sally, Superman, Batman, Captain America, the Joker, and—

Where in the hell did Darryl find a life-sized Oogie Boogie costume? Never mind.

Benny stopped caring and tried to see anything in the pressed mass around him. "How can we even find Kelly out here?" Benny huffed in exasperation. "She could be anywhere!"

"She's a soul eater," Keith replied, staring down the way. "She's exactly where she should be." He walked away from the stage, down a jogging path parallel to the river on his left, and pointed. "Right there."

And there she was, sitting on a ledge up some stone stairs, on a patch of grass above the jogging path with an excellent view of the river, next to a tent with more actors popping in and out. She wore a wicked black lacy mini-skirt, lacy black sleeves, and huge-black velvet fairy wings flopping out of her back. She surveyed this city of fools with a vicious smile of smug condescension- *not even bothering to hide who she is anymore.* Benny couldn't see how he ever could have seen her as Kelly.

She tried to kill me.

Benny quivered and he stepped back, afraid she'd see him. "What do we do?"

"Kill her and it's over."

KILL her? *Could he do that?*

"How? She's—"

"She's alive. That means she can die. She sent the Puka to kill Taylor and Connor and God knows who else, so she owes me one. Ripping her head off ought to pay that back."

Benny gulped. Keith's dark side was...very dark. The air shimmered around them again as The Veil rippled, getting weaker by the second. Keith saw it too. Looking up he judged the time.

"It's not full sunset yet. We have that long to get her." He held Benny on the shoulder. "You up to this Benny?"

Benny. He'd been called that as long as he could remember. And you know what, he had never liked it. Not at all. After going through Ghostland he never wanted to be called that again. "Finn" was a one-syllable name, so was Keith. Such names were sharp and carried power.

"My name is Ben."

Ben watched as Keith blinked, that face of, *Where did that come from?* But, it felt right. Keith agreed, looking right at him and...approving.

"Yes. It is."

They both moved into the crowd, towards *her.*

FORTY-EIGHT

Keith's return trip through Ghostland had been even more nauseating than Benny's. After all he'd been out for barely ten minutes before having to jump right back in. It was almost enough to make a man swear off supernatural holidays forever.

Nah.

Keith hadn't been to Halloween by the River for years and forgot how crowded it got. The Greenbelt was packed to overstuffed with people milling in every direction. Pixies with sparkle hair on the left, giant bananas on the right. *And since when did underwear become a Halloween Costume?* All of them drinking. *It's barely dusk, people! Have some self-respect!* But fliers posted on every lamppost proclaimed it all:

The City's only Dusk to Dawn Halloween Celebration! No Cover before the Sun Goes Down!

Keith's Scream tattoo itched as the twilight orange gave way to deep red, making the sky looked like it was on fire. Keith wondered how to handle Kelly when he grabbed her. *Screw it, ancient killer fairy or no, she's in a mortal body. But... best to keep Benny out of sight.* Motioning to Benny to hide behind a concessions tent, Keith moved forward into the crowd, maneuvering into a blind-spot so he could approach Kelly without being seen.

Had Keith had more time to think it over, he might have given his next move more sophistication, might have remembered that he was just about to reenact Dan Aykroyd in the first five minutes of *Ghostbusters*, when he saw the librarian ghost, and just yelled "Get her!" But he didn't think it over, and his anger honestly didn't let him care. Fixing on Kelly, Keith made his move, running right up the stairs to throw her to the ground and put his foot in her neck. He charged...and almost made it.

WHOOSH

Keith hit an invisible wall. He landed in a heap with a bruised ego, just like Dan Aykroyd in the first five minutes of *Ghostbusters*. Kelly never even looked at him.

"Do not touch me." Such a soft voice, barely rising above a whisper, slowly turning to him and Keith groaned. "But Elder Mac Cumhaill, this would have been so much more convenient had you just let your own house kill you."

Keith got up, ignoring the pain as Kelly eyes now fixed on him.

"You are every bit the coward you deride in others," She said, flinging hair over her shoulder as the quintessential temptress. "You're worse, as you're a hypocrite. Your pain would be such a feast, but please tell me you brought the young Mac Cumhaill all the way back here for me."

Keith inhaled and stared her down. "You won't see him again."

"Won't I? He's here. I can smell his terror."

Keith gritted his teeth but said nothing. He had no intention of revealing Benny or getting into a battle of witty repartee. He just had to grab her.

"He can hear me, I know he can," she said. "Good, for he'll want to hear this. Benny is the perfect metaphor for this helpless time. A frightened loner, terrified of his own people. Community used to be a mortal's greatest strength. Your clans shared fire, protected each other. But now? You're *all* loners, selfish and huddled, addicted to your electronic alchemy and oblivious to any humanity around you.

You don't even know your neighbors name, let alone if he's alive or dead. The 'community' that protected you before is exactly what you've extinguished."

Kelly stood up. "And you? You think it was anything other than an accident of birth that put you above your nephew?" She stepped down to the street. "I might have picked the wrong prize all along. My greed lusted for the death of the little Mac Cumhaill, but my vanity blinded me to the real failure of your clan. You. The Sun is about to set, and the Night demands the Last to Die."

Keith felt the air darken.

>CLICK<

Oh no you dont!

>CLICK<

Stop! That memory hadn't beaten him yet and neither would this monster, who even now drilled anger into his eyes.

"You should beg me for mercy Elder. I've spent eternity stealing the grace of guilty mortals."

"You should beg me," Keith responded. "I stole the grace of an innocent one."

Keith blocked out the crowd, the plaza, and the whole stinking city as he sucked in his breath. Kelly just smiled.

"Then prepare yourself."

WHOOMP.

A sucker-punch from behind. Keith didn't need even one guess who. Darryl, wearing the same clothes he had worn the day before with bloodshot eyes and hair in desperate need of a comb. His left hand shot out to hit Keith in the gut, knocking Keith over against the tent and into the grass. Darryl stood over him with eyes wide with anger.

And a wicked serrated blade in his right hand.

Uh oh.

Behind him, Kelly laughed. "Greed is so sugary a sensation! Clan O'Grady is already muddled by selfish want. But now I've kindled a new sensation inside him, which he will return to me tenfold."

322

Keith jumped to his feet, ribs hurting, as Kelly's next word dripped from her lips.

"Rage."

Darryl pointed his blade right at Keith's neck, and spoke, his voice raspy and slurred.

"I think this will permanently end our partnership."

Keith sighed. "I suppose you wouldn't listen if I said you've been corrupted by an ancient Celtic succubus who overloads emotions so she can feed off them, and eat your soul in the process?" Keith whispered.

Darryl just stared.

The blade stabbed right for Keith's chest—

Damn it.

Keith jabbed Darryl's arm away at the elbow and twisted, a quick disarming move he'd done a hundred times. It usually worked, except when the blade was held by a supernaturally possessed lunatic. Darryl's grip *didn't* break, and the blade slashed across Keith's forearm, causing Keith to yelp as he switched tactics to loop a leg behind Darryl's knee and tripped his stance, sending him floundering to the ledge. Keith's fist slammed Darryl's face, but he still didn't drop the blade.

Screaming, Darryl slashed blindly, slicing Keith's other arm in a lucky flail, earning another yelp.

Screw this. Keith jumped away when a hand caught his foot and sent Keith tumbling to the rough cement. Keith disentangled his legs just in time to see Darryl's bleeding hands grip his blade with white-knuckles, wearing the scowl of a furious monster. Keith knew one of them wasn't going to leave this alive.

So he ran.

Stumbling on four limbs, Keith tried to get some distance between him and the blade. If he could get some footing, he could outrun Darryl. There were so many people here, all he had to do was get lost in them. He cut through the street and pumped his legs fast through the crowd. *Just lead them away from Benny—*

A HUGE black form lurched over him, giving Keith a minor heart attack. His eyes focused on...The Headless Horseman?

Of course, Darryl hired a horseman for a dumb photo op. Sitting on a humongous horse, the actor looked at Keith from underneath a fake severed head. Fortunately, an actor was all it was.

Clippity Clop

Crud.

Keith looked behind him. Back-lit against the failing sunset, Keith's eyes filled with spots as he saw another rider, charging at full gallop. Headless.

Clippity Clop.

The Dullahan charged right at Keith, who was caught with nowhere to run and no time to get there. The Herald of Death had him in his sights and Keith knew it.

I wouldn't have had the heart to kill Darryl anyway. I can only hope Benny gets away.

Clippity Clop

Frenzied laughter burned Keith's ears as Keith clutched his arms to his face and tensed for the impact. The rider roared in triumph!

And passed right through Keith, who fell only a chill breeze. Keith whirled to see the rider disappear back into the shadows from which he came. With hurried hands he checked his face and found no wounds or blood anywhere.

But it had me cold. I was right here. But Keith had a horrible thought. *Unless it didn't come for me.* Keith turned around, finding the seething form of Darryl plowing through the crowd, panting with wild anger in his eyes.

And blood oozing down his face.

Oh... Darryl.

FORTY-NINE

$\int$ UNSET BURNED THE SKY orange. Winds spun the clouds above into ever increasing circles.

And in front of him, Keith's last friend had been marked for death. Off in the distance, Keith thought he heard a howl. *Not yet.* Keith screamed mentally.

But time had run out. Keith spun on his foot as Darryl's serrated blade flew by him. Darryl's face radiated hate that Keith could literally feel. There could be no saving him this time. Keith couldn't reposition as Darryl charged again, giving Keith no time as Darryl hurled himself forward with a ferocious scream of rage. Keith reacted with a tripping tackle, meant to get an assailant on the floor with your knee at his back. It wasn't designed for armed assailants, and Keith did it without thinking. He shouldn't have. Darryl fell in a tangle of legs, face pressed to the pavement, arms trapped underneath him. He grunted with pain as he hit. He didn't move.

Keith immediately knew why. His heart raced with *Oh no please tell me I didn't just*—

Keith hurled Darryl over onto his back to see the serrated blade—

Not embedded in Darryl's chest. It had been pushed flat at the last second. Darryl's eyes squinted in pain from a huge bruise to the head, but he'd live. *Thank god.* Keith threw the blade out of reach and stood up, gasping for air. He saw Benny peeking in the back. *Good. Stay there.*

And he saw Kelly, staring at him in complete anger. Keith smiled.

"I'm sorry, did something ruin your master plan? "

Kelly's eyes flickered and Keith dared to laugh.

"Oh don't even try to scare me, Honeybunch. I've done scary, lived scary, breathed scary, and you are most definitely not scary."

Kelly's eyes flared gain, but...then she smiled.

"You've stopped nothing, MacCumhaill,. No one escapes the Rider's verdict."

A shadow fell over everything as a black mass knocked Keith to the ground. A black smelly mass that Keith knew all too well. *Smells like a horse.* Black mane whipping in the setting sun, a black rippling form pounced over Keith, grabbing the ground as a stalking feline. With horses head.

GET UP! Keith fumbled to his feet, getting up after the monster at Darryl's throat. He'd stop it! Keith grappled the monster with two arms and swung it around.

And stared into his own eyes. Not-Keith. Mouth open in a mocking laugh and eyes red with flame. Keith's hesitation cost him as Not-Keith backhanded him across the face and a vice-grip locked around Keith's throat, squeezing with the force of a hydraulic vice, pressing him against the asphalt. Keith saw stars.

Darryl's serrated blade appeared in Not-Keith's other hand. Keith pushed away, against a brick wall as the blade's bloody tip reached for his left eyeball.

Not-Keith stared back at him, eyes spinning red, mouth open in glee, mocking Keith's helplessness. That laugh, that god-awful laugh, enjoying his complete dominance.

Then spinning the knife around in his left hand, Not-Keith flung it backhanded, impaling Darryl's prone body through the heart.

Keith screamed, a single blast of red rage for one last dead friend. Not-Keith jumped off of Keith, his form melting into a feline crouch that landed a few feet away, then leaping up and away into the towers of the city, leaving only a mocking laugh drifting in the evening air. Keith almost ran after it, but couldn't take his eyes off Darryl, blade sticking out of his chest. Keith's vision went red.

If I have to choke him with my own blood, I'm going to kill that SOB.

At that moment, the sun's final sliver passed beneath the horizon. The faintest glimmer of golden rays touched the sky, then the day was gone.

A chilled breeze blew across the square as everything suddenly went ghastly quiet...except for one sound just on the fringes of mortal hearing. A howl. Keith looked from Darryl to Benny approaching him, staring at Darryl's motionless form. Someone had to say it. It may as well be Benny.

"Last to die."

The breeze buffeted into a gale, blasting wind and dust from every crack and spinning dust devils high above the plaza. The orange glow of sunset vanished, leaving a deep *RED* covering everything, draining all color.

Another howl, as if from the bones of the earth. Everyone around heard it, looking in shivers and fear, but Keith felt it more than anyone as his eyes went to the red sky and the caption of his SCREAM tattoo involuntarily rolled across his mind, something he'd memorized long ago:

The sun was setting...

Suddenly the sky turned blood red, there was blood and tongues of fire above...

And I sensed an infinite scream passing through nature.

Samhain had arrived.

FIFTY

THE NEXT SOUND EVERYONE heard was singing.

Singing?

But so much more than that. Every mortal sense revolted against an unnatural pressure that flowed down the street, engulfing everything, and anyone it touched...shivered.

The twilight sky pushed down, a claustrophobic ceiling of vicious clouds churning with a thousand faces. Every streetlight popped and went out, leaving only the red of the dying dusk.

And the *singing*.

What the Hell? Keith expected a great many sensations tonight, but that one absolutely went over his head. Singing... lyrical voices... a sweet wordless melody. It soothed the ears of the gawking crowd, their faces turning to the sound, coming from deep in the darkness. Keith remembered— *Wasn't the river over there?* But that thought quickly evaporated as a fog seeped off the river.

A *glowing* fog, with singing forms inside. Female forms, slowly, patiently, walked towards them all. Every mortal eye froze on the approaching forms silhouetted against the glowing mist. Slender.

Graceful. Not a soul in the crowd moved, until one of them stepped through into the clear air, and Keith just stared.

That was not the Dullahan. Nor the *Sluagh*.

It was a nurse.

A very sexy nurse. Tight dress stretched over a lithe form, super-model legs, unbuttoned top revealing a supple neck. Red lips high-lighted silky black hair that spilled over the shoulders beneath a white nurse's cap. Her face wore a luscious smile that promised...lots.

Then another Sexy Nurse stepped out. Then another, and another. Over a dozen.

Oh no.

At least that's what Keith thought as every other male in atten-dance dropped whatever they were holding and ogled the newcom-ers. The intoxicating hum flowed like honey as the harem of nurses stepped with the precision of runway models into the gaze of a hun-dred bug-eyed males. The women at the party were just as mentally stunned as the males. *Maybe they see something different.* One man stepped forward, his legs involuntarily moving towards the enticing singing. Other men followed. The nurses raised their arms towards the approaching men, faces smiling in alluring welcome.

Keith found himself immune, his own hormones quite asleep. *Going to the Land of the Dead and back again in 24 hours would tend to do that.* But try as he might, Keith couldn't think of a way to stop this, not when mortals surrender themselves so freely. Keith could only watch as silky arms of the nurses wrapping around willing men, who surrendered utterly to their deep kisses.

Clippity Clop

Keith's ears throbbed, his head pounded. The approaching foot-steps banging as nails into a board.

CLIPPITY CLOP

A brush of air. A maniacal laugh. A smashing of hooves. Keith's ear exploded in pain as a WHOOSH passed right in front of him, a gargantuan snorting mass galloping off into the darkness. His head flared with pain and he went to his knees. The singing was too loud, the flashing lights too bright. Keith trying focusing on anything, as he blinked tears out of his eyes.

Finally, the pain faded, and aching muscles pulled up his head to look at the wide mass of people at this Halloween Party. *Who would die? Who had the Dullahan claimed?* Keith looked, and gasped.

Every face was covered in blood.

Every. Last. One.

Even as Keith watched, the nurses pulled the men backward into the fog until they hit the edge of the river, water rippling just a footstep away. Completely entranced by the chorus, the men watched blankly as the nurses, and every porcelain inch of their busty forms—

Liquified.

Bodies of supple flesh melted into pools of green swirling water as hands of rotten seaweed wrapped around mortal necks, and the nurses morphed into several long snouted howling beasts made of sickly green kelp with crocodile-esque jaws that sank around the heads of the helpless men and twisted with vertebra shattering **cracks.** The rotten forms then jumped backward into the water, carrying their broken prizes with them.

Some survived long enough to drown.

That broke the spell. Anyone human who wasn't already dead opened up with a full throated scream. Except Keith. His encyclopedic mind ran through hundreds of monsters of myth and fable until he recognized this one, a water-monster that delighted in using a pleasant guise to lure weak-willed fools to a watery grave.

So that's what a Kelpie looks like. Another time and place and Keith might actually have been fascinated as fog rose out of the river, plunging everything into a thick haze as it climbed up walls, unfurling as a smothering blanket. People screamed as it touched them, there was no other possible reaction as senses revolted against the chill of the grave, even as unnatural figures started materializing out of the fog. This time the *Veil* didn't merely open.

It dropped entirely.

Hundreds of ghosts crossed over from the *Other Side*. Translucent figures of men, women, and many things that would never be called human at all, monsters with gangrenous limbs never meant for this world, stepped over and took lurching steps into mortal land.

Keith would have waited an eternity to see this, as the ghosts flowed with an unholy compulsion to one spot.

Darryl's body.

Oh lord.

The mortal form of Darryl O'Grady still lay where he fell, blood pooling and running into the cracks in the pavement. Keith saw Darryl's eyes closed in... serenity? Now the ghosts approached and closed in. No doubt anymore. Keith knew he had to run. This was never meant for the eyes of a mortal. He had to get Benny out of here too! But Keith MacCool had to see this. He would see it even if the very sight struck him dead on the spot. Keith had lived his whole life just to see what was going to happen right now.

So he watched, watched as a horde of spirits surrounded Darryl's body and raised their blank faces to the sky... and started to keen a lonely note to the heavens. Everyone who heard it fell to their knees, hands over their ears. Keith collapsed with them, his knees turned to jello, tears streaming down his face. With great personal pain he spared a glance at Benny... looking like his guts were about to spew all over the street.

Darryl's body started to glow.

A white emanation enveloped the entire form. Bright, but so cold Keith's blood cooled even so many yards away. The ghosts cried even higher, sending the surrounding mortals into panic, desperate to cleanse their ears. It didn't help.

Darryl's glowing body levitated ten feet into the air as the light got brighter and the ghosts screamed louder. Keith couldn't dare even blink as his skin prickled and his eyes watered. He saw everything.

He saw Darryl's eyes open, stark white orbs, staring out into eternity. His mouth opened in a silence matching the keening of the ghosts. His white light froze as cold as a glacier, pulsing in a mockery of a heartbeat as Keith stared at what Darryl had become. A corpse, impossibly thin, starved, wearing a mane of motley white hair. Tatters of a white robe clung to the frail body. Skin stretched over gnarly bones, over a face lost in death. Unmistakably Darryl O'Grady.

Death incarnate.

For a precious second Keith met its eyes, and saw Darryl's face blink in consciousness, and...terror. Then eyes glazed over in corpse white. Blank. The wailing stopped as the Last to Die finally joined his flock.

The Ankou had risen.

FIFTY-ONE

DARRYL WAS THE ANKOU.

Undulating tendrils of fog coiled through the twilight air as Darryl/Ankou raised rotting arms to the sky, and every mortal left in the plaza ran for their lives.

Keith didn't, even as Darryl rose as a white angel of death. Keith didn't have the luxury of fear. He stopped it last night at the mall, and he'd stop it again. Without a quiver of hesitation he stepped up to stare Darryl/Ankou right in its blank white eyes. Darryl stared back with no emotion whatsoever.

Sorry Darryl, I can't let you go any farther. Keith raised his hand in the absolute STOP, presented boldly. *They still expect mortals to run. Darryl, you're dead. You're not hurting anyone else.* Keith stared down the monstrosity that wore his friends face, and didn't move.

Darryl/Ankou did. A cold hand of rotting leather grabbed Keith's exposed palm, and crushed it.

PAIN

Jolts of shock raced up his arm and buckled his knees as a cold mass gripped Keith's soul. He could *feel his heartbeat freezing.* Keith

333

ripped his hand out of the death grip, leaving pieces of his skin still frozen to dead knuckles as he fell backwards, clutching his freezing hand and gasping for breath as his heart fluttered. Darryl/Ankou swatted him like a broken scarecrow, flinging him ten feet away. Keith fell in a heap, his exposed flesh bringing fresh fires of pain with every touch. He fumbled to his feet and stumbled away as Darryl/Ankou reached for him again. Keith's eyes blurred from so much cold. From somewhere far behind, he heard Kelly laugh, as if she could read his thoughts in mocking delight, and Keith realized his mistake. No, the Night did not expect him to run.

It expected him to die.

TEN MINUTES AGO, KEITH had told Benny to hide.

That was a long time ago.

Since then Benny saw Darryl come after Keith with a wicked blade, saw Darryl die by a monster with Keith's face, then saw a pack of supermodel nurses turn into seaweed sea-monsters to eat a pack of drunken beer-swirling idiots as a killer white fog released a hoard of spirits into the middle of downtown Big City. The ghosts flowing into his city, hearing beating hearts and smelling warm blood, and the city disintegrated into panic.

Now Benny watched the Ankou rise, hovering in the fog as a desiccated angel with a face of a *Game of Thrones* White Walker and hair of Gandalf in a wind machine.

Oddly enough Benny wasn't afraid, even though he thought maybe he should be. Fear had kept him safe his whole life, but now he didn't want to be safe, he wanted his uncle. So Benny ran to Keith even as spirits made sloppy grasps at him through the fog. But Benny didn't stop until his hands wrapped around Keith's shoulders. Darryl/Ankou floated right above him, a body of white leather stretched over too much bone, and close enough to wring the life out of then both. Benny heaved Keith to his feet with what

334

little muscle he possessed. *Damn it. Keith, you had to stick your hero complex out too far!*

Someone laughed at him. Kelly. Benny saw her mini-skirted form still sitting on the ledge above the sidewalk, clapping. Her black form hopped down to street level, red-hair fluttering in the twilight wind. "There's our little man!" Benny had had ample experience with being laughed at as well. He wasn't going to succumb this time even as his brain started to buzz, a black smudge worming its way in...

"Your anger was delicious," Kelly mocked. "What are you feeling now?"

Benny had too much adrenaline to feel anything, actually. The beast with Darryl's face moved toward them with rotten arms extended as Benny just heaved Keith backward. The Ankou's radiance bathed him in the filth of the *Other Side*, a foulness one strengthened since the sun had passed. That aura now drew a swarm of ghosts around Darryl/Ankou, a thousand faces. All the dead of the year. Benny stared at them all. The sight was... amazing. For a precious second Benny actually just watched as the vision of white death orientated on Benny and Keith, craggy arms reaching as it pushed itself through the air towards them on lifeless feet hovering a foot off the ground.

Benny came to his senses as grasping fingers reached for Keith's exposed neck. Benny yanked him further away, but Keith was so heavy.

I'm not going to make it.

Benny finally found his fear as the Ankou rose above him, seeking to throttle Benny with boney fingers. He squinted as the leathery arm swung—

It missed.

Or rather, something blocked him. Benny opened his eyes to see a ghost standing in front of him, interposing itself between Benny and Darryl. *A ghost? Who?* Benny focused in the dim light, gasping as he beheld a flickering pale form of an impossibly tall, bald man wearing a T-shirt announcing "Fright Zone."

The ghostly apparition of Connor blocked the Darryl/Ankou.

A ghost in a Spiderman costume appeared next to him. Quentin.

And another, Scotty, wearing the sweat pants and T-shirt Benny had seen in his nightmare so very long ago.

This was Halloween, when every spirit of the last year was free to walk the Earth again, every soul who had died in the last year, ALL of them. Now they lined up to protect Keith and Benny as Darryl's corpse blinked with dead eyes, flummoxed long enough for Connor to turn around to Benny. He looked so...friendly. Exactly how he would have been in life. Connor reached out with a wispy arm to touch Benny's shoulder and lead Benny's gaze around to—

Captain Jack Sparrow. Or rather, the dead version of him, and beside him...

Bridget. *She made it back! But who's that next to her?*
Kelly.

Ghost Kelly, Benny reminded himself, wearing torn clothes from the car accident nearly a year ago, not the dominatrix tease that stood mere yards away cheering for his death.

None of them let the Ankou pass. They stepped up, forms bright and powerful against the cold of the Ankou. In response the corpse reached out a leathery hand to grab Scotty, whose mouth opened in silent pain. Benny gasped for him. *Ghosts can't feel pain. Unless they're resisting something.*

Benny watched as Scotty... dissolved, his human form fraying into smothered cold light in the Ankou's hand, then caught by the currents of ghosts to join the mass behind the Ankou. Gone. Connor and Quentin pulled away. Their forms so much paler, weaker.

The Ankou adds ghosts to his Horde... It would steal every ghost it found. Benny spun to Jack and Bridget. *They had to get out of here! It would—*

Be enough time to escape. Jack wrapped milky arms around both MacCools in a foggy bear hug, then with a breath of air, pulled them away. Benny's sensations drowned in flying, of moving over the ground impossibly fast. They flew out of the greenbelt, out of downtown. The howl of the Ankou drifted to nothing as it vanished in the distance, a mournful cry for lost prizes.

But so many mortals were left behind, their screams lingering for a long, long time.

FIFTY-TWO

THE FIRST ONES DIED before they even knew.

The actor playing Jason Vorhees just stood there like an idiot as a leathery brown humanoid jumped on him in a guttural scream, pointed claws piercing his back and sinking a mouth full of piranha teeth into his neck. The actor died before he hit the ground. Beside him, Leatherface lived long enough to turn tail and run blindly into the haze. The humanoid jumped to him from Jason before he made even two steps. The monster seized Leatherface's head with two oversized filthy hands and broke his neck with a skull twist. The RedCap feasted on each corpse in turn.

Meanwhile, the Headless Horseman bellyflopped to the asphalt after his horse bucked and panicked. Watching his horse bolt out of sight through the fog, his vision failed under a cool shadow. Looking up, the actor saw... a severed head, in the hands of a headless rider. The head opened its mouth into a maniacal grin of yellow teeth as the black horse spectacularly reared up above the actor, giving him only a second to cry out before a curtain of black took him. For even the Spirit of Death can take offense.

It wasn't the only one. A rush of steamy wind announced yet another monster, with stamping hooves raking fire against the earth, quickly disorientating some pretty-boy vampires who had lost sunglasses and all dignified demeanor in their mad dash to escape. The demonic horse made sure to find them, and laugh at them. Vampires, the would-be Scariest Monsters of our time. They had never even heard of a Puka, but looking inside the darkest corners of their memory, the Puka knew everything about them, turning into a ten foot tall reptilian with bulging eyes and forked tongue.

All their corpses fell to the pavement, faces frozen into screams. Samhain gazed with greedy eyes on mortal life, and drank its fill.

ACROSS TOWN, AN OLD man scowled at children running across his lawn in their superhero outfits. Preposterous nonsense and he would have none of it! No pumpkins in his yard or candy at his door. Not even a porch light. He met anyone daring to approach him with a merciless scowl he had held for 20 years and the neighborhood knew better than to test him.

He turned his back to the street when a small form dared to step foot on his grass. He looked with dismay as it even dared approach his front door! He yelled that he had no candy with enough profanity to reduce this urchin to tears!

It didn't work. The child walked to stand on his very steps! With a huff the man turned to slam his door in the child's face. That would drive him off! Except his foot was stuck. The little beggar had grabbed his leg! *Why that...* The old man wound up a backhand to send the little fool to his knees, only to stop in mid-swing as he saw-

Teeth. Scaly skin. Glowing red eyes. And far too late, he realized this was no child.

As it sunk razor teeth into the flesh of his leg, his scream carried across the block.

A YOUNG COUPLE. TOO young.

She actually fell for the whole thing. He said *"You be the Lion Tamer and I'll be the lion."* The "Lion Tamer" being a short skimpy number of course, something you'd see at a "gentleman's club" advertising "Steve Irwin Night." This little suit (emphasis on "little") showcased her legs (that went all the way up) and exaggerated a chest that was absolutely real. She even got to wave the whip around so she didn't notice his eyes crawling over every exposed inch of her.

She'd likely be cold tonight. Good. Just give him an excuse to wrap her in a lion hug. He was warm and toasty in his fuzzy lion suit. He'd be sure to use the fuzziness to his full advantage later as he got a few drinks into her. He laughed to himself, this year was going to be a HELL of a Halloween.

But awfully foggy this year. The walk from the parking garage to the downtown bar scene shouldn't have taken more than a couple minutes, but all the lights went out, and what was up with that wind? His lion's ears had blown off three times already. Not that he minded a little dark with his main squeeze, in fact the eeriness of it all obviously made her nervous. Good, that should let him get away with an arm around her waist...

"What was that?"

"What was what?" She thought she saw something? How could she see anything in this dark?

"My god, what's that!?"

By the time he saw it, it had already ripped his throat out.

FIFTY-THREE

BENNY OPENED HIS EYES, shivering. He looked around. Trees rustled above him, arms waving against the wind that blew the dust into his eyes and ghostly howls into his ears. Where were they now? In the woods?

No, just farther down the greenbelt. No people, no lights, just trees stretching into the cloudy sky above picnic tables and rusted Frisbee golf stations. Beyond the trees he saw a few emergency lights of downtown smothered by thick-curtained fog. He'd never realized how dark the city was with all the lights out. There was nothing to see in the dark anyway. They'd...*flown?* about a mile. Out of the way for now, at least from the Ankou.

I can't get used to that word. It's Darryl for God 's sake!

There were other things to get used to. Churning clouds dominated the sky, forming a twisting funnel touching both horizons that induced a panicked, vertiginous feeling of falling *upward* the longer one looked at it. And ghosts were everywhere, hundreds of spectral figures ran in a silver ribbon across the night sky. A milky way of moaning souls flowing across the atmosphere.

Real Halloween.

Benny turned as Keith groaned. He had landed on his face, unconscious. Benny saw his hand close-up for the first time, a mess of red-raw skin. Benny squirmed just imagining how much it had to hurt, but he did have one idea, pulling off his right shoe, peeling off his sock and stuffing Keith's hand into it. At least now it would not touch the bare ground, maybe blunt the pain, but Ben had to wonder:

If Keith couldn't handle this, what chance do I have?

To emphasize the point he heard screaming through the trees, from people running hell bent for leather away from something. Benny tried to yell but his throat didn't want to work. *NOT THAT WAY! Too close to the fog!* They wouldn't have heard him anyway. As the runners passed under low branches, hooked rotting hands popped down through the fog to dig claws into their faces. The runners had a second to scream as their feet left the ground and they vanished into the dead tree branches, muffled screams lost on the wind.

"DAMN IT!"

"Benny? You kiss your dead sister with that mouth?"

Keith woke up for a moment, thank God. But then he closed his eyes again, leaving him alone.

Not alone. Benny felt a hand on his shoulder. Bridget's. Benny took a moment and looked at the ghost of his sister, just looked. A transparent smoky mist with the same hair, same eyes. She hadn't aged a day. *Of course she wouldn't. She's a ghost.* But a ghost with unmistakable consciousness. She still watched over him.

So did Connor, appearing in a flicker of blue mist next to Bridget. Then came the misty forms of Jack, Quentin, and *I guess that's Taylor. Never actually met him.* Everyone killed by the Puka. Benny couldn't help but *gulp.*

What do I do now?

Connor lifted a wavering arm to point. Benny followed to see a path going back into town, apparently he knew where Benny should go.

342

Benny didn't argue. He heaved Keith to his feet and started walking through the yellow murk of the emergency lights, letting Connor, or Connor's *ghost*, lead the way. Keith stumbled in grogginess, but he could walk on his own, clutching his hand. Connor lead them out of the park and back into downtown. He passed a couple blocks and several closed doors.

Does Connor even know where he's going?

He did. Connor pointed to an open door in a huge several story building. A hotel? People were already there, Benny saw a dozen or so run in through a double glass door amid frantic shrieks. Something about the wise action of "hiding from monsters behind a glass door" tickled Benny's mind, but looking at the river of souls flowing above him, any place was better than the great wide open. He ran to the door and shoved Keith in. The interior opened up into a lobby with desks and couches. Benny pushed Keith behind an overturned table and pulled his legs out of sight of the street. In a quick glance around Benny saw paper skeletons on the wall, orange ceramic pumpkins on the desks and a life size cardboard stand-up of Dracula holding two mugs of beer in either hand. Flanking that was a poster of a flagrantly out of proportion werewolf with a keg of beer on one shoulder and a bikini-clad screaming girl on the other. "Screaming" insofar as she had the devil's grin on her.

Benny took a moment to breathe, seeing the other people hiding in here, human eyes peeked out from under tables. They were safe, for the moment. Connor, Jack and Taylor all hovered outside, flickering in and out. Except...

They were dripping. Their ghostly forms rippled as tiny droplets of...ghost water peeled off their transparent flickers and fell upward, to be pulled into the ghost highway above them, out and away.

They're being pulled. The Ankou is calling them. They're resisting, but they're getting weaker the longer they resist.

And just like that, Quentin vanished. Too weak from confronting Darryl, his form never did completely resolidify. As Benny watched helplessly, Quentin's Spiderman form dissolved

343

into smoky water and flowed upward into the river above. Benny kept track of his mist for barely a second as it got caught up in the ethereal river, then lost him. Benny inhaled, but could do nothing. *They'll all be taken, one at a time. Even Bridget.* The very idea exploded Benny's anger, making his skin boil red.

NO. I won't let them have Bridget!

So mad was he, he only then realized that in staring at the ghosts, he'd never actually closed the door to the hotel lobby, and a thick wave of silky white fog rolled right in.

Carrying a creature with it.

What was THAT? Benny didn't recognize it for the life of him, even as it opened a mouth of crooked fanged teeth to have him for dinner.

PAIN

Keith's eyes shot open to the agony of his hand. For a scarce moment he thought he had gone blind as he blinked all around, seeing nothing but darkness and blurs. Then he remembered the lights going out. Then he remembered...Connor and Jack? They pulled him away, taking him on another ghost ride like he experienced chasing the *sluagh* to the mall. Now where was he, inside? *Sure, except its awfully foggy in here.* Fog rolled everywhere, undulating like a milky octopus looking for flesh to grab. *And why is there a sock on my hand?*

Grrrrr.

Then Keith saw the monster in the door, and that woke him up real quick. It was an opium nightmare with four legs of a panther yet the face of a gorilla. Black claws tore divots in the floor as the monster opened his maw to release an ear-ringing shriek. It stunk of musty blood that Keith could smell even from over here. Nauseating. Worse, Keith had never seen anything like it before. None of his books or folklore marathons ever showed him anything like this. *I know why.* Some monsters survived the cultural shifts to exist in whatever form, like the Redcap. But others were too forgotten for

344

even that, existing so far back to be a legend of a legend, swallowed by time. Such monsters tended to have no use for mortals at all, other than to chew on their bones.

This particular monster looked at Benny like his bones were very tasty indeed.

Benny! Keith couldn't get up in time. But after all they'd been through, to watch his nephew die in a hotel lobby? Keith wouldn't let it! He—

Watched.

Benny is standing his ground.

THE BLAST OF STINK hit Benny in the face. It scared him.

He was far too familiar with that emotion, as he'd been scared nearly his whole life, as long as he could remember. But... he also remembered the other Benny, the one that beat Marcus to within an inch of his life. He... *remembered* where that strength came from, remembered where he could find it again. He wasn't going to run and hide anymore. On the contrary he locked eyes with this beast, daring it to stare back. Nothing could hurt Benny without his permission. Nothing whatsoever.

The Beast disagreed, snarling and growling with blazing eyes. Benny stared back with every bit as much anger. Benny was scary. This was Halloween, and he would be damned if he would be scared by a growling animal, albeit a 1600 pound one.

You can't scare me, and you're not getting in.

With a blank glare, the black beast growled... then leaped away, seeking easier prey.

Benny exhaled as the black beast vanished. One monster was down but there were so many more. To prove the point more screams came rolling down the street. Benny stepped back inside the door, this time closing it firmly as he turned around and let it sink over him.

My God, I did it.

345

KEITH HEAVED HIMSELF UP. *My God, he did it.*

Keith's hand still hurt like hell, but he'd done the *HallO'Scream* with raging food poisoning before, and he could sure as hell handle a burned hand, especially with Benny needing help.

Or did he? Stumbling over, Keith went to the window to see the monster disappearing into the fog. It wasn't coming back. Keith then looked at the fog coiling into every corner and the river of ghosts curling through the sky, to do circles around the moon.

Magnificent.

Except this time it was more than crossover at the *HallO'Scream,* it was the whole freaking city, and people were dying out there.

"Hide! Zombie!"

Someone was still outside! Keith ran to the door, stretching his head out over the sidewalk to see two girls dressed in black leather running down the street, being chased by—not a Zombie, but a formless vapor with skeleton hands. *How could they goof that up?* But Keith already knew how, knew how people are generally decent, but also generally stupid, especially when they're being chased by a full-torso vaporous apparition. Take lazy people out of their comfort zones and they're as ignorant as a cowboy in a Verizon store.

Keith waved the girls inside, but they refused, instead they ran around a corner with no possible cover. Keith yelled after them and pounded his raw fist against the brick of the building in frustration. Everyone in this whole stupid town was going to die. Well, Keith would MAKE THEM listen, damn it. He turned around to face everyone hiding in the hotel lobby.

"Get up!"

Everyone stared blankly, shivering and whimpering.

"WILL YOU GET THE HELL UP?"

No. They would not get the hell up. They sobbed and cried. *Oh for the love of...* Keith knew his yelling wasn't making things a damn bit better, but this wasn't any time to be nice. These idiots were going to die! Except... Keith took a good long look at these scared, frightened people, and realized they weren't looking at him. Keith turned to Benny.

"They're looking at you."

FIFTY-FOUR

Benny saw the crowd looking at him.

Men and women came up from overturned tables, watching him with wide eyes. A frazzled head of hair peeked up from behind a couch, face a smear of tears and diva make-up. "How... did?" the girl tried to ask but her voice gave out. She couldn't speak, but she could stare. Benny didn't like being stared at. He'd prefer the horrors outside. But now everyone stared at him, pleading with their eyes for help. Even Keith was looking at him, expectantly.

Me? They want me to save them? In the center of a room full of people staring at him, Benny found the old antisocial panic yet again. He just fought off a monster damn it, he couldn't be afraid of people. Benny breathed and looked around, taking in dozens of men and women, a frightened mass of humanity. They weren't moving. Benny knew he'd have to do the unthinkable.

Talk to them.

"I... I know how to get out of here."

They listened.

"This isn't going to be like anything you've done before. They can only chase you if you run. So we're not going to run."

Benny hadn't spoken that many words in front of a crowd since speech class. Meanwhile Keith had gone behind the registration desk, finding a first aid kit to give his burned hand something better than a sock. Keith wrapped his hand with some gauze and pretended not to look, but Benny saw Keith's eyes:

He thinks I can do it.

Another scream from outside- and Benny looked across the street at a young girl, college-age with black hair, jeans and blue jacket, running for her life from a floating ghost apparition straight out of *Raiders of the Lost Ark*. Benny actually thought *Whoa that's cool,* but the girl apparently wasn't an Indiana Jones fan and had no idea what was going on. Screaming, she saw the light inside the hotel lobby and ran for it. She wasn't going to make it.

Benny didn't have time to argue with himself. He ran.

The fog was so thick it pulsed across the air. More people were running in the streets but there were not enough places to hide. With cackles of fanatical laughter, skeletal arms hooked out to ensnare helpless men and women, carting them high into the air where they disappeared into the fog, their screams vanishing with them. Benny ran into the heart of it all. He reached the girl as even more screeching apparitions tore at her hair, and Benny realized he had forgotten something.

Bridget remembered, and was next to him. Benny felt something in his hand.

A pumpkin. The one item no one else in this dumb city ever thought they'd need on Halloween. In fact, Benny had no idea why this street would even have one. In this city they were usually smashed underfoot. It must have been rescued from the lobby of the hotel. It was amateurishly carved with triangle eyes and smiling mouth, but it carried a fierce glow. The owner had foregone candles and went with glow sticks. Smart.

Holding the radiating pumpkin high before him, Benny shoved it right into the mass of ghosts. The skeletal horrors whipped out bony hands to grab black tresses of hair, but the orange light parted the ghostly mass like Moses and the Red Sea. Again, Benny could see what it saw:

BLINDING EYES. Eyes with no form, a spirit with no face. Unblinking with angry living flame that would not let him pass.

With a shriek the spirit hooked upward and away. Gone.

Benny pulled the girl behind him and ran back to the hotel.

KEITH'S EYES BORED IN on Benny. *He can do it.*

The ghost gave a last discouraged scream as it disappeared into the sky. Keith saw Benny gasp and stagger a bit as the connection cut. *Was he holding his breath the whole time? But it worked.* Pumpkin in hand, Benny got the girl back to the hotel, panting with exhaustion. Keith broke into a smile that usually only appeared in the depths of the *HallO'Scream* prop room or a midnight movie showing of *Master of the Flying Guillotine*.

"That, ladies and gentlemen, is what Halloween is all about." Together they could do it. Together they could—

SCREEEECH.

Keith's hands went to his ears. A screech like ripping metal set off pain sensors he didn't even know he had. Several people in the hotel collapsed, holding their ears against an excruciating sound that they had never heard before. Keith, however, *had* heard it before. He gritted his teeth as he looked up into the buildings, into the urban steel jungle of the city now surrounded in a sea of fog and found what he was looking for. Benny's ruckus with the pumpkin was bound to get his attention.

It perched on a ledge like a gargoyle with a wind-blown mane of serrated black hair, eyes of red flame. The Puka's eyes fell on them all, and the howl ceased. Like an acrobatic feline the black form jumped from building to building, then landing in the street without a sound, crouching like a tiger, mane flaring in the wind atop a horse's head.

Eyes set on Benny.

"STAY AWAY FROM HIM!" Keith screamed as his memory burned with flashbacks of Jack, and Aiden, and Darryl. Now it wanted Benny. Keith wasn't going to let that happen. Benny already backed up as Keith pushed him behind some of the people and placed himself out in front of the crowd gathered at the hotel door. It hurt his body to walk, even to breath, but there wasn't any kind of pain in this world that could stop him now. The puka stared at him, flexing muscles and opening horse lips to reveal jagged monster teeth.

Laughing at him.

Keith didn't care. The horse/feline hybrid almost slithered across the pavement, its breath making steam in the night air. Keith never took his eyes off it as he stepped away from Benny, interposing himself between the monster and his nephew. He didn't speak, he didn't need to.

I think we're about to have a serious disagreement.

The puka's eyes whirled as the horse rose into a 7-foot tall black-maned humanoid with a wicked evil grin. Keith flicked his head around to nod to Benny.

Take over.

Keith turned back to the monster that had wrecked his haunted house, killed every friend he had, and threatened his nephew with bodily harm. His words spat through clenched teeth.

"I dare you. Scare me."

WHOOSH

BENNY SAW KEITH'S DETERMINATION and knew what was about to happen. He tensed as Keith stomped straight up to the Puka and dared it to do anything about it. If possible, the Horse smile turned even wickeder.

WHOOSH

A blast of bitter wind with the stench of a cesspool engulfed Keith in a storm of dust that tore him off the ground, sending him tumbling end over end into a vortex of laughing skulls over the streets, out of sight. Gone.

"KEITH!" The gale evaporated, and Benny heard a horses laugh echoing down the dark street, then Benny was alone. He turned around to face the crowd, then gulped as everyone looked right at him.

I'd better be worthy of my name.

FIFTY-FIVE

BENNY SCANNED THE SKIES for another second before surrendering. Keith wasn't coming back, and he was on his own. *I can't do this alone!*

Except he wasn't alone, he was at the head of a couple dozen people, who now all looked to him. That was a lot of staring.

What do I do?

Benny's choice was taken from him as demonic shrieks came around the corner and the entire crowd ran back inside the hotel. Everyone cowered in the lobby as howls jiggled the windows and claws scraped against the glass.

Benny caught a good look before they disappeared, seeing that these spirits were nothing human. Animal snouts, apparitions with grasping lobster claws and spider legs. Nameless fears that hadn't been released in mortal land for 100 generations. One of them had a spider's head and eight full grown squirming spider-legs, and several girls muffled their cries at the sight. A grown man screamed in mortal terror as it passed the windows.

SPIDERS? Benny seethed at the man behind him. *You're six feet tall and you're scared of a spider?* Benny silently cursed as he took a good long listen to the shivering and sobbing in the room. Benny finally understood why Keith got infuriated so easily this time of year. None of these people had ever been scared, really petrified, a day in their life. Petrified was the back-stairwell of the high school. Petrified was getting trapped in the locker room shower by bullies with a gleam in their eye. Benny knew all too well what it felt like.

Maybe that was exactly what made him stronger than anyone here.

I know something no one else in this room does. I know HOW *to be scared. I've had a lifetime of practice.*

Benny's confidence reasserted itself. No, monsters weren't scary, not one damn bit. People, on the other hand—

"Benny?"

What? Who said his name? Who would even know his name? Benny looked around and finally saw a petite girl scooting across the floor toward him. Black hair, small eyes. She leaned in to whisper.

"You're Benny Bensel aren't you? Bridget's brother?"

Benny nodded. "Uh...yes." *And you are?*

"You were in the HallO'Scream when it burned down. I was worried. No one knew if you were in it."

Her again! The girl Kelly had pointed out as the expert on Finn MacCool. She hadn't gone to the mall, she went the other direction. *That's where I saw her, at the HallO'Scream two days ago. And before that, a locker across the hall, had math class same time of day. Name was...can't remember. But ...*"You were worried for me?"

"I asked Bridget to introduce us last year. I'm...I'm Piper."

"Of course you are," Benny said, embarrassed.

"You ...stopped that monster." She said with expectant eyes. "How did you do that?"

Errr. "I...uh..."

Piper didn't wait for an answer as her excitement broke through her terror. "Can you get us out of here?"

"I don't...I think so. Sure."

Way to sound confident there. But seriously, what are these people expecting? Benny looked at Piper, then at his hands. He was still

354

holding the pumpkin he'd used against the specter. He didn't remember bringing it back in, but the lobby had even more. *Odd. They must be leftovers from somewhere else, somewhere that didn't need them anymore.* Benny's memory wasn't up to Keith's standards, but he did remember every business that had carved pumpkins out on Halloween. The only one remotely near here would be—

It clicked. Why Connor had led him to THIS particular city block.

And Taylor's ghost materialized before Benny's eyes, flickering, transparent, still very dead. He pointed.

Benny nodded and looked to Piper. "Can you keep everyone here for me? I...I thought of something." Piper nodded, and Benny got up to walk behind the hotel counter towards the back door. It opened into a dark alley of gritty gravel. The lights were still out, but Benny knew where he was. Leaving the hotel, he ran down the alley to the left, looking down side streets, looking for one building in particular. He found it, right where it was three nights ago.

The *Scare Asylum.* Closed, shut down, but exactly what Benny needed.

Benny ran to the back door, expecting it to be locked and having to pound it down with five guys, but when he touched the knob... it opened wide, creaking on rusty hinges with all the flare of a 30's horror movie. Taylor's ghost held the doorknob on the other side, inviting him in. Benny nodded, looked around for thirty seconds, then ran back to the hotel.

The crowd was waiting for him, still shivering under the tables. Benny walked up to the nearest ones, and shivered too. But he spoke to them anyway.

"Look...uh...I can get some of you out of here. Maybe. I kinda know what's going on out there, which is likely more than you know. You might want to stay here and ride this out. I don't know if that will work or not, but the more of you that come with me the better. You might find what I'm going to do stupid, but ..."

He had to sell this. To everyone.

"But I don't."

The crowd hesitated.

SELL IT.

Benny inhaled, and searched his mind. "A friend of mine told me, very recently, that bullies 'get you' twice. Once when they pound you, then again when you spend the next decade hiding from them. So ask yourself right now how many times tonight you want to be 'gotten.'"

Benny knew Connor would like that.

"Make up your mind fast, because I'm leaving. If you want to help then follow. If not stay here." Benny sounded meaner than he wanted to, but he didn't want to wait anymore. He turned around to go back to the *Scare Asylum.* He didn't know how many of the people would follow him.

They all did. With Piper in the lead.

Benny led them down the alley and around the corner into the open door of the *Scare Asylum.* Benny funneled them all in. Taylor's ghost reappeared. Benny looked at him, unsure what to say. "Thank you," seemed appropriate. Could Taylor even hear him? The flickering figure nodded, but also looked tired, and blurry...

Oh no. He used up his strength helping us! Now he can't—

With a breath of wind, Taylor's ghostly eyes rolled upward as his face blanked, no longer able to resist the pull from above. Benny reached for him but there was nothing to grab as Taylor's form melted upward. Gone.

Benny choked, but got control. Turning around, he closed the door and walked back to the room he wanted. The *Scare Asylum*'s costume area. Masks filled a wall. Costumes lined various racks and laid across tables. Zombie suits, furry monsters, executioner's robes. An entire horror movie's worth of haunted house supplies. Benny started by opening a big chest full of effects make-up and dumping the contents all over a huge work table in the center of the room. Fake blood, liquid latex, brushes. Then he looked to Piper, who had been standing next to him, and swallowed his fear. He spoke to her.

"Can I...uh... use your face?"

Not the kind of thing to say to a girl. But she understood. Desperate to escape, the crowd was silent as Benny smeared ghoul gray make-up all over Piper's face, followed by thick black circles around her eyes and blood running out of her ears. Keith taught him everything he knew, and now Benny taught the crowd, directing others to duplicate what he was doing to Piper. He also pointed at the wall of masks.

"If you're not up to getting dirty, pick a mask. But not just anything. Pick something special."

People started fingering the latex hoods. Benny took a break from Piper to look at the wall, searching the rows for something he remembered from his last visit with Connor and the two girls. Finding it, he yanked it off the wall and threw it at the six-foot tall redneck who embarrassingly exposed his fear of arachnids five minutes earlier. A Spiders head.

"Pick the one that scares you."

Piper's face was done 90 seconds later, and she led a dozen girls in spreading out their personal stashes of make-up all over the floor to contribute to the communal supply. Benny got to work on the next volunteer as Piper did most of the talking. Benny didn't like talking to people.

But he did know Halloween.

CREEEEEAK.

The front door to the *Scare Asylum* opened.

Benny stepped out first. He took a moment to see his reflection in the glass doors. Ash blackened his eyes into hollow orbs, shading his face into a blackened skull hiding inside a hood. His gray hands held the orange glow of a pumpkin. Gripping it tightly, Benny walked into the street.

Behind him, another dark robed figure stepped out, a young woman wearing the tatters of a ghoulish bride. Then behind her stepped a zombie. Then a demon, then a skullface, until an entire motley assortment of Halloween monsters stood on the sidewalk facing the street. Swamp beasts. Furry monsters, and one monstrosity with a spider's head. Everyone's hands were full of anything that could glow: pumpkins, glowsticks, even cellphones with Jack O'Lantern apps.

As a group they witnessed skeletal apparitions sailing through the streets, chasing any mortal they saw.

Piper stepped closest to Benny. She swam inside the folds of a black gravekeeper's robe, her face hid under an ashen skull. She saw the swooping horrors above her and stopped, scared. Everyone was scared as they saw what waiting for them. A tsunami of ghosts soared above them with bloody hunger in their eyes. Someone choked on a sob.

Benny felt every last chill. Especially his own.

This isn't how I thought I'd spend this Halloween. Courage didn't come easy, especially when he had to provide it to everyone else. *I can't flake out now.* But with snarling ghosts in front of him, and a crowd of staring mortals behind him, he almost did. Almost, until another ghost materialized right in front of Benny, separate from the screaming hoard. The crowd didn't react, so maybe it appeared only for him. This wasn't a monster.

It was Jack.

Connor's transparent image stood next to him, but it was the ghost of Jack Cavanaugh, standing on the street corner in his Captain Sparrow outfit that motioned to Benny. In his head Benny could hear Jack's voice in the perfect warble of Johnny Depp:

The problem is not the problem. The problem is your attitude about the problem. Savvy?

Connor spoke next:

And if someone asks you if you're a god, you say YES!

A moan curled through the air and Benny saw that Jack couldn't resist anymore. He rippled, then drifted upward into the ghost river. Benny gasped and looked to Connor, expecting him to follow right behind, but Connor just looked to Benny, saluted with his right hand, and walked into a shadow to disappear. *Connor can still resist the pull.*

358

Benny was pulled back to the present with a warmth in his hand. He looked down to see Piper's lithe zombie hand holding it. The crowd shuffled up behind her.

No sense putting this off. Benny spoke to Piper softly, putting every effort to channel Jack's confidence. "We're doing this. Stick it right in their face and don't back down."

Piper's eyes whirled in a kaleidoscope terror. "But...I don't know how to be scary!"

Benny turned to look at the assemblage of costumed monsters behind him. People so tall that Benny had to look up to see them. They obviously felt the same way.

"I do."

Benny walked into the street and a skeletal phantom with glowing red eyes shrieked directly towards him, spreading bony arms with sickle claws. The crowd cried out, but Benny yelled back at them.

"Ever been to a haunted house? Well you're in one now."

Several terrors barreled down on Benny, claws extending to rend him into pieces.

"And YOU'RE the monster!"

Benny shoved his pumpkin high and defiant, letting loose with a rip-roaring guttural ROAR. A full chested guttural scream of righteous anger, screaming like a maniacal killer. Nothing articulate. Pretty dumb actually. But contagious, and the crowd screamed right along with him, ROARING loud and proud. Inharmonious, but loud, and a touchdown cheer if Benny ever heard one.

The red-eyed phantom fumbled and vanished into the night.

More ghosts swooped in on them but the crowd raised pumpkins in challenge right back at them. Benny screamed until he went hoarse. His voice couldn't give out yet! A soothing hand on his shoulder drew away the pain. Flickering blue. Bridget. Benny looked at her wispy form, and as their eyes met he fell into one last vision, the last gift from his dead sister.

Screams, of a hundred thousand shrilling voices, taunting the mortals with promises of pain.

But screams answered back, from the mortals! Mortals with faces painted as black skulls with snarling faces, marching down the road with their fists in the air. They screamed their challenge against the night. And where they went, the spirits fled. The mortals marched and drove the terrors from their village. They scared away the Night. And cheered. For themselves. For their lives.

Scary was survival.

Benny gulped in air as the vision passed. A massive gust of dust roared across Benny's eyes, blinding him for a moment, when his eyes cleared, Bridget was gone.

So was everything else. No ghosts. No apparitions. No screaming dive-bombing skeletal terrors.

Looking around Benny saw faces hidden under the make-up that were, dare he say, smiling? *People who deal in monsters cannot be afraid of them.* Something only a Haunted House Connoisseur would know. Now these people weren't afraid, they *were* monsters. Vicious, wrathful monsters, and they wanted their city back.

They had earned one street.

Benny pulled the crowd away from the *Scare Asylum* and into the now deserted street. Across the way he saw people peeking out from closed doors, eyes alive with hope. The monster crowd waved them over and shared whatever they had, quickly making their faces into personifications of ugly. Someone had a tiki torch and using it they made more torches out of whatever was lying around. Benny put the torch bearers in front of what now numbered over two dozen skull-faced lunatics. *For being dumb enough to take on the living dead, that's exactly what we are.* New recruits ready, Benny moved forward, following the silver river of ghosts in the sky, a river converging somewhere ahead.

The crowd followed Benny, Piper staying on his right. He saw her smiling, daring to hope she'd survive this horrible night.

"Finn... Finn MacCool never had it that hard," she said.

Flashback to *The Burner spewing liquid flame all over scorched rocks bubbling exposed skin—* Benny smirked. "You'd be surprised."

"Where do we go now?"

"To the next street."

"This is unreal," Piper said, quiver in her voice. "What happened to Halloween?"

Benny looked upward to the river of ghosts in the clouds.

"It came back."

FIFTY-SIX

WIND! GRITTY DIRT SLASHED Keith's eyes as a vortex of dust tumbled him end over end. Clouds and buildings swept by as the wind propelled Keith impossibly fast. Wherever Keith had been before, he knew he wasn't there anymore.

THUD.

Keith landed face first with an explosion of dust on a dirt road. Thick trees lined either side under the night sky, with the rustling of dead branches the only sound under dark clouds. As he climbed to his feet, he heard moans of the dead, and not just that. The air had a musty presence that vibrated against him, worming its way into his skin. The *Other Side.* Not a shallow pocket this time, but deep within its bowels, a layer so deep that the dead were almost physical entities.

To prove the point, a skeletal apparition solidified out of spinning fog and took a swipe at him. Keith ducked as talons swept over his head and the skull-faced spirit flew off into the clouds. Keith watched for it to return, almost missing the *next* ghost swooping from behind. Keith rolled on the ground as the spirit overshot and disappeared into the trees surrounding the road, trees with sharp edges daring Keith to skewer himself upon them.

Clippity Clop

And there's the Dullahan, Keith thought. *Couldn't have Samhain without him.* Keith looked down the dark road but couldn't see anything more than dozen yards away. A thick fog obscured everything.

CLIPPITY CLOP

That's not the Dullahan!

Keith had two seconds to jump into a ditch as a black rider tore by like a screaming banshee, hooves pounding like steam hammers and slicing a sword where Keith's neck had been a second before. Keith coughed up leaves as he rolled over and the black caped rider turned his massive horse around to take another charge. This time Keith took a good long look, seeing this rider had a head, right on his shoulders where it belonged. This wasn't the Dullahan, just a killer. With a really sharp sword.

Keith jumped the other way as the rider pounded by, this time landing in a prickly briar patch that stuck him with a hundred prickly points. Keith yelped but disentangled himself, looking around for an escape, but seeing nothing but endless road and impassable forest on either side.

Just like a room in a haunted house, Keith thought. Claustrophobic confined space against a galloping terror in the dark, oppressed by pain on all sides. The rider turned around one more time, a black hooded rider in a fluttering cape, like so many monsters Keith had seen before.

No, this was *exactly* like a haunted house, a house meant especially for Keith.

The Puka wants a rematch.

It wanted to kill Keith once and for all, the only haunted house owner to survive it. Well, Keith would give him everything it wanted and more. "As I was saying before I was interrupted," Keith yelled into the night air, "Scare me!"

Ruuuuuumble. The *Other Side* rippled with Keith's proclamation, and now he drew it all in: the hum, the whispers, the ambiance of this living haunted house. Keith collected it all into his mind. Bridget had shown him how to bend this place to his will, and now Keith wanted to be scary.

And Keith had been scaring for a long, long time.

Clippity Clop. The rider came charging for the third time. The ground rumbled under the pounding of the monster hooves, shaking the very bones in Keith's legs. The rider burst out of the fog, sword held high in a muscled arm to slice Keith's head from his shoulders. Eyes oriented on Keith—

Who was holding a shotgun.

BOOOM!

Metal, blood and grit flew everywhere as the rider exploded off the horse, falling onto the road with a flop of dust. His horse carried on, flying past Keith as a four-legged earthquake and off down the road into the fog. Vanished. Keith chambered another shell and spat at the heap on the ground. "The maniacal black knight cliche doesn't scare us anymore. It had something to do with the invention of gunpowder." Keith angrily held the shotgun up high with one hand. "This is my boomstick!"

The crumpled rider wriggled. Not dead yet. Bones crackling, it sat up in an unnatural position. Keith pointed his weapon as the rider made the sound of a—

Cackle. Out of the pile of shredded clothes and metal crawled a skeleton. Rickety bones hurled itself at Keith in *Jason and Argonauts* style, happening so fast that Keith didn't even have time to wonder why a musty skeleton summoned by a Celtic horse would even know what a *Jason and Argonauts* skeleton cackle was supposed to sound like.

BOOM. Keith blew off an arm and several ribs in a cloud of boney dust, but the skeleton just knocked the shotgun away as it clamped down on Keith's neck with broken teeth, its sharpened fingers digging in to rend Keith's flesh from his bones. It just made Keith mad. Keith grabbed the skull with two hands and looked straight into the empty eyes with a furious glare.

"Scare THIS!"

With a shriek of anger the skeleton was ripped away by the grip of several twisting branches, monstrous trees that were not there a moment before. Thick roots wrapped around white bones and dragged the screaming Harryhausen refugee several feet into the air. The skeleton thrashed against the rough bark of the branches, but was completely overwhelmed, just like in one of Keith's favorite movies. The same one with the "boomstick" as a matter of fact, featuring a lone mortal trapped in a dilapidated cabin besieged by haunted trees in a dead forest, trees who happily attacked any expendable movie extra, especially shrieking females.

Or skeletons. Keith winked— and the branches ripped the corpse apart, sending bones fragments all over the dead leaves of this haunted forest. Keith shouted in victory and looked through the trees and saw horse-eyes watching him in anger. *Nope, didn't like that at all.* Good. Keith would give it something to get angry about. A push of Keith's *will* melted the forest away to reveal the churning clouds of the *Other Side*. Nightmares, terrors, and winds surged around Keith as red flaming eyes appeared in the clouds around him, full of hate.

"Puka's Night is it? Trying to be scary?" Keith sneered.

If the Puka wanted a battle of scares then Keith would give it one. Terror versus terror, fright versus fright. Keith was a haunted house creator and now he stood inside the ultimate haunted house with an unlimited budget, unlimited scares, and all the actors he could imagine. On this Halloween Keith was exactly where he wanted to be, in a battle against the Celtic mascot for Samhain, a battle of fright to the death.

So Keith shattered the cold air in a furious challenge.

"How about if I scare YOU?"

No one knew more about Halloween than Keith.

No one.

FIFTY-SEVEN

KEITH ONCE WISHED HAUNTED houses could be real. Now he knew they could be.

A whirlwind of images pummeled him, assaulting every sense at once. In this deepest swirl of the *Other Side* every thought turned into reality. Every monster turned real.

WHOOSH

The whirlwind spun away, and Keith found himself in a graveyard. Titanic tombstones jutted up from dead earth, cracked stone with Celtic swirls. A chapel of death under a cold moon.

Keith took in the grim scene. The fear of death crossed every culture, fear the Puka would use against him. Looking, Keith saw the Puka perched atop a tall pillar, black limbs digging into the stone like a stalking vulture, eyes of red hate lost in a whipping black mane.

BOOM

The earth exploded at Keith's feet. A grave had blown outward, leaving a gaping crater sick with the filth of rot and decay. Every sense screamed for a healthy mortal to *Run for your life! The Filth will infect you!*

Keith stayed right where he was, even as a disgusting corpse pulled itself out of the crater, a slime-ridden monster with a half-rotted face and no eyes, just sticky holes where something should have been. It hissed with a mouth full of dirt as it crawled upright and lurched toward Keith.

RUN YOU FOOL! Keith's primitive hind-brain screamed at him to get out of reach, to flee from the sickening mass. As this monster chomped its dead teeth in another *hiss,* Keith thought that yes, running away would be a very good idea.

Just not tonight.

We ARE scary.

Keith's hand touched his arm, caressing a tattoo under his jacket to mold the *Other Side* around him. The graveyard vanished under a torrent of fog. Hell, a snow-filled blizzard as in seconds every tombstone lay buried under a foot of snow straight out of the Scandinavian depths. Keith vanished with it. He now wore rusted armor with a rotting cloak and horned helmet. Underneath lay a corpse of dark leather skin stretched tight over bare bones. Muscled hands held a chipped battleaxe dripping with black blood.

It was Halloween after all. Now Keith had his costume.

The ghoul kept growling toward him, zero thought behind his gouged eyes. Keith laughed. No, the Puka had never been to Norway. He wouldn't know about a *Draugr,* the Viking revenant who guards his tomb for eternity, coming from a culture that held death with honor and had so little fear of corpses that it burned them.

Keith cleaved the ghoul's head in two.

The creature disintegrated into black smoke and *Draugr*/Keith continued his forward momentum to jump right into the Puka with axe high in the air. It chopped down with undead strength of a 1000 years—

Shattering the stone pillar as the Puka vanished into gray smoke.

Keith spun to see the Puka appearing behind him, bringing his axe around just as Puka backhanded him with the strength of a pile driver. Keith knocked down icy tombstones like bowling pins until he hit a snowdrift several yards away, his *will* collapsing under the pain and *Draugr* body evaporating. Keith struggled to his feet amongst broken tombstones, but grinned maliciously as the Puka growled in pain too. Grisly ichor leaked from an axe wound. The *Draugr* had been too fast.

You weren't there when Ireland learned about the Vikings the hard way? Keith fumbled with the tombstones. Getting footing was hard with the snowy rocks shifting beneath his weight, and his raw frozen hand acted up again. But Keith felt other pain. Not his, the Puka's. Keith could feel it. Almost follow it...

BOOM.

Another grave exploded, wiping away Keith's blizzard wasteland, shifting the scene to...a desert of bones, baking under a hot red sun. Bleached skulls and ribcages stretched to the horizon as yet another corpse crawled out of the new hole in the ground. Not slimy this time, but baked, dried up, the parched shell of a poor soul left to die in the middle of nowhere. Dried leather skin creaked as rusted arms reached out to grab Keith before he could get back on his feet. This desert mummy squirmed across the broken bones and would be on Keith before he could do a thing about it. The corpses face was a near solid mass of fossilization, blocky teeth grinding together. Revolting.

Keith growled with anger and pushed his will outward again.

I eat revolting for breakfast.

The desert vanished. Rippling into existence now was a thick rain-forest in murky air, sultry heat of a jungle at dusk, Asian lamps hanging from trees. In the midst of soggy dirt and tangling undergrowth, the petrified corpse reached for Keith only to find that he had vanished. Where Keith had been...

Was the head of a dark haired woman.

Just the head. Beautiful almond eyes, smooth face trailing a flail of waist-length black hair on one end... and a writhing mass of intestines on the other, writhing around her head like Medusa snakes.

Sitting in a tall tree of this rain forest, the Puka...blinked.

With a tentacle FLASH, the writhing mass attacked the corpse, its whipping innards slithering around its neck in strangulation. The monster reached right through the fleshy tendrils to grab the snarling head directly, but the tentacled intestines overwhelmed it as flailing flesh wrapped around every limb, then *squeezed*. The mummy croaked as its head popped off and rolled into the dank forest. The rest of the corpse disintegrated as it hit the ground. For a moment, there was no sound but the chirping of forest animals...and an angry growl from the Puka, unable to see anything of Keith or this dark-haired woman inside the thick black smoke. It peered closer...

Getting a front seat view as the beautiful dark-haired female head sprang from the cloud, smiling with a mouth of fanged teeth as her black entrails propelling her through the air.

That...squirm, belonged to a *Penanggalan.* One of the more erotic monsters from southeast Asian folklore. Keith always wanted one for the *HallO'Scream,* now he *was* one. Keith's *Penanggalan* self launched across the night sky, crossing the distance to the Puka in milliseconds and sinking razor teeth into a thick horse leg. The Puka screamed as it was hurt again. Muscles flexed as it knocked the head away. Keith's form disintegrated under the power, but this time he controlled his fall and landed feet first, watching the Puka leap to another tree far away. The Puka didn't like that one damn bit. Keith's bloodlust burned as his mind whipped through a never-ending encyclopedia of horrors his brain had filed away over decades. He hadn't even begun to fight.

Neither had the Puka. Psychic pressure buzzed Keith's head as red glowing eyes sunk into him. Puka burrowed, trying to find another primal fear. Keith pushed back.

Give me your worst.

The rain-forest whisked away into the mists of the *Other Side* as yet another location of mortal terror set the scene. Mortals had so much to be afraid of, so many buried instincts we never even think about until they stare us in the face. So small, so fragile.

So edible.

Grrrrrr.

Keith found himself human again, standing in a craggly forest with tall trees and crunchy leaves, surrounded by a dozen pairs of shimmering yellow eyes.

Grrrrrr.

Something was very hungry indeed. Yellow eyes stepped forward on four legs. Wolves. BIG wolves, muzzles dripping with gore as Keith's mind fought a terror deeper than conscious thought itself: Fight or Flight, the terror of knowing you were about to be dinner to a hungry predator. 50,000 years of homo sapiens' compulsion to SAVE YOURSELF rammed Keith right between his eyes as he moved to run into the dark—

Except Darkness was a primal fear too, the terror from pre-history when man's domain extended no farther than the edge of a campfire. Whether by clawed horrors in the stone-age or by urban predators that would kill you for your android phone. Keith felt the Puka's mockery at the smallness of man.

YOU EXIST TO BE EATEN. The Puka pressed against Keith's mind. *RUN FOR YOUR LIFE AND DIE!*

Keith considered as the mangy wolves closed in, saliva dripping on the crunchy forest floor.

Nah.

Fear of being devoured by a predator? That went back farther than homo sapiens. A *lot* farther. Keith knew just how far back.

The Puka didn't.

So Keith vanished.

The wolves stopped. They sniffed the air, confused.

THUMP

A massive vibration shook the ground, rippling the leaves, stopping the wolves in mid growl.

THUMP THUMP

The ground rumbled as if hammered by massive footsteps, for that's exactly what they were. Wolves *yelped* as a gigantic three-toed scaly leg smashed out of the trees to squish one wolf into pulp. Then a reptilian muzzle the size of a mid-sized sedan scooped up another one to crack lupine bones between serrated teeth, *Keith's* teeth as his Tyrannosaur scattered the wolf pack with the roar of a steam engine, *crunching* wolf after wolf. Keith's predator pitched its head to ROAR at the sky in triumph and advance on the Puka. This is what scary was about!

Never seen a dinosaur have you? They're older than Samhain! Older than Ireland!

OLDER THAN YOU!

Keith hurled his jaws down to engulf the Puka. The psychic *buzz* in Keith's head faltered as the Puka finally—

Freaked.

Gibbering desperation pushed it up and away to escape. Keith wouldn't let it! The *buzz* of connection led Keith straight into the monsters mind. The Puka shrieked as it tried to break the connection, but Keith drew up his entire sense of self and PUSHED.

I've got a scare room for you!

Cornered in a claustrophobic pipe. Trapped!

And a predator is outside, a HUNGRY predator. Massive jaws the size of an SUV clamp right outside your tiny hole. A dinosaur so wild with hunger that it smashes against your small drainage pipe again and again, tearing away corrugated metal. Teeth chew in frantic twisting. It smells your blood. It knows you're in that hole.

But you can't escape! The other way is blocked with rocky debris that pokes you as you squeeze against it hoping for the slightest space between you and the chomping teeth! But the jaws are so big! You've all but surrendered to your fear, knowing that when its frenzied strength rips away enough of the pipe, it will clamp its jaws down on YOU.

And now the hole is even bigger! You kick your legs back and back, trying to squeeze back against the rocks, but there's nowhere left to squeeze to! The reptilian jaws can reach too far in and clamp down on your thrashing leg, serrated teeth puncturing all the way to the bone!

SCCCCRRRREEEEEEEAAAAACCCCKKKKK

The Puka screamed. The black mass slithered out of Keith's mind. Keith yelled with exhilaration as he now pressed in again. "Scream for me!" Keith shouted, now back in human form.

The Other Side rippled again into a 360 degree panoramic theater. The ground fell away in hurricane winds as all sense of *real* versus *fantasy* whipped away. The next battleground focused as Keith pressed forward all the harder with even more nightmares that his anger fed his mind faster than he could use them.

"SCREAM!"

FIFTY-EIGHT

A̶n̶ ̶e̶t̶e̶r̶n̶i̶t̶y̶ ̶a̶g̶o̶, in a moment perfect beauty in Benny's TV room, Benny knew exactly when he would permanently purchase *Cabin in the Woods* for his coveted DVD collection:

The SWAT Team of weapon laden tough guys charge into the hall of elevators, just in time for every door to open in a synchronized :::*ping*::: swamping the bad-guys in a tsunami of horror movie monsters including but not limited to: a man-eating tree, a giant vampire bat, a howling soul-sucking ghost, and a 50-foot long snake. Seeing them all at once in a ten-second orgy of blood on his big screen TV, Benny just about cheered.

Seeing it all in person on the streets of his city, Benny about heaved. *This isn't funny.*

But the ghosts also showed the way. Benny's party just had to follow the river of spirits in the sky. The crowd moved through the streets as fast as their fragile courage would take them. *They're getting the hang of it,* Benny thought, *but my kingdom for a dozen HallO'Scream veterans.*

And speaking of horror movies, a death scream cut the air, the shriek of a man who'd seen his whole life pass before him and knew the finale was mere seconds away. It came from a massive courtyard intersection of major hotels and office buildings. Benny and his crowd ran ahead to the source. Piper remained at Benny's side, holding a pumpkin before her, drawing off his courage. She'd need it. What they saw wasn't a ghost.

A mad cross between a bear and a carnivorous lizard with four black eyes and six sets of claws. The beast took two sniffs of the air and looked up directly at the crowd of costumed mortals with a growl. People gulped, and stepped back.

"No. One. Move." Benny enunciated, keeping perfectly still. The beast's mouth of notched teeth opened as it regarded Benny's crowd. They started to inch back...

"DONT MOVE."

A girl wearing a red devil face and fright wig whimpered, eyes locked on the beast. "But that's a monster!" she whispered. Benny rose up as high as his legs allowed. He stepped forward.

"So are you!"

The beast's four eyes whirled as Benny closed the distance with his pumpkin in front of him. With smaller steps, his group joined him. Benny dared peek his head at their reflection in a store window: Skulls. Bigfeet. Slashers.

Monsters.

The slobbering beast growled, then shuddering with...fear?

He doesn't know what we are.

"Charge him."

To Benny's pride, his crowd let loose a shout like half-crazed banshees. The beast leaped back with a *yowl*...then jumped down a dark alley. The crowd cheered, slapping each other under their gruesome monster masks. Benny tensed and led them around the next corner.

Every living inch of it swarmed with ghosts, skeletal corpses swirling in the sky and around buildings in undulating laughter as

374

they hooked skeletal arms around screaming men and women and threw them into murky clouds. Other people died as ghosts plunged claws into chests to stop their hearts, killing them where they stood. Dead bodies collapsed in the road, lifeless. . .until transparent spirits rose from the corpses, and were pulled irresistibly into the river of souls stretching across the sky.

Benny's entire troupe of drafted haunted house actors gulped. So did Benny. *This wasn't in the MacCool job description.* Piper squeezed his hand. *How long has she been holding my hand?* Didn't matter, the point was made. *We're in this together, and its now or never.* Benny started in slow—

Until a girl ran right across the street from them, screaming for her life.

"SUZANNE!"

A woman yelled behind Benny, dressed in a brown monk's robe with face painted in orange and black pumpkin face. She pushed her way to the front, reaching for the girl. "Suzanne! Run to us!"

The running girl looked and saw the woman. "Megan?" College-aged, dressed in only shorts and jacket. Her bare legs with white boots skidded for traction as she ran from a skeletal horror pursuing her. Hands of petrified bone slashed her legs and she fell to the pavement, screaming as the hands dragged her into the fog.

"NOOOOO!" Megan tore out of the crowd, slicing her flaming torch in her right hand like a lightsaber and screaming in furious anger, bashing any skeletons that got near Suzanne. The specter shrieked and fled. Suzanne clutched her bleeding legs as Megan leaned over to help, turning her back to the specter that now came back with friends. As she looked down, Megan never saw as a dozen spirits dislocated their jaws impossibly wide—

Benny did. He dove for Megan, pushing her down as a swarm of petrified hands clawed them from every side and a seven-foot-tall decomposing humanoid of parched leather came out of the fog. Protruding bone pushed out of broken skin and a single blank eye fixated on Megan. She never even had time to scream as it reached down to swallow her head whole—

ROOOAAARR. The Halloween crowd screamed in the face of death. Benny found himself surrounded in a ring of pumpkins as his crowd charged forward. A man painted green with monster claws took swipes at the ghosts, daring them to get closer. A woman with a painted wolf's face snarled with blackened teeth. A couple of rubber monster masks in black leather stood side by side, holding pumpkins out with one hand, waving torches in the other.

Like a river curling around an unmovable rock, the fog steered clear. One last *ROAR* from the scary humans and the fog fled completely, skittering around every corner. Benny breathed as hands reached down to help him up. Suzanne tried to stand but cried in pain at every movement, her lacerated legs leaving a trail of blood right on the street. Several people helped her up, letting her lean on them.

For one precious moment it was just so...quiet, just quiet breathing under a black sky of stars. Benny looked around as the silence coaxed dozens of whimpering forms out of hiding. From out of apartments and locked cars, came more sobbing people running for the safety of the crowd.

How many do we have now? Benny didn't know, but everyone taught the newcomers fast. People smeared make-up on faces and more than a few new people had masks of their own, scary ones at that. A demon skull, a bear skin rug, and even a Darth Vader mask. *I guess that'll work.* Benny finally had a moment to look around. This corner had been busy, too many people when it was attacked and now corpses littered the ground. Wispy spirits lifted up from the bodies, flowing upward into the river of ghosts above him. Benny shivered, but—

Save the living first, he thought as one more huddled mass bumped him with a moan. Hurt, bleeding, he nursed a wounded arm and had a heck of a beaten face. Benny reached for him to get him into his crowd. *This guy needs help.*

He looked into the face of Marcus.

An entire life shot between their eyes in two seconds. Especially what happened last night, as Marcus still sported the bruises. All of them. But this wasn't the Marcus Benny knew, that man was gone.

This Marcus bent over in pain, but held up his eyes long enough to see Benny, who looked into his eyes and saw none of the arrogance, none of the self-importance, like part of him was dead. The lingering black funk on his soul was unmistakable.

Kelly's had her way with him too.

Benny just looked at him. *What sensation did she leech off of him? Dominance? Aggression? His behavior over the last year makes a lot more sense now. He's just another victim.*

Benny looked down. A lifetime was a long time to be mad. Knowing what he now knew, none of it meant a damn. He now saw Marcus as he really was. Not so hot, not so bright, and very shaken. Benny didn't need any courage speak to him.

"Ah...You need help?"

Marcus swallowed. "Yes. And, I can... I can help."

Yes he could. Marcus had worked in the *Scare Asylum.*

"I've got just the face for you," Benny said as the crowd passed forward some make-up. "It's not a vampire either."

"Benny, I'm sorry...for..."

"So am I." Benny looked him in the eye as he held tubes of make-up in his hands. Ashen Grey. Blood red. "Stand still, let me put a face on you." Marcus nodded, and winced as he knelt down. As he did, Benny could see the street behind him.

A ghost stood there.

Connor. Arms folded in satisfaction, he nodded with a smile. Benny smiled back, and got back to Marcus.

"And my name is Ben."

A scream came from several blocks away then cut off with blood-curdling finality. Everyone looked up to see a pale light glowing from somewhere beyond. Benny gathered his crowd around him, pulling them close. Chasing off a few skeletons was one thing, but until they confronted the Ankou, they hadn't won anything.

It approached.

FIFTY-NINE

KEITH WAS MORTAL. MORTALS are born to die. So much fear of death. So much desperation to save yourself from it. So many reminders of how close death actually is. With every prick of pain. With every drop of blood.

Every breath you take.

SUFFOCATION!

Keith's body fell under waves of cold salty water. He clawed in desperation to breathe! His lungs burned as his body thrashed for any air, but the waves pulled him down. DOWN.

Keith's mind fell under the maelstrom of seering wind as nightmare after nightmare flooded his senses. He held on, barely.

Water filled Keith's lungs, choking him even as more weight pushed him down, away from the only light he could see, far above on the surface, now so far away.

Except it wasn't the water pushing him down. He was being PULLED. Prickly claws grasped his ankles, pulling him farther down into the reach of smiling women with bodies of seaweed.

378

And mouths of piranha teeth.

Not Kelpies again. Keith wouldn't fall for this, but the images barreled in so fast that they were only blurs. The Puka once had the entire Halloween holiday as his own. How many nightmares could scare entire generations? How many mortals could die in an eternity? The Puka knew all too well, and more terrors assaulted Keith from all five senses.

Cold water had suffocated him, but now he was suffocating against cold dirt, pressed down with the strength of an elephant. Thick leather arms pushed him flat and his bones cracked under the strain.

Jagged teeth ripped Keith's flesh, pulling his muscles into shreds as a gargantuan humanoid pulled red juicy blood from Keith's body to sedate a horrible hunger.

Being eaten alive!

Mortals are born to die. The Redcap will happily send you on your way. Keith's mind split between the two conflicting visions, each one a nightmare of death tearing his sanity out at the roots. His heart pounded as he reached for control, contracting his mind into a ball of white hate to fight back against the two horrors, even as he was assaulted by a THIRD!

Death.

The body withers. The heart falters. The hourglass sand empties and breath itself stops. From age or by neglect the end is the same.

DEATH.

Shriveled flesh goes numb. Fingers get cold. Feel your heart skip, stutter. FEEL YOUR HEART STOP.

Body is devoured by worms. Born to die Born to...

Born. Keith almost had a memory of his birth. A lifetime ago. But lifetimes always end, and he really knew what happened next:

Death is only the beginning.

See what awaits on the other side.

See the bony hands of Death reach for you, the spirits of those already passed, waiting across the threshold. Waiting to grasp your spirit with the clutch of cold death, waiting for their feast in death that they could never have in life.

Even death doesn't protect you here. Scream as the Purgatory of the Dead reaches for you.

Scream as your spirit is devoured by the Sluagh.

Scream in Fear.

Keith could have. Should have. Maybe even would have, but he simply had too much vindictive pride. Keith knew fear as a weapon of survival, the primeval Fight or Flight. Choose flight? That *might* save your life, *might* let you escape. *FLEE!*

Keith chose Fight. October 31st made a good night for fighting. He had plenty of nightmares of his own:

Burning house, flames everywhere. And you're in the middle of it all, wearing a full-face breathing apparatus that fogs as you gulp huge amounts of air. Fire all around you as you struggle to escape.

Then the air cuts off. Struggle against the mask. Heavy gloves make for fumble fingers as you squirm against the straps. GET IT OFF!

You won't make it.

Celtic monsters. What did they know about fear? The most dangerous tool they ever heard of was the wheel and axle, but in this new world there were so many more terrors even Celtic killers needed to fear. Keith would introduce them.

Kelpies, water spirits. Enticing mortals to their deaths under the waves. Such cold water, freezing your skin to the bone. Mortals should fear them.

Except there was so much more in the water than mortals. In fact, there were so many creatures that claimed dominion over the water, and everything in it. No, the kelpies have no idea about this New World. They have no idea they're supposed to be afraid to be back in the water.

The suffocation vanished as Keith wrapped himself in the *Other Side*...and evaporated. The kelpies screamed as he slipped out of their grasp, thrashing as they searched the water for him.

They weren't going to find him.

The water beneath the kelpies surged as a massive undertow pulled them away. The kelpies pushed away but couldn't swim against the suction of an entire ocean forcing them down, down into a black maw the size of a house.

The maw shined with several rows of pointed teeth out of a Lovecraft nightmare.

But they weren't teeth, they were... plastic?

Pollution, an entire pulsing mass of industrial plastic, the waste of civilization, clogging the water, full of corpses of sea-life that had been caught, trapped, and died ensnared amid plastic bottles, plastic bags, plastic rope. The mass moved with sickly purpose to consume, ever hungry for more of the ocean, more life to corrupt.

You want to suffocate me? I'll suffocate YOU.

The Kelpies shrieked against the mass, just in time for the massive Cthulhu tentacles of shiny rotten plastic to wrap around them, dragging them into the open maw of human waste that closed with a CHOMP. Muffled screams barely escaped as the monstrous mass retreated into the depths.

The mane of flailing black hair leaped back into view as the horse-head monster roared with a challenge. It now came after Keith all the harder with eyes glowing with hate.

Redcap straddling him, ripping into him with savage claws and animal fury! So much pain. This monster defined pain for an entire culture. The first of the slashers would FEAST on blood!

The first of the slashers maybe, but not the most exciting. Keith knew of another, a monster defined by pitiless brutality. Keith usually hated celebrities, but now he would make one exception.

Especially if in space, no one could hear you scream.

Keith vanished! Evaporated into the mists and the Redcap roared in furious hate! It clawed and growled with hands dripping blood, looking for its lost victim. It looked everywhere!

Except behind itself.

A long shadow dropped over it, a black mass whose skin reflected the depths of empty space, a sightless head trapped in eternal grinning teeth. The Redcap spun to face the new creature behind him—

Freezing in stupendous shock at a monster with one set of jaws that opened to reveal another, a monster that took but a moment to drink in the Redcap's own bewildered fear before the inner jaws of the Alien shot out to crack the Redcap's skull wide open.

Keith pushed into the Puka's mind while he had the advantage, pushed into the glowing red eyes of death, daring the horse-head freak to do anything about it.

You haven't seen anything yet!

Demonic faces of the Sluagh writhed in laughter as they thrashed the pitiful mortal soul. Mismatched faces and crooked skulls contorted to mirror the contortion of their own black souls. They smothered Keith.

They expect you to run. Why wouldn't you?

Odd time for it to come up, but Keith's broken hand still hurt. A ripple of his *will* soothed the pain. And more as Keith took full advantage of the moment as his right arm extended out into a metallic tool with a buzzing blade.

A chainsaw blade now slashed across the heads of the *Sluagh* in a scream of internal combustion.

PAIN! The pain of sharp metal wielded by a mortal who was just too dumb to know he was supposed to be afraid, and who had watched entirely too many 80's cult horror movies. A mortal with a chainsaw, mowing down the Sluagh with a malevolent smile on his face.

You're *NOT* in Ireland anymore!

Undead faces howled as the scream of the metallic beast on Keith's arm tore through them, carving an arc of shredded death, and the Sluagh howled from something they thought lost forever: Agony.

Keith cackled with glee. "Swallow my soul, will you?" His chainsaw arm reached high in the air in a cacophony ROAR of black exhaust. His other hand reached behind him to pull a double-barrel shotgun from a holster on his back. He spun it around one finger before pressing the barrel right into the mouth of a crackly white convulsed face of the nearest undead spirit with mismatched ears and crossed eyes.

"SWALLOW THIS!"

BOOM

IN ANOTHER REALITY, AT the end of a huge autograph line, an actor at a nameless Comic Con signed an old collector's DVD of a movie called ***EVIL DEAD II*** with the autograph "Bruce Campbell."

Taking a pause, he looked up into thin air and smiled.

THE *OTHER SIDE* CONVULSED as Keith pushed the Puka backward, drawing every dark corner of his mind into yet another monster. Sharp clawed hands formed for a corpse with stretched skin and mottled green stringy hair. Jagged teeth blazed through jaws forever frozen open in rigor mortis, wrapped under the rotting robes of royalty, embroidered with regal gold of the Chinese emperors. Centuries old.

Keith struck with white hands glowing a sickly yellow, strangling the Puka in painful livid ferocity.

"COME ON!"

The Puka shriek in animal torment. You bet that hurt! Getting your soul sucked out by the *Jiangshi* always did, an undead monstrosity from the absolute other side of the world from the Celts. This monster feasted directly on your *chi* to suck it right out of you. Keith's bony fingers dug into the Puka's flesh and sucked hard.

In one moment of perfect clarity, Keith saw the Puka writhing in pain.

Burn, you damned animal. This is MY century. BURN! Keith pressed all the harder.

No one knew more about Halloween monsters than Keith. No—

SMASH

A tsunami's worth of wind blasted Keith right between his eyes. Control of the panorama ripped out of his grasp as the impact rang his head.

That...hurt.

Keith reached blindly but his *Will* slipped through his fingers under the pain. Heavy winds blew away everything and Keith's vision filled with—

RED FIERY EYES.

The entire sky was wiped away by an overpowering horse-head, flaming eyes as bright as twin suns cooked the scorching landscape beneath them, burning right through his eyelids. *I've made him mad.*

Keith hit the dead earth face down like a sack of bricks, and choked on a cloud of grit coating his lungs. A monstrous shadow fell over him, and the Puka's anger squashing him with the roar of an oncoming train, the black presence suffocating his mind

Yes, the Puka was mad.

>CLICK<

NO! You can't hurt me with that anymore!

>CLICK<

YOU CAN'T

Keith's hands gripped the dead dirt in resistance. Keith wouldn't let himself be taken by that again! The Puka disagreed.

CLICK

Pain cracked his head wide open.

CLICK

Keith screamed louder than ever before.

CLICK

His resistance shredded as sounds barreled their way into his mind, the sounds of death.

The sounds of Failure.

HIS failure.

The pounding wouldn't stop, the PAIN wouldn't stop. Keith stumbled to his knees under it all. *Get Up Damn You!* But the black pushed him down. The Puka laughed at his weakness. Keith couldn't move even one millimeter. In his mind's eye he saw Not-Keith again, pressing itself into every painful corner of Keith's awareness.

Your century? The voice blasted in Keith's head. *Let me show you your century!*

WHOOSH

A force threw Keith back into cold air, ice crystals carving a thousand pinprick slices against his face. Tumbling at hundreds of miles an hour, the landscape melted away beneath him, lost into the fog and whirls of the *Other Side.* Keith opened his eyes in pain to see dirt, trees, and small houses sweep past. He recognized this place, moments frozen in time from the grainy photographs in the *Hal-lO'Scream.* A century ago. This purgatory recorded mortal life, but this new scene opening before Keith wasn't a scare.

It was History.

Boys in threadbare coveralls ran around country farms, using burlap sacks as masks. Other kids were wearing paper sacks drawn with children's paint into black cats, witches, wild animals and scarecrows. The terrors of the open field, of the rural. Halloween circa 1900.

The wind sliced it all away as they moved forward in time. Now the cities have encroached. Families now live in concrete, abandoning the farms and fields to rust under the care of nostalgic grandmas. The culture changes, and Halloween changes with it. The scarecrow costume is gone, lost when we left the fields. So is any terror of the black cat, as it's now domesticated and living in every apartment highrise, not scary at all.

Further forward in time. Under a thousand wisps of history, Keith saw the neglect of a culture, the willful ignorance of how scary the Dark used to be. How quiet.

The Big City is anything but quiet. LIGHTS! SOUND! Movies. The 1930's. An entire pantheon of monsters is born on the silver screen. Dracula, Frankenstein, the Mummy, each earning a parade of Halloween costumes. Everyone wants to be Dracula, with kids creating any monstrosity they can out of paper mache and linen.

They run through the streets in black clothes, emulating their terrifying heroes.

But no one wants to be the Invisible Man. He disappears as a Halloween costume before he even starts, and maybe heroes get too popular. *Abbot and Costello Meet Frankenstein?* Frankenstein isn't so cool anymore. History barrels onward to the—

1950's. The S pace R ace h as c aptured t he i magination. *It Came From Outer Space* introduces the Invading Alien. Too complicated for burlap and paper, but now you can buy pre-fabricated costumes! Who has time anyway to build anything anyway as a brand new invention shows all the classic monster movies on Saturday night TV? Over and over people watch monsters on a grainy black and white screen, and over time, they get kinda washed out. You can't be scared of what you let into your family room every weekend. And everyone on TV is supposed to be a pretty face. Monsters are too ugly.

So gone are the green witches. Why be a monster when you can be gorgeous? Leading to the—

1960's! And we get a marvelous new product: Plastic! Plastic masks, plastic pumpkins. Plastic costumes of whatever we desire! Be a Starship Captain! Be a President!

At the expense of the Ghost costume. With vinyl plastic masks, who would suffer the indignity of wearing a sheet over their head? Gone. We also lost the Mummy, always your grandmother's costume anyway. But before you can mourn, here come the—

70's and 80's! With the introduction of the slashers! Leatherface. Michael Myers, Jason, Freddy. They're all scary! They're all in hundred nightmares and huddled slumber party movie marathons.

At least at first. In the 1990's the m ovies c ome too fast, in s o many numbers that no one even bothers to give them a name anymore. *Nightmare on Elm Street VI. Friday the 13th Part VII.* Who cares if they're scary or not? Besides, they're ugly. Girls want to be monsters too, and look what the Halloween stores have for us in the 21st century! Freddy Krueger dresses! Jason mini-skirts! Sexy is in! Just ask these new sexy vampires in fishnet stockings that now inundate our media-players.

Sexy.

Plastic. Welcome to the 2000's. So what is left of our scary night?

Good news is, we didn't lose the slashers. We just put them in glamor makeup and miniskirts and made them dance on stage.

Bad news is, we lost everything else. Halloween, neutered by an entire century, and only a few people even care that Halloween should be scary or even remember when it was.

And most of them are dead.

The images vanished. Keith found himself high in the air breathing in frantic gasps, his throat scarred with frost as he flew through the present day, but in a city coated in red death, the red of hate. At a dizzying velocity Keith found himself trapped on the Puka's back, soaring past towering buildings close enough to scrape his skin. Keith couldn't close his eyes against the pressure, even as the Puka turned his equine snout 180 degrees around to laugh at him—

With Connor's face, laughing his head off as he whisked Keith over Connor's *Fright Zone*, scorched and broken, police tape whipping in the wind. A friend he had failed to protect. The Puka changed again—

To Aiden. Dead for being too stupid, furiously screaming at Keith as the Shriek Bootique flew beneath them, still flashing gaudy pink strobe lights. Aiden growled and sent a punch right into Keith's gut, who didn't even have time to wheeze before—

Darryl's face. Downtown, where even now a hundred dead mortal souls screamed in agony. Darryl's red eyes lashed out with... laughter? "SEE I told you. I TOLD YOU!"

And then they were over the *Hall'OScream*. Baked under harsh glare Keith saw it for the burned out ruin it was. Where Jack had died. Because he failed.

Jack's overwhelming muscle twisted Keith around, forcing him to see every burned inch of the *HallO'Scream*, grinning with blocky horse teeth the entire way.

Failed.

FAILED.

NO! Keith gritted his teeth and dug his hands into Jack's eyes, forcing pain to the animal he knew lay beneath. The Puka's black mane flailed into the wind as the horse head returned and Keith wrapped both arms around the Puka's neck and squeezed, summoning everything he had left. *You won't get me. YOU WON'T!*

The Puka threw him off in mid air.

Keith tumbled end over end through cold icy air before bouncing in a tangle of limbs across sharp-edged gravel. He skidded to a stop in...

A parking lot. Bright sign. His vision cleared too slowly to read it, even as he felt the ripple of the *Other Side* forcing itself in. Was it making another nightmare? Every square inch of skin was sliced and bleeding, but Keith had to get up, pain or no pain. He struggled to his feet, ready for anything.

Almost anything. He stood in front of a convenience store.

THE store.

Keith's last shreds of determination drowned in stark hysterical fear. *No, I can't go back in there!* He turned to run.

A half second too late, as with a *WHOOSH* of ethereal suction, the doors opened and sucked Keith in, his arms grasping at nothing.

SIXTY

THE CENTER OF THE city rose above Benny like tombstones. The streets were devoid of life. The Ankou had already been here. Every corner brought Benny's Halloween posse closer to a *chill* somewhere ahead. Anyone with any sense had escaped long ago.

Escape wasn't Benny's plan. His crowd had swelled to a minor mob. Piper held pace at Benny's right side as they walked deep into the city, daring anything undead to come near them. Ben Mac-Cool Bensel had led his aspiring Halloween saviors this far. He'd take them the rest of the way, even if they were attacked by the hounds of hell themselves.

Hell hounds would have been preferable to what now appeared around one last corner. A lifeless white pall bathed the street in a cold pale glow. Above them, the river of ghosts keened and converged on a point just out of sight. As the white pallor flared all the brighter, several members of Benny's group gasped and nearly dropped their pumpkins as it came into view.

The Ankou.

Its lanky frame hovered a foot off the ground, dragging tatters of a white robe. White hair blew all around the face that alternated from a white skull to flesh and back again. A skull that wore Darryl's face. So cold.

Behind the Ankou formed ranks of spectral forms forming from the river above, faces of a thousand dead stretching as far back as Benny could see, some very same faces Benny had seen alive only a day before! Blank-eyed actors from Connor's *Fright Zone* stood next to stone-faced vampires from the mall, behind victims of the Kelpie Greenbelt only hours ago. Now as Benny's breath froze in the frosted air, the Ankou laid blank eyes on him and Benny's band of costumed heroes.

They blanched.

Benny couldn't blame them. Raised on Harry Potter and Katniss Everdeen, they had never seen anything like this in their lives.

This was the Last to Die. The True Ghost of Halloween.

And it was hungry.

A blast of arctic wind blasted them all, making the entire crowd step back. Torches dropped onto the pavement as eyes stared with blank faces. Benny even saw Piper as a petrified statue, incapable of even a scream to warm her soul. Benny almost joined her as the Ankou stared him down.

This monster even brought Keith to his knees! Why couldn't he stop it? Benny thoughts entered near panic until a single thought entered his head.

Because he tried to do it alone. But Benny wasn't alone, he'd brought a whole crowd a Halloween terror with him. Cold or not, they were with him. Gripping his own pumpkin with both hands, Benny shoved it before him. The Ankou stopped. The decayed face of Darryl/Ankou peered at Benny...then reached for him with a flaking arm.

Don't.

Move.

Benny wanted to. His soul screamed *Escape! Run!* But Benny had done that too many times already. This time he wasn't moving.

390

His crowd was.

Another pumpkin joined him on his left, then another on his right, and as Benny stood firm his monster crowd stepped up on every side, adding their light to his. In the center of a dozen flaming pumpkins Benny remembered more images from Ghostland. *The Irish shared their fire.* Now his monster crowd shared theirs as the flaring orange drowned out the pale white, dispelling the cold.

The Ankou...fluttered, and retreated.

Benny's heart surged and all but ran to push the Ankou even further back. The rest of his crowd shook off the fear and joined the push until the Ankou lifted itself several feet off the ground and almost flew off—

SCREECH

Benny's hands flew to his ears as a black shadow covered the street, a deep darkness that penetrated the soul and nauseated right to the bone. Benny gripped Piper, who almost heaved as she, and most of his crowd, fell to their knees.

That wasn't the Ankou.

Benny could barely lift his head as a black stink settled into his bones, but saw the source of the scream sitting high in the air on a theater marquee, putting out a shadow that stretched across the street to engulf Benny's crowd. Black hair fluttered in the wind as her legs dangled in fishnet stockings and a black dress that flared out like fairy wings. They *were* wings, of a fairy. With Kelly's face.

The Leananshee laughed with condescension. Benny knew that sound anywhere.

He hated it.

Kelly, or "Not-Kelly" as Benny now knew her, laughed across the intersection as she floated down on leathery bat wings from her perch. Her red hair had twisted itself into a crown as her eyes dazzled like emeralds, radiating sensuality as heat off a bonfire to muddle mortal minds with lustful fantasies. The Leahanshee, the optimum of Irish Feminine Beauty.

All Benny saw was the monster who had killed his sister. Not-Kelly smiled at him.

"Do they know how scared you are?" She intoned. "You're not hiding in your basement this time. We both know that's where you'd rather be. Your fear is thick enough to," she leered, "taste."

Benny looked at her with angry eyes, dispelling her black shadow to face her directly. He still gripped his pumpkin, its tiny candle warming his hands. His rage warmed the rest of him as he just stared her down.

"Nothing to say?" Not-Kelly said, walking to him in a runway strut, expanding her dark shadow to blacken everything around him. Its cold void started sucking the heat out of every mortal body.

"You don't need to say anything at all, young Mac Cumhaill," she spoke softly as she stepped closer. "It's so much better if you just...stopped feeling anything at all."

Benny felt the black leeches again, the invisible tendrils that sucked away his sensation, feeding her. *NO!* He wouldn't let that happen again, whether he was alone or not.

Except, now he wasn't all that cold. Something had interposed itself between him and Not-Kelly.

Bridget. Her flickering form blocked out the dark shadow, her glow driving away the leeching black. Looking at Bridget, then back at Not-Kelly, Benny finally had something to say.

"It took me way too long to figure it out, but I've never been alone."

Benny took the hand of his dead sister, and the black funk ran screaming from his mind. Kelly's smile vanished as Benny's monster crowd clawed back to their feet.

"Yes, the lost sibling returns. Except this is Samhain, and her year is up!" Her devil's smile returned. "The Last to Die takes *all* the souls."

The Ankou! Benny remembered. He collects the dead. *All the dead!* The floating corpse with Darryl's face reached forward with hands radiating a cold white. *It wanted Bridget.* Benny felt the grip on his hand slacken. Wispy threads on Bridget's jacket pulled away as if by a giant vacuum cleaner and Benny gasped in horror as Bridget's eyes went blank.

She started to flow toward the Ankou, who awaited her with arms opened wide.

"STAY AWAY FROM HER!"

Benny shoved himself between Bridget and the Ankou, shoving his pumpkin into the face of the monster. The Ankou's face contorted and Bridget's hand became solid enough to grab again. Ghost or not, Benny held on and pulled her out of the Ankou's reach. Benny wasn't going to lose her again.

Bridget's eyes became aware again, and Benny looked to her with an unspoken understanding.

You've protected me. Now its my turn to save you. Benny presented himself firmly and forced the Ankou back. He didn't need anyone's help, not to save his sister as he held Bridget and didn't budge.

Kelly flared with anger. The storm, the ghosts, and the cutting wind all blanked out as Kelly's scream surged over everything. "You don't have the strength to be a man!"

Benny straightened.

"Tonight, I can be whatever I want to be."

The mist curled around Benny, and one more ghost stepped into the scene. It wore leather pants and long braided hair as it walked right up to Benny and— merged.

As in Ghostland, Benny saw through the eyes again. Or now, Finn MacCool saw through his, as did every MacCool who had ever lived from a millennium ago until now, an unbroken line marking the generations going so far back as to be only legend, whose current generation lay at Benny's feet. Benny WAS Finn MacCool. And on Samhain that was the scariest thing of all.

SIXTY-ONE

THE DARK FUNK OF the *Other Side* pressed against Keith's consciousness. Stuck like a fly in glue, he couldn't turn away.

The woman screamed for her life.

The thief hid behind her, his gun pressed into her forehead, daring Keith to step any closer.

GET OUT yells the thug, wide-eyed and frantic. He's panicking. The police got here too fast. Keith got here too fast. The idiot grabbed whoever he could to escape.

I SAID GET OUT!

Skin is pock-marked with open sores. He's a meth head, too fried to talk to. Keith doesn't have to talk to him anyway. He just has to get the woman out of here. She's sobbing, about to panic too. Too many guns! She's going to bolt! Don't set her off!

Keith gagged against the smell of gasoline and floor cleaner. His body itched against his detective uniform with his gun weighing heavy in his hand. His *real* hand.

This wasn't a hallucination. This was happening.

Again.

Keith has to disarm the idiot before he hurts the woman. Just wiggle a little closer! Catch the eyes of the woman, let her know she can get out of this!

Get the meth head's attention in the wrong place, keep his eyes on the firearm, pointed right between his eyes, and make sure that's all the idiot sees! Good. He's forgetting the woman! His gun is drifting away from her head...

Keith couldn't breathe couldn't move couldn't scream as he lay trapped in a living replay that forced him to relive every moment. He knew what was coming and couldn't stop it. Not again. *I can't LIVE THIS AGAIN!*

A horse laughed.

Control his attention! Give him nothing to go off of. Distract him!
Keith could do this! The woman watches him and understands! Trust me, Keith screams with his eyes! Trust me!
Wait, was that movement—
Behind me?!
>CLICK<
A gun at his ear! The thief had a partner, hidden in the back! How did Keith not see him?
>CLICK<
His gun misfired! His revolver is cocking again. SHOOT HIM! SHOOT HIM!
BOOM
BOOOOOOOM

Loud. Keith's ears rang and eyes squinted, not wanting to open them, not daring to see. DON'T!

Splattered blood. Shattered glass.
What happened? The woman. Standing with a bullet in her head. SHE'S DEAD
Very dead.
But her corpse still stood there, bullet hole right between her eyes, which were wide open and blazing with furious anger at Keith. Rais-

ing a bloody hand in savage accusation, she screamed with the hate of thousand lifetimes.

YOOOUUUU!!!!!

Keith stared helplessly as the woman's eyes impaled him. His guilt forbade looking away even as the woman started to spasm. Her eyes rolled back into her head as her body convulsed in a standing seizure, shaking her until she finally disintegrated in an explosion of dust.

Leaving behind a ghost, a specter ten feet tall, wearing the ragged remnants of her burial dress blowing in a furious wind as the ceiling and the entire floor of the store fell away into a sea of black. Still visible inside the decrepit corpse, the petite woman's face glared down on Keith with a mouth of fanged teeth and unhinged her mouth wide enough to swallow Keith whole.

YOOOOOUUUUU!

>CLICK<

Keith's eyes glazed over as the gigantic face of Not-Keith lorded over him with a triumphant laugh.

>CLICK<

Pain. So much pain. Keith didn't know if he was alive or dead. He didn't care.

She's dead!

>CLICK<

The woman rose before him in a freezing whirlwind, wide-eyed and screaming.

You FAILED!

>CLICK<

Keith had been trapped with this guilt for too long, for years, and he couldn't live with it one second longer. Why would he want to live with this guilt anyway?

Give me one damn good reason!

Pummeled by ghastly images of a dead woman, Keith honestly couldn't think of one. The whirlwind swirled with one dead face after another, screams of the dead who stoked his guilt. Now the red eyes of a horse-headed monster drilled into him, eyes that had been mocking him for days, eyes now in the face of Not-Keith, standing as a monstrous giant.

YOU FAILED! LIVE YOUR LIE!

The red eyes pushed him down against the dirt, or whatever made up this ghostly land, suffocating Keith against his own flesh.

DIE BY YOUR LIE!

Keith gasped, pushed back, but it was true. He'd lived his lie for such a long time, the lie that he wasn't afraid, the lie that he wasn't guilty.

DIE!

Now finally asked himself the question that had kept him up for years:

Maybe I deserve to die. Yes, maybe he did. He had failed, and someone died for it, and he lied to the worst person of all, himself.

DIE!

Giving in would be so easy. Flight, run away, lay down and expire. Maybe he wanted to. But then amidst the pain, and guilt, and fear... another thought popped into his head.

Maybe that's why I survived this long.

One advantage to fear, it let you know you were still alive. Maybe Keith had spent years nurturing his own it because it reminded him what was at stake, reminded him how perilous it was to be a mortal. Keith also knew something about fear even the Puka didn't.

 No matter how scared you get, there's always something scarier. Hundreds of smothering fears attacked mortals every day. The Puka could imitate them, but it couldn't *experience* them. That was another kind of terror altogether, that's what makes mortals hide behind a false face when it's all they could to avoid the urge to just **scream!** Keith fought that urge every day.

Now he stopped fighting.

Keith dropped every false face, every mortal wall, every lie, and *screamed* face to face with every fear that terrorized modern mortals from the moment they were born:

The fear of a bill they could never pay.

The fear of a broken car they could never fix.

The fear of the bank account they could never settle.

The fear of the house they could never afford.

The fear of career they could never replace.

And the fear of seeing the same face of the same dead woman, in his dreams every single night. The fear of falling asleep and knowing its waiting there. EVERY NIGHT FOR THE REST OF YOUR LIFE.

The fear of failing, at absolutely everything.

FEAR

Keith screamed, right into the Puka. Keith's hands clawed deep into the black skin and into the Puka's eyes. The Puka squirmed under his hands as the *Other Side* panorama of nightmares spiraled around them both. The ground formed, then they flew, to land in a graveyard, which disappeared into a black forest, then melted into an office cubicle maze. The Puka dug talons into Keith's flesh but Keith held on, pushing and screaming as the Puka tried to escape in a jump far away. Keith twisted limbs and smashed it back down to the dead earth to grab the Puka's preposterous horse head by the ears, and SCREAMED.

Keith was *too mad* to ever keep quiet ever again.

Too incensed.

Too infuriated.

Too exhausted.

Too spiteful.

Too vindictive.

Too much.

TOO MUCH.

His scream echoed, reverberated, and tore open Keith's own ears in ripping pain.

But he screamed his lie out of him.

Yes an innocent died. But Keith finally admitted what he never could before:

She was dead before the bullet hit her. I saw her eyes go out.

She died of fear.

I SCARED HER TO DEATH!

Keith's scream blasted into the Puka's eyes, loud enough to shatter them.

Silence.

Keith's eyes open with a start. He lay on cold wet grass, under a mortal sky. Looking at his hands, he saw he still furiously clutched the gray skinned, mangy furred head of a mummified horse, its face frozen in unadulterated horror.

The Puka was dead.

Keith collapsed next to it, under a sea of autumn stars.

Sixty-Two

F**INN MACCOOL STEPPED OUT** *of the mists to find himself in another Night, another Samhain. There's always another Samhain.*

There's always another MacCool to defend it.

Ben MacCool Bensel stepped forward, wearing the spirit of Finn Mac Cumhaill, a ghost born under a jagged land, honed in the daily struggle to survive. Kelly just stared at what Benny had become. The darkness of the leananshee undulated around her like a terrified octopus. She was scared.

In response, Ben/Finn pulled a razor sharp Celtic sword out of the ether, and sliced off one of Kelly's smoky tendrils in a double-handed stroke.

Kelly shrieked as the tendril disintegrated, the first real pain she had felt for thousands of years since the last time she fought a MacCool. Ben-Finn pressed forward, his sword slicing through the air again, and again, taking off tendrils with every attack. Kelly's black fairy wings quivered with agony as she fumbled and fell to the pavement. She looked up at Ben/Finn's upraised sword as Benny looked down on her and kept slicing.

"You think this holiday is about fear?" He shouted. "We know it better than you ever did! Every Halloween fanatic you killed, they all knew something you never will! Halloween is about *LIFE!*"

Slice

"We don't wear costumes to take lives, but to save them!"

Slice

"We stand up to the biggest baddest monsters Samhain has and *we shove them right back down!*"

SLICE

Kelly's black foulness fell away with every hit, and her form melted. Her supple hands wrinkled into blackened flesh with hideous claws and bone spurs. Her body shrank into a pathetic shape; so skinny, so hungry, and starving. The leananshee in her true form, a famished female still wearing Kelly's green eyes, still desperate for one morsel of human sustenance.

Ben stood over her pitiful body and forced words into her ears.

"Each Halloween is another year to remember you're still alive. To *earn* your life for another year!"

Kelly now totally collapsed into a quivering pile of wings and hair. Lightning crackled above as Ben walked over to stand by her head, sword at the ready. Behind him, the crowd stepped up to form around both Ben and Kelly, their pumpkins bathing the circle in orange light.

"That's why the Irish beat you," Ben continued. "Because they loved being alive more than your monsters loved being dead. Because Halloween lets us celebrate *being* alive. It's so easy, you knew how easy you could lose, so this time you killed off anyone who might know how to fight back. And you went after the MacCools personally, hoping for moronic revenge."

Ben looked her right in the eye.

"So tell me you had nothing to do with Bridget's crash."

Looking up from the street in obvious agony, Kelly's face broke into a demonic smile. Benny raised his sword in a killing blow. Kelly screamed—and surged, grabbing the sword in a blur of black smoke. Her fangs screamed right into Ben's face as her other hand snaked over his throat, seeking to crush it. Ben tried to throw her off, but the Ankou moved in. Darryl's white corpse had been hovering behind Kelly, now the midnight wind sent its burial shawl billowing into the air as it advanced against the Halloween crowd. Kelly summoned what was left of her black aura and pointed a furious finger.

"Consume them all!"

The Ankou moved against the mortals. Locked with Not-Kelly, Ben couldn't intervene. Could they stop it without him?

Just this once, Ben thought, looking to his Halloween posse, *Put away the iPhones and actually celebrate being alive!* For one moment, the crowd looked to bolt. Only a moment.

It *didn't* run, it advanced. Just like Ben had taught them. With Piper in the lead they stepped right into the Ankou's cold light, pumpkins and torches raised high as a *RooOOOAAAAR* surged across the plaza. Skull faces and demon masks shouted in defiance, flinging their orange light forward, scattering every ghost left in the street. Darryl's blank eyes just stared, barely conscious inside the skull of thin flesh. The Halloween crowd dared the white monstrosity to take them. It couldn't. Raising decomposing hands to his face, it gave a high-pitched shriek of a thousand dead skeletons. For a moment Ben saw through its face, through the glow and the rot to see Darryl underneath. Poor greedy Darryl. Horrified. Trapped just as much as anyone. Just the dumb fate to be Last to Die. Ben looked it in the eyes.

You know what scary is now, don't you?

Darryl blinked, and beheld Ben in...recognition?

And resignation. He evaporated, his ghastly form floated away into the darkness of the street.

Kelly screamed in anger. Ben shoved her off, freeing his sword with a single swipe and slicing Kelly across her midsection. Kelly collapsed in agony as a stream of black sparkling dust dripped from her wound. Ben backed up to his monster troupe. Under Kelly's pain and frustration, she still wore a face to kill.

Clippity Clop.

Something else obviously agreed. Somewhere behind the clouds, Benny heard a maniacal laugh, and horseshoes striking pavement.

Clippity Clop.

Kelly's face looked to the horizon, her black hair flying around her as her black aura rose again a nauseating radiance, her face re-forming into the smooth porcelain of Kelly. Soft. Pretty.

Condescending.

"Mortals are born to die, Benny. No matter which mortal shell you wear, the Rider will eventually take you as he did your sister. If you're not taken by my hand, you'll be taken by his!"

Clippity Clop

Ben/Finn now saw the sparks of the galloping hooves, sizzling ferocity as the Dullahan tore down the city street. But it wasn't the only ghost, as Bridget had appeared next to him, holding his hand and standing firm against the oncoming death rider. And next to her appeared the *other* Kelly, ghost Kelly, the actual owner of Not-Kelly's stolen body. Benny gazed at her, and read a message in her silent eyes. He turned back to Not-Kelly.

Clippity Clop

"Yes, Samhain is a reminder of how mortals have to fight to earn every day of life. But since you stole a mortal's body, what will happen to you?"

Not-Kelly's face turned to him. *Clippity Clop* got more furious.

"Who exactly is the Dullahan here to take?" Ben gleaned as the hysterical laughter charged right at him. Not-Kelly leered in victory as the tempest of the Dullahan tore over them both in a swarm of dust and shrieking—

And passed right through. Ben checked himself. No blood.

Clippity Clop

With a gust of wind and hooves striking sparks from pavement, the rider turned around and hooves caught purchase on cracked asphalt. The black horse reared up with a snort of flame, and the headless rider flaunted his own head with its frenzied grin on its face. When the horse came down, Ben locked eyes with the severed head.

It winked at him.

Not-Kelly looked at the rider, then Benny, then back again, her eyes frantic. "You haven't the bile to kill me! You don't have the will to finish this! You're not worthy of your name!" Green eyes dripped with a condescending smile as she said one last word.

"Benny."

Ben stood right over her, lowering the sword. The Finn presence dimmed, and Ben felt his own mind, his own body.

"I don't know if I'm worthy of my name or not."

Not-Kelly smiled in victory, until Ben leaned in with a triumphant leer.

"But my sister was!"

Not-Kelly screamed as the Dullahan as dumped its bucket all over her, plastering her face in a grotesque smear. Her ghoulish hands futilely tried to rub it away, smearing the blood in hysterical terror as Ben rose over her in anger.

"And my name is BEN!"

He smashed his pumpkin over her head.

Kelly's bloody form hit the pavement with a *thud,* sprawled in flaming ash. With a cackle the Dullahan spurred his snorting mount. His hand reached out and grabbed a black shadow rising out of the body, a flailing mess of ghostly hair and limbs. For a split second Benny saw the Leanan's real face, a demonic bat frozen in terror as it struggled against the clutch of the Dullahan, which reared up on his horse and galloped off, laughing with glee until it disappeared into the night, dragging the Leananshee with it. A scream echoed through the clouds.

Gone.

Benny's awareness slowed as streaks of ghostly matter flew past him. Mirages of monstrous faces vanished into the sky and the distance around him. The crowd charged, passing on both sides as they ran ahead, past the square into the streets beyond blazing with light. Against their surge, the darkness peeled away like paper in a seering fire, recoiling, retreating, and taking all remaining ghosts with it. Scared away by cheers. So many cheers.

It was over.

SOMEWHERE ELSE

Finn Mac Cumhaill knelt in the stream, washing the blood from his face, the ash from his arms. Then he stood up in the dawn of the new day. Samhain had passed.

The wheel of seasons turned. The days turned dark now as the wind promised cold gusts of winter to come. But light would return with the spring, and an entirely new year awaited the Land of Eire.

After Samhain was Imbolc. Then Beltane. Then Lughnasadh, then back again. The seasons never stopped. Finn had earned another year until the next Samhain. Another year until The Night came again. It would be as terrifying as dreadful as ever, or perhaps for now, just a little less.

Finn got up to walk amongst the people, feeling their smiles. He laughed with all of them in the morning light with the Hall of the Irish Kings still standing tall. They took him into their nearby homes. There to meet his new wife.

There would always be a dawn after Samhain.

So long as you fought for it.

SIXTY-THREE

QUIET. STARS TWINKLED ABOVE, visible behind the giant towers of the city.

Ben sank to the street, sitting on hard cement. Everything started to blur all over again. He needed sleep so terribly bad, but he couldn't.

Some ghosts hadn't left.

The *Sluagh* were gone, retreated behind folds of *The Veil*. Other predators slunk away into whatever hole they had crawled out of, but wispy reflections of people remained. Not monsters or beasts, just people. Now out of the Ankou's negative influence they raised their eyes with awareness. Ben saw Quentin and Taylor drifting through the streets. They weren't leaving, just walking through the town, then into the residential areas. They were going...

"Home."

Ben turned to see Keith walking up next to him. He was dirty and bloody as he moved with a limp and a serious splotch of gray in his hair. But it was Keith.

"You, you're OK? But you were..." Ben, paused, remembering his terror seeing Keith being ripped off the street.

"I got better," Keith said, completing the pause. "I needed to get something out of my system."

Ben looked at Keith, understanding. "Do I get to hear a stupendous story of your fearless bravery?"

"You do, and I'm going to sit you down and make you listen to the whole thing, as soon as you tell me *your* awe-inspiring tale," Keith took in the street. "And yours isn't over yet."

Ben turned back the ghosts still flowing through the streets, but now with purpose.

"What's happening now?" Ben never had time in the last three days to think far ahead. He'd forgotten more Halloween history than he'd ever remember.

"The other part of Halloween," Keith answered, waving at the ghosts as they flew overhead to parts beyond. "The happy part."

Ben looked incredulous. "Happy part?"

Keith nodded, and motioned to a ghost approaching them.

Darryl. No longer the decaying angel of death, now a glowing figure of white. Keith muttered a single word.

"Closure."

Members of Ben's Halloween horde had come back to the plaza. Exhausted, but still wearing the costumes and monster masks. Now they finally dropped them in the street as they saw the ghosts still there. Not just any ghosts. As Ben watched, Darryl/Ankou approached the ghost of a young girl, dressed in ordinary shirt and pants. She stood right there with other ghosts, staring as a young man approached her out of the crowd, walking with timid steps towards her and reaching out a trembling arm in hesitation. A quiver went going through them both as they touched, then embraced as family. Separating with a smile, the young girl turned to Darryl behind her, who had been waiting patiently. Touching his open hand, she floated into the sky and disappeared into the sky.

Escaping Purgatory. Ben thought. *Joining the next existence.*

Other people came out from behind locked doors, eyes red with tears, but reaching with baited courage towards other ghostly figures, families being reunited. Ben watched in fascination.

"They get to go home," Keith said softly, as Darryl's ghost took the hands of more smiling spirits and released them. "That's what ghosts are supposed to do on Samhain. They get to go home one last time, and the Ankou ensures they get there safely."

Ben looked as Keith sat down on the street curb, groaning in pain as more ghosts said their goodbyes before flying off into the night, then back to Darryl. "Is he..." Ben couldn't think of the right word. "OK now?"

"Yes," Keith answered. "He's doing his job now. A guardian to be respected, not a villain to be feared."

Ben watched as Darryl released more spirits, moving slowly, waiting for each spirit to give its final goodbyes before offering his own hand. Darryl's face no longer lay stretched over a spectral skull, but as a glowing phantom he still looked creepy. "Even if its Darryl?"

Keith gave a resigned laugh. "Who better to collect every single ghost of the last year than a bean-counting accountant?"

Ben admitted that yes, that did make a serendipitous amount of sense. He got lost in the scene so much that he almost missed a ghost walking out of the pack towards him. Keith saw it too and immediately stood up as they both recognized the face.

Kelly. Ghost Kelly, walking toward Ben with a smile on her face. Ben stood rigid for a moment, reminding himself that this was the actual Kelly, the real one. She mouthed something, the words getting lost on the wind, but Ben could lip-read.

Thank you.

Kelly rose into the air, out and away, towards the suburbs.

"Where?" Ben asked talking out loud, as he followed her vanishing form.

"She's going to her own family." Keith replied. "She hasn't seen them in a long time."

"That's right. She died almost a year ago," *Good god, her family never even knew.*

Keith reached gently to Ben's shoulder. "That's where we need to be too. Home. Someone's waiting for us. And we only have this night. Darryl is going to be very thorough. It's now or never."

Someone? Ben knew instantly.

Bridget.

"We better beat her there," Keith smiled seemingly as happy as ever despite his multiple wounds. Ben took stock and found that he hurt all over too. Crud, didn't anything slow Keith down?

SIXTY-FOUR

FINDING A RIDE HOME took an endeavor in and of itself. Keith didn't need to be told his car was long gone, likely towed away the day before. *Screw it. I totaled it anyway.* Several members of the monster posse helped out, finally getting the MacCools back to their home in the suburbs. How long had it been since they had been here? Keith couldn't recall.

Pulling himself out of the car and walking up the steps to their front door, Keith noticed Ben hesitating in the driveway. He was looking upward, at the bedroom window on the right.

Hers.

Nothing moved in there, but Keith looked around to see other houses being visited. Spirits flew down from the misty sky to land on sidewalks and walk to their homes like angels of grace. Doors opened with creaking anticipation. Scared faces peaked around corners, looking at...well, *gawking* at what awaited them on their front porch.

Hope you have trick or treat candy ready, Keith smirked. *The afterlife will never be the same.* Keith thought. *If the citizens of this town didn't appreciate Halloween before, they damn well would now.*

Cautiously, after all that had happened so far during this fantastic night, the ghosts were welcomed into their old homes. Keith watched, then put his hand on Ben's shoulder as they walked together through their front door.

Silence.

Keith felt Ben's heart race as they passed the foyer. Walking into darkness (the lights still didn't work), the hardwood floor squeaked with every step, the same squeaks that had kept Ben awake for so many nights. In fact, this was the exact time Ben should have been terrified to be down here. But now Ben took the lead to look inside every room they passed, with Keith behind.

*She wouldn't have made herself too hard to find, her favorite chair was...*around the corner. Keith stood at Ben's side as they entered.

Bridget's ghost sat in the cushy loveseat. She raised her eyes as they entered, and smiled. Keith nodded, but stepped back. This was Ben's moment.

THERE SHE WAS.

Ben had been seeing Bridget for days now, but so rushed. Now he had all night, No, he had ONE night, she was here to say goodbye.

The Ankou... Darryl will be here soon. Don't waste the time you have left. Don't waste Halloween.

Ben didn't. Walking into the TV room, he approached Bridget even if he didn't know quite what to do. Bridget did, jumping out of the chair and giving him a huge bearhug. Ben didn't want to let go. He didn't have to, Halloween went on until sunrise, and Darryl had a whole city of ghosts to collect. He might not get here for hours. Plenty of time to say goodbye. Ben used it well. Keith had stepped out. He was good at that.

Alone, in the darkness of Halloween night, Ben sat down in his comfy couch next to the blue ghost of his sister.

He stayed there for a long time.

When the Ankou finally approached his door, Ben let him in.

SIXTY-FIVE

NOVEMBER 1ˢᵗ

ᴀɴᴅ ɪꜰ ᴛʜᴇʀᴇ ᴡᴀꜱ any day that Keith *really* hated, that would be November 1st.

It always had to be so damned shiny, transforming hard-bought Halloween decorations into passe left-overs. At least Christmas had a whole week to wind down until New Years, and some lunatics kept their holiday lights up through February! But Halloween got no grace period whatsoever, nothing except the day of the year farthest away from the next Halloween, and complaints from the neighbors to get your unsightly gravestones out of there.

Ben didn't like November 1ˢᵗ either, except maybe this year the withdrawal wouldn't be as ragged.

For everyone else life had already moved on. Standing a street corner next to the *Scare Asylum*, Ben watched as people walked around him on a quiet Sunday morning, as if nothing whatsoever had happened last night. Christmas lights were already up, hanging off of storefronts next to plastic snowflakes advertising "Beat Black Friday!" Ben hated *that* even more.

"What is wrong with these people?"

"It'll take more than a holocaust to stop the merchandise machine," Keith said beside him, carrying a pile of horror masks back inside Taylor's haunted house. "We love normalcy, and Halloween is just one holiday with plenty more barreling in right behind it. We want everything to be the same, every day, every year. "

"But they have to remember *something* about last night!"

Indeed, fires burned, paramedics ran about with body bags, a few sirens here and there. But...

"Your Halloween Posse will. They'll have each other to help. I highly recommend you Facebook all of them. As for the rest," Keith waved a hand at the city, "They'll remember whatever they want to."

Ben grunted. Things weren't going to be the same for him. Not by a good long stretch.

"I still see him."

Keith walked up and looked. Ben could tell Keith still saw him too. Severed head, maniacal laugh. Not even Death gets a rest. He worked 365 days a year, even November 1st. After all, people die everyday and someone had to mark them. Both MacCools had seen him earlier that day chasing an ambulance down a busy street. Except this time, he wasn't riding a horse.

He drove.

A midnight black 1976 Chevy Nova with a raging engine that sounded like a chainsaw jump-starting a drag-racer. Burning grease and tires spinning, the Dullahan's new Ghostmobile jumped through traffic, passing through people and automobiles like a gust of wind, holding his severed head out the window. No one else saw a thing as he spun down another street in the general direction of the hospital. Except as the Dullahan passed the MacCools his brakes squealed with a grave curdling *SCREECH,* stopping right there in the intersection, cars driving through his spectral form without a ripple. Ben stared in amazement, until the severed head turned itself towards the MacCools.

And winked.

416

"With the hyper-frantic drivers in this city, he won't have a moment's peace," Keith remarked as the Ghostmobile spun off again. "But glad to see he's taking kindly to the modern age."

Ben didn't know what to think. "That's your car!"

"You were expecting the Headless Motorcyclist? Yes, that mush face stole my car."

Ben actually laughed "Well your car was *dead* wasn't it?"

"Very dead." Keith laughed. "The culture changes. The monsters either change with it or fade away. That guy is a survivor. I think we'll be seeing him for a long time." Keith closed the door to the *Scare Asylum* and sat on a nearby bench, seemingly unconcerned with anything. Ben, however, looked around the mess left of downtown and still couldn't accept it.

"How can people just go on?"

"They only remember it as a fuzzy bad dream, which only gets fuzzier in the light of day," Keith said. "A merging of the living and dead isn't something mortals are meant to remember."

"But so many people died. How do they explain that?" Broken windows, destroyed buildings. And a lot of dead. Not as many as there could have been, but still.

"They already have," Keith waved. "How do they ever explain it? A riot in the bar district? Arsonists? Anything will do. Always has. Halloween 1984 in Detroit. Nearly 300 arson fires. In one night! They named the whole thing 'Devil's Night.' Makes you wonder if something else really happened, doesn't it?"

"So this has happened before," Ben considered.

"Could be. Maybe it'll happen again."

Ben had to digest that one.

"Most of them know as much as they need to," Keith continued. "Mortal Land can't handle more problems than it already has."

Ben dropped it as the city proved the point before his very eyes; cleaning up the mess and moving on. Nothing got in the way of civilization. *Not with Black Friday less than a month away.* He watched the traffic fly by, one car at a time.

"Things might change." Keith offered. "Maybe last night taught them something. Maybe it didn't. But I bet we'll have a lot bigger turn out for the *HallO'Scream* auditions next year."

Ben huddled on the curb. "I can't think about a haunted house right now. Last night was..."

"The best haunted house we've ever seen," Keith finished.

Ben considered that. "And we had to ruin it."

Both MacCools laughed, then Ben felt Keith stand up and hover over him. He still needed to be protective, even now.

"Need to see her grave again?"

Bridget's grave. He used to visit it a lot. But now...

"No," Ben saw Keith start to ask a question, but cut him off. "That's not where she is anymore."

Strong answer. Keith rose up, as if he was... proud? Keith would see him as a little boy for a while yet, but he saw progress. Ben would have to work on that, but he meant what he said. Bridget had an adventure of her own now. Keith understood and sat back down, relaxed. After being pummeled by a giant monster horse, only Keith could pull that off.

"You haven't told me what happened to you. What happened to the Puka?"

Keith's eyes flickered. Anger? No. *Resolution.* Some emotion Ben couldn't put his finger on.

"We had a meeting of the minds. It found out that there was something a lot scarier than it was." Keith said, staring down the street as his stone face appeared, letting Ben know that was the end of that conversation. Keith started the next one.

"So BEN MacCool, this is the first day of the rest of your life. Given it any thought?"

Ben considered. "Been thinking of letting Dad know what happened. Don't care if he believes me or not. Then, I'm getting off my rear and getting into the University for the spring semester."

Keith almost applauded. "Excellent. Yes, you've seen quite enough of the HallO'Scream's basement. You'll like natural sunlight. It can be very invigorating, in the proper month," he said with a smirk.

"What are you going to tell my Dad?" Ben asked.

"I talked to him this morning. Seems Darryl never actually had time to finalize the deal to scarf up the HallO'Scream. So guess what. It's still ours. Good thing too. Needs a big fix-up."

"It's a wreck! And Darryl was the money! How can we fix it?"

"PUH LEAZE! You know your dad better than that. He never leaves any investment uninsured. And he's quite happy you survived the 'riot.' As for the house? Just ash and scorched carpet on the 2nd floor. Give me a trashbag and two crowbars and I can clear that out over a weekend. I'm going to turn that place inside out and make it the best gosh-darn haunted house in this time-zone. This town hasn't seen anything yet!"

Ben was mildly shocked. "As if nothing happened?"

Keith got up and stepped forward, completely serious. "As if *everything* happened. As if you and I are the best people to make sure that it doesn't happen again, by making sure people remember what they're supposed to be afraid of. To be one last bastion of scary against the eternal wimpification of Halloween."

Ben frowned as he gestured to the smoking mess that was downtown. "I don't think anyone will be in a mood to go to a Haunted House for a good long time."

Keith only grinned. "Of course. That's what the cycle of holidays is for. The complete spectrum of human sensation. Thanksgiving is the gluttony. Valentine's is the sappiness. Fourth of July is the need for big loud booms. Every holiday is there to satisfy some emotional need. Life is meant to be felt, remember? By the time October rolls around, people will be in the mood for a rip-roaring scare all over again."

"You left out Christmas."

"Did I? Considering decorations were already for sale a month ago, I'm certain it can take care of itself. Let's say it's about the need for family, or about being Halloween's prudish brother. They're both doing the same job, as they both appropriated the old pagan holidays. But they go about themselves differently. Christian holidays are long term, passive protection, keeping old monsters of those days forgotten, never getting enough energy to escape. Halloween is the active protection, teaching us how to fight if or when the monsters *do* escape."

Ben nodded. "Christmas is the defense. Halloween is the offense."

Keith looked down the street, at Christmas lights in a store, on sale even now. "And Halloween is absolutely necessary to keep Christmas from butting itself all the way into August. But that's another story."

Indeed.

Keith stood right next to Ben. "And speaking of next year. I'm making a major change."

Ben looked up. "You just said you're not abandoning the house!"

"Heaven forbid! Oh no. The MacCools need it. The world needs it. It's just that from now on, I'll have conflicting responsibilities." That word earned a crinkle of confusion on Ben's face. Keith laughed.

"You are the heir to MacCool, worthy of your name. And we're going to make sure you stay worthy. Yes, we're going to get you out of your dad's house, we're *both* getting out. I'm going to do something I should have done a while ago. You're going to get yourself into college, make friends, and actually meet and kiss a real girl. You did get the number of that girl from last night I trust?"

Ben's face turned to abject shock. Keith laughed again. "How did I know? We've been under the same roof for a long time. But don't get off-topic. Yes, you're going to do all that and more, but we're always keeping Halloween as our highest priority. We wouldn't be ourselves if we didn't. There's always another Halloween."

Keith leaned in.

"So I've got a favor to ask."

Keith asked. Ben listened.

Ben thought long and hard, and said yes.

"I'll need help," Ben added after thinking it over.

"You'll get it. You've got your Halloween Posse, as I said," Keith got up to leave when another thought barged into Ben's head.

"Wait! I've got one question."

"Only one?"

"Last night. How did you find me after it was over?"

"I had help. Connor led me to you."

CONNOR! Ben had forgotten all about him! Had Connor escaped the Ankou? Ben never saw him get sucked up. *That means...* Ben had a prickly feeling up his spine as he asked his last question.

"Is Connor ...?"

Keith grinned an evil grin. "Ask him yourself. He's right behind you."

ONE YEAR LATER

OCTOBER

OPENING HOUR WAITS FOR no man, living or dead.

The last rule of Haunted Houses is that they are never completed. No amount of preparation in July ever prevents a single working day in October from stretching out 18 hours or more. Props always break. Special FX lights always short out. Only a taskmaster with an encyclopedic memory could even attempt to control the never-ending war with entropy. Keith MacCool's memory was second to none, but Jack had been some of the best help he could ask for (insufferable Captain Jack Sparrow uniform and all). He'd be a hard man to replace, but the show had to go on.

Now Keith stood in his prop-strewn command center of the new *HallO'Scream*. Commands bellowed through the air, costumes haphazardly flung around, and a single voice exercised control. But it wasn't Keith's.

"Where are the orange lightbulbs?"

"Why aren't the fog machines on the 2nd floor turned on?"

"Who's in the Zombie Room tonight? AND WHY AREN'T THEY IN THE ROOM?"

Actors ran in everywhere to get into position. Keith enjoyed watching from afar. Different year. Same noises. This would always be home even if this time he played a different role. He pushed himself through the mess as best he could. He had to find—

"Piper!" There she was, wearing a delightful t-shirt embroidered with *Creeping It Real*. Ben's girlfriend had the frazzled hair that came with trying to keep a box of cats safely in the box (a better metaphor for handling the *HallO'Scream* he had yet to hear), with a clipboard in one hand and a cellphone in the other. Keith squished himself right up to her, making sure he had her full attention. A full police detective uniform would do that.

"Where's Ben? I have some very important people who demand to make his acquaintance, and they're not there to admire the noose in the Midnight Forest."

Piper's eyes flashed to Keith in exasperation. "I know! He knows! He just ran back to the Tunnel to fix a strobe light."

Keith wasn't impressed, "The Fire Marshall is coming now! And he's not coming through the Tunnel, he's going to walk right up to the front door and start grilling the ticket booth about why there's flammable gauze in the Corpse Lab! Get Ben out here!"

"He's coming!" Piper all but yelled as she fumbled with a walkie-talkie hooked to her shirt collar. Keith took the time to soak the night all in: Synthesized ghost moans piped over cheap speakers, the sting from hot fog burning his lungs, sensations that had defined his existence for years. He'd miss them. For four days a week anyway. He'd still be here on the weekend, in costume, scaring the bejeezus out of anyone and everyone. He'd never give that up, not for all the full-sized candy bars in his trick-or-treat bag.

Piper shouted again into her walkie-talkie, getting no results as Ben still did not materialize. Several actors ran by asking for clarification, each one with a red-light emergency (at least to them). Piper solved each mini-crisis with sharp hand gestures and piercing eyes, stamping out the fires only to see others spring up like undead that wouldn't die. Yes, she'd do good at this job. Ben was lucky to have her, if he would just show up from whatever skeleton he thought needed more bloody gore.

"Piper—"

"I'M LOOKING!" she interrupted. Exasperation contorted her face as she dropped the walkie-talkie. "Why does this have to happen now? They know we're about to open!"

"Of course, they know," Keith gave an open mouth smile. "They want to catch you at your absolute best, not after you've had time to hide all the combustibles and yank the extinguishers out from whatever closet you hid them in. Either you're ready for a fire right now, or you never will be. For some reason they're jittery about fires occurring in our quaint little elementary school."

Piper's eyes narrowed. "This was your idea wasn't it? You told them to come right now!"

Keith laughed. "Part of the new job, sweetheart. Your police liaison is allowed to play dirty. Especially when it's me."

Piper's eyes crawled over Keith's spotless detective uniform, scouring it for the slightest flaw with which to impeach his character. Keith knew she wouldn't find one (other than for a rather large white bandage peeking out from above his collar). He took this job seriously.

"He's your nephew. You can't fail him."

"It's because he's my nephew that I have to push him. And its not me. I'm just the guy who drove the Fire Marshall all the way from the Big City. I got to turn on the flashing lights on the car too. Really cool at dusk. Great advertisement. I should've thought of that years ago. But it has to be someone, like me, who has this place memorized inside and out to tell our heroic Fire Marshall where you guys like to hide all the contraband. AND because I'm the devious schmoe who used to hide it from The Man in the first place."

"You're a fiend."

"Yes, I am. And a master shapeshifter into many other horrors as well." Keith nodded to her, dipping his head in old school chivalry. Her exasperation melted long enough to smile back. Keith continued. "But tonight I'm just a public servant, and I haven't been back on the job long enough to earn a screw-up. So help me out here. Where is Ben?"

"He'll get here. Meanwhile, stall the inspector with one of these." Piper fished through a box of t-shirts, producing one with dazzling orange/red lettering:

HALLO'SCREAM

Scary is Your Survival

Keith scowled. *I told him if I saw another t-shirt, I'd burn it.*

"Whose idea was *that?*" he enunciated, loudly.

"Mine" said a voice echoing from the far side of the room. There he was, finally, materializing from behind a poster for *ALIEN* that flawlessly concealed the door between the prep-area and the first floor. Ben dragged a box full of spray-paint cans, extension cords, and duct tape. Three haunted-house essentials. He dropped the box on the captain's chair, beneath the *SCREAM* poster that lorded over the room. He stared Keith in the eye, wearing Keith's old leather jacket.

Keith looked him over. "Looks good on you. Ready?"

Ben looked at the bandage on Keith's neck. "Show it to me."

Keith's eyes narrowed. "If you don't mind, it's still a bit tender."

"I bet it is. And if I don't see it, I'll tell the inspector you used to store the acetone next to the space heater."

"You wouldn't dare!"

"Just one peek, then we can greet our illustrious guests."

"Was your midterm in Economics above a B?"

"With this place as my final project? Please. The other students come to me for help."

"All I needed to hear." Keith reached up to unbutton the collar of his uniform and open his shirt, exposing a bandage that went up his neck and down a shoulder. Symmetrical to the SCREAM tattoo on the other side. Keith's fingers delicately peeled back the upper bandage, revealing...

426

A black humanoid, crouching on a cliff-face with spindly limbs, muscular body marked with Celtic runes. Black mane of hair whipping in the mountain wind.

And the head of a horse.

Ben leaned up on his tip-toes to get a good inspection, as if it needed his approval, then stepped down.

"You never told me a Puka was your favorite Halloween monster," Ben said as Keith buttoned himself back up.

"You didn't ask." Keith smirked.

"Neither did he." They both laughed. Until Keith's face froze with dead seriousness.

"Now show me yours."

Ben smirked, and took off the leather jacket, revealing a bandage going up his right arm. He peeled it back halfway. Keith leaned in to set his eyes on—

"Best image of Finn MacCool I've ever seen."

"Should be." Ben said, straightening up and covering his arm.

"And the other one," Keith said, making Ben freeze.

"I didn't tell you about that one."

"You didn't have to."

Ben paused for a moment, then rolled up his other sleeve.

Bridget.

Keith nodded, and Ben pulled the jacket back on.

"Bring em on."

Keith rose up to his full height, looking over the crowd of actors and craftsmen, too many of whom were doing nothing but gawking at the two MacCools. A room full of teenagers dressed as robed-executioners, zombies, and one guy putting on a RedCap suit, fumbling with oversized leather gloves ending in wicked hooked claws. Keith grinned. Oh yes, this was going to be a *real* scary year.

Keith grabbed Ben by the shoulders and spun him around to the crowd, sweeping his hand and raising his voice in the booming MacCool shout they all knew too well.

"Well, don't just stand there gawking," Ben shouted. "Go out there and scare something!"

The actors scattered as Piper reached over and gave Ben a kiss on the cheek. Keith laughed as she ran off to fix yet another scare room catastrophe.

"If Connor could see you now," Keith sneered. "What would he say about *that?*"

Ben leaned back with the devil's grin. "He'd congratulate me for winning back *Scariest House of the Year.*"

"I saw the RedCap," Keith replied.

"That wasn't it. I contracted for some extra help this year. Call him a ringer."

Keith frowned. "I'd know anyone worth hiring."

"And you know this guy," Ben said. "He's doing a bang-up job on the second floor. He's a natural. There's no other house that can do this. You saved the *HallO'Scream,* but I'm going to immortalize it."

"How?" Keith glared.

Ben laughed. "Well, there's one more T-shirt you haven't seen yet." Ben pressed a black tangle into Keith's hands. "Read."

Keith did, his eyes widening.

He can't possibly mean—

Ben smiled. "He told me himself. Haunted House Connoisseurs never die. They—"

"—come back to haunt their house," Keith muttered, staring down a hallway.

"The *Fright Zone* is gone, so I offered him a place here," Ben continued.

Keith looked at the shirt again, then sank his head back in a luxurious diabolic laugh.

"Connor never knew when to quit," he giggled as the surprise wound down, his mind already swirling with new possibilities, grinning an evil grin matched only by Ben's own.

"This town is going to learn what scary *really* is," Ben sneered.

Keith peered around the room, as if... looking for something in the shadows.

There, under the SCREAM poster, he thought he saw a flicker. Maybe just a shadow from the bustling actors.

Maybe it was something else.

Keith stuffed the shirt into a pocket. This one he'd keep.

HALLO'SCREAM

One Hundred Fake Ghosts. And One Real One

THE END...

ACKNOWLEDGMENTS

When Halloween Was Green came about in a flash of compulsion many years ago while walking the family dog on a chilly Autumn night, a flash that demanded "You will write a novel." Unfortunately it didn't include the slightest hint about the plot, the characters, or any narrative.

"Well, can you at least tell me the setting?" I asked the empty air, which earned me one word:

"Halloween."

It took two years of researching and note-taking before I even wrote the first sentence. It then took another three years of fumbling to complete the overweight first draft. At that point it was happy circumstance that I had both a wife (Valerie) who was a self-published comic book writer, and a mom who was a professional editor and has published several historical novels of her own (under the pen name Karen Lockwood). Both of them worked through the entire novel to get it into reading shape, as did a horde of beta-readers who took on the harrowing early drafts of this novel: friends at home, friends online, friends from work, friends from college that even now I haven't seen in years. Every one of them had a personal contribution which made its way into these pages (If you're reading and know where to look, you'll see your fingerprints).

Then, over many years of attending sci-fi conventions, fan Q&As, and book signings, I've had the good fortune to meet established and very patient authors such as Jim Butcher, Kim Harrison, Patricia Briggs, and Larry Correia, all of whom took the time to take an aspiring author aside and give him valuable creative advice. If I would have any advice to give to the next author, it would be to surround yourself with as many voices as possible, as they will see the blind spots that you will not. Reach out.

Any thank you must include also author Katie J. Cross for introducing me to Blue Harvest Creative, and to Vern at Blue Harvest Creative for pushing this project through, giving it the cover and interior design that it deserved. Here's to the next novel.

About The Author

     Bernard K. Finnigan decided in the 6th grade he might want to be a novelist, then spent the next three decades doing anything but. Besides getting his Bachelors and Masters in Education from the University of Idaho, he's worked as a burger flipper, furniture mover, substitute teacher, balloon vendor and Ambassador to the World at Disneyland. He honed his Halloween skills as a special effects make-up artist in Los Angeles and working for professional haunted houses throughout Idaho in the 1990s. Bernard is now a home-haunter who spends the off-season as a nuclear worker at a local national laboratory, occasionally uploading homemade educational science films to YouTube. He lives with his family in Idaho, where on October 31st he's been known to pass out full-sized candy bars. This is his first novel.

r

Made in the USA
Monee, IL
31 July 2023

40175192R00254